Love Bytes

Carolyn Lampman

RED CANYON PRESS

Love Bytes

Printed in the United States of America

Formatting: Wild Seas Formatting
(http://www.WildSeasFormatting.com)

Cover art: Kelly Martin

Proofreading: Emilee Bowling

Published by

RED CANYON PRESS
4530 W. Mountain View Dr. Riverton, WY 82501
Willow Creek
carolynlampman13@gmail.com

Dedication

To Jennifer and Katy, who read Love Bytes in its infancy and showed me the villain of the piece.

To Bru, who pointed out it might be virtual reality, not time travel. As usual, he came through when I wasn't sure what was going on.

To Ayme, who makes my words shine, and Emilee, who adds the final polish that makes the whole thing glow. I couldn't do it without you!

To Dawn, who let me use her name because it was so perfect. You truly are one of the most beautiful people I know.

To Ed Dowie, the best P.A. ever, who also let me use his name. Thank you for all your help and support!

Most of all, to the real-life Annie Bedford and the family she had wrapped around her little paw. They are truly one of God's brightest spots in my life.

Prologue

Kenzie Armstrong frowned at the sunlight streaming in through her windshield as she drove into the mountain parking lot. The occasion called for huge gray thunderheads billowing up over the mountains and a cold Wyoming wind whistling down through the canyon. The day was too bright and cheerful for burying a boxful of worn-out dreams.

The parking lot contained only one other car, but Kenzie knew that wasn't likely to last. People came from all over to visit "The Sinks," locals as well as tourists. There was something irresistible about a raging river mysteriously disappearing into a mountain then reappearing as a placid pool half a mile down the canyon. No one knew exactly where the Popo Agie River went while it was underground; some speculated that the pool had a different source. Frankly, Kenzie didn't care. All that mattered to her was that nothing the river took underground ever resurfaced in the pool. Even Brad should be satisfied with that.

Kenzie couldn't help a flash of resentment as she picked up her shoebox of treasures and slid out from behind the wheel. Just because they were getting married next week didn't give Brad the right to control her life. He still insisted their fight was merely one of the minor tiffs their premarital counselor had warned them might occur as their wedding date approached. But it hadn't felt like a tiff to her. In fact, she was so irritated with his high-handed manner that she'd left her engagement ring at home in her jewelry box.

The fight started when Brad hacked all her social media accounts and changed her name from Kenzie Armstrong to McKenzie Marriot. She'd been livid, but when she'd taken him to task, he acted so contrite, she almost believed his assurances that he had done it to save her the trouble later.

That was, until Kenzie discovered he'd deleted half of her contacts — the male half — and then she lost it! Most of them were just friends and classmates, but Brad had somehow managed to make *her* feel guilty for having any masculine connections other than him. In the end, he'd succeeded in convincing her the only way to show she truly loved him was to get rid of everything her old boyfriends had given her. She wanted to tell him what he could do with his unreasonable demands, but as usual, Brad had manipulated the situation so that she couldn't refuse. Just last week, he'd donated a huge box of sweaters, jewelry, and original artwork to a church rummage sale. Every ridiculously expensive bit of it had come from women who fancied themselves in love with him.

Kenzie glanced down at her meager love offerings. They were pathetic by comparison. Even so, tossing them in the trash bin as he'd suggested was unthinkable. If she had to get rid of them, it was going to be in her own way. That's why she had come here, to this magical spot: to dispose of them with a full measure of dignity...and a touch of drama. With a rueful smile, she locked Brad's car and started across the parking lot. *Maybe he has a point,* she thought. *Maybe I am clinging to the past.*

She paused for a moment at the head of the trail that led down through the trees to the water's edge, near the mouth of the cave that swallowed the rushing river. No doubt that's where the occupants of the other car were, and hers was a task that required privacy. Kenzie turned and walked up the hill, past the visitors' center, to the observation point above the river. From there, a visitor could watch the Popo Agie somersaulting its way down over a jumble of boulders in a foaming, frothing race to the bottom, where it disappeared into the mountain.

After a quick glance over her shoulder to make sure no one was looking, Kenzie slipped around the wooden barricade and scrambled down the bank. She clambered over several slippery boulders and finally settled on a large rock at the very edge of the river.

The roar of the tumbling cascade drowned out all other sound; Kenzie felt as though she was completely alone, with only the violence of the river for company. The isolation was comforting as she settled the box in her lap and prepared to say goodbye to her past.

Steeling herself, she closed her eyes and reached into the box. She smiled softly as her fingers closed around a plastic squeaky toy. Her beau had promised to win her a huge stuffed animal at the carnival. She'd wound up with the world's funniest-looking rubber ducky instead. They'd laughed and joked about it for months afterward. The ridiculous toy had never failed to bring a smile to her face and new lightness to her heart.

Today, the silly grin on its face made her feel a bit better. She dropped a light kiss on its odd little topknot and set it in the water. It bobbed up and down as the current swiftly drew it toward the rapids. The duck vanished and then popped up a few seconds later farther downstream, bouncing around in the wild white water like an absurd yellow cork until it disappeared, taken down into the darkness by the power of the river.

Next, Kenzie opened the lid of a little tin box painted to look like cloisonné. Tommy had sent it to her as a souvenir from Hong Kong. She pulled out one of the Chinese fortune sticks inside and read: "Change is coming." Kenzie smiled. *No kidding,* she thought as she closed the lid. They weren't even married yet and Brad was already turning her world upside down. After running her fingers over the smooth surface once more, she drew back and threw it down river where the water was most turbulent.

With a sigh, Kenzie returned her gaze to the shoe box again and pulled out a long necklace made entirely of apple seeds. She ran its length through her fingers, savoring the feel of it. The memory of a lazy summer day and innocent young love flowed through her mind like molten honey, warm and sweet.

An image of twinkling brown eyes danced before her as the necklace pooled into her hand, and her fingers closed over it. For a long moment, she held it over her heart then slowly released it into the raging torrent at her feet. It disappeared into the flood without a ripple.

Her other keepsakes followed suit: a bit of lace from her prom dress, a silver thumb ring, a polished agate, a braided leather bracelet, her journal. One by one they disappeared from sight, taking her memories with them. Soon the box was empty, and Kenzie stood watching the last of it, a small dried daisy, swirl around and around in a tiny pool of shallow water next to the rock. A great emptiness threatened to overwhelm her, as though she had somehow lost much more than a few worthless trinkets. Sudden tears filled her eyes.

It was definitely time to go. With a sharp twist, she turned toward the high bank and the path at the top. Through blurry eyes, she miscalculated the distance from one rock to another. Her shoe slipped on the slick surface, and the box flew out of her hand as she grabbed at the empty air, trying to catch her balance. She teetered for an impossibly long moment, then pitched headlong into the river.

When Kenzie surfaced, she tried to scream, but her mouth filled with frigid, choking water as she went under once more. The current tumbled her down over the rocks like a rag doll. The second time her head broke through the surface, the mouth of the cave loomed before her. The last thing she saw was the rock wall racing toward her with terrifying speed. She slammed into it like a race car hitting a barricade. Then, mercifully, everything went black.

Chapter 1

Rainbow Falls

Kenzie floated in a blissful cloud of warmth. It was at odds with the throbbing pain in her head and the aches in various parts of her body. For the life of her, she couldn't remember coming to Brad's house and climbing into his hot tub, but she had to admit it felt rather nice. So did Brad, for that matter. As a general rule, he wasn't a cuddler, but there was no mistaking the hard plane of a masculine chest against her back and the feel of his arms around her.

Maybe she'd play possum for a while longer. With her eyes closed, she could almost imagine the waterfall she heard was real and not one of Brad's silly nature CDs. It was so nice to float here in his embrace, letting the warm water soak away her aches and pains. They fit together like two spoons, so closely entwined that his mustache tickled her cheek.

Suddenly, Kenzie was wide awake. Brad didn't *have* a mustache! Her gaze skittered down to the long, muscular arms that held her in place. Three parallel scars ran down one bulging bicep and disappeared into the water — scars that definitely did not belong to Brad.

Panic and adrenaline hit at the same time. With a hard, backward thrust, her elbow connected with his solar plexus, and she scrambled forward out of his grasp. His sharp grunt proved her aim had been accurate, but she hadn't gone more than a step before a large hand closed around her wrist. She struggled with all her might, but his grip was too strong to break.

"Wait!" he gasped, obviously fighting for breath as he captured her other wrist and held her immobilized.

Kenzie stared at her captor in horror. His dark hair hung in lank strands clear to broad muscular shoulders, and a heavy beard obscured the lower half of his face. With a painful grimace, he rose to his feet, and Kenzie stared in shocked dismay. The man stood well over six feet tall and was built like a block of granite. He was also stark naked except for a small round stone that hung from a rawhide string around his throat.

Kenzie could see dozens of scars beneath the water droplets covering his arms and chest. He looked as though he'd been through a war. Fresh terror washed through her. She wouldn't be the first woman to disappear without a trace from the area around the Sinks. Many people thought it was the work of one man, a man who had been convicted of murder and was currently sitting in the Rawlins prison. But they hadn't been able to prove he was the so-called Great Basin Killer. Could this man be the one responsible?

No. No, he was too young. He'd have been in grade school when the first girl disappeared. Maybe he was one of the right-wing militants that sought refuge in the mountains. Whoever he was, he was obviously dangerous. After a moment of stunned immobility, Kenzie began to struggle in earnest.

"Whoa, now," he said. "No need to get excited. You're safe here."

"Let me go!" This was the sort of situation she'd been taught to deal with during her self-defense training. Shifting her weight to one foot, she snaked the other around the back of his leg and jerked his feet out from under him. He went down with a surprised curse and a mighty splash.

Kenzie didn't even look back, just headed for the opposite side of the pool as fast as she could. She hadn't gone more than a few steps when a wave of dizziness hit her, and she pitched forward into the water. Disoriented and confused, she floundered around trying to find her footing. With no warning, a pair of strong hands plucked her from the water and set her on her feet.

"Here, now. No sense trying to drown yourself." His voice was deep and gruff, the kind that sent shivers of apprehension racing down her spine. "I'm not going to hurt you."

"Then get your hands off me, Buster," she snarled through clenched teeth.

"No problem." He raised his hands and backed away. "Never meant you any harm. And the name's Whiskey Jug Johnson, not Buster."

Kenzie glared at him. *Whiskey Jug?* Who did he think he was fooling with a crazy name like that? "What am I doing here?"

He shrugged. "Beats me. You came over the falls. By the time I fished you out, you were close to dead."

"What falls?"

"Rainbow Falls," he said, pointing to the curtain of water that fell from the rocks.

Kenzie looked at the rainbows sparkling in the mist that surrounded the falls. It was beautiful—and completely unfamiliar. There was a waterfall farther up Sinks Canyon, but there was no hot pool behind it. Besides, she'd never heard of Rainbow Falls. In an area known for its scenic hiking trails, it hardly seemed possible that a natural wonder this amazing would go unmentioned.

None of this made any sense. Kenzie started to rub her forehead and stopped abruptly when she encountered a large bump. No wonder her head hurt! With gentle fingers she explored the injury. "What happened to me?"

"Like I said, you came over the falls. At least, I think you did. I was filling my canteen, so I didn't actually see it. You made a pretty good splash when you hit, though, and it spooked my horse. He lit out like I'd set fire to his tail. When I looked back at the pool, there you were, floating face down in the water. I figured you were a goner when you weren't breathing, but once I got the water out, you started again." He gestured to the hot pool. "I brought you here to warm you up."

"This is crazy. The last thing I remember was falling into the river..." Kenzie swayed as dizziness assailed her once more.

Before she realized what was happening, he'd scooped her up in his arms. "I don't think you should be up yet. That's a pretty nasty bump you have there," he said.

"Put me down!" Kenzie's command might as well have been the wind blowing in the trees for all the effect it had on him. Short of jabbing her thumbs into his eyes, she was powerless to stop the big galoot. "I may not be able to stop you from raping me," she said, willing her voice to be menacing rather than pathetic or pleading, "but it won't be easy. I'll fight you every step of the way and do my best to leave scars that you'll carry for the rest of your miserable life!"

"Rape!" He practically dropped her on the rocky ledge and backed away as fast as the water would allow. "I wasn't—I'd never... What the hell gave you that idea?" His shocked look appeared genuine.

"What else was I supposed to think? You were restraining me!"

"I was holding you up! You were unconscious. You'd have drowned if I hadn't."

"Right, and you took your clothes off to do it." She stared pointedly at his bare chest. "That makes all kinds of sense."

"I didn't want to get my buckskins wet." He glanced down at himself and blushed. "Look, I have a cache on the other side of the waterfall. Will you be all right by yourself for a while?"

Kenzie blinked in surprise. "You're leaving?"

"Only for a few minutes. Will you be all right?"

"S-sure."

"Good." He gave her a reassuring smile. "Just rest now. I'll be back before you know it."

Kenzie blinked at him in amazement as he crossed the pool. She closed her eyes and looked away from his nakedness as he climbed out of the water on the other side. When she looked again, he had disappeared through the mist.

Kenzie frowned. *Cash?* What in the world did money have to do with anything? Was she dealing with a Rambo-type character here, a commando left over from the War in Iraq or

Afghanistan? More than one soldier had come back from war, forever changed. Maybe he was just plain crazy. Running around in the mountains without a stitch of clothes on wasn't exactly sane.

It was clear the man thought the head injury had muddled her thinking. As she fingered the goose-egg-sized lump on her forehead, she wondered uneasily if he was right. Nothing made any sense and her head ached abominably. Still, she couldn't very well stay here, calmly waiting for him to return.

The pool was surrounded on two sides by high, steep banks and on a third by a sheer rock wall. Kenzie frowned. The only easy way in or out was the way her captor had gone, and she didn't dare take that route. Could she manage to keep her wits about her long enough to climb the steep embankment? A critical surveillance of the two banks was not promising, but she had to try. Though she wasn't quite sure where she was, the highway couldn't be too far away. Maybe she could see it from the top.

Normally, Kenzie would have been able to scramble up the bank without much trouble, but today her whole body hurt. Gingerly, she stood up and tested her balance. For the moment at least, the dizziness seemed to have passed. The cool mountain air hit her as soon as she left the warmth of the pool, and she shivered. Just what she needed: a case of hypothermia on top of everything else! Telling herself the exercise would warm her up, she took a breath and started to climb. Every muscle protested as she clambered awkwardly up the hillside.

By the time Kenzie reached the top, her misery had increased tenfold. She was covered with goosebumps and hurt in more places than she could count. The exertion hadn't done a thing to warm her up, and her wet clothing clung to her like an icy second skin. Still shaky from the climb, she sat on a large rock for a few minutes to catch her breath and to think. There was no sign of human habitation in the unending wall of trees, not even a forest service privy. She listened intently but only heard the roar of the waterfall behind her. Either the highway was deserted, or it was farther away than she had anticipated.

Turning around, Kenzie examined the string of unfamiliar pools below her. Her last hope that she was close to her car vanished. She plunked down on a boulder and surveyed the scene below. It was obvious this place wasn't part of the Sinks at all. Instead of cascading down the mountainside into a cave at the bottom, the water here came straight out of the cliff and fell into a clear pool. It wasn't just the river, though. Nothing about this place was even remotely familiar. She rubbed her face in confusion. Where in the world was she?

On the other side of the waterfall, movement on the far bank caught her eye. Squinting down into the trees, she saw Whiskey Jug Johnson. He was dressed from head to toe in buckskins, complete with fringes. Probably thought he was Daniel Boone or something. The only thing missing was the coonskin cap. In spite of everything, she was inclined to believe him. Not that she thought he was sane — far from it. She just felt he really hadn't meant her any harm. Unless he was one heck of an actor, he'd been truly aghast at her suggestion that he was a rapist and had appeared embarrassed by his nudity.

Then she realized what he was doing, and a cold chill ran through her that had nothing to do with her sodden clothing. He appeared to be digging a trench of some sort. A grave? The Great Basin Killer popped into her mind again, and her heart began pounding. They'd only found one of his victim's bodies. The others had disappeared without a trace. As her chest tightened, and her breath began coming in short gasps, Kenzie dropped her head between her knees and willed herself to be calm. The last thing she needed was a full-blown panic attack.

He's too young, she reminded herself. *The disappearances stopped twenty years ago. This man couldn't have had anything to do with them. Besides, he couldn't dig a grave with only a tree branch.* Still, there was something very odd going on here, and she wasn't about to stick around and find out what it was.

Kenzie rose shakily to her feet. It was definitely time to leave. Unfortunately, she didn't know which way to go.

Though she wasn't sure exactly where she was, she had to be somewhere close to the Sinks. Surely, she could find her way back there or even to the highway, where she could flag down a passing car. Kenzie glanced up at the sky, silently blessing the Girl Scout leader who had taught her how to tell directions. The sun had just passed its zenith and started its descent into the west. She knew the town of Lander was northeast of the Sinks, so she turned her left shoulder to the sun and set out.

About twenty minutes later, Kenzie discovered a well-worn trail at the edge of the forest. Relieved, she followed it back through the trees. It was sure to lead to a campground or something. As she walked, her clothes gradually dried in the warm summer sunshine. Only her feet remained damp and uncomfortable in her sneakers. Even so, she was glad she had chosen to wear them rather than her sandals.

Following the trail through the forest didn't take a lot of concentration, and Kenzie found her thoughts turning to her predicament. Though the trees, rocks, and streams were just as she would expect them to be, nothing was familiar. The falls and the two pools were obviously nowhere near the Sinks. So how did she wind up here, wherever here was? There were those who thought there was a whole underground river system connected to the Sinks, since more water went in than came out. Was it possible that the river that formed the falls, and the pools was part of that system? For all she knew, she could have been in the water for a day or more. Her thoughts went round and round, without getting any closer to a reasonable answer. All it did was make her headache worse, so she pushed the thoughts away and concentrated on finding her way out of the mountains.

While the sun continued its steady progress across the sky, Kenzie trudged through the forest, crossed meadows, climbed hills, and even forged a couple of small streams. At times, the trail grew faint. She lost it once, when she had to cross a huge granite outcropping, but managed to locate it again on the far side. The trail seemed better defined after that, and her hope resurfaced; she must be getting closer to civilization.

By the time the sun went down in the west, Kenzie felt as though she had walked twenty miles. She was tired, hungry, and thirsty. Her feet hurt almost as bad as her head. Worst of all, she was cold again. Without the sun, the mountain air cooled rapidly. Her T-shirt and shorts did little to keep her warm.

The trail was becoming more and more difficult to see, and she knew she would have to stop soon or risk losing it altogether. Before long, it was full dark, with no moon to light the way. Millions of stars dotted the heavens, but their feeble light couldn't penetrate the inky darkness that surrounded her. Kenzie shivered. Summer nights were cold in the mountains.

The worry that she had managed to keep at bay all day long suddenly returned with a vengeance. Without a tent and sleeping bag or proper clothing, how in the world was she going to keep warm? She couldn't even start a fire, nor did she have a clue what to do about her growing hunger and thirst. She hadn't seen any berries and wouldn't have known which were edible even if she had. Only a fool would drink from a mountain stream without purifying it first.

Suddenly, light flickered through the trees ahead. As she drew closer, she realized it must be someone's campfire. *Thank heavens!* She'd managed to find a campground. Buoyed by the prospect of a warm fire, some proper directions, and maybe even some food, she strode out of the trees and into the clearing.

After the darkness of the forest, she was momentarily blinded by the bright light of the fire. Even so, she could see someone sitting on the other side. "Hello," she said with a falsely bright smile, "I'm Kenzie Armstrong, and I seem to be lost."

"I'll bet you're hungry too," said a deep, vaguely familiar voice. "Come on in and have a bite to eat."

Kenzie's stomach tightened in horrified panic as the man behind the fire stood up. With a million acres of forest and hundreds of campers on this stupid mountain, she'd managed to stumble across the one camp she didn't want to be anywhere near. Running away was useless; he'd catch her before she went ten feet. As closely as he was watching, she'd never be able to overpower him, either. Once again, she was in the clutches of the terrifying and mysterious Whiskey Jug Johnson!

Chapter 2

"Come sit by the fire and warm yourself," Whiskey Jug said, pointing to a log on Kenzie's side of the campfire.

"I'm not that cold," Kenzie said. He undoubtedly knew it was a lie—she was shivering so hard he could probably hear her teeth chattering—but he pretended to accept it. The temptation to bolt back into the woods was strong, but if she ran, he'd just bring her back. Besides, she was tired, cold, and hungry, and his fire drew her like a magnet. It was warm, and the tantalizing smell of cooking meat wafted toward her, beckoning to her with invisible tendrils.

"Supper will be ready soon," he said, as if he'd read her mind. "Hope you like rabbit."

Since Kenzie had never eaten rabbit, she had no idea. Not that it mattered; anything that would fill her stomach was fine with her. She nodded and said nothing.

Whiskey Jug put another piece of wood on the fire and turned the spitted rabbit over the flames. The silence stretched, broken only by the popping of hot pitch and the occasional hoot of an owl. Kenzie edged closer to the fire and held her hands out to it. Its heat felt good against her chilled skin. *There's no way to escape him without a head start,* she reasoned, *even if I did know where I was going—and I don't.* Her stomach grumbled. As long as he stayed on his side of the campfire, maybe waiting until after supper wasn't such a bad idea.

But how in the world was she going to keep him over there? Somehow, she didn't think he'd be overly impressed if she threatened him with her self-defense training. Even if she lied and said she had a black belt in karate, there was no guarantee he'd consider that a deterrent. For all she knew, he had one himself and would promptly challenge her to a match right here in the forest.

A slight smile curved her lips as she pictured the ridiculous thought. Suddenly, almost as if he'd read her thoughts, he raised his head and stared straight at her. The fathomless dark eyes were impossible to read in the dancing firelight, but his intent expression made her heart skip a beat and her throat tighten.

"Mr. Johnson," she began in what she hoped was a businesslike tone. "I think we need to get a few things stra—"

"Shhh!" He rose to his feet and strode purposefully around the fire, his long legs eating up the ground between them.

Kenzie's flinching recoil nearly sent her tumbling backward off the log as she put up her hands to protect herself. "No!" she cried.

"Quiet," he hissed, then jumped the log and disappeared into the dark forest behind her.

She whirled around and stared after him in open-mouthed amazement. The man was definitely a lunatic. After several long moments of silence, a distant crashing sound reached her ears. Kenzie wondered uneasily what Whiskey Jug was doing. Had he seen someone? The scuffling noise could be two men fighting. For a moment, she felt a spurt of hope, but then she realized there was no certainty she'd be better off with anyone else. For all she knew, these mountains could be the hiding place of a whole regiment of survivalists who didn't care for company. Whiskey Jug Johnson might be the best of the lot.

A high-pitched snort sounded back in the trees, followed by a sharp curse and the sound of heavy bodies smashing through the underbrush.

Kenzie's eyes widened in sudden comprehension. It wasn't another man Whiskey Jug was fighting, but an animal of some sort. Her stomach jerked. Grizzly bears and mountain lions had both regained much of their former territory in these mountains during the past few years. Even the wolf packs that had been reintroduced to Yellowstone Park had made their way to Sinks Canyon.

What if the animal came after her? Scanning the camp for

some sort of weapon, she realized with a slight shock that she'd never seen Whiskey Jug Johnson with any sort of gun. *What kind of self-respecting militant goes around unarmed?*

The sound of something moving toward her threw Kenzie into a panic. With her heart thumping, she grabbed the first broken branch she could find and retreated across the clearing. As weapons go, it wasn't much, but it was better than nothing.

Moments later, Whiskey Jug emerged from the trees, leading a large black horse. "Now we won't have to walk," he said, with an air of deep satisfaction.

A horse was about the last thing Kenzie had expected. She lowered her branch. "Where did he come from?"

"I expect he was attracted by the light, though I can't say I know why. I figured the dunderhead would be halfway to Mexico by now."

Kenzie vaguely remembered Whiskey Jug mentioning that his horse had run away. "He's yours?"

"Yeah. He bolted when you came over the falls. Dang fool hasn't got the brains God gave a tree stump." Whiskey Jug pulled a rifle out of the scabbard and leaned it up against the log before turning his attention to the saddle.

"Oh," Kenzie said with dawning comprehension. "Your gun was on the horse!"

"Yep. Maybe I should start taking it with me when I dismount. It's the third time this week he's taken off like that."

"He seems calm enough now."

"For the moment, anyway. I've had a devil of a time breaking him." A log shifted in the fire, sending a shower of sparks into the air. Whiskey Jug tightened his hold on the reins as the horse jerked back. "Dammit, Bear Bait, hold still. That fire isn't going to hurt you."

Kenzie raised her eyebrows. "Isn't Bear Bait kind of a strange name for a horse?"

Whiskey Jug shrugged. "I called him that so much it kind of stuck." He pulled the saddle off and threw it over the log where Kenzie had been sitting. "It's about all he's good for."

"But he's beautiful," Kenzie protested.

"Looks don't count for much out here. Dependability and endurance are a whole lot more important when your life's at stake."

"I suppose that's true, but how often does your life depend on a horse?"

Whiskey Jug frowned. "A man doesn't last very long in these mountains without one. No other way to get around."

"No other way to —?" Kenzie's look of confusion cleared as she glanced around in sudden comprehension. "Oh, I get it. We're in the wilderness."

Whiskey Jug gave her a long look. "Where did you think we were?"

"Within walking distance of my car. But that can't be," she said, thinking aloud. "The nearest wilderness is miles and miles from Sinks Canyon." She rubbed her forehead. "This gets more confusing by the minute."

"That's just what I was thinking," he muttered under his breath.

"Pardon me?"

"Nothing." He turned back to his horse. "That rabbit ought to be about done. Why don't you give it another turn?"

Kenzie looked dubiously at the fire. "How do I do that?"

"Just turn the spit." He glanced over his shoulder at her. "You might want to put your club down first, though. It's easier if you have both hands free, and you're in no danger now."

Kenzie blushed. She'd forgotten she was still holding the stick. It was obvious from the sarcasm in his tone that he didn't think much of her choice of weapon. "Actually, I thought you might need it for kindling in the morning when you want to get the fire started again," she said with airy nonchalance, then dropped it into the wood pile.

"I don't plan on letting the fire go out tonight."

"You don't?"

"Nope. Gets cold up here, and we've only got the one blanket. Think maybe I'll leave a good buffalo robe in my cache by Rainbow Falls from now on."

Whiskey Jug's reference to money didn't make any more sense now than it had at the waterfall, but Kenzie decided to ignore it as she concentrated on turning the rabbit. The spit wobbled a bit but stayed firmly wedged in the forked branches Whiskey Jug had stuck in the ground. The last thing she needed was to dump their dinner into the fire. That kind of thing would make a hungry man lose his temper, and Whiskey Jug didn't look like the type that was long on patience anyway.

Kenzie straightened from her task and caught sight of what looked like a canteen hanging from the saddle horn. Her thirst suddenly intensified a hundredfold. "Is that" — she cleared her parched throat — "Is that water?"

He glanced over his shoulder at her. "You thirsty?" When she nodded, he disentangled the strap and handed her the canteen.

Kenzie practically snatched it from his hand, unscrewed the lid and lifted it to her mouth. It was warm and had a slightly musty flavor, as if it had been in the canteen a long time, but it tasted like ambrosia to Kenzie.

"Go easy on it," Whiskey Jug said as she gulped the contents. "It's all the water we've got."

Kenzie took one more swallow before handing it back to him. "Thanks." She wiped her mouth a little self-consciously. "I hadn't had anything to drink all day."

Whiskey Jug frowned as he put the lid back on the canteen. "Why is that? You crossed half a dozen streams."

"Yes, but I didn't have a filter with me, and they were probably full of all kinds of deadly critters."

"Like what?"

"Oh, you know, giardia bacteria, maybe even amoebas. The last thing I need is dysentery!"

He stared at her for a long moment then turned back to his horse. "Right."

A sudden thought occurred to her. "Umm, where exactly did that water come from?"

"The pool by Rainbow Falls. I had just filled the canteen when Bear Bait took off."

Kenzie suddenly felt a little queasy. "I don't suppose you purified it first?"

"What?" He turned to stare at her.

"Purified. It means... Oh, never mind." *It's probably just fine,* she thought, eyeing Whiskey Jug's strong physique. *He doesn't look like he's been sick a day in his life.*

The smell of the cooking meat drew Kenzie's attention and sharpened her hunger until it was almost painful, but she didn't have the slightest idea what to do next. There wasn't a table to set, or even any plates. How would they eat?

Kenzie glanced hopefully at Whiskey Jug, but he appeared to be concentrating entirely on Bear Bait. He ran his hands up and down the animal's legs and over its flanks and back, apparently checking for injuries. It didn't look as though they were going to eat until the horse had been cared for. Maybe if she pitched in, the work would get done faster.

"Is there anything I can do to help?" she asked.

Whiskey Jug looked up in surprise. "I don't know. I guess you could bring me the picket if you want. It's in my saddlebag."

"All right," Kenzie said, heading for the saddle. "What does it look like?"

"It's a leather cuff hooked to a chain."

His words stopped Kenzie mid-stride as images of manacles chained to a bed crystallized in her mind. "A...a leather cuff?"

"I fasten it around Bear Bait's leg and drive a stake into the ground through the end of the chain. It's the only way I can get him to stay put. He'd be halfway down the mountain if I used hobbles. Figured out how to crow hop the first time I put them on him."

Embarrassed by her lurid imagination, Kenzie was glad he'd turned back to his work. Brad always teased her that her face was an open book; she didn't need Whiskey Jug reading that particular passage.

When she finally reached the saddle, she paused in surprise. Though the leather looked new, the styling was very old. In fact, it looked like a museum piece. "Is this a replica?"

"No, it's a Pollard. I had him make it for me two years ago when the trapping was good. Can't say that I ever heard of a saddlemaker named Replica."

"No, I mean a copy," she said reaching into the saddle bag. "It looks like something right out of the eighteen hundreds."

"What do you mean?"

"I don't know a lot about horses, but I did some research on saddles for a project I was working on. This saddle looks like it was made in the eighteen nineties."

Whiskey Jug stopped what he was doing and rested both arms on the back of the horse as he turned to look at her. "It was made in 1866," he said.

She laughed. "Yeah, right." He raised his eyebrow, and her smile faded. "You're serious, aren't you?"

"I bought it from a saddle maker in Cheyenne last summer," he said, staring at her, challenging her to dispute his claim.

Kenzie was the first to look away. *He's crazy, but he's harmless,* she reminded herself as she reached into the far saddlebag. *At least, I hope he's harmless.* "Here's your picket," she said, pulling it out. A bright yellow object dropped to the ground, and she bent to retrieve it. "Hey, my duck!"

"It's yours?"

"Until I threw it away, it was." She gave it an experimental squeak. Bear Bait snorted and threw up his head.

"Dammit. I take back everything I ever said about you!" Whiskey Jug grabbed the bridle before Bear Bait could bolt. "You're too stupid to use for bear bait!" He glared at Kenzie. "What the hell is that thing doing here, anyway?"

"It's just a toy. My boyfriend won it for me at a carnival. He was trying to get one of those big stuffed animals, but for some reason his aim was lousy that night." Kenzie was suddenly aware of how silly it must sound. "It was all kind of a joke," she finished lamely.

Adam let go of the bridle and started grooming the horse. "I would have thought you were a bit old to be playing with toys. Or little boys, for that matter."

"He wasn't a little boy, he was my boyfriend. You know, the guy I was dating? My significant other?" When Whiskey Jug still looked blank, Kenzie resisted the urge to roll her eyes. He was going a little overboard with his 1800's fantasy. "How about my sweetheart?"

"Ah." Whiskey Jug nodded. "He was courting you."

"Uh...right."

"This...toy seems an odd sort of gift for a man to give his intended."

"Oh, he wasn't my fiancé. In fact, we each went our own way soon after that."

"Small wonder," he muttered, fastening the leather cuff above Bear Bait's foot.

Kenzie decided to ignore the remark as she watched him drive the picket spike into the ground. "Do you want me to turn the rabbit again?"

"No, we best eat it while there's still some juice left in it," he said, wiping his hands on the legs of his pants and moving toward the fire.

Kenzie experienced a momentary twinge of revulsion as she watched him handle the rabbit without cleaning his hands — the same hands he'd used to wipe down his horse. By the time he'd cut the rabbit in half, however, her hunger overcame her distaste, and she accepted her meal with gratitude.

Though there was a blackened crust on the outside, the meat was surprisingly good. Kenzie ate every bite and licked her fingers when she finished.

"I never had rabbit before," she admitted. "I'd heard it tastes like chicken, but I never really believed it."

"Does it?" Whiskey Jug asked, as he rose to his feet and

stretched.

"Does it what?"

"Taste like chicken."

"Don't you know?"

He shook his head. "Nope. Not too many chickens running around up here in the mountains."

"What do you eat, then?"

He shrugged. "Mostly deer, elk, and moose, with an occasional bear thrown in for a change."

"You eat bear?" she asked, revolted by the thought.

"Yep," he grinned at her. "Keeps me from being puny."

"But surely you had chicken before you moved up here."

"Lived up here since my pa bought me at a rendezvous in the Wind River Country." He pulled a wicked-looking knife out of the sheath at his waist and tested the sharpness of the blade against his thumb. "I wasn't much more than knee high at the time."

Kenzie's mouth dropped open. "Your father *bought* you?"

"More or less. Pa traded Crazy Charlie a jug of rotgut whiskey for me." He flashed her a lopsided grin. "That's where I got my name."

"Selling children is against the law!" Kenzie exclaimed.

"Maybe back East, but around here, folks pretty much do what they want."

"I think that's terrible!" Kenzie was aghast at his blatant disregard for the law.

Whiskey Jug whacked off a pine bough. "What's so terrible about it? All Pa did was make everybody happy. Crazy Charlie didn't want me. Hell, he couldn't even remember where he'd found me for sure, and my ma had been hankering after a baby."

"What about your real parents?"

Whiskey Jug shrugged. "Probably dead. Can't quite figure out what white folks were doing out here back then anyway."

"Maybe Crazy Charlie kidnapped you."

Whiskey Jug chuckled and shook his head. "From where?

Back then, the closest civilization was St. Louis. Crazy Charlie is harmless, but he's not one to go to any extra work. Besides, what would a lone trapper want with a little boy? Makes no sense."

Kenzie frowned. This man was truly convinced he was living in the nineteenth century, and his fantasy was oddly complete. No doubt if she asked, he could tell her all sorts of convincing tales of growing up in the mountains. The strangest part was that it all sounded so completely real. "If your mother was hankering for a baby, I find it hard to believe she named you Whiskey Jug."

"She didn't."

"Then, what's your real name?"

"Doesn't matter." Whiskey Jug cut another bough and tossed it into the pile. "No one ever calls me by it. Don't suppose I'd answer to it if anyone was to use it any more than if they were to call me Mr. Johnson."

"What are you doing?" she asked as he picked up the pile of pine boughs and moved them closer to the fire.

"Making us a bed."

"Us?" she squeaked. "There's no way I'm sleeping with you."

He raised an eyebrow. "Then where do you plan to sleep?"

"Right next to the fire."

Whiskey Jug snorted. "You won't last five minutes." He glanced at her bare legs. "Especially in those clothes. You'll cook on one side and freeze on the other."

"I don't care."

They stood glaring stubbornly at each other for a long moment, then Whiskey Jug sighed. "Look, I don't plan on taking liberties with you, if that's what you're afraid of," he said. "We can spoon, if that will make you feel better."

"What?"

"You know, spoon. We put our heads at opposite ends of the bed." He demonstrated by putting his hands together, fingers to palms. "That way, you'll only have to sleep with my feet."

Kenzie glanced from him to the bed of pine boughs and back. Sleeping on the cold hard ground with no blanket really didn't appeal to her. Besides, if rape were his plan, he'd have already done it. "All right," she said doubtfully.

Whiskey Jug didn't even acknowledge her capitulation, just finished arranging the boughs. He spread the horse blanket over the needles then shook out the gray wool blanket that had been rolled up behind his saddle and lay it over the top.

As tired as she was, Kenzie had to admit it looked rather inviting. She stood staring at it, uncertain what to do next.

"You can go to bed if you want," Whiskey Jug said, picking up his rifle. "I'm going to take a look around." With that, he strode out of camp and into the dark, silent woods.

Kenzie stared after him for a moment then scrambled into bed. It wasn't terribly comfortable and smelled strongly of horse, but it was better than nothing. She gazed up into the star-studded sky and concentrated on relaxing. A hundred camping trips from her youth floated through her memory. Instead of sheep, she and her sister had taken turns counting the satellites that sailed across the night sky.

Kenzie smiled to herself. Tonight, there was no one to dispute whether a light belonged to a plane rather than a satellite. She was still looking for her first one when Whiskey Jug returned and crawled under the blanket. True to his word, he put his head at the far end of the makeshift bed.

Kenzie continued to scan the sky, but she saw no movement; all the stars stayed firmly in their places. The longer she searched, the more uneasy she became. Surely the law against any kind of motorized travel in the wilderness didn't extend to outer space. She shifted slightly and turned her gaze in a new direction.

"It's Adam."

Kenzie started at the sound of his voice. Somehow, in her search of the heavens, she'd almost forgotten he was there. "Wh-what?"

"My name. It's Adam."

"Adam Johnson," she said experimentally. "It has a nice sound."

"You seem restless," he said. "Sometimes the ground is too hard, even with pine boughs under you."

"No, it's not that. I'm just looking for satellites."

"Satellites?"

"Yeah, you know, little lights that move across the sky," she said with a touch of sarcasm in her voice.

"Oh, you mean falling stars," he said after a long pause. "You may as well go to sleep. They come later in the summer."

Kenzie grimaced in the darkness. Oh, of course, how could she have forgotten? They didn't have satellites back in 1868! Suddenly, she was determined to find a satellite just to see how he explained it away. She continued to search the heavens until her eyes finally began to get heavy, but never once did she see what she was looking for. Her last thought before sleep overtook her was as irrational as it was frightening: What if she had somehow become caught up in Whiskey Jug Johnson's fantasy?

Chapter 3

Adam "Whiskey Jug" Johnson slowly opened his eyes. The blinking lights on his control panel flashed in odd syncopation with the loud ringing of the doorbell. He rubbed his face and sighed deeply. It always took a minute or two to orient himself when he came out of his computer game. Late afternoon sunshine coming in through mullioned windows made intricate patterns on the golden oak floor of his office. He blinked in surprise and glanced at his watch. Had he really been inside his program that long?

"Just a minute," he called, stripping the gloves from his hands. The bell continued its insistent clangor as though he hadn't spoken. "Damned interfering woman." He removed the helmet from his head and set it carefully on the specially padded pedestal next to him on the desk.

He dropped his hands to the push rims of his wheelchair. "Yeah, yeah, I'm coming." With powerful strokes, he backed out of his computer station and propelled himself across the living room, to the door. He twisted the lock with a quick flick of his wrist before turning back toward his instrument panel.

"Come on in, Annie," he said, disapproval heavy in his voice.

"My, aren't we in a cheerful mood this evening!" The small, shapely blonde held three plastic bags of groceries in one hand and a gallon of milk balanced precariously in her arms as she wrestled with the door. "What's the matter, miss your nap this afternoon?"

"Annoying sounds make me grouchy. Some idiot was leaning on the bell." Adam flipped a couple of switches and studied the readouts on one of the screens.

"Sorry about that," she said cheerfully. "I had my hands full."

"What are you doing here, anyway? My surgery isn't until Wednesday, and you know I don't like to be disturbed when I'm working."

"Somebody has to pull you out of that computer once in a while." She closed the door with an elbow and crossed the room to deposit the bags and milk on the breakfast bar. "I knew you'd forget to get food, so I picked you up some groceries while I was doing my own shopping."

Annie glanced up at the blank screen attached to the hanging cupboards above her head. Reaching under the counter, she pressed a button. The empty hall outside flickered into view. "You know, Adam, Todd installed that security camera for a reason. The whole idea is for you to find out who is outside *before* you unlock the door. What if it hadn't been me?"

"I knew it was you. Nobody else comes by." He tapped out a string of numbers on the keyboard. "Don't know why your husband thinks I need a security system, anyway."

Annie leaned her back against the counter and crossed her arms. "Gee, I don't suppose there's a burglar alive who'd be interested in the four zillion dollars worth of computer equipment you have in here, not to mention what you're working on."

Adam snorted, "As if they'd have a clue. I doubt if there's a handful of people in the world who'd recognize simulated reality."

"Maybe not. On the other hand, there are some very bad people out there that would pay just about anything to get their hands on the first program capable of mimicking the real world, not to mention the creator of that program."

"You worry too much."

"And you don't worry enough. Want some supper?"

"Annie, go home to your husband and kids."

"Can't. Todd had a security system to install up in Jackson, and his partner's gone on vacation. Zoey and Seth offered to go along and help."

"Too bad you didn't go with them."

Annie smiled. "What, and ruin all Todd's fun? Three long, lovely days of listening to his teenagers bicker back and forth. Now what about that supper?"

"I don't suppose you'll go away until you're satisfied I'm not starving to death, will you?"

"Nope." Annie grinned as she straightened and pushed away from the counter. "You know, you really ought to be grateful to me. In the long run it will save you time. You won't have to stop and fix yourself something or put your groceries away."

Adam just grunted and focused his attention back on his calculations. For the next half an hour, there was little noise in the apartment, aside from the clicking of computer keys and the occasional cupboard door closing or sounds of meal preparation from the kitchen.

"This makes no sense," Adam muttered to no one in particular.

Annie scooped grilled cheese sandwiches out of the frying pan and slid them onto plates. "What's wrong?"

"A new character showed up today."

Annie looked up as she opened a bag of chips. "That's happened before, hasn't it?"

"Yeah, but this one's different." Adam scanned the screen in front of him. "It doesn't belong, only I'm not sure if it's a malfunction of the Character Generator or the Reality Guard."

"Let me guess, the Character Generator creates characters, right?"

"Exactly, and it's not the first time I've had trouble with it. I put it in so people could add whatever character they wanted to their story. All the famous ones like Davy Crockett and Marie Antoinette worked just fine, but the others didn't."

"What do you mean?" She set cutlery on the table then walked across the room to look over his shoulder.

"When I first tested it, I tried to build a character based on my father. Instead, I got a senile old trapper who calls himself

Crazy Charlie."

"You're kidding! He told you his name was Crazy Charlie?"

Adam nodded. "Yes, and to be honest with you, the name fits. Charlie looks like my father and has some of his mannerisms, but that's where the resemblance ends. Although, I have to admit, he does seem to know a lot about being a mountain man, and sometimes he even gives me good advice. Most of the time, he lives in a fog, confused and slightly disoriented. I never know when he's going to show up or what he's going to do."

"Wow, are all the characters like that?"

"Thankfully, no. To be honest, the early ones were worse than Crazy Charlie. They looked and sounded like real people but were more like cardboard cutouts—kind of one dimensional. That's when I realized people act the way they do because of their experiences. It's like newborn babies. At first, they have very little personality, but they develop it surprisingly fast when they start to interact with other people and the world."

Annie looked intrigued. "You figured out a way to give them experiences?"

"In a manner of speaking. I discovered it was a matter of cortex stimulation and frontal lobe interaction, so I created some nanomatter bytes by interacting with the character, which I then programmed to—" He grinned at the look on her face as her eyes began to glaze over. "Never mind the technical stuff. Suffice it to say I developed a bank of character traits for players to choose from. In *Fantasy Quest*, players can create a person by filling out a character chart of sorts. That creates a realistic character which further develops as they interact with the player inside the game. The more you play the game, the more real they become."

"And is your glitch one of those basic characters?"

Adam shook his head. "That's just it. Everything about the glitch is perfectly normal. Highly developed, in fact."

"Except…"

"Except it's out of sync. The clothing, speech, attitudes… Everything is wrong. That's why I think the Reality Guard might be at fault, instead of the Character Generator."

"What does the Reality Guard do?"

"It keeps everything true to the time and place of the setting. For example, if you tried to put a horse-drawn freight wagon into a modern setting, the Reality Guard would change it into a semi."

Annie glanced at the screen. "So, have you figured it out yet?"

"Nope. I can't find anything wrong with either the Character Generator or the Reality Guard." He shrugged. "If worse comes to worst, maybe I can change it from the inside."

"From the inside?"

He nodded. "I'll go back in and try to reprogram the glitch by interacting with it."

"Are you crazy?" Annie squeaked. "What if the whole program winds up crashing when you're inside?"

Adam chuckled. "Then I'll find myself sitting here staring at a blank screen just like I have every other time it crashed." He grinned as he reached up and switched on another monitor. "Don't worry, Annie. It's only a glitch. It's not even in my main program."

"What do you mean?"

"Look." He moved his mouse and tapped the button a couple of times. Suddenly, a bright picture sprang to life on the screen. Bold letters flashed across a moving landscape, announcing *Fantasy Quest*. "This is the program I'm putting together for Microcom. The other one I use to test out ideas."

"You mean like the Indian village?"

"Exactly like that. I'm not sure what caused the glitch or where it is, but it doesn't represent any danger. Not to change the subject, but I'm hungry. Is that meal you promised me about ready?"

"You're trying to distract me."

"Moi?" He gazed up at her with a look of wounded innocence. "Now, why would I do that?"

Annie put one hand on her hip and shook her head. "Honestly, I don't know why I bother with you."

"Because you can't resist the urge to try and save me from myself."

Annie made a face. "I think you're a lost cause."

"Probably, but I'm glad you haven't given up on me."

"Oh? And why is that?"

"Because," he said, whirling his chair away from the computer console and rolling toward the table, "you make a killer grilled cheese sandwich."

She laughed as she followed him. "And the way to a man's heart is through his stomach, right?"

"Something like that." His eyes brightened as he lifted one corner of his sandwich. "Ah, ham and cheddar with Dijon. Tell Todd he'd better be good to you or I'll steal you away from him for your sandwiches alone."

She smiled as she sat down and shook out her napkin. "Not a chance."

"Why not? I'm handsome, charming, and a great conversationalist."

"Not to mention ridiculously rich," she added. "No, in spite of all that, I'd have to turn you down even if I weren't madly in love with my husband. No woman could compete with your computers. She'd be a fool to even try."

Adam gave a dramatic sigh. "Ah. Well, then, I guess I'll have to settle for your sandwiches." He took a bite and closed his eyes as he chewed. "Mmm. Heaven on Earth."

"Flatterer."

Adam winked at her and took another bite.

After dinner, Annie loaded the dishwasher and finished putting away the groceries while Adam went back to his computer.

"That's that," she said at last. She dug through her purse until she found her keys, with the distinctive silver key chain shaped like Cinderella's glass slipper. "I'll pick you up for your appointment with Dr. Dowie at one-thirty."

"I suppose you will, whether I want you to or not."

"Darn right. Until the doctor gives you the ok to drive again, I have you under my thumb." She walked to the door. "I left you some lunch in the fridge. All you need to do is microwave it. If you know what's good for you, I won't find it there tomorrow — and I will check."

"Do you know you're a bully?"

Annie grinned. "That's what big sisters are for."

"You're not my sister."

"There you go, splitting hairs again." Annie opened the door and blew him a kiss. "See you tomorrow."

He watched her walk down the hall on the surveillance monitor. At the corner, she turned around, stuck her thumbs in her ears, and waggled her fingers at the camera before waving and disappearing from sight.

Adam laughed out loud. Annie was a treasure. Hers was not the first face he saw when he opened his eyes after the attack that had left his legs paralyzed and useless, but it was the only one he remembered from his long, pain-filled recovery. They'd started out as patient and physical therapist, but somewhere during the months of painful exercises, they'd become friends.

A year later, they met by chance at a snow cone stand on a hot August afternoon. By the time all the syrupy ice had been consumed, Annie's kids were taking turns sitting on Adam's lap and squealing in delight as he whipped his chair around the park's many walkways, at top speed.

The next week, Annie and her husband, Todd, took Adam to watch his first wheelchair race. It was love at first sight, just as Todd had predicted. Before Adam knew what was happening, Todd had enrolled him in a gym and started him on a rigorous training regime.

Adam sighed and rubbed his left shoulder. Now here he was, ten years later, a washed-up has-been. Racing had been the one thing that made him feel whole again. The trophies he'd won were secondary to the satisfaction of competing with other highly trained athletes. A dislocated shoulder and massive tendon damage ended his career. Even Wednesday's surgery wouldn't make his shoulder whole again.

He turned his chair toward the computer console once more. At least he still had this. Computers had been his passion long before he'd been chained to the chair. Though he'd built his first computer at the age of ten and created his first breakthrough software package at fifteen, his real love was virtual reality. *Fantasy Quest* was the first program to go a step beyond, into the world of simulated reality, where the player actually interacted with the program, instead of just moving through the landscape. It was projected to completely revolutionize the world of gaming when it went on the market in February.

Still, it was *Beta Quest*, his test program that drew Adam. Early on, he'd realized he needed a place to try out new ideas, without contaminating *Fantasy Quest*. To that end, he created a program inspired by some of the brightest memories from his childhood and the time he'd spent with his father.

Charles Trelane Johnson had been fascinated with the life of his great-grandfather, a mountain man named Whiskey Jug Johnson. From the time he was small, Adam and his father had embraced the life of the mountain man once a year at one of the many rendezvous reenactments throughout the west, where they'd reveled in the primitive living conditions and mountain-man festivities.

When it came time to create a place where he could try out new ideas, the world of the mountain man had seemed the natural choice. He'd created the setting and his own persona, based on what he knew of the real Whiskey Jug Johnson, who had been bought at a rendezvous and raised in the mountains by a white trapper and his Arapaho wife. From the beginning, Adam had felt comfortable amid the pines and high, rocky peaks of the Great Snowy Range. The mountains welcomed him like an old friend when he sought solace there after the fiasco of his last race.

"Ok, Ms. Glitch, where are you hiding?" Adam muttered as he focused on the screen in front of him." He scrolled through the programming.

Kenzie wasn't the first character to show up unannounced, but she was the first he didn't seem to have any control over. Adam's ability to influence the characters in *Beta Quest* was limited, but he had become fairly adept at changing them in small ways. To date, his most complex character was a self-appointed uncle named Jesse Three Dogs. Adam couldn't keep the old man from drinking too much whiskey, but when the alcohol wore off, Jesse became the quintessential wise old Indian—just as Adam had intended.

Kenzie, however, had defied all attempts to change her. Adam's first inclination had been to convert her to the proper century by acting as though he didn't have a clue what she was talking about. So far, it hadn't been overly successful. Though he hated the thought of it, Adam knew he was going to have to delete her from the program. The only problem was, he couldn't find her anywhere in the programming. He rubbed a hand over his face. The only way to deal with the glitch was inside *Beta Quest*. Hopefully, interacting with her would make her conform to the setting, though it was odd that the Reality Guard hadn't already taken care of her anomalies.

For some reason, Adam didn't experience the flash of irritation he usually did when things didn't go as he'd planned. Instead, he felt something very much like anticipation. There were worse things than hanging out with a computer glitch, especially one who looked like Kenzie.

Chapter 4

Dawn was painting the eastern sky with a vivid pink brush when Adam opened his eyes. This was usually his favorite time, when the entire day stretched out ahead of him, fresh and full of possibilities. Today, he felt nothing but misgivings as he watched the golden rays of the sun slice through the first blush of sunrise.

Though *Beta Quest* existed only inside his computer, it followed the natural rules of the universe. The woman, Kenzie, couldn't be deleted from here, and he couldn't change the course the program chose to follow. It was part of the excitement of the game and one of the biggest advantages *Fantasy Quest* would have over the virtual reality programs that had come before. He'd modeled his program after the holodeck that had been part of a popular TV series during his youth. Maybe Kenzie shouldn't come as a surprise. Characters were always getting themselves into predicaments in that imaginary world and having to figure it out. Just like Captain Piccard and Data, he'd just have to play it out and see what happened.

Kenzie lay curled hard against the warmth of his legs. Obviously, lying next to the fire, covered with the single blanket, hadn't been enough to keep her scantily-clad body warm. She'd been tossing and turning ever since he'd entered *Beta Quest*. It was sheer torture. Every movement reminded him how long he'd been without a woman and how good this one looked to him. Even with a vicious sunburn and covered with cuts and bruises, she was appealing. At any rate, she was better company than Bear Bait. *Who do you think you're kidding?* whispered an insidious little voice inside his head. *You'd think she was beautiful in a roomful of pretty women.*

Adam pushed the notion away with a sigh. It didn't matter what he thought of her; he'd programmed *Beta Quest* so that no one could use it as a sexual playground, including himself. Kenzie seemed to have gotten over her initial terror, but she obviously didn't trust him. Of course, that went both ways. He didn't exactly trust her either, with her little yellow devil duck and elbow of mass destruction. Everything she said and did reinforced his first impression. What computer character worried about getting dysentery from a canteen or was frightened by the mere mention of a horse picket? Nope, there was no doubt about it: he had a crazy woman on his hands.

It was hard to say why the program had created a glitch with bats in the belfry. Whatever the cause, he was stuck with Kenzie until he figured out what to do with her. The tribe thought there was great magic in such people, that they were to be protected and revered. Could that be where she'd come from?

Almost as if his uneasy thoughts disturbed her slumber, the woman stirred against him and threw her arm over his legs. His reaction was instantaneous and nearly painful in its intensity, just as it had been when he'd awakened with her in his arms at the hot spring. Adam ground his teeth as irresistible images of lovemaking tumbled through his head. It was definitely time to go. The last thing he wanted to do was trigger the Sex-Hex and shut the whole thing down. Carefully, so as not to wake her, he disentangled himself and crept from his warm bed into the sharp mountain air.

An involuntary shiver ran through him. Usually he draped the warm blanket around his shoulders to ward off the early morning chill as he built up the fire. Thankfully, it only took a few minutes to rekindle flames from the embers. As he warmed his hands, he scanned the clearing. Bear Bait looked half asleep, completely ignoring the squirrel that chittered at him from a nearby tree.

Adam glanced over his shoulder at Kenzie. She didn't appear to even realize he'd left. A single hand lay curled next to her cheek, and she slept with a slight smile on her face. A magpie flew overhead, his raucous call loud enough to wake the dead. Kenzie didn't even stir.

The only food he'd brought along was some buffalo jerky and a canteen of water. Another glance at Kenzie, and the blanket draped across her slender frame decided it for him. Jerky would be good enough for him, but she looked half starved. She should be safe enough here while he went to find something for their breakfast.

Adam had programmed certain rules into the structure of *Beta Quest* in order to maintain the illusion of reality. Characters had to sleep, and they had to eat. In *Fantasy Quest*, the players could choose to have grocery stores or cupboards full of whatever they wanted. But in his own little kingdom, Adam preferred to provide food for himself.

There had always been game here, though at first it had been fairly scarce. He never knew if the animals had increased or if his hunting skills had improved, but it was rare that he came home from a hunting trip empty handed. In the tradition of the mountain man, he used every part of the animal, jerking meat he couldn't eat fresh and making clothing from the hides and sinew.

Adam slung his powder horn around his neck then picked up his rifle and checked to make sure the powder was dry. With a final look at the sleeping woman, he crossed the clearing and entered the woods on silent, moccasined feet.

He hadn't gone far when he came across fresh deer signs. After a moment of hesitation, he decided to follow. Though he wouldn't be able to take the extra meat with him this morning, they weren't so far from his cabin that he couldn't come back and get the rest later in the day. He'd need plenty of meat if Kenzie stayed.

As he stalked the deer, plans revolved in his mind. The first thing he'd have to do was find Kenzie something more appropriate to wear. Maybe some of his mother's things would work. They'd be a mite large, of course, but maybe if he dressed her in the clothing of the period, she'd start to act accordingly. At least the clothes would hide her body. There was only so much enticement a man could take, and he was about at the end of his tolerance. Who would have thought he'd find shorts and a T-shirt so sexy?

A slight movement in the trees ahead drove all other thoughts from his mind. Moments later, Adam crept to the edge of a meadow, where a young buck grazed peacefully, the twin points of his antlers still swathed in their summer velvet. Adam raised the Hawkins to his shoulder and sighted down the barrel.

Just as he squeezed the trigger, a scream split the air. The lead ball kicked up dirt inches behind the deer, who bounded across the meadow toward the safety of the trees on the opposite side. But Adam didn't see it. He was already running toward camp, his heart pounding in his throat. All he could think of was the cougar he'd sighted yesterday, a large lioness with a den of hungry cubs to feed. One small, unarmed human wouldn't stand a chance against the big cat's fangs and claws.

Cursing the shot he'd wasted on the deer, Adam stuck a patch and ball in his mouth to moisten them and poured powder down the barrel of his gun as he ran. On an off stride, he hit the butt of the rifle on the ground to tamp the powder then slammed the wet ball and patch down the barrel with his hand. As he seated the ball tight with the ramrod, he wished he had a Winchester repeating rifle so he wouldn't have to load on the run like this. The entire process had taken little more than a minute, but it seemed like an eternity.

His long legs covered the remaining distance in record time, leaping obstacles in his path and dodging trees. A frightened whinny sounded close at hand, and Adam's stomach lurched in panic. Had the marauder finished with the woman and turned its attention to Bear Bait already? With images of horrible carnage racing through his mind, he burst into the clearing, the Hawkins already swinging into place against his shoulder.

It took a second for him to realize there was nothing to shoot. Bear Bait pulled and jerked on the reins that Kenzie held in her hands. The saddle sat on his back at a cock-eyed slant as though the cinch hadn't been tight enough when someone tried to mount. Adam's incredulous gaze snapped to the woman, who was covered with a liberal coating of dust and had a long, ugly scratch on one leg.

"You tried to steal my horse!" he accused. In a few quick strides, he crossed the clearing and grabbed the reins out of her hands. "Give me those."

"I-I just..." she stammered.

"I don't want to hear it," he snarled. "Get the hell away from my horse. It's going to take a miracle to get him calmed down after this."

"Look, I'm sorry. I didn't mean to get him all riled up like this. He hardly let me get a foot in the stirrup before he blew up."

The look Adam gave her should have scorched her. Kenzie started to speak but appeared to think better of it and withdrew to the bed of pine boughs on the other side of the fire. She never made a sound during the entire time it took for him to put the saddle on properly and quiet the horse.

When he turned at last, she watched him with wary concern as he put out the fire and started to break camp. "I... I don't know what to say."

"No, I don't suppose I could expect you to apologize for stealing my horse." His voice dripped with heavy sarcasm.

Kenzie had the grace to blush. "I'll admit it was a pretty stupid stunt, but when I woke up and realized I was alone... Well, I guess I didn't think it through. It just seemed like such a perfect opportunity to..." Her voice trailed off uncertainly.

"To what? Escape?"

"All right, yes. That's exactly what I was trying to do. Every prisoner has a right—no, an obligation— to escape if they can."

"Prisoner! Is that what you think?"

"What am I supposed to think? You followed me all afternoon even after I made it quite clear I didn't want anything to do with you."

"I was trying to protect you!"

"From what?"

Adam gazed at her in pure astonishment. "From what? Holy hell, this mountain is crawling with wild animals that would just love to make a meal out of a tenderfoot like you."

Kenzie snapped her fingers. "Oh, that's right. I forgot this is 1890. How silly of me."

"It's 1868," he said, beyond exasperated, "and I don't see what that has to do with anything."

"Haven't you heard? Most of the wild animals are gone, hunted to extinction by men like you."

"Only the beaver, and they were never very dangerous unless you backed them into a corner. There are still cougars and grizzlies aplenty. I suppose you're going to tell me you have nothing to fear from them, either."

"I saw a documentary just last week that said grizzly bears are basically vegetarians and rarely eat meat."

Adam snorted. "Somebody should tell the bears that."

"What is it about people like you that makes you want to kill helpless little animals?"

"Hunger."

"I guess I should have expected something like that from a living anachronism. There are laws against hunting out of season, you know."

Adam stared at her for a long moment then shook his head and went back to breaking camp. "Crazy woman," he muttered under his breath.

Kenzie sighed and rose to her feet. "Look, I obviously went about this all wrong. All I really want to do is go home. Can't you understand that?"

He glared at her. "Listen, lady, you don't want out of here half as bad as I want you gone."

"Then maybe we can strike a deal. If you'll just take me to the nearest town, I'll pay you."

"With what? I know damn well you weren't carrying any money yesterday."

"My fiancé will be glad to pay you whatever you ask when we get back to civilization."

"Fiancé! I thought you sent him on his way after he gave you the duck."

"No, that was Mark. This is Brad, Brad Marriot. Maybe you've heard of him?" she asked hopefully.

"Can't say that I have."

"Suffice it to say he can afford any price you name."

He snorted. "And you figure I've got nothing better to do with my time than go gallivanting all over the countryside looking for this beau of yours."

"Don't worry; I'll call him the minute we get into town. He'll have the money there in no time."

Adam raised an eyebrow. "He comes when you call?"

"He will this time. I'm sure he's worried sick. How much do you want?"

Adam turned away. "I hate town. I wouldn't take you there for a hundred dollars!"

"All right. How about two hundred, then?"

Adam blinked. *Two hundred dollars! Where does she think she's going to get that?* His eyes narrowed. "How can I be sure I'd get my money?"

"You have my word."

"The word of a horse thief?"

She frowned. "I left my ATM card and my checkbook in the car..." Suddenly, her face brightened. "I know! I'll give you my tennis bracelet for collateral." She unfastened it from her wrist and handed it to him. "It's worth a lot more than two hundred dollars."

Rainbows of light danced across his palm as he gazed down at the gold and diamond bracelet in his hand. Maybe Laramie was exactly the place she needed to be. She'd probably fit right in with the motley group of misfits there. Besides, he was curious about where this was all going to lead. It wasn't the first time things had come out differently than he expected in *Beta Quest*; just look at Bear Bait.

"We're leaving in ten minutes," he said, slipping the bracelet into his possibles bag. "Best get yourself together, 'cause I'm not waiting."

Kenzie didn't argue, just nodded her head and hurried off into the woods. Five minutes later, she was back, her hands and face damp and her hair curling in wispy tendrils around her face.

Adam resisted the urge to sigh. He'd given her time to answer the call of nature, and she'd decided to wash up in the frigid creek instead. The woman was a total idiot. "Here," he said, tossing her a piece of jerky.

"What's this?"

"Breakfast. Probably not what you're used to, but that's all there is until noon."

"And then?"

"Then we have more jerky." Adam shoved his rifle into his scabbard and swung up into the saddle. "We'll stop at my cabin to pick up supplies. Should make it to Laramie tomorrow some time."

"Are we going the whole way on horseback?"

"Unless one of us sprouts wings, we are." Adam took his foot out of the stirrup and extended his hand toward her. "Here, I'll give you a hand up."

Kenzie approached the horse uncertainly. "How do I get on?"

"Stick your left foot in the stirrup, grab my arm, and swing up behind me." When she did as he said, Adam leaned down and grasped her arm just above the elbow, certain that he'd crush the delicate bones of her hand. The strength of her grip on his arm surprised him as she swung up behind the saddle.

"Why don't you have a four-wheel drive?" she asked as she settled. "Surely, you need it when you come out of the wilderness."

Adam frowned. *ATM, four-wheel drive, a tennis bracelet… for pity sake, why isn't the Reality Guard working on her? Can I trigger it from here?* he wondered. A wagon or a buggy were about the only things in *Beta Quest* that had four wheels and could be driven. "Wouldn't be much use up here," he said finally. "A travois does the same thing, and it's easier to get from one place to another."

There was a long pause, then she gave an exasperated sigh. "All right, have it your way. I give up trying to talk to you."

It was fine with Adam if she didn't talk all the way to Laramie. He was used to silence — liked it, even.

What he wasn't used to was the feel of a female form against his back. For the most part, the cantle on the back of the saddle kept them separated, but whenever they crossed rough terrain, she'd put her arms around his waist and cling to him like the bark on a tree.

It was silly, it was distracting, and it was completely unnecessary. Adam found himself going out of his way to cross gullies, climb hills, and traverse creeks that he could have just as easily avoided.

They reached his cabin shortly before noon. Though Kenzie didn't complain, it was obvious the long ride had taken its toll. Her movements were slow and awkward when he helped her dismount. While he gathered a few necessary items, she wandered around the meadow with a slight limp, peering back into the trees. From the way she walked, Adam could tell the tender insides of her thighs were chafed and raw, probably covered with a rash, caused by the leather of his saddle. There wasn't much he could do for her except maybe put some bear grease on it. He considered it for a minute but then shook his head. No, she'd probably object to the smell.

One thing he could do, though, was get her into appropriate clothes. He ducked back into the cabin, crossed the dirt floor, and pulled a hide-wrapped bundle down from where it hung near the ceiling. The clothes were his mother's, or at least a virtual copy of them. Though she didn't quite have her husband's and son's enthusiasm for the mountain-man life, Barbara Johnson had often attended rendezvous with them.

Discovering the one-room, utilitarian cabin in *Beta Quest*

had been a surprise to Adam. Finding his mother's rendezvous clothing had been a shock. He'd never figured out why they were here, but at least they were in good shape. The mice couldn't get to them suspended from the ceiling that way, and the smoke from the fireplace should have kept the bugs out.

"Mr. Johns—uh, Adam?" Kenzie's voice came uncertainly through the door behind him. "Um, could you tell me where your bathroom is?"

Adam turned to look at her, his eyebrows raised. His subtle attempts to change her obviously weren't doing much good. Maybe it was time to bring out the big guns. "My bath room?"

She nodded. "I need to use it."

"You don't have time for a bath." He turned back to the bundle of clothes. "Besides, the closest thing I have to a bath room is the hot spring behind Rainbow Falls, where I found you yesterday."

"No, no, I mean the toilet. You know, your outhouse."

"Ah." Adam could almost feel her embarrassment. "Haven't got one."

"Then what do you—I mean where do you go…"

"Out in the trees."

"Oh."

There was a long moment of silence, then he heard her moving away. *Damnedest computer glitch I've ever seen*, he thought with a shake of his head. The smell of cedar and smoked leather surrounded him as he unrolled the bundle. The dress he'd been thinking of was right on top. His father had bought it for his mother at a rendezvous they'd attended on their honeymoon. Adam remembered seeing her stroke the soft, white leather and run her fingers through the fringe more than once. He'd been picturing Kenzie in it since the idea had occurred to him that morning.

Regretfully, he laid it aside. The dress was the last thing Kenzie needed. Riding into Laramie looking like an Indian would be worse than showing up the way she was. At the bottom of the pile lay a rumpled calico dress his mother had worn to her last few rendezvous. It was too big for Kenzie, but at least it was white-women's clothing, and she'd be decently covered. He rolled up the buckskin dress and put it in the Dutch oven to keep the mice away. Then he gathered up the cotton dress and went to find Kenzie.

He found her walking back and forth across the meadow.

"I decided to get some exercise while I had the chance," she said. "Is it time to go?"

"We'll leave as soon as you change into this." He handed her the calico. "It'll be too big for you, and it's a little out of style, but—"

"A *little* out of style! Good grief, things like that weren't even in style when my great-grandmother was a kid."

A muscle tightened in his jaw. "It'll be better than going to town that way. At least you'll be decent."

Kenzie glanced down at her clothing. "Since when are a T-shirt and shorts indecent?"

He folded his arms across his chest. "If you don't change, I won't take you to town."

"Oh, for cripe's sake. How the heck do you expect me to ride a horse in a long dress? The darn thing must have ten yards of fabric in it."

"Other people do."

"Have you ever tried it?"

He uncrossed his arms. "Hell no, but I don't ride in my underwear, either. You can't convince me your legs don't hurt from rubbing on the saddle."

Kenzie glared at him then glanced at his legs. "Don't you have an extra pair of pants I could borrow?"

"You mean my britches?"

"Yes." She crossed her arms and lowered her voice in a near perfect imitation of him. "If you don't lend me a pair of pants, you won't get your two hundred dollars."

His eyes narrowed, and his jaw hardened. "Threats don't work on me."

"They don't work on me either, so why don't we just skip

that part and come up with a compromise?" She softened her expression and dropped her aggressive stance. "Look, I'm not trying to be difficult. I just can't ride in that dress. The pants don't have to be anything fancy, and I'll pay you an extra twenty dollars for them."

"Twenty dollars! Hell, all I've got is an old pair of buckskin britches."

"All right, fifty, then. Please, Adam."

"How come you keep calling me that?" he growled.

"It's your name, isn't it? Personally, I like the sound of it a whole lot better than Whiskey Jug."

He glared at her a moment longer then turned and disappeared into the cabin. Several heartbeats later, he emerged with a wad of buckskin in his hand. His expression as he stalked toward her didn't invite comment. Ignoring the warning, she smiled and held the pants up to her waist, then she looked up at him. The legs were dragging on the ground.

With a sigh, he took them from her and pulled his buck knife from the sheath at his waist. He sliced a foot and a half of leather off each leg then tossed the pants to her and walked back into the cabin with the scraps.

By the time Adam emerged a few minutes later, Kenzie had slipped into the buckskin trousers and was trying to secure them around her waist.

"Here," he said, tossing her a rawhide string. "You'll have to use this for a belt. We're leaving as soon as I get the canteens filled. Be ready."

Not only was she ready when he returned, she'd even loaded the extra supplies into the saddlebags. But if she was expecting a thank you, she was sadly disappointed. He merely grunted and handed her a piece of jerky for lunch.

The afternoon passed much the same as the morning, with little conversation and a great deal of hard riding. Kenzie felt ready to drop by the time Adam stopped for the night. She didn't even have the energy to complain when he gave her the third meal of jerky. In fact, she could hardly stay awake to eat it while he fixed two beds, one on either side of the fire. *That must be why he'd brought the extra blanket along.*

As Adam lay down on his own bed he glanced at his rifle and then over at her. "Don't even think about it," he said in a threatening voice. "It's not loaded."

"What if we get attacked by wild grizzlies?" she asked sarcastically.

He turned his back to her and pulled the blanket up over himself, not even bothering to answer.

Kenzie crossed her eyes and stuck her tongue out at his back. Then, feeling more than a little silly, she climbed into her own bed. Unlike her companion, she did not fall asleep right away, in spite of her exhaustion. Her bed was freezing cold. Kenzie wondered why he'd bothered to make up two beds; it really was much warmer sharing the single bed. Oddly enough, she no longer worried about him trying to take advantage of the situation. He was interested in only one thing: getting rid of her. She studiously ignored the little niggle of hurt that accompanied that thought and turned her attention to falling asleep.

The next morning, Adam woke her at the crack of dawn. The sun was just beginning to peek over the horizon as Kenzie heaved herself up behind the saddle and settled in to chew on her breakfast jerky. She promised herself a huge meal as soon as she got to town and was solvent again.

The remainder of the trip took two hours but seemed much longer to Kenzie. She drooped behind the saddle, too exhausted to hold herself upright. Several times, she caught herself just as she dozed off. With the mood Adam was in, if she fell off the horse, he'd probably just leave her there. That was her last thought before she fell asleep against Adam's back. She awakened slightly when one of his big hands closed over the two of hers where they clasped each other around his waist. A smile touched the corners of her mouth as she drifted back into dreamland.

"Well, there's Laramie," he said at last. "Where exactly do you want me to take you?"

Kenzie jerked awake and pretended an alertness she didn't feel. "The nearest phone will be fine. One of the truck stops should—" The words died in her throat as she leaned forward and peered around his broad back.

The mountains and the surrounding prairie looked pretty much the same as they always had, but the town sure didn't. It resembled a movie set of the Old West, complete with clapboard building fronts, hitching racks, and horses. No, that wasn't quite right either. The town was too dirty and smelly, too realistic for a movie set. There were more tents than actual buildings lining the narrow street, which seemed to be paved with inch-thick dust and piles of horse droppings.

Kenzie felt a tickle of recognition and a deep chill of foreboding as she gazed at the busy little frontier town. It didn't look like a movie set; it looked like 1868!

Chapter 5

"Where exactly do you want to go?" Adam repeated, glancing over his shoulder.

Kenzie stared at the street in wide-eyed shock. Either Whiskey Jug Johnson had been telling her the truth all along, or she was having one whale of a hallucination. "This is Laramie?" she asked, hoping it wasn't.

"Yep." Adam looked back at the street and grimaced. "Ugly, ain't it?"

Kenzie's mind whirled with confusion and possible explanations. Insanity? An elaborate hoax? Time travel, for heaven's sake? Each thought was crazier than the last. She fought down a wave of panic. One thing was for sure: this wasn't the way home. If there was one, it lay behind them, on the mountain.

"Where do you want me to take you?" Adam asked, his growing impatience obvious in his voice.

"About a million miles from here," Kenzie murmured. She pinched the bridge of her nose with her thumb and forefinger. "What would you say if I told you I wanted to go back to the mountain?"

He put all his weight on one stirrup, turned halfway around in the saddle and stared at her in stunned amazement. "What?"

Kenzie gave him a weak smile. "I changed my mind?"

"Changed your mind!" His complexion darkened, and his eyes flashed. "You stole my horse, wrecked my extra pair of pants, promised me a small fortune to bring you to this hell hole, and now you've changed your mind?"

"You can keep my bracelet."

The look he gave her would have sent a grizzly running for cover, but he didn't say a word, just turned back around and nudged Bear Bait forward with his heels. Though the horse was less than enthusiastic, they proceeded down the street, dodging pedestrians and other horses. They stopped in front of a large tent with a wooden false front and a string of horses tied to a makeshift hitching rack. Adam swung his right leg over the saddle horn and vaulted to the ground.

"Where are we going now?" Kenzie asked as he tied Bear Bait to the hitching rack.

Adam didn't even glance her way. "I don't give a damn what you do. I'm going to get drunk."

"Wait!" Kenzie called as he disappeared through the door. It took several anxious minutes to dismount as Bear Bait danced around, impatient to be rid of his load. By the time she finally made it through the door and into the dim interior of the tent, Adam had disappeared.

It was a saloon, though it didn't look much like the ones she'd seen in the old westerns on TV. The whole place had a temporary look about it. Everything, including the bar, was constructed of raw, unfinished lumber, with crates and barrels forming the supports underneath. The only light came from the semi-translucent canvas walls, though several unlit lanterns hung from the center beam. The whole place seemed to be filled with smoke, noise, and unwashed male bodies.

A group of the most disgusting men she'd ever laid eyes on were gathered near the far wall, laughing uproariously at something. Kenzie shuddered and looked away. She was sure she didn't want to see whatever it was they were so interested in.

"You can turn your tail around and head right back out that door," a distinctly unfriendly voice hissed. "This place ain't for the likes of you."

Kenzie turned in startled surprise. A woman stood next to the door, hands on hips, glaring like an unfriendly bulldog.

"Are you deaf? I said get the hell out of here!"

Kenzie glanced behind her to see who had made the woman so angry, but there was no one there. "Are you talking to me?" she asked in astonishment.

"No, I'm talking to the cross-eyed mule next to you," the woman said sarcastically. "I hear the Golden Goose down the street is hiring."

Kenzie stared at the woman in open-mouthed amazement. Even to twenty-first century eyes, her profession was obvious. She wore heavy makeup, including several fake beauty marks, and her brassy blonde hair looked none too clean. All that was missing were ostrich plumes and a red satin dress. "I don't want a job. I'm looking for someone."

"You can look for him somewhere else. Clancy don't need any more girls, 'specially not ones that look like boys."

"You don't understand. I'm looking for Whiskey Jug Johnson."

The other woman gave a very unladylike snort. "Whiskey Jug? Lordy, you can't even come up with a likely name. Enough of your lies. It's high time you skedaddled." The other woman reached for her, a no-nonsense look on her face.

"I know he's in here somewhere." Kenzie desperately scanned the room. "He couldn't have—there he is!" she cried in relief as she caught sight of his familiar profile at the far end of the bar. She darted past the woman at the door and threaded her way through the patrons of the saloon.

Kenzie reached Whiskey Jug just as the bartender handed her tennis bracelet back across the bar to him. "Can't tell for sure, but it looks like paste to me. Diamonds ain't quite so bright."

Adam sighed. "I was afraid you'd say that."

"Of course it's real!" Kenzie said indignantly. "It was a gift from Brad."

Adam glanced at her. "Oh, hell!" he said, then turned away and took a healthy swig out of the bottle in his hand. "I was hoping you'd wandered off to blend in with the other lunatics."

"I'm glad to see you, too," she said. "Look, I'm sorry I—"

"Listen here, missy." The brassy blonde arrived with blood in her eye. "You can't just come in here and steal my customers."

"I'm not trying to steal anybody. Whiskey Jug and I are old friends, aren't we?" Kenzie looked up at him with a smile that could have melted solid ice. It appeared to have no effect.

"Do you know this little tart?" the blonde asked indignantly.

Whiskey Jug wiped his mouth on his sleeve. "Never saw her before in my life."

"I didn't think so." The blonde smiled with grim satisfaction as she grabbed Kenzie's arm.

"Come on, Adam," Kenzie said in her most conciliatory tone. "I can explain—"

He ignored her, fixing his gaze on the mirror hanging on the tent pole behind the bar instead. He paused, with the bottle halfway to his mouth, and stared intently into the glass. "Damn!" he muttered, slamming the bottle back on the bar with a crash.

For an instant, Kenzie thought he was coming to her aid, but he didn't even glance her way. She looked into the mirror, wondering what had caught his attention and saw several men on the far side of the room, laughing at something on the floor.

With a fearsome scowl on his face, Whiskey Jug turned and strode back across the tent, toward the group. They never knew he was coming until he grabbed the two closest to him, knocked their heads together, and dropped them, unconscious, to the floor. Another man in the group threw a punch that hit Whiskey Jug's stomach, but it seemed to have little effect. A second later, the man joined his friends on the floor, felled by a blow to the jaw by a ham-sized fist.

As if on cue, the entire saloon erupted into violence, with bodies and furniture flying hither and yon. Stunned by the sudden turn of events, Kenzie watched the fight in helpless dismay. Adam fought like a madman. One by one, the other men wound up on the floor. *What in the world lit his fuse?* she wondered.

Just when it looked as though Whiskey Jug would be the

last man standing, Kenzie caught a movement out of the corner of her eye. The blonde had Adam's whiskey bottle in her hand and was sneaking up behind him.

"Look out, Adam!" Kenzie yelled.

He turned toward the sound of her voice, just as the bottle crashed down on his head.

Kenzie winced as he hit the floor with a thud. Feeling more than a little responsible, she rushed to his side. Using the techniques she'd learned in first aid, she rolled the huge body toward her and gingerly settled his head in her lap.

"Out cold," the brassy blonde said with satisfaction. "One of you boys run and get the sheriff, before this polecat wakes up and tries to light out of here without paying for the damages."

"What damages?" Kenzie said indignantly. "All you have to do is set everything upright again. Nothing got broken except Adam's head."

"Thought you said his name was Whiskey Jug."

"It is, but—"

"Whiskey Jug?" One of the bodies next to the tent wall stirred and sat up. Kenzie was surprised to see long, black braids shot with silver; leathery, brown skin; and an advanced state of drunkenness. A pair of eyes so dark brown they looked almost black blinked a couple of times before focusing on the man in Kenzie's lap. "Whiskey Jug."

"You know him?" Kenzie asked in surprise.

The old Indian nodded. "The son of my sister."

Suddenly, Kenzie understood. Those men had been tormenting the old man; that's what they'd been laughing about. And Adam had seen his uncle in the mirror. No wonder he'd gone berserk.

Adam groaned and opened his eyes. He peered up at Kenzie in confusion for a moment then frowned fiercely. "You still here?"

Kenzie shrugged. "I didn't want to leave and miss all the fun," she said dryly.

"What did you hit me over the head for?"

"It was her." Kenzie said, nodding toward the blonde. "I tried to warn you."

"He was bustin' up the place," the blonde said defensively. "There's the sheriff now. We'll just see what he has to say about it." With a flip of her skirt, she stalked off to meet the sheriff at the door.

Adam struggled to sit up, closing his eyes against the pain. "Where's Jesse Three Dogs?"

"If you mean your uncle, he's right there."

Adam's eyes popped open, and he turned to look. A smile lit his face when he saw the old man was safe and sound. After a moment, his smile faded. "You're drunk."

"Good whiskey," Jesse said, patting an empty bottle that lay next to him on the floor.

Adam sighed. "It always is."

The sheriff arrived, bristling and ready for a fight. "All right, what the hell is going on here?"

Adam jerked his thumb over his shoulder at the men he'd dispatched. "These cowpokes decided to rough up the old man."

The sheriff stroked his mustache. "Way I heard it, you started the fight."

"I just evened up the odds some."

"He was only defending his uncle," Kenzie said.

The sheriff looked back and forth between Jesse Three Dogs and Whiskey Jug. His eyes narrowed suspiciously at Kenzie. "Uncle?"

"On his mother's side." Kenzie ignored Adam's warning look. He obviously didn't know cooperation was the best way to deal with law enforcement. "Surely, you can't blame him for protecting his family."

"Don't pay her any mind." Adam tapped his temple. "She's got rats in her attic."

The sheriff nodded. "I can see that. Probably shouldn't bring her out in public." They both ignored Kenzie's indignant gasp.

"What about the damage he done?" The blonde made a sweeping gesture of her hand that took in the other patrons of the saloon, now slowly coming to.

"That's right. Betty here says you owe Clancy a hundred dollars for bustin' up his saloon."

"That's a barefaced lie," Kenzie said indignantly. "This place was a wreck when we came in."

Adam pulled out Kenzie's tennis bracelet. "All I've got is this."

"Don't you dare give that floozy my bracelet!" Kenzie made a wild grab for it, but Betty was faster.

"Watch who you're calling a floozy," Betty said, holding the bracelet up to the light. "At least I ain't crazy." She squinted at it for a moment then made a rude noise. "This thing ain't worth a plug nickel. Don't even look like real diamonds."

Kenzie jerked it out of the woman's hand. "That shows how much you know about it."

"I know enough not to be taken in by shiny glass." Betty crossed her arms in front of her and glared down at Adam. "You must have something of value."

"Not unless she pays me the two hundred and fifty dollars she owes me," he said, jerking his head toward Kenzie.

Kenzie felt like a butterfly pinned to a display board as a dozen eyes swung her way. "I… I don't have any money. That's why I gave him my tennis bracelet for collateral."

Betty turned back to Adam with disgust. "I guess I'll have to settle for whatever cash money you have on you, then."

He shrugged. "I just spent the last of my money on a bottle of whiskey."

"That's so," the bartender said. "He tried to trade me the bracelet for some vittles."

The blonde transferred her angry gaze to the sheriff. "You're not going to let him get away with this, are you?" she demanded indignantly.

"Nope. You folks will have to leave. We don't need your

kind here."

"That's it?" the blonde squawked.

He shrugged. "Not much else I can do, Betty. Can't make the man give you something he ain't got, and you know we don't have a jail yet."

"What about the damage he caused?"

The sheriff glanced around at the former combatants, who were starting to get to their feet. "Fighting tends to develop a powerful thirst. I expect you'll get your money fast enough seeing to these fellas." He focused on Adam again. "In the meantime, you have exactly ten minutes to clear out of town."

Adam shook his head as though to clear it. "Time we headed back to the mountain, Jesse." He swayed slightly as he stood up.

Kenzie frowned up at him. "Are you all right?"

"I've been worse." He winced as he reached a hand down to help his uncle up. "Did you ride to town, Jesse?"

"Yes."

"Good. Let's get out of here before something else happens." He headed toward the door without a backward glance.

"Does the woman go with us?" Jesse Three Dogs asked.

"Damned if I know," Adam threw back over his shoulder. He reached inside his shirt and touched the talisman around his neck.

"I'm sure as heck not staying here," Kenzie said and followed him outside, with Jesse Three Dogs bringing up the rear.

Jesse's 'ride turned out to be an ancient mule with a blanket and two large bundles draped across its back. The poor animal looked as though it had already made one too many trips up the mountain. Kenzie had her doubts about whether he'd survive another. She forgot all about the mule as Adam untied Bear Bait from the hitching rack. His movements seemed slowed and almost clumsy as he mounted his horse. When he was finally in the saddle, he sat for a moment with his eyes closed.

Kenzie wished she knew how to convince him to take her back up the mountain, when he opened his eyes. "What are you waiting for?" he asked with a growl. "The sheriff said ten minutes."

Kenzie hid her surprise. "Uh, right. I was just giving you time to get settled." It was a good thing she'd had practice getting up behind the saddle. Adam gave her very little help, beyond moving his foot out of the stirrup so she could put hers in.

"Are you sure you're all right?" she asked, settling herself on the horse.

Adam pulled Bear Bait's head around and nudged his ribs. "I'll live."

Kenzie gave the broad back in front of her a worried frown. "Maybe you should see a doctor before you leave town."

"Damn interfering woman," he muttered.

Kenzie swallowed the rest of her sentence. So what if he passed out? It wasn't like he was driving a car, after all. Other than the jingle of the bridles and the creak of saddle leather, it was a silent trip out of town. Neither Jesse nor Adam seemed inclined to talk as they left the prairie and headed up the mountain. Kenzie wasn't about to make waves of any kind.

Several miles later, Adam began to slump forward in the saddle. Thinking he'd fallen asleep, Kenzie reached up and shook his shoulder. "Adam, wake up."

Instead of rousing, he listed to the side for a long moment, then tumbled to the ground.

"Adam!" she cried in alarm. The combination of the loud noise and the loss of half his load was too much for Bear Bait. With a high-pitched snort, he took off at a gallop. Kenzie lost her hold on the saddle and fell off. Her terrified scream was cut short when she landed in the dirt with a bone-jarring thud.

For several minutes she lay there, too stunned to move as horrible pain radiated from her tailbone upward through her body; she couldn't even breathe. Hot tears trickled down her face. She was going to die here without ever knowing whether she was suffering from a wild hallucination caused by traumatic brain injury or if she had done the impossible and traveled back in time.

"Whiskey Jug? Whiskey Jug?"

Through the haze of her pain, Kenzie heard Jesse Three Dogs calling to his nephew. How could she have forgotten? Almost without realizing it, she took a deep breath and rolled over to look. Adam lay in a crumpled heap on the ground where he'd fallen.

Kenzie groaned as she struggled to her hands and knees. She knelt there panting for several minutes as she took stock of her various aches and pains. For one thing, she could breathe again. Her backside hurt like the devil, but she wasn't paralyzed. Apparently, she'd just had the wind knocked out of her.

Jesse Three Dogs had climbed down from his mule and knelt down next to Adam. He rolled the big man onto his back and glanced at Kenzie. "You are all right?"

"I guess so," she said, rising gingerly to her feet. "I don't think anything's broken, except maybe my butt."

Jesse nodded wisely. "It is often the way when you get bucked off a horse."

"How's Whiskey Jug?"

"I don't know." Jesse knelt next to him and put his ear on Whiskey Jug's chest. "The dark spirit has not stolen his breath, and his heart is strong."

"Maybe he passed out from getting hit on the head."

"I think it is from his wound."

Kenzie raised her brows in surprise. "What wound?"

"The one that bleeds down his side," Jesse said, pointing to the dark stain on the side of Adam's shirt and pants. "You will have to do it."

Kenzie pulled her gaze from the blood stain. "Do what?"

"Help him." Jesse held out his shaking hands. "I cannot hold the knife steady."

Kenzie swallowed hard. "A-all right, but you'll have to tell me what to do."

Jesse pulled Adam's knife from the sheath at his waist and handed it to her. "First you must cut his shirt open so we can see where he is hurt."

Kenzie stared down at the knife. "I'm not sure—"

"It is not so hard as you think." He helped her insert the blade under the edge of Adam's shirt and showed her how to cut through the soft leather without hurting the man beneath it.

With a quick slice of the sharp knife, Kenzie slit the buckskin of Adam's shirt. She placed the knife on the ground and peeled back the leather. "Oh no," she whispered. Adam had been neatly sliced from the top of his shoulder almost down to his rib cage. Unable to soak through the buckskin, the blood had spread out until his entire body seemed to be covered with it. The pain must be terrible. A lump formed in her throat. He wouldn't even have been in Laramie if not for her. If Whiskey Jug Johnson died, she'd never forgive herself.

Kenzie looked around frantically, hoping for a miracle. There was nothing to see, not even Bear Bait. It was miles to the nearest doctor, and they had no way to get there except to ride atop an ancient mule. Panic reared its ugly head. She was stranded a hundred and fifty years in the past, with the one person she knew bleeding to death in front of her.

Chapter 6

Kenzie stared down at Adam's blood-covered body. We've got to get a doctor." Her voice sounded shaky, even to herself.

"It would take too long," Jesse Three Dogs said. "He has lost much blood. We must work fast."

"I don't know what to do," she wailed. "The first-aid class I took was so long ago that I hardly remember anything. What if I do something wrong and he dies?"

"If you do nothing, he will die anyway."

Kenzie knew it was true. Willing herself to be calm, she took a deep breath and tried to remember her first-aid class.

"We have to stop the bleeding," she said, looking around for something to press against the wound. One glance at Jesse convinced her he'd have nothing sanitary enough to even consider using. After three days on the mountain, her own clothes were just as filthy.

As her gaze fell on Adam's buckskin shirt, she bit her lip. It was probably home to a billion germs, give or take a couple of million, but it was comparatively clean. Besides, it had already been against the wound. Using it to apply pressure wasn't going to increase the chance of infection. The damage was done.

Praying she wasn't making a dreadful mistake, Kenzie used Adam's knife to slice off a good-sized chunk of his shirt and tried to wad it into a ball. When that didn't work, she folded it several times, taking care to keep the soft side out, then pressed it down on the wound with both hands. After a few minutes, she lifted the edge and peeked underneath. "It's not exactly what I'd call absorbent," she said. "But it seems to be working. I wish we had some disinfectant of some kind." She pressed the leather pad back over the wound. "I still don't understand how this happened."

"It must be someone knifed him during the fight," Jesse said.

"But I didn't see a hole in his shirt," Kenzie said in surprise.

Jesse rose and walked to his mule. "It was only big enough for the blade to pass through. That is the way of good buckskin." He retrieved his canteen, and what was left of Adam's bottle of whiskey, from his saddlebag. Then he knelt next to her. "When the bleeding has stopped, we must clean the wound."

Kenzie's eyes widened when she saw the bottle. "Alcohol, just what we need!"

"Use strong spirits, keep bad spirits away."

Kenzie smiled slightly. There was one for the medical books. Her smile faded as she eyed the canteen dubiously. "I sure wish we had more water. I don't think it's going to be near enough to clean him up."

Jesse shrugged. "Plenty more water in the creek."

"What creek?"

Jesse nodded toward a thicket of willows at the bottom of the hill. "This time of year, it runs clear. It is good water."

Kenzie had her doubts about that. During dozens of camping trips, she remembered her father saying it wasn't what you could see in the water that would hurt you; it was what you couldn't see that caused problems.

As her gaze traveled past the mule, her mind suddenly focused on the pack tied to its back. "You wouldn't happen to have a pan with you, would you, Jesse?"

"I have."

"Good, if you can build a fire, we can heat water in it to help wash off the blood."

After a moment, Jesse nodded slowly. "I will build fire. We will need it to keep Whiskey Jug warm anyway."

As he shuffled off to do her bidding, Kenzie had the distinct impression he thought she'd lost her mind. To him, cold water would have worked just as well. On the other hand, it was completely useless to boil water without a cloth of some sort to clean the wound. Even if they did get it clean, what in the world were they going to bandage it with?

The panic she'd been holding at bay surfaced again. If she didn't come up with something, Adam was going to die. The thought caused a strange tugging at her heart. Somehow, her perception of him had begun to change over the last three days. *Think, Kenzie, think!* She did a mental inventory of everything she had with her, which wasn't much: a T-shirt, shorts, underwear, shoes, and socks. *Socks! Of course.*

Kenzie glanced down at her lavender anklets. She could wash the worst of the dirt out in the stream then kill the germs by boiling them.

Adam lay still as death beneath her hands as Jesse built the fire and fished a pan out of his pack. She cautiously lifted her leather compress and looked beneath it. The bleeding seemed to have stopped. Stiffly, she rose to her feet and limped down to the stream. Removing her shoes and socks proved to be far from easy. Her injured backside radiated pain every time she moved.

By the time she managed to get her socks washed out and had hobbled back up the hill, Jesse had the fire going and water heating. He was working off to the side on some sort of contraption. She dropped one of her wet socks into the pan of water and went to check on her patient. Kenzie groaned as she eased herself down into a sitting position. What if she'd done permanent damage to her tailbone? She was beginning to agree with Adam's assessment of Bear Bait.

With a sigh, she settled herself as comfortably as possible and lifted the compress she had left on Adam's wound. Even to her untrained eye, the need for stitches was obvious. *I am in way over my head,* she thought. *What I wouldn't give for a cell phone and access to 911 about now.* The full impact of her situation crashed in on her. It wasn't a dream or a hallucination. She was stuck in 1868. She gazed down at Adam's bloodied torso. This man was the closest thing she had to a friend. Ok, maybe not a friend exactly, but he was the only person she knew here. If he died…

Kenzie didn't even want to finish the thought.

She looked at the pan of water and wondered how long it would need to boil before it was sanitary. It had a way to go yet; wisps of steam were just beginning to curl toward the sky. On the other hand, all the bad nasties were already at work in the wound. She glanced down at the bottle of whiskey. The smartest thing to do was to get the disinfection process going as soon as possible. Wiggling the cork out took several long moments, but it finally came loose with a pop. Kenzie gingerly poured a small amount along the length of the wound.

Adam's eyes jerked open. "Holy hell!" He tried to raise himself up on his elbows.

Kenzie put both her hands on his chest and pushed him back down. "Stop that," she said sharply. "You'll start bleeding again if you aren't careful."

He winced as a fresh wave of pain washed over him. "Dammit, woman! What do you think you're doing?"

"Tending to the knife wound you forgot to tell us you had," she said. "What in the world were you thinking? You could have bled to death."

"It's just a pin prick. What the hell did you do, anyway?" he grumbled. "It feels like you covered my shoulder with gun powder and set it afire."

She held up the bottle of whiskey. "This was the only antiseptic we had on hand."

"Jesus! You poured straight whiskey on an open wound?"

"I didn't have a whole lot of choices."

"You could have left well enough alone." He laid his head back and closed his eyes against the pain.

Kenzie glanced down at the second sock. "I suppose I could wash the worst of the blood off while we're waiting." She poured water from the canteen onto the cuff. It shouldn't matter if the sock wasn't sterile, as long as it didn't come near the wound. "I'll be as gentle as I can," she said softly and began to gingerly sponge blood from the undamaged areas farthest from the knife wound.

66

"He is awake?" Jesse Three Dogs asked from behind her.

Kenzie sighed. "He was, but I think he's passed out on us again. It's probably a good thing. He needs stitches." Kenzie poured more water on the sock. "I don't suppose you know how to sew up a wound."

"I have seen it done."

"You have? Where?"

"Fort Steele. Whiskey Jug did not like it."

"No, I don't suppose he did. Without anesthesia, it must have hurt like the very devil."

Jesse Three Dogs looked pensive for a moment. "There was no one named Anna."

"No, no, anesthesia isn't a person, it's—" Kenzie made a face. "Never mind that. What did the doctor use to sew him up?"

"I do not know. It looked like sinew."

"So much for that idea," Kenzie said with a sigh. "We're fresh out of sinew."

"Horse tail."

Kenzie glanced over her shoulder in surprise. "What did you say?"

"Hair from the tail of a horse."

"I'm sorry, I don't—"

Adam opened his eyes again and glowered at his uncle. "You're not sewing me up with horse hair!"

"Say, that's not a bad idea," Kenzie said, ignoring Adam's indignation. "Too bad Bear Bait headed for the hills. Do you think mule hair would work as well?"

Jesse nodded. "It is shorter, but it will work."

"What the hell do you know about it?" Adam demanded.

"I am the one who took you to the fort and held you down so the doctor could do his work," Jesse reminded him calmly. "I will do the same again."

"The hell you will!" Adam started to raise himself up on his elbows again.

"Oh, no you don't," Kenzie said, firmly pushing him back

down.

"Do not worry, Whiskey Jug. The cut is not so bad as last time."

"And she's no doctor!" Adam snarled.

Jesse appeared unperturbed by Adam's churlishness. "That should make you happy. You did not like the doctor. The woman will do a good job."

Kenzie's stomach clenched at the idea. "Oh, but I don't—"

"Do not worry," Jesse said. "Whiskey Jug will lie still for you."

"Tell him, Whiskey Jug." But Kenzie's words fell on deaf ears. Whiskey Jug appeared to have slipped back into unconsciousness.

Jesse rose stiffly to his feet. "I will go find my needle and make sure it is sharp."

"You have a needle?"

Jesse nodded. "I have all that is needed," he said cryptically.

No matter how she protested, Kenzie was unable to change Jesse Three Dog's mind. He listened politely while he plucked several long black hairs from his mule's tail and sharpened his bone needle. When she had finished the long list of reasons why she couldn't do it, Jesse showed her his trembling hands.

"You must," he said simply.

With a defeated sigh, Kenzie gave in and used the sterilized sock to clean the wound. Then she bathed the entire area with whiskey and mentally tried to prepare herself for what was yet to come. It was little use. She could tell herself that it was the same as hemming a skirt until the grass turned purple. Her better sense knew darn well it wasn't.

Jesse handed Adam the rest of the bottle of whiskey. "It is time. You will drink this, then we will begin."

For a moment, Kenzie was tempted to ask for a drink herself to steady her nerves. Instead, she retrieved the bone needle and one of the long black hairs. As she threaded the needle, she marveled at the long thin tip. *Who would have thought a piece of bone could be made so sharp?*

Adam took one last, long swig and put the bottle down with a thump. "Might as well get started if you're going to do it," he said with a growl. "It'll be dark before long."

Kenzie glanced at Jesse, who nodded and moved into position. The thought of him holding Adam immobile was ludicrous. He was half the younger man's size and twice his age. On the other hand, Jesse Three Dogs had a talent for making the impossible seem possible. After all, he'd somehow convinced her she was capable of sewing up an injured man with a piece of bone and a few strands of a mule's tail.

Kenzie dipped the needle and tail hair in the boiling water, counted to sixty then bent to her task. Just as she had feared, there was no way she could convince herself it was fabric she was working on. With every jab of the needle, blood welled from the hole and her stomach rolled. True to his word, Jesse held the younger man immobile, though Kenzie suspected it was because Adam was afraid of hurting his uncle if he moved violently. On and on, she sewed, one stitch at a time, pulling the sides of the gaping wound together in a crooked red line.

About the time she started on the second strand of hair, Adam passed out. It was a little easier after that, though not much. More than once, she had to stop and swallow the bile that rose in her throat and will her stomach not to heave. She used up the second hair and started on the third. At last, with barely two inches of her makeshift suture left, she came to the end of the cut.

With hands trembling almost as violently as Jesse's, Kenzie handed the old man the needle and surged to her feet. She barely made it to the willows by the creek before she threw up. One advantage of eating lightly was that it didn't take long to empty her stomach, though the dry heaves lasted a bit longer. When the retching quit, she collapsed on the grass. She lay there, eyes closed, until the nausea went away and the shaking subsided.

The smell of cooking food finally roused her. She was

surprised when her stomach growled in response. The sun was setting in the west as she sat up. From this distance it was impossible to know what Jesse was stirring in the pan. Probably some strange Indian concoction. She'd heard they ate all kinds of obnoxious things like crickets and roots. The thought brought back her queasiness, but she knew she'd better at least try to choke down whatever it was.

With a sigh, Kenzie rose and made her way down to the stream where she washed her face and rinsed out her mouth. Jesse looked up as she limped back into camp.

"Whiskey Jug sleeps," he said simply. "You did well."

"I don't think I'd want to do it for a living." Whatever was in the pot made odd popping noises as it cooked. She tried to see what it was, but a nearly impenetrable curtain of steam rose from the bubbling mass. It reminded her of the time she'd watched her great-grandmother make soap out of fat and ashes. Kenzie swallowed hard. "That fire sure feels good." She crossed her arms and rubbed her hands up and down them. "It's getting kind of chilly."

Jesse nodded. "It will be even colder tonight."

"I hope you have blankets."

"One."

Kenzie glanced toward Adam. "We've got to keep him warm."

"We will put him on the travois so he will not have to lie on the cold ground," he said, gesturing toward the contraption he'd been working on. "We will all share the blanket. Between us, Whiskey Jug will stay warm."

"Great." Adam might stay warm, but she sure wasn't going to. The travois would hold two normal sized people in a pinch, but Adam wasn't built along normal lines. There was no place for her and Jesse Three Dogs to sleep but on that same cold hard ground. Kenzie thought longingly of the bed of pine boughs Adam had made the night before.

Jesse gave his pot one final stir. "Now it is time to eat. We will save some for Whiskey Jug."

Kenzie stirred uneasily and tried to keep her face neutral as he pulled a tin bowl out of his pack and dipped her out a bowlful.

"The daughter of my father fed it to Whiskey Jug from the time he was young," Jesse said with the shadow of a smile. "It is said among my people that this is what made Whiskey Jug grow so big."

"Really?" Hadn't Adam told her it was bear meat that gave him his size? Kenzie's stomach gave another queasy roll as she gingerly accepted the bowl. "What exactly is it?"

His smile deepened into a full-fledged grin. "Your people call it mush."

Chapter 7

"I need a break." Kenzie said, leaning against a boulder beside the trail.

Jesse Three Dogs glanced back over his shoulder. "A break?"

"I need to sit down for a while."

"It is only a little farther to a stream, where we can water the mule and rest."

"I don't care if it's only ten feet; I can't go another step. You go on ahead, and I'll catch up." Kenzie tried not to snap at him as she gingerly worked her way down to the bottom of the rock, taking care not to sit on her injured hip. They'd been on the trail since shortly after dawn, climbing steadily over increasingly rough terrain. *You'd think the old man would at least have the decency to look a little tired,* she thought grumpily.

"What is wrong?"

"Nothing a good long soak in a hot tub and a bottle of aspirin couldn't fix," she muttered, resting her back against the boulder's solid surface. "I thought walking would help, but it only seems to make my backside hurt worse."

"You could ride the rest of the way to the stream. The mule won't mind."

Kenzie grimaced. "No, thanks. As much as it hurts to walk, sitting on your mule would be a hundred times worse."

"You could ride with Whiskey Jug."

"On the travois?"

He nodded. "There is room."

"I'm not so sure about that," she said with a wry grin. Adam's huge body sprawled across the horse-drawn stretcher like a blanket. "Besides, I'm kind of afraid to jostle him."

Jesse shrugged. "It would not hurt him to wake up."

Kenzie frowned as worry curled around the edges of her

discomfort. Adam hadn't opened his eyes since early morning, when she'd managed to spoon-feed him a few small bites of mush. "Do you think he's all right?"

Jesse shook his head. "It is too early to tell."

"Maybe it'll be better when we get him home."

"It is possible." He rubbed the mule's neck. "That is why we must get there soon."

Kenzie sighed. "All right, I get the point. Give me your hand so I can get up." The gnarled hand grasped her arm and pulled her to her feet with surprising strength. As Jesse Three Dogs walked away from her, Kenzie marveled for the dozenth time at the change in him. The slightly pathetic old man of the day before was gone with the last of the whiskey fumes. The trembling hands were steady now, the bent shoulders straight. An air of competence surrounded him, and in his eyes lurked the wisdom of the ages.

By the time she hobbled her way to the travois, Jesse had somehow managed to move Whiskey Jug over. "Are you sure this is a good idea?" Kenzie asked doubtfully.

"You cannot walk farther, and Whiskey Jug will not mind. His wound is on the other side."

"All right," she said. "I'll take your word for it." The empty space wasn't large, but it looked like a small piece of heaven to Kenzie. "Thanks," she said with a sigh as she settled into the spot next to Adam's big body. The abrasions from her wild ride down into the cave at the Sinks were still painful, and her bent, bruised, or broken tailbone throbbed. Add to that various aches and pains from riding for the better part of three days and then sleeping on the ground, and there wasn't a part of her body that didn't hurt.

"That is better?" Jesse asked.

"Much better. Thank you." Kenzie wiggled a little more snugly into her space and closed her eyes. "Let me know when we get there."

A few minutes later, the travois started moving with a bump and a jerk. The sensation of the poles dragging along the ground was a little strange, but soon her exhausted body began to relax. Adam's restlessness had kept her awake much of the night, just as she had thought it would. Though his injury had prevented much tossing and turning, his pain-induced mumblings and groans never left any doubt about his suffering. It had been a long, uncomfortable night for all of them. As the steady motion began to lull her senses, her eyes drifted closed.

The next thing Kenzie knew, she was fighting her way through layers of sleep toward consciousness. Staring up into the wrinkled face of Jesse Three Dogs, she tried to gather her scattered wits and focus on what he was saying. "Wh-what?"

"We are here."

She rubbed the sleep from her eyes and looked around the clearing. The sun was shining through the tops of the trees behind Adam's cabin. "Good grief, how long did I sleep?"

"Long enough for sun to cross the sky. I not bother you."

As her mind cleared, Kenzie suddenly became aware of a hard wall of warm flesh beneath her cheek and pressed against the length of her left side. In her sleep, she'd cuddled against Adam's body and pillowed her head on his shoulder. His arm was curled loosely around her in a possessive fashion that somehow made her want to burrow even closer. The sensation was heavenly and completely inappropriate for someone who was a week away from being married.

"I certainly didn't intend to fall asleep like that," she said as she struggled out of Adam's slack embrace and sat up. Maybe her unconscious mind had mistaken Adam for Brad.

"You are feeling better?" Jesse asked.

Kenzie rotated her shoulders experimentally and stood up. "I still feel like I've been run over by a bulldozer, but I guess I'll survive."

Jesse gave her an odd look, then unhitched the travois from the mule and lowered it to the ground. "We will each take a side and drag Whiskey Jug into the cabin," he said.

"All right." Kenzie bent over and lifted the travois pole on her side. "Oomph," she grunted. "Not exactly a featherweight, is he?"

Jesse Three Dogs didn't answer, but his face showed the strain as the two of them dragged the big man across the clearing. Kenzie's breath was coming in short gasps, and her arms were aching by the time they reached the inside of the cabin.

"Boy, do I feel sorry for the mule," she said as they set the travois down next to the bed in the corner. She bent over, put her hands on her thighs, and tried to catch her breath.

Eventually her breathing eased, and she looked up at Jesse. "So, how do we get him into bed?"

"I think we will have to put his bed on the floor," Jesse said, pulling furs from the bed and laying them on the hard-packed dirt. "I do not think we could lift him that high."

Kenzie gave a wry grin. "We'll be lucky if we can get him off the travois."

"You lift his feet," Jesse said, pointing to Adam's moccasins. "I will move his shoulders."

It took several more minutes of concentrated tugging to transfer him to the pile of furs. When they were finally finished, it was all Kenzie could do not to collapse on the floor next to Adam and go back to sleep. The image was far too enticing, and she bit her lip. If snuggling up to his solid bulk made her feel safe, she told herself, it was only because the exhaustion and stress of the last few days had taken their toll.

"It is time to look at Whiskey Jug's wound," Jesse said, kneeling next to the makeshift bed. "We will need water."

"I'll go get it," Kenzie offered, thinking fresh air and activity would clear her head.

Jesse nodded, and Kenzie slipped through the door, out into the last of the afternoon sunshine. She paused to listen for a moment then grabbed the bucket and headed toward the sound of the creek. It only took a second to find the well-worn trail through the woods. The trees closed in around her with comforting familiarity. It felt just like walking through a mountain campground in her time. She could almost believe she was back in the twenty-first century, where she belonged.

A sudden crackle in the underbrush brought her head around with a snap. Kenzie peered anxiously into the gloom. Nothing moved. After a few seconds, she shrugged and moved on down the trail. It was probably nothing more than a squirrel, she told herself, feeling silly for being so jumpy.

Even so, she had the uneasy feeling that something was watching her the whole time she filled the bucket. A half-forgotten memory rose from the back of her mind. Weren't you supposed to make noise to scare the bears off? It couldn't hurt. Kenzie started whistling and headed back up the trail. The sound quavered nervously as she approached the spot where she'd heard the noise.

Kenzie's whistle cut off in mid-note, and her eyes widened in horror as she saw a huge black shape back in the trees. Her brain said, "*Run!*" but her feet stayed rooted to the spot, every muscle in her body frozen with fear. The scream building in her throat sounded more like a whimper as it escaped her lips. This time, there was no mistaking the crashing for a squirrel. The animal gave a menacing snort and moved through the underbrush toward her.

As quickly as it came, the paralysis disappeared, and Kenzie took flight, her screams echoing through the forest like rifle reports off a canyon wall. The crashing in the woods matched her pounding footsteps. The animal was chasing her. Fear lent speed to her feet, and Kenzie ran even faster. Suddenly, her toe caught on a tree root, and she pitched forward, skidding along the path until she came to a stop, sprawling face-first on the forest floor just as the creature crashed through the brush ahead of her.

Kenzie covered her head with her hands, cringing in the dirt as she tried to prepare herself for the first fang or claw to pierce her body. In her state of panic, it took several seconds for her to realize the sound of the animal's feet beating a hard tattoo on the trail was receding. Instead of attacking her, it was running away! Astonished, she raised her head just in time to see shiny, black hind quarters and a long, flowing tail disappear around a corner of the trail far ahead.

Bear Bait!

Kenzie didn't know whether to laugh or cry as she picked herself up out of the dirt and went looking for the bucket she'd dropped in her haste. Funny how her opinion of Bear Bait had changed in the last few days. Far from thinking Adam had misnamed the animal, she now wondered at his forbearance. That horse was a menace!

By the time she'd filled the bucket a second time and made her way up the trail again, Bear Bait was standing by the corral, with his head through the fence, calmly munching the grain Jesse had put out for the mule.

"Oh, fine, now you show yourself. Why couldn't you have done that before you scared me half to death?" Kenzie sighed with exasperation. "I suppose you'll blow sky high if I try to catch you." The horse ignored her, and she tipped her head to one side. "On the other hand, if I managed it, Whiskey Jug might be grateful enough to help me get home." She set the bucket down. "What the heck," she said. "It's worth a try."

Kenzie approached cautiously, taking care to make no sudden moves. Bear Bait seemed to be watching her out of the corner of his eye but made no attempt to get away. "It's ok, boy," she said quietly. "I'm not going to hurt you."

She talked soothingly as she inched her way forward. Bear Bait continued to watch her for a few moments then went back to eating. In fact, he allowed her to walk over and pick up what was left of the reins. The twin strips of leather were much the worse for having been dragged through who-knows-what for the better part of two days, but there was enough left for her to pull his head back through the fence.

Much to Kenzie's surprise, the animal was completely docile as she led him around the edge of the corral and through the gate. She briefly considered unsaddling him but decided to quit while she was ahead. If the process proved to be as disastrous as her attempt to saddle the beast, she might not live through it. The saddle and bridle looked as though they'd had a pretty rough time of it, but Bear Bait showed no visible ill effects from his adventure. Surely waiting a little longer until Jesse Three Dogs could unsaddle him wouldn't matter.

Jesse looked up when she entered and stared at her in startled surprise. "What happened?"

"I found Bear Bait out in the woods."

"He gave you trouble?"

She glanced down and grimaced at her disheveled appearance. "You could say that. At any rate, I got him into the corral but wasn't quite sure how to unsaddle him. How's Whiskey Jug?"

"I do not like the looks of his wound, but it is early yet to tell."

Kenzie frowned. *An infection could easily kill him.* "What will we do if it gets worse?"

"We will have to get help."

"You mean like a doctor? Whiskey Jug will have a fit."

Jesse Three Dogs smiled. "There is one Whiskey Jug will not mind."

"Maybe we should go get him."

Jesse shook his head. "We would have to go to him, and the mule needs to rest. Besides, Whiskey Jug's wound may improve over night." He glanced at the fireplace, where a pot bubbled over the fire. "We will eat soon. Then you must sleep."

Kenzie resisted the urge to sigh. Mush again. Jesse's diet was no more varied than his nephew's. It had been a relief to eat it last night, instead of jerky, and quite filling for breakfast, but she was ready for something else.

"This will help your pain," he said, gesturing to the coffee pot gently steaming next to the fire.

"Good. I could use a cup of coffee."

"Not coffee. Tea."

"Really?" Kenzie wondered how they brewed tea back in the old days. Tea bags were years in the future, and she couldn't imagine Jesse Three Dogs carrying around a tea bob like her grandmother had used.

There was silence between them as Jesse went about his business, and Kenzie settled herself on the bed. "What is this dozer animal you speak of?" he asked, glancing up questioningly.

Kenzie blinked in surprise. "What?"

"When you woke up, you said you felt like one had run over you."

Kenzie's brow wrinkled as she thought back to her first waking moments. "Oh, you mean bulldozer?"

Jesse nodded. "It is not one I have heard of before."

"It's not an animal; it's a big machine they use to move dirt…" She trailed off. It was just plain silly trying to explain twenty-first-century technology.

"Ah." Jesse nodded as though her explanation made perfect sense. "Whiskey Jug also talks of such things."

"What things?"

"Your dozer bull sounds like the machines of his dreams." Jesse shook his head. "Buffalo Horn said they were dreams of great magic."

"Really?" Kenzie raised her eyebrows in surprise. Dreaming about futuristic machines was the last thing she'd expect from the volatile Whiskey Jug Johnson. On the other hand, steam locomotives would be the stuff of nightmares for someone who rarely came out of the mountains. "Maybe it was something he saw when he was a little boy, before he came here."

Jesse nodded. "It is possible. I will go take care of the horse if you will watch the mush."

"Sure thing," Kenzie said, peering into the coffee pot. The steam was too thick to see clearly, but it looked as though something were floating in the water, something stringy and green and very un-tea-like. She shuddered and turned her attention to the mush.

By the time Jesse returned fifteen minutes later, Kenzie had managed to find a bottle of molasses and Adam's dishes, such as they were. Two tin plates and cups that didn't even come close to matching were the sum total of his crockery. *Must not entertain much,* Kenzie thought with a wry grin as she set them on the rough wooden table and prepared to dish up the mush.

"Look what I found," she said, pointing her wooden spoon toward the molasses as Jesse came in. "We can have sweet mush."

"That is the way Whiskey Jug likes it."

She glanced toward the pile of furs and sighed. "If only he'd wake up and eat some."

Jesse nodded wordlessly and made his way to the fireplace. "This will make your pain not so bad," he said, pouring some of his concoction into a tin cup.

Kenzie thought of the long green strands she'd seen in the murky liquid. "Uh... Yeah, I'm actually feeling a whole lot better now. Thanks anyway."

"You still limp when you walk," he pointed out.

"Right, but it's mostly from stiffness. It doesn't hurt at all anymore."

Jesse Three Dogs looked disappointed. "It is true what is said among my people, then."

"What?"

"That white women are weak and cowardly."

Kenzie bristled. "We're not weak *or* cowardly. I just don't want your tea, that's all."

Jesse turned to dump the tea back into the pot. "I thought we had misjudged your race, but—"

A sudden image of the many people, white and brown, who would be killed in the next few years ran through Kenzie's mind. Maybe if the two cultures had understood each other better, there would have been less conflict. Changing one man's image of the whites probably wouldn't make that much difference. On the other hand... "Okay," she said with a shrug. "I guess it couldn't hurt."

Jesse beamed as he handed her the cup. "Be very careful. It

is still hot."

"No kidding!" She moved her fingers gingerly over the surface, trying to keep from burning herself on the hot metal. Staring down into the dark liquid, she could almost imagine it really was tea. Aware of Jesse's intent gaze fixed on her, Kenzie blew across the top and took a cautious sip. It had a strange, bitter taste. Surely the man wouldn't have any reason to poison her. "What exactly is in this, anyway?"

"It is willow bark tea."

Kenzie frowned. Why did that sound so familiar? Acknowledging that Jesse Three Dogs had very cleverly manipulated her, Kenzie finished the tea, and they sat down to eat. By the time they were done, she was beginning to feel very sleepy. "I think I need to go to bed," she said with a yawn.

Jesse nodded knowingly. "It is the tea. You should take the bed. I will sleep on the floor next to Whiskey Jug."

"Thanks," she said, picking up the blanket they had slung over the travois. With a yawn, she settled down into the bed and snuggled under the blanket. That willow bark tea was something else. Not only was she pleasantly drowsy, the pain was virtually gone. For the first time in five days, there wasn't any part of her that ached. As she closed her eyes, a thought clicked into place, and she suddenly remembered what you got when you boiled willow bark. Far from trying to poison her, Jesse Three Dogs had given her a good strong dose of aspirin.

"Grizzly!"

The hoarse shout brought Kenzie out of a sound sleep with a jolt. She jerked upright in bed, with her throat tight and her heart pounding. Confused and disoriented, she had no idea where she was. Then Adam's thrashing and moaning brought her attention to the pile of furs near the bed. Jesse Three Dogs was trying to keep the younger man still but was having little luck; Adam tossed and pitched like a bucking bronco.

"What's wrong?" Kenzie asked, her voice breathless with

alarm.

"His head is filled with bad dreams," Jesse managed to gasp. "He will tear his stitches."

With sudden comprehension, Kenzie scrambled out of bed and joined the fray. Less than a minute later, she went flying as Adam's arm caught her off guard and flung her to the side. She landed with a thump on the dirt floor, the jarring thud shuddering through her body in an intense wave of pain as her abused tailbone protested yet another attack.

Kenzie's eyes narrowed, and her lips thinned to a determined line. "All right, buster, if that's the way you want it, two can play at that game." Her self-defense training had taught her numerous ways to disable a man. Since most of them depended on causing intense pain, they wouldn't work with a man who was already out of his head. Still, there might be a way.

Her bruised body protested mightily as she worked her way around to his head. "Hold on to him, Jesse. I'm going to try something." With the heel of her hand, she gave Adam a hard chop behind the ear. Her aim was perfect, with her blow landing exactly where she wanted it to.

Any normal man would have crumpled into a heap on the spot. Adam opened his eyes and stared up at her with a hurt look strongly reminiscent of a boy whose pet hamster had suddenly grown six-inch fangs and turned on him with no warning.

"You hurt me," he said accusingly.

"I-I'm sorry," she stammered. "I didn't mean —"

With the speed of a striking snake, he reached up, folded his right arm around her head, then jerked forward. Kenzie somersaulted over his shoulder and landed flat on her back on top of the furs, narrowly missing Jesse Three Dogs, who scrambled out of the way.

Before her stunned senses had a chance to react, Adam locked his arm around her like a steel vise and tucked her against his undamaged side. She didn't recognize the language he spoke or understand the sharp question he asked, but Jesse's reply seemed to soothe the demons that haunted him. He hugged her closer, then relaxed into sleep once more.

Carefully, so as not to disturb Adam, she turned her head and peered at Jesse. "What was that all about?"

"Whiskey Jug asked if the grizzly was gone and if you were safe."

"He thought I was being attacked by a bear?" Kenzie could feel the uneven rise and fall of Adam's chest and the heat that emanated from his body. She reached up and touched his flushed face with gentle fingers. "Good grief, he's burning up with fever."

Jesse nodded worriedly. "I think it is time we take him to the village and let the doctor see him."

"The village? You mean we're going all the way back to Laramie?"

"No, we will go to the village of my people. Buffalo Horn's medicine is strong. It will be light soon. We will leave then."

"I'll help you get ready," Kenzie said and slowly started to extricate herself from Adam's slackened hold. She was almost free when he suddenly tightened his grasp and pulled her back down.

Kenzie didn't understand any of what he muttered over the top of her head, though she thought she recognized the words *haw-hase* and *grizzly*.

"He still thinks you are in danger." Jesse Three Dogs gave her a rueful smile. "I think it will be better if you stay and keep him calm."

Kenzie shook her head. "He must have me confused with someone else. I can't think he'd want me here; he doesn't even like me."

"Whiskey Jug is not one to show his true feelings."

She glanced doubtfully up at the mountain man who held her so tightly. "How do you know he means me?"

"He said he must save the *haw-hase*." Jesse shrugged. "It is the name he has always called you."

Kenzie sighed. "All right, I'll stay here, but leave the door open so I can call you if I need you."

"It is a good plan," Jesse said with a wise nod as he turned to go.

"Jesse," Kenzie asked curiously. "What exactly does *haw-hase* mean, anyway?"

There was a glint of humor in the old Indian's eyes as he glanced over his shoulder at her. "It means crazy woman."

Chapter 8

Kenzie jerked awake. Once again, she found herself in the crook of Adam's arm. It flashed across her mind that she had cuddled with the volatile and surly Whiskey Jug Johnson more in the last two days than she had with her handsome fiancé in months! She dismissed the odd thought as soon as it occurred to her. She couldn't deny it had been pleasant, but the last thing she needed was a case of runaway hormones caused by stress and lack of sleep.

"Whiskey Jug is not so wild now."

Startled, Kenzie twisted around and looked up at Jesse Three Dogs. Belatedly, she realized it was the travois stopping that had awakened her. "He does seem quieter, doesn't he?"

"Is he better?"

Kenzie could feel the heat of the big body next to her. Shifting slightly, she reached up and felt Adam's forehead. "I don't think so. He seems even hotter than he was last night. How much farther to that Indian camp?"

"We are almost there," Jesse Three Dogs said. "It is just over this hill. I thought you would wish to ride into camp on the mule."

"I'm not sure I'm up to riding yet," she said uncertainly.

Jesse nodded with approval. "That will be even better."

"What will?"

"If you walk in, leading the mule."

"Why would I want to do that?"

"Your injuries will feel better if you get up and move around."

Kenzie's eyes narrowed suspiciously. Something about the way he said it made her doubt the truth of his words. On the other hand, Jesse Three Dogs wasn't given to idle conversation. There must be a very good reason for her to abandon the travois before they entered the village. "All right," she said with a sigh. "If Whiskey Jug will let me, I'll do it your way."

Slowly, Kenzie began to extricate herself from Adam's slackened hold. She was almost free when he muttered something and shifted in his sleep. She froze, expecting him to pull her back, as he had every other time she'd tried to escape. This time, however, Jesse spoke harshly in his native tongue. Adam's features settled into a dark scowl. Looking down at the mutinous set of his jaw, Kenzie was astonished when he muttered something and let his confining arm fall away.

"What did you say to him?" Kenzie asked as she got stiffly to her feet.

Jesse hesitated for a moment then tossed her the mule's lead rope. "It is probably better you do not know."

"In that case, I don't *want* to know," Kenzie said with feeling. Considering how quickly he'd told her what *haw-hase* meant, it must be bad. Kenzie's tone was not lost on Jesse Three Dogs, who smiled and nudged Bear Bait with his heels. After a few hard tugs on the rope, Kenzie got the mule moving and followed Jesse over the crest of the hill.

At the top, she caught her breath in stunned surprise. A beautiful valley stretched below them in peaceful splendor. Grass flowed in a rich, green carpet across the wide floor and up the mountainside until stopped by a thick pine forest. The forest continued up the mountain to a broad gray rimrock that stretched to the north for miles. An Indian village was nestled on the banks of the winding stream that meandered through the bottom of the valley. It looked like something out of a picture book about the Old West. It also looked impossibly far away.

"Can't I just ride the travois down the hill?" she asked plaintively.

Jesse glanced back over his shoulder. "The hill is too steep. The mule will need guidance. You can ride on his back if you like."

Kenzie considered it briefly then sighed in defeat. The

insides of her thighs still burned where the skin had been rubbed raw against the leather of Adam's saddle, not to mention her aching tailbone. "No, thanks. I'd rather walk."

Jesse Three Dogs merely nodded and began the descent. The hill was steep and the path they took through the trees a winding one. At first, it was all Kenzie could do to keep up; her sore muscles protested every movement. Gradually, the stiffness began to abate, and she found it easier to follow Bear Bait down through the trees.

About halfway down the hill, they came out into a small, open meadow. Kenzie closed her eyes and turned her face toward the sun. The warmth felt good after the cool shade of the forest. She smiled as the mule's nose bumped her from behind. He obviously recognized the trail and was anxious to get home to the village.

"Just give me another minute," she said, reaching over her shoulder to scratch the animal's head.

It was hard to say how long she stood there. Time ceased to exist as she absorbed the warmth of the sun and inhaled the comfortingly familiar smells of the mountain. A soft breeze sighing through the trees masked all sound, except for the call of a distant crow and the soft snuffle of a horse nosing the grass beside her. The small sound brought her eyes open with a snap. A cry of shocked surprise escaped her lips before she had a chance to stop it.

She was surrounded by half a dozen Native American men on horseback. They all stared at her with identical enigmatic expressions in their fathomless dark eyes. The faces could have come from the Wind River Reservation in her time, but an aura of danger surrounded them like a cloud. As she stared at the lean, hard-muscled bodies, she realized these men were some of the fierce warriors of the plains she'd learned about in her history class—and they had no reason to love whites.

Kenzie tried to smile, but her face refused to cooperate. Frantically, she sought Jesse Three Dogs with her eyes. Apparently unaware that she no longer followed, he was clear across the meadow, about to enter the woods on the far side.

"J-Jesse," she called, her voice cracking into a squawk that didn't carry two feet. With a nervous little laugh, she cleared her throat and tried again. "Jesse!" she yelled, hoping the note of rising panic wasn't as obvious to the men as it was to her.

He glanced back over his shoulder then wheeled Bear Bait around and trotted back across the meadow. As greetings and smiles flew back and forth between Jesse Three Dogs and the others, Kenzie realized they were friends. In fact, they were probably from the village in the valley. They might even have been watching when the travois cleared the brow of the hill and had come to investigate. Suddenly, Kenzie knew Jesse wanting her to lead the mule had something to do with meeting these men. Though she had no idea what he'd been thinking, she found she'd much rather be on her feet and mobile when she met them than helpless on the travois with Whiskey Jug.

She watched as Jesse apparently explained Whiskey Jug's injury in great detail. One of the men dismounted and lifted Whiskey Jug's shirt to survey the damage. It was impossible to tell if Jesse mentioned her part in Whiskey Jug's misfortunes, but after a few curious glances, the men ignored her altogether. Finally, with a few sharp words, the man remounted his horse, and the entire party turned toward the trees on the far side of the meadow. Jesse Three Dogs rode with the other men, leaving Kenzie to follow behind with the mule.

"Don't worry about us," she grumbled at their backs. "We'll be just fine as long as a bear doesn't decide to have one of us for an afternoon snack." The mule balked, apparently dissatisfied with the length of their rest. The more she tugged on the halter, the more the mule set his feet. A glance across the meadow showed the last of the Indians disappearing into the woods.

"Come on, you stupid mule," she said with a nervous yank. "I won't find the way to that village alone." In desperation, she reached back and gave the animal a hard swat on the rear with the end of the rope. With a snort, it lurched forward. Adam groaned as the violent motion jolted the travois, but Kenzie didn't dare stop the mule to see if her patient was all right as she hurried across the meadow. It was a good thing she'd refused the dress Adam had offered her. She imagined herself tripping over the long skirt and rolling down the hillside. The buckskin pants fit remarkably well — better, in fact, than when she'd first gotten them, or so it seemed. One more odd thing in her life.

Though the men never stopped to let her catch up, Kenzie never quite lost sight of them through the trees. She began to suspect they knew exactly where she was and adjusted their pace accordingly. Of course, she had no delusions about why they bothered. If it hadn't been for Whiskey Jug Johnson on the travois, she had no doubt they would have left her behind.

By the time they reached the village, Kenzie was thoroughly disgruntled. Within minutes, they were surrounded by a crowd of women and children, all jostling each other as they vied for a better position to view the newcomers. Though they were openly curious about her, it was obvious they were far more concerned about Whiskey Jug Johnson than they were about having a strange white woman in their midst.

Kenzie glanced around apprehensively, searching the crowd for Jesse Three Dogs. Where in the world had he gone? A nervous quiver was just starting in her stomach when he came out of a tipi. The man with him had the same strong features and flowing gray hair, but that was where the resemblance ended. An aura of power surrounded the stranger as the two men walked toward the travois.

Without a murmur, the crowd fell back to let him pass through, strongly reminding Kenzie of Moses parting the waters of the Red Sea. Like the others, he inspected Adam's wound. After several minutes of firing what sounded like sharp questions at Jesse Three Dogs, he barked out orders, and several men came forward.

As they lifted Adam off the travois, the Indian turned his head and looked straight at Kenzie. She felt seared by the intensity of his dark eyes as he again spoke to Jesse Three Dogs. Then he turned and followed the men carrying Adam into a nearby tipi.

"Buffalo Horn says Whiskey Jug's woman has done well," Jesse said. "You are welcome in his home."

"Whiskey Jug's woman!" Kenzie squawked. "Where the heck did he get that idea?"

But Jesse Three Dogs was already hurrying away toward the tipi Whiskey Jug had disappeared into. Kenzie glanced at the crowd of women and children still gathered around. It was impossible to tell what they were thinking as they stared at her, their faces expressionless. A flicker of unease fluttered in her stomach. Though she didn't know exactly what Jesse had told Buffalo Horn, these people probably knew she had something to do with Whiskey Jug's current condition. What if they held her responsible?

"Wait for me," she called after Jesse.

After the brightness of the sunlight outside, it took a moment for Kenzie's eyes to adjust to the dim interior of the tipi. It was surprisingly roomy, far bigger than Kenzie would have ever guessed from the outside. An elderly woman appeared to be building up the fire in the center of the floor, while two other women hovered around Adam, settling him onto a pile of furs off to one side.

Buffalo Horn dismissed them with a wave of his hand and knelt next to his patient, on the floor. Kenzie moved closer as the man lifted the buckskin shirt to better examine Whiskey Jug's injury. It was the first good look at the wound Kenzie had had all day. The entire ragged length was puffy and red, the swollen skin dented every so often by the uneven stitches. Kenzie bit her lip. Unless she was very much mistaken, it was badly infected. So much for her rough-and-ready sterilization methods.

She felt a touch on her arm and turned to find one of the Indian women at her elbow. The old woman smiled and gestured toward another pile of what must be buffalo hides a few feet away. Kenzie glanced toward Adam again then reluctantly followed the woman and obediently seated herself on the hides, ready to jump back up if Buffalo Horn needed her help controlling Adam. These were his people, she reminded herself. His family.

When Adam didn't move while Buffalo Horn finished slicing off what was left of the buckskin shirt, Kenzie didn't know whether to be glad or to worry. He hadn't exactly been the best of patients the last two days. Either he was well enough to recognize Buffalo Horn, or he was too sick to fight anymore.

Without glancing at any of them, Buffalo Horn began barking out sharp orders. The women scurried around the tipi, bringing him an odd assortment of things as he asked for them. From a leather bag, he took a handful of something and threw it on the fire. The flames flared then settled, with only an occasional sputter. Smoke rose from the fire, filling the enclosure with the pungent aroma of burning herbs. Though the smell was not unpleasant, Kenzie began to feel slightly dizzy. As her tired muscles started to relax, she wondered muzzily if it were some kind of herbal anesthetic.

Buffalo Horn picked up a tightly wrapped packet. With careful fingers, he untied the thong and unfolded the layers of leather. Almost reverently, he lifted a long thin knife from the soft deer hide and placed it on a rock so that the blade extended into the fire. Through an almost dream-like haze, Kenzie watched Buffalo Horn mix the ingredients the women had brought him.

When the knife blade glowed red hot, Buffalo Horn took it by the bone handle and plunged it into a container of liquid. The hissing spit sounded abnormally loud and Kenzie closed her eyes, unwilling to watch the medicine man lance Adam's wound.

It would have been almost pleasant to drift in the darkness if Adam's occasional moans of pain hadn't reminded her what was going on beyond her closed eyelids. She gritted her teeth against the sound. After several long minutes, the big man was quiet once more, and Kenzie cautiously opened her eyes.

Buffalo Horn had finished his work and was packing away the tools of his trade, while one of the women covered Adam tenderly with a blanket. As Buffalo Horn rose to his feet, he murmured something to one of the women, who tossed another handful of herbs into the fire. Without another glance at Adam or Kenzie, he left the tipi.

Kenzie looked at Adam. He was resting comfortably for the first time since she'd stitched him up. She settled down in her pile of hides. Though the buffalo hair appeared coarse, it was quite soft and the bed surprisingly comfortable. Maybe she could rest her eyes for just a minute.

"No!

The belligerent voice brought Kenzie out of her doze with a jerk.

"Get that damn thing out of my face!"

Kenzie's momentary disorientation disappeared in an instant as a wooden bowl came flying at her. She ducked, and its contents splattered on the tent wall behind her. Her gaze turned to where Adam lay, slightly propped up and half covered with a buffalo robe like hers. A woman knelt next to him, a startled expression on her wizened face. Kenzie glanced at the wall behind her and grimaced at the mess dripping down the side of the tipi. The woman must have tried to feed him.

As Kenzie sat up, another of Buffalo Horn's women approached the first with a bowl of food. They held a low-voiced conversation for several minutes, then the two women traded places. They had barely settled when Adam sent the second bowl after the first. In spite of his apparent alertness, it was obvious he wasn't cognizant of where he was or what was going on.

Kenzie sighed. "All right, I'm coming." Mindful of her stiffness and the aches and pains that tormented every part of her tortured body, she crawled the short distance between her bed and Adam's.

She pantomimed eating to the two women, then pointed from herself to Adam. "If you'll give me some more food, I'll give it a try." They gave her a doubtful look then glanced at each other. After a moment, the older one shrugged and nodded.

Kenzie touched Adam's shoulder. "It's time you settled down and stopped giving everybody such a hard time."

Whiskey Jug turned toward the sound of her voice. "*Haw-hase?*"

"Yeah," she said with a wry grimace. "It's me, your resident crazy lady." The older woman handed her a bowl of stew and a spoon that appeared to have been made from some sort of horn. Kenzie took a spoonful and blew across it to cool the liquid. "You really should eat this lovely stew these nice ladies cooked for you."

"You hit me," he said accusingly.

Kenzie could feel herself blushing. She'd hoped he wouldn't remember her aborted self-defense move. "Yes, I did, and I'll do it again if I have to. Now be a good boy and open your mouth."

He looked grumpy for a long moment then obediently accepted the spoonful of stew.

"There, now. That wasn't so bad, was it?" she said, dipping the spoon back into the bowl.

"I can't let you wear my ma's dress."

Kenzie frowned. "What are you talking about?"

"I kept thinking how pretty you'd look in it," Adam said, pushing aside the spoonful of stew she offered him.

Kenzie peered at him. His eyes had a glassy look in the dim light. "Do you have any idea where you are, Whiskey Jug?"

He sighed. "But the folks in Laramie would run you out of town on a rail if you showed up in an Indian dress."

"Oh, great," Kenzie said. "I might as well be talking to the wall."

"Guess I'll have to let you wear the white woman dress Pa

got at the rendezvous."

Kenzie set her jaw. "I'm not doing anything unless you eat some more stew."

He glared at her. "Damn contrary woman."

"Look who's talking. Now eat, or I'm leaving."

Whiskey Jug's expression grew darker still, but he accepted the spoonful of stew, and the next, with no comment. In fact, half the bowl disappeared before he pushed it away.

"So tired," he muttered as he sank back down into the furs and closed his eyes.

Kenzie felt his forehead and was relieved to find it cooler. Buffalo Horn's medicine seemed to be having the desired effect.

The elder of the two Indian women took the bowl from her and replaced it with another filled with stew. She pointed at Kenzie and pantomimed eating.

"Thank you," Kenzie said with a smile. Then she rubbed her stomach. "I am rather hungry, now that you mention it." The stew was delicious and left her feeling comfortably full and sleepy. It didn't take much convincing from the old woman for Kenzie to seek her own bed once more.

Adam did not awaken again that day. When darkness fell, Buffalo Horn came to check on his patient. It was hard to tell, but Kenzie thought he looked pleased. During the long night that followed, Adam slept restlessly and awoke several times. Since Kenzie was the only one in the tipi he would take food or water from, she slept in fits and starts. Though Adam appeared to be growing stronger, he was still delusional.

The next day was long and difficult, but Kenzie refused to leave Adam's side. If he died, she'd be stranded here in the village, with people who might not look too kindly on her without him. Even if they were inclined to help her, she couldn't communicate with them. How could she make them grasp what had happened to her when she didn't understand it herself?

By late afternoon, she was exhausted. The old woman finally sent her to her pile of furs and indicated it was time for her to rest. Kenzie reluctantly agreed, thinking she'd only rest a moment or two and then return to her patient's bedside.

Kenzie had no idea how long she slept before she woke with a start. It had to be sometime after sundown, because the tipi was dark except for the glow of coals from the fire pit. For a moment she wondered what had wakened her. Then she heard it again. Adam was muttering in his sleep.

She made her way across the darkened tipi. Her patient seemed to be sleeping, but she could see his brow furrowed as though he were in pain. She reached out and felt his forehead. Suddenly, Adam's eyes popped open, glittering up at her in the dim light.

A slow, sensuous smile slid across his face. "*Na hate*," he murmured softly in an unfamiliar tongue. Without warning, muscular arms surrounded her and pulled her down into a tender embrace. Kenzie was afraid to struggle. What if she reopened Adam's wound? The thought barely had time to flit through her mind when his mouth claimed hers in a soft, coaxing kiss, and she ceased to think at all.

"*Hicka!*" At first the sharp command failed to penetrate the sensual haze that surrounded Kenzie. She was only aware of Adam and the pleasure coursing through her.

"*Hicka!*" The sound of a slap rang through the air and Kenzie tumbled out of Adam's arms. The old woman stood over them, glaring down at them with a look of severe disapproval.

Adam blinked up at her and rubbed his bare arm. "You didn't have to hit me so hard, Red Blanket."

The old woman shook her spoon at him as she delivered what appeared to be a long lecture in her native tongue. Adam looked sullen as she continued to scold but never interrupted. At last, apparently satisfied that she'd chastised him sufficiently, she handed Kenzie the spoon and gestured to the kettle of stew on the fire.

"You feed Wheesky Jug." Then, with one last fearsome scowl at Adam, she turned and left the tipi.

Adam grimaced and turned his gaze to Kenzie. "You're still here."

"Where else would I be?"

"I don't know. I guess I thought you'd go back to where you came from."

"I would if I could," she muttered as she dipped a fresh bowl of stew from the pot. She schooled her face into a smile as she turned back toward her patient. "Why don't you try some of this fabulous stew Red Blanket made for you?"

He gave her an odd look. "How did we get here?"

"When you started to get violent, Jesse Three Dogs decided you needed to see a doctor, so he brought you here." She dipped the spoon into the fragrant stew and brought the spoonful to his mouth. "I'm glad you're really awake this time. I was afraid you were still out of your head."

"What do you mean violent?"

"You started thrashing around. It took both of us to subdue you that time." Kenzie thought it best not to tell him quite how that had been accomplished, since he seemed to have forgotten. "You've been yelling about grizzlies and trying to protect me ever since."

He looked startled. "How long has that been going on?"

"Off and on for a couple of days."

"Red Blanket says you've taken care of me since I got here," Adam said.

"I didn't have much choice."

He frowned. "Why not?"

"You wouldn't let anybody else near you except Buffalo Horn, and he didn't seem inclined to nurse his spoiled brat nephew." She gave him another spoonful of stew. "Besides, I didn't have anything better to do. This tipi isn't exactly full of entertainment options."

"Thanks," he said gruffly.

She shrugged. "You'd have done the same for me."

Adam gave her an enigmatic stare. "What the hell gave you that idea?"

"Well, I guess because you've been trying to take care of me since we met, even when…" Kenzie faltered as she remembered her part in the events leading up to his injury. He could easily hold her responsible. Maybe he did.

"You know," she said, "Red Blanket and I are getting to be friends, even though she doesn't speak much English. It's amazing how fast I learned to understand her sign language. I suppose she's your aunt, and Buffalo Horn is your uncle?"

"More or less." He looked thoughtful as he chewed and swallowed. "I don't remember much of anything after we rode into Laramie. I seem to recall finding Jesse Three Dogs in the saloon."

"Right. That's where you got knifed."

He blinked. "Knifed?"

"You got into a fight with the cowboys who were harassing Jesse Three Dogs. He was…um, sort of under the weather, and they were taking advantage of the situation. You managed to get the best of them all, but not before one of them knifed you." Kenzie nodded toward his injury. "Being the stubborn person that you are, we didn't know about it until we were halfway to the mountain. If Jesse hadn't forced me to sew you up with a couple of strands of hair from his mule's tail, you would have bled to death."

Adam stared at her, his face a study of confusion and astonishment. "Maybe you'd better tell me the whole story."

"All right, but you have to promise to eat while I do." Kenzie shoved another spoonful into his mouth before he could answer. "You know, I was kind of nervous about what I was eating at first." Her mouth formed a rueful smile. "I think Jesse Three Dogs knew it too and couldn't resist the urge to tease me. I realize now how silly that was of me. This stew is really quite delicious."

"Mm. It's a specialty of Red Blanket's," Adam said around a mouthful. "She says it makes you strong and cunning."

"Really. What is it?"

"It's called Cee-cee."

"Oh? What does that mean in English?"

Whiskey Jug gave her a wolfish grin. "Rattlesnake."

Chapter 9

"I need to take a bath." Kenzie pantomimed washing her hands and arms to Red Blanket.

The other woman nodded and pointed to the container of water near the fire.

"No, no. I meant a whole-body bath." Kenzie pretended to scrub her body and legs. "Oh, please understand me."

Red Blanket shook her head. "*Nockoo.*"

"*Nockoo?*" Kenzie frowned in confusion. "What in the world does that mean?"

"It means the water is too cold to wash in," came a deep voice from behind her.

Kenzie whirled around. "Adam, you're awake! How are you feeling?"

"Like I got hit in the shoulder by a porcupine. How long was I asleep this time?"

"Nearly a day. Are you hungry?"

"Not really."

"You sure?"

"Yes, I'm sure," he said irritably. "I ought to know if I'm hungry or not."

"All right, I believe you." She gave him a considering look. "Will you do something for me?"

Adam narrowed his eyes. "That depends on what you had in mind."

"It is possible to take a bath, right?"

He shrugged. "It is if you aren't picky about warmth. The only place around here would be the creek, and it's a mite chilly this time of year."

"At this point I could bathe in glacier runoff. What about soap?"

A ghost of a smile crossed his face. "Now, that I can get

you." He said a few words to Red Blanket.

The old woman looked at Kenzie then shook her head and headed for the flap of the tipi. Kenzie could have sworn she heard the word *haw-hase* as Red Blanket ducked through the opening and went outside.

"I take it that means no," Kenzie said, disappointment heavy in her voice.

Adam grinned. "No, it just means she's going to get your soap for you."

"But she thinks I'm crazy."

"Why do you say that?"

"She called me *haw-hase*."

Adam raised an eyebrow. "So?"

"Oh, come off it, Adam. Jesse told me it means *crazy woman*."

He gave her a startled look. "When did he do that?"

"Right after you tossed me on the ground."

"What?"

"At the cabin. Remember I mentioned you were out of your head with fever and kept hallucinating about a bear? When you got unmanageable, Jesse and I had to hold you down so you wouldn't tear your stitches."

He was incredulous. "And I threw you on the ground?"

"I think you took exception to me hitting you."

Adam frowned. "You hit me?"

Kenzie felt the heat rush to her face. "Well, yeah... We had to stop you. I was afraid you were going to hurt Jesse, the way you were flailing around." She pretended to study the pile of furs she'd slept on. "Anyway, my self-defense training didn't work on you."

He rubbed the back of his ear. "None of this makes any sense."

"You had a fever. It's not unusual for a high temperature to cause hallucinations. That's all it was."

Whiskey Jug looked pensive. "There's something very odd going on here."

"Oh, for —" Kenzie shook her head in frustration. *Honestly, he's as thick as a post,* she thought.

Red Blanket's return saved Kenzie from another futile argument. Without a word, the older woman handed her something that looked like a small sweet potato. Kenzie looked at it blankly then glanced up at Red Blanket. "I don't understand."

"It's your soap," Whiskey Jug said with a grin.

Kenzie raised an eyebrow. "My soap?"

"Yep. Just smash it with a rock and start rubbing on it."

"Oh, right, and that's when the whole tribe turns out to laugh at me."

He chuckled. "It's called soap weed. You'd probably recognize the plant it comes from."

"I would?"

"Ever see yucca?"

Kenzie frowned. "It's a tall, spiny plant that lives in the desert, right?"

"Right, and this is the root. The Indians have used it for soap for hundreds of years."

Kenzie looked doubtful as she glanced back down at the root in her hand. "Ok, so where do I go for my bath?"

"Just a minute. I'll ask Red Blanket. The camp may have moved since the last time I was here."

Adam and Red Blanket conferred for several minutes. Even though Kenzie couldn't understand what they were saying, it was obvious Red Blanket wasn't comfortable with her guest's proposed bath. Adam finally seemed to convince his aunt, and with one last shake of her head, Red Blanket gestured for Kenzie to follow her outside.

As soon as the flap fell after the two women, Adam gingerly lifted the bandage on his shoulder. He stared at the wound in astonishment. It mirrored the incision the surgeon had made, but it was sewn together with odd little stitches. He couldn't quite tell what they were made of, but it didn't look like any thread he'd ever seen. He could almost believe it was from the tail of Jesse's mule, as Kenzie had said.

Adam pulled the bandage back over the wound and stared up at the smoke hole in the top of the tipi.

What the hell is going on?

Three days ago, he'd left *Beta Quest* in Laramie City right outside the saloon. Everything inside the program should have stopped. It hadn't. In fact, it appeared that a significant amount of time had passed; Kenzie had a very convincing story of all that had happened. He — or at least his body — had been present and had reacted to what was going on around him. How could that be?

Then there was the wound on his shoulder. It was an exact copy of the surgery the doctors had performed, though it had been closed in a completely different manner.

The residual effects of anesthesia always gave him odd dreams. This time they'd been a confusing welter of *Beta Quest* snippets with one very vivid dream he'd had of Kenzie sleeping in his arms, snuggling into his warmth and making sweet little sounds of satisfaction. His memory of that particular dream is what had brought him back to *Beta Quest* almost as soon as he'd hit his front door. Adam grimaced as he thought of the fit Annie had when she came back from her errand and found him hooked up to his computer. She wouldn't be much happier if she knew he was there again today.

Still, there was much here that needed to be explored. With the release of *Fantasy Quest* less than six months away, he had to know what had happened to his prototype. Was he dealing with a simple glitch, or had the program gone through a major transformation?

Adam frowned suddenly and rubbed his hand over his face, half expecting to find himself clean-shaven. The beard and long hair he sported inside *Beta Quest* were still there. Not everything had changed, then, and so far there didn't seem to be any danger. His first inclination was to just delete the program, but he couldn't. Whatever had happened here could have ramifications in *Fantasy Quest*. His best bet was to wait and see what happened. It was going to take careful study, and Kenzie Armstrong was the key.

After the soft-muted light inside the tipi, the sunlight outside was almost painful. Kenzie blinked several times, and the camp came into focus around her. Other than a few curious stares, people went about their business, undisturbed by the strange white woman in their midst.

Pots bubbled over small cooking fires while women knelt nearby, stretching and scraping hides or grinding a fine powder between two stones. Small children and dogs frolicked among the working women, receiving smiles and an occasional word of encouragement.

There was no sign of the men who had escorted her to camp. They were probably off hunting or something. Of course, she hadn't seen any men except Adam and Buffalo Horn since she'd arrived. For all she knew, they could be out fighting a war somewhere. Even Jesse Three Dogs was strangely absent.

Red Blanket led her out of the village and down through a thicket of willows, to a wide stream at the bottom of the hill. The water was so clear Kenzie could see the rocks and moss on the bottom. Though the tell-tale dimples swirling in the water indicated a fairly strong current, it looked almost calm. The crystalline depths were so inviting in the warm sunshine that Kenzie smiled in anticipation.

Red Blanket took the yucca root from Kenzie and squatted next to the stream. She laid the root down on a flat boulder and smashed it to a pulp with a fist-sized stone.

"I use that on my hair, right?" Kenzie eagerly gathered up her tangled locks and pretended to wash it.

Red Blanket nodded then gave the creek a dubious look. "*Nockoo*," she said again.

"I know, it's cold," Kenzie said, "but I feel so grungy I don't care what it feels like as long as it's wet and will get me clean."

Red Blanket gazed at her a moment longer then shrugged and turned away. Kenzie was almost certain she heard the word *haw-hase* again as the older woman shuffled away.

"Yeah, you're probably right," Kenzie muttered as she unbraided her hair. A cautious look around as she kicked off her sneakers convinced her she was alone. Skinny- dipping in ice water was bad enough. A peeping tom would make the miserable experience complete. Those trees across the creek would make a perfect hiding place for one. She stared at the spot for a long moment, probing the shadows for a hidden menace. Then she shook her head and looked away. *Talk about paranoid!*

With a quick twist, she grabbed the bottom of her shirt and pulled it off over her head. The buckskin britches weren't far behind. She felt horribly exposed, standing there in her skimpy underwear, but she still hesitated. Inviting as it looked, Kenzie knew Red Blanket hadn't been exaggerating about the temperature of the water. From experience, she knew her body would adjust quicker if she just plunged right in.

Gritting her teeth against the cold, she stripped off her underwear, grabbed the yucca root and waded quickly out into the stream. The thigh-deep water was so cold Kenzie could hardly catch her breath, and she couldn't force herself to wade any farther into the stream. A deep, painful ache settled in her legs, and gooseflesh popped up all over her body.

"Holy catfish!" she gasped. "I thought I was kidding about the glacier runoff."

She scrubbed her body and washed her hair in record time, but her skin had a blue tinge when she finally staggered out of the stream. Shivering uncontrollably, she struggled into her shirt and pants. The cotton of her T-shirt and the buckskin stuck to her damp skin, but the warmth it had absorbed from the sun was welcome. Her hair hung down her back like an unpleasant wet blanket. Bending forward, she swung it over her shoulder and tried to wring the water out. "What I wouldn't give for a towel and a hairdryer right now," she murmured.

Though her drying method left something to be desired, Kenzie managed to get the worst of the water out. Her natural curl was already taking over, and there was little she could do with the tangled mass. Even braiding was out of the question without a comb or brush. With a sigh, she reached over and broke a couple of sticks off a nearby bush. She twisted her wet hair into a rope, wound it into a knot on top of her head, and secured it with the sticks. Hopefully the sticks would hold her hair in place the way pencils had at home.

Though the warmth of the buckskin had disappeared, Kenzie was grateful for its protection on her lower body. The T-shirt clung damply to her curves and did little to stop her violent shivering. Her jaws were beginning to ache from the constant chattering of her teeth. As she picked up her underwear and turned back toward the creek, she thought longingly of the blessedly warm fire in Buffalo Horn's tipi.

Soon, she promised herself. *Soon*. Her numbed fingers felt awkward as she spread her underwear on a rock at the water's edge and began scrubbing them with the yucca root.

Kenzie had just about decided her socks were a lost cause, when a sudden noise brought her eyes up with a start. She scanned the woods on the other side of the stream, looking for the source of the sound. The hair on the back of her neck began to prickle as she saw a movement back in the trees.

"Who's there?" she called out.

For a long moment, there was no answer. Then a man stepped out of the shadows. Though he was dressed like the men who had brought them to the village, Kenzie was almost certain she had never seen him before. A man like this would stand out in a crowd. Two eagle feathers woven into the long hair that hung loose about his shoulders, and the polished bone breastplate that covered his naked torso, as much as the gun he carried in one hand, marked him as a man to be reckoned with. Tall and regal, he stared at her with an almost predatory gleam in his dark eyes.

"A-are you from the village?" she asked, pointing her thumb back over her shoulder toward the tipis that were hidden by the trees at the top of the hill.

He uttered not a word as his gaze raked her from the top of her head to her bare toes. Kenzie wondered uneasily how long he'd been standing there watching her. "I'm finished here now." Kenzie scooped up her wet underwear and surged to her feet. "I'd better be getting back," she said, backing toward the village. "I'm sure Whiskey Jug will be wondering where I am. We're guests of Buffalo Horn, you know."

Kenzie had no idea if he spoke any English or if the names she uttered meant anything to him. All she cared about was putting as much distance between the two of them as possible. When she finally reached the edge of the willows, she turned and fled up the hill. She didn't stop until she had reached the safety of Buffalo Horn's tipi and Whiskey Jug Johnson's protective presence.

"Adam!" Kenzie said breathlessly as she ducked through the opening. "I was washing my clothes down by the creek just now and…" Her voice trailed away as her eyes adjusted to the light, and she realized for the first time that Adam was not alone. Buffalo Horn and Jesse Three Dogs sat on either side of him. From the censorious look on Adam's face, Kenzie was pretty sure she'd interrupted something important.

Adam frowned at her. "Uh, Kenzie, we're kind of busy right now —"

"Sorry," she said with an apologetic smile as she sidled by the men and hurried over to her pile of furs. He obviously wanted her to leave the way she came. Too bad! Ignoring him, she picked up the buffalo robe and wrapped its shaggy warmth around her. No way was she going back outside. Not with that scary stranger still out there.

Adam gazed at her for several seconds. She could have sworn she saw his lips twitch before he turned his attention back to the other two men and their low-voiced conversation. Drat the man anyway. He knew how blasted cold she was, and he thought it was funny. At least he hadn't been able to say, "I told you so," with his uncles here.

It wasn't long before her shaking subsided and her body temperature began to rise. As the warmth crept outward along her limbs and sleepiness invaded her mind, she found herself marveling at how wonderful the buffalo robe was. The best thermal blanket in the world couldn't even begin to measure up. *Maybe I've stumbled onto something here,* she thought as her mind continued drifting toward sleep.

There were buffalo ranches in the west that had brought the animals back from the brink, and buffalo meat was fast becoming a low-cholesterol alternative to beef. Where there was meat, there were hides. Buffalo robes could be the next big yuppie craze. A little tough to pull off, maybe, with all the animal rights activists and environmentalists in the world, but with the right ad campaign—

A sudden stream of light invaded the interior of the tipi as a tall Indian ducked through the doorway and straightened. Her strange rambling thoughts came to an abrupt end as she jerked into full wakefulness. It was the man she had seen across the stream.

"Eagle Feather?" Adam appeared to be shocked to see the other man, but Buffalo Horn and Jesse Three Dogs greeted him with every sign of delight.

Kenzie pulled the buffalo robe closer around her and sank back into its depths. So far, nobody in the village had paid much attention to her, except when they needed help with Adam. *There's no reason for this encounter to be any different,* she told herself.

At that moment, the man they called Eagle Feather dropped a bundle to the ground. "The white woman left these by the creek," he said in English.

Adam glanced down at Kenzie's sneakers then over at Kenzie. "Eagle Feather brought your shoes back," he said.

"Thanks," was all Kenzie could manage. It sounded like a frightened squeak even to her own ears.

"Kenzie's a little shy," he told Eagle Feather, "but she appreciates you returning her shoes."

"She is your wife?"

Adam shook his head. "No, she's a stray I found wandering around the mountain."

As Eagle Feather cast a speculative glance toward Kenzie, she shrank even farther back into her buffalo robe. After a moment, he turned his attention to the three men by the door and ignored Kenzie for the rest of his visit, which lasted entirely too long, in her opinion.

At last, Eagle Feather, Buffalo Horn, and Jesse Three Dogs all rose and filed out of the tipi.

Adam grimaced as he settled back down onto his bed. The visit had obviously tired him. "You can come out now."

Kenzie peeked out of her buffalo robe. "Is Eagle Feather gone?"

"For now."

"What do you mean *for now*?" Kenzie asked in alarm. "Is he coming back?"

"Unless things have changed, he will." Adam readjusted himself into a more comfortable position and closed his eyes to sleep. "Eagle Feather is Buffalo Horn's son. He lives here."

Chapter 10

Eagle Feather was back.

Frowning, Adam removed his helmet and stared at the computer screen. Eagle Feather was one of his creations that had turned out to be a little too realistic. From the first, he'd seen Whiskey Jug Johnson as a rival. He'd been fiercely competitive in everything from hunting to winning favor with Buffalo Horn. Adam had finally deleted Eagle Feather from the program to restore peace.

Adam glanced at his watch. Ten to four. The vibrations of the timer he'd attached to his wrist had alerted him to the time, exactly the way he'd hoped it would. Without it, he'd have never made it out of *Beta Quest* before Annie arrived. She'd decided he needed rest after his surgery and had promised to shut all three of his computers down completely and remove them from his apartment if she found him so much as cleaning a keyboard.

He unhooked himself from his computer, switched off the monitor, and wheeled his chair over to the recliner, where he was supposed to be resting. He only had a few minutes to get himself situated before Annie stormed his door. Usually, maneuvering himself out of his chair and into the recliner took only a few seconds. It was a bit more taxing with only one sound arm. Luckily, Annie had gone to pick the kids up from school; she had a bad habit of showing up early if she had nothing to keep her occupied. As it was, he barely had time to settle himself before the bell rang, and he heard her key in the lock.

Zoey Bedford swept into the room, with Annie in her wake. "Adam, tell Mom it's all right if I stay with you and do my homework. She thinks she needs to be here to fix your dinner and stuff, but I could do it. If I go home, my idiot brother will be on the internet, talking to his stupid friends, and I won't be able to look up Sam Houston, and I'll probably get an F and be grounded for the rest of my life. Please say ok."

"Ok," Adam said, without blinking an eye.

"Huh!" Annie shook her head as she closed the door. "I swear you'd help Zoey rob a bank if she asked. She has you wound around her little finger, just like she does her father."

Adam gave her a wounded look. "All she wants is a little help with her homework."

"Last time you helped her, she wound up with the most complicated science project I've ever seen. It took her two and a half months to finish it, and I didn't think I'd ever get all of that paraphernalia out of my extra bedroom."

"Yeah, but I won first place, Mom," Zoey reminded her. "Besides, don't you have kickboxing tonight?"

"I can miss it one week."

"There's no need for you to miss your kickboxing night," said Adam. "I've been babysitting Zoey since she was six years old."

Annie gave him a sardonic glance. "A six-year-old isn't quite the same as a sixteen-year-old."

"Maybe not, but you know you can trust me to keep her out of trouble."

Annie snorted. "I seriously doubt that, but I'm not worried about you keeping her under control. I'm worried about her keeping *you* under control. If I leave her in charge, you'll have that blasted helmet on your head before I'm even out of the building."

Adam tried for a look of wounded innocence. "I've behaved myself so far, haven't I?"

"I wonder." Annie's eyes narrowed, and she looked around suspiciously. "No books or magazines. The TV remote is clear over there. What exactly *were* you doing before we got here?"

"Doing?"

"I've never known you to sit and twiddle your thumbs, Adam. I find it more than a little strange that you're sitting there with nothing to occupy your time."

Damn. He hadn't even considered that. Sometimes the woman was way too perceptive. "I was napping," he said.

"Sure you were." She glanced toward the dark computer screen suspiciously.

"Aw, come on, Mom. You act like Adam's a prisoner or something," Zoey said indignantly. "He doesn't have to do what you say."

Annie looked chagrined. "You're right," she said after a moment. "I'm sorry, Adam. I don't mean to treat you like a child."

"But you can't resist," he said with a grin. "It's that mother thing you've got going. Don't worry; Zoey will fix me her gourmet macaroni and cheese dinner then trot off to do her homework. Meanwhile, you can have your workout and be back here before bedtime."

"He's right, Mom," Zoey said, pushing Annie toward the door. "Adam and I will be fine."

"Well…" Annie hesitated, but she was clearly tempted.

"Please, Annie," Adam said softly. "It's bad enough that you have to take care of me. Don't make me feel even guiltier by putting your life on hold."

"Oh, Adam," she said. "I don't want you to feel that way."

"Then, go. Have a good time. Zoey and I will be fine."

Annie glanced indecisively back and forth between Adam and her daughter. After a moment, she threw her hands up in the air. "Ok, you win. The two of you are on your own. I'll be back sometime before ten."

Zoey and Adam shared a conspiratorial grin as the door closed behind her. "She's such a worrywart," Zoey said, shaking her head. "What do you want in your macaroni and cheese?"

"Surprise me."

Zoey grinned even wider. "Feeling adventurous, huh?"

"Yep. So, how's school?"

As she cooked the meal, and all through dinner, Zoey

regaled him with stories about school, her current boyfriend, and the latest plan to convince her parents she needed her own car. Adam listened with sincere interest, and Zoey regarded his occasional comment or suggestion as valued input. The hour passed in comfortable camaraderie.

"Well," Zoey said as she finished loading the dishwasher, "guess it's time I hit the books." She gave him an apologetic look. "Mom told me to take your phone."

"Seriously?

Zoey nodded. "She says you need your rest and that you can do more work on a cell phone than anybody else could on a computer."

Adam pretended to look hurt. "I'd never—"

"Yeah, right. She also told me not to take no for an answer." She held out her hand and wiggled her fingers. "Come on.

"Fine." Adam took his phone out of his pocket and tossed it to her then settled more comfortably into the recliner. "I'm going to see what I can find on TV. Hand me the remote, would you?"

Zoey picked up the remote from the entertainment center. She started toward Adam then stopped and glanced toward his computer station with a pensive look. After a moment, she pointed the remote at the computer and pressed the power button a few times. The Tv turned on and off, but nothing else happened.

"What are you doing?" Adam asked, clearly amused.

"Just checking to see if you have this thing programmed to turn on your computer."

Adam chuckled. "You have a suspicious mind."

Zoey shrugged as she handed him the remote. "Maybe so, but I wouldn't put it past you to do something like that. Mom said not to let you near your computer tonight."

"I promise I won't get out of this chair until bedtime," he said with a smile. "In fact, you can use the laptop in my office for your research. That way I won't be tempted. There's nothing on this one. Besides, I'm planning on channel surfing, and that's bound to be pretty distracting."

Zoey gathered up her books. "All right, if you're sure you don't need anything."

"If I do, you'll be the first to know."

"I'll see you later, then," she said, and disappeared into his office.

Adam spent a few minutes flicking through channels on the TV, listening intently to sounds coming from the other room. It wasn't long before he heard what he'd been waiting for.

"Hey, cool." Zoey stuck her head out the door. "Adam, is this file called *Zoey's Mix* for me?"

"Absolutely not! I put all your favorite music together for the girl next door."

"An old lady lives next door," Zoey said with a grin. "And she's deaf as a post. Can I use your wireless headphones?"

He sighed. "I suppose you might as well, though I'm still not convinced Mrs. Potter won't like the mix."

"Thanks, Adam. You're the best." She disappeared through the doorway again.

He waited a few more minutes, until he heard the sound of her fingers tapping on the computer keyboard. "Zoey?" he called. When there was no response, Adam grinned to himself. So much for his self-appointed guardian.

With another glance at the door, he pointed the remote at his computer and pushed the "mute" button. Instantly, a computer desktop appeared on the TV. He clicked a button and said, "Call Scott Martin."

On the fourth ring, the answering machine kicked in. "Damn," Adam muttered to himself as he listened to the message. "Scott," he said when the beep sounded, "this is Adam Johnson. I've run into a bit of a snafu with my current project, and I'd really appreciate—"

"Adam, I'm here." Scott broke in. "Man, it's good to hear your voice."

"Yeah, yours too." Adam smiled. He and Scott Martin had

been close friends ever since they had tied for first place at the National Science fair in high school. They spoke the same language of higher mathematics, science, computer programing, and gaming. "I needed to bounce something off you. I hope I'm not interrupting anything."

"Not really. I was just trying to work out a stubborn equation. It can wait. What's up?"

"How much do you know about SR?"

"Simulated Reality? Not a heck of a lot. I know the theory behind it and basically how it works, but that's about all."

"Good. I need a fresh perspective about a glitch in my beta program."

"What kind of glitch?"

"Actually, there's more than one, but they all seem to center around a character that showed up last week."

"Showed up?"

"Yeah, I know it sounds weird, but it's happened before. I came up with a Character Generator so players could create new characters inside the game. In the beta version, they sometimes just sort of appear. I refined it in my final version, but I never fixed it in the beta program. It hasn't been a problem before."

"But now it is?"

"Yes, because this character doesn't fit."

"What do you mean, 'doesn't fit?' Is it an alien or something?"

"No, it's a woman named Kenzie Armstrong."

"A glitch named Kenzie?" Scott sounded surprised.

"So she says. But that's beside the point. She's about a hundred fifty years out of sync. The setting of the game is 1868, but she acts as if it's modern day. Nothing I've tried has changed a thing."

"Why not just delete her?" Scott asked.

"I tried to, but I couldn't find her anywhere in the programming." Adam closed his eyes. "I wasn't overly worried about it until last week when I had surgery on my shoulder. By the time I got home from the hospital, I'd been gone for three days. When I logged into *Beta Quest*, I expected everything to be where I left it, but it wasn't. Three days had passed, and all the characters claimed I'd been there the whole time."

"The game went on without you?"

"Apparently. Even stranger, I had a wound on my shoulder in almost the exact same place as the incision the surgeon made."

There was a moment of silence on the other end. "Ok, now *that's* weird. Are you sure this new character is causing all the trouble?"

"That's the thing; I don't know if she's just one more aberration or if she's the catalyst."

"Maybe you'd better start from the beginning and tell me everything that's happened."

As Adam told the story of his adventures with Kenzie Armstrong, his sense of unreality grew. Strange as it all seemed while it was happening, in retrospect it sounded even more bizarre. From her entrance via Rainbow Falls to the unexpected return of Eagle Feather, nothing she did made sense.

"I see what you mean about her," Scott said. "Have you ever had aberrant characters before?"

"Oh, sure. There were plenty at the beginning, but they were different."

"How?"

Adam considered this for a moment. "They had obvious flaws in their humanity. There were pieces missing. Kenzie is completely real. If the setting were present day, she'd fit in perfectly."

"How do the other characters react to her? I mean, do they accept her?"

Adam thought of Betty and Eagle Feather, of Jesse Three Dogs and Buffalo Horn. "After a fashion, they do. I mean, they seem to think she's a little strange, but they act pretty much as I'd expect them to around an odd character."

"You said the game continued on even when you aren't

there. Do you know what happened?"

"I talked to a couple of my more advanced characters for a few minutes this afternoon. I gather that, up until Kenzie appeared, the whole program stopped the minute I left it. That's why I'm becoming more and more convinced that she's the cause of it all."

"Did you ask what you—or rather, your *body*—was doing while you weren't there?"

"Jesse Three Dogs said I spent most of the time unconscious, though apparently there were moments of semi-consciousness."

"And what happened then?"

Adam frowned. "It sounded as if I acted like the unsuccessful characters in the program."

"What do you mean?"

"I reacted to stimuli, but only in a primitive sort of way."

"Like…"

"I objected pretty strenuously when they tried to sew up my wound."

"Not surprising."

"Apparently I only reacted when Kenzie was there." Adam saw no reason to repeat Jesse Three Dogs's story of how he'd held her in his good arm for the better part of two days any more than he saw a need to explain the rather potent attraction he felt for his computer glitch. It had no bearing on the situation, anyway.

"Hmmm." Scott sounded pensive as he mulled it all over. "Have you thought of putting her in your other program to see what happens?"

"You mean put her in *Fantasy Quest*?" Adam said in surprise.

"Not in the original. Surely you have a master you can make copies from. You could set up the same scenario, create the same character, and then sit back and see what happens."

"Damn, why didn't I think of that?" Adam said in awe. "It's so simple it never occurred to me."

"Too close to the problem, that's why."

Adam grinned. "I knew there was a reason I called you. You always give a fresh perspective."

"Hey, that's what friends are for. Just doin' my job," Scott said. "I fully expect you to return the favor when I hit a wall."

"Any time, my friend. Any time. Which reminds me, are you still willing to test out my new Zeta-server?"

"It's ready?"

Adam smiled at the note of excitement in his friend's voice. "We start in-house testing next week. You should be getting yours about the same time."

"Do you really think it could expand enough to hold a zetabyte?"

"Theoretically, though it's going to be awhile before we need that much data storage," Adam said. "Right now, it's big enough to hold *Fantasy Quest*. Even with all the peripherals, that's only a few terabytes."

Ten minutes later they said their goodbyes, and Adam hung up the phone with an impatient glance at the clock on the wall. Annie wouldn't be back for another hour, and any delay seemed intolerable. He knew better than to risk her wrath, though. If she caught him on the computer, she was perfectly capable of making good her threat of removing what she saw as a roadblock to his recovery.

Idly, Adam used the TV remote to download his e-mail, but there was nothing of any importance. With a sigh, he switched off his computer and resolutely turned his attention to the TV. He was still flipping through the channels, trying to find something of interest, when Annie finally arrived.

"How was kickboxing?" he asked.

"Great! We had a match night," Annie said with a satisfied smile. "Melissa Roberts will think twice before she challenges me again!"

Adam chuckled. "I'm forever grateful you never took up wheelchair racing. You get downright vicious when there's competition involved."

"It only seems that way to wimps." She glanced around. "What did you do with my daughter?"

"She's in the other room, working on her homework. I told her she could listen to my wireless headphones, so she probably didn't hear you come in."

"Might as well let her work while I get you settled for the night. Now, stop," she said when he made a face. "I know you don't like it, but the less you stress that shoulder, the sooner it will heal."

"I was just thinking maybe I'd stay up a bit longer," Adam said.

"Sorry, buddy, not tonight. In case you've forgotten, you just got out of the hospital."

Adam gave in to the inevitable. He knew it was useless to argue when Annie switched into her mother mode. For some reason, he never minded her occasional high-handed management of his life. Maybe because he knew she meant well. And maybe because, tonight, he knew she was right, even though he had no intention of following her orders.

As it was, Adam meekly allowed her to help him through his nightly routine, with only one small sardonic comment about her tucking him in. She gave him a flippant reply, collected her daughter, and left him alone, with a cheerful wave and a promise to be back in the morning. He lay in the darkness long enough to give them time to reach their car and drive away before he switched on the bedside lamp.

Cursing his useless left shoulder, Adam hefted himself out of bed and into his chair. Weary and hurting, he wondered how wise this all was as he loaded *Fantasy Quest* on his extra computer and transferred his SR equipment. Once inside the game, though, all was forgotten as he lost himself in his fantasy.

Creating another Kenzie Armstrong—or at least a character that looked and sounded like her—was easy; yet this Kenzie was decidedly different. She didn't try to run away, steal his horse, or talk about satellites. When he offered her his mother's clothes, she was thankful, and when they arrived in Laramie, she didn't follow him into the saloon. In fact, within a few minutes of their arrival, a grateful fiancé showed up to claim her.

No matter how many times he started over, or what scenario he put her into, she acted just as she was supposed to — completely different from the Kenzie in *Beta Quest*. As the night wore on, and Adam tried everything he could think of, one fact became blindingly clear: Though this Kenzie looked exactly the same, she didn't interest him one bit.

When he finally dropped into bed, just as dawn was breaking over the horizon, he was no closer to understanding what was going on than he'd been before, and he was no closer to figuring out if the Kenzie glitch posed a serious problem for the future of *Fantasy Quest*. His only option was to go back into the program and play it out to see what happened. Adam relaxed against the pillows, closed his eyes, and drifted off to sleep with a smile on his face.

Chapter 11

"Red Blanket say he is better," Jesse Three Dogs said, gazing doubtfully down at his nephew. "He still sleeps."

"I know, but Buffalo Horn seems to think it's normal." Kenzie stared at Adam with a thoughtful expression. "Whiskey Jug hasn't eaten since yesterday sometime. Do you think I should wake him up?"

Jesse nodded. "He cannot get well if he does not eat."

"Adam. Adam." No reaction. Kenzie bit her lip. If she shook him, she might hurt his wounded shoulder. After a moment's hesitation, she touched his face. "Whiskey Jug?" He turned his face into her hand but otherwise showed no response.

"You don't think he's worse again, do you?"

Jesse shook his head. "If Buffalo Horn and Red Blanket say he is getting better, it is so. He will wake when he needs to." He gazed down at Kenzie thoughtfully. "But it is time for you to go outside. The morning is of great beauty. If you stay away from the sun, you wither and die."

Kenzie grinned. "I'm not a plant."

Jesse Three Dogs did not return her smile. "Whiskey Jug does not need watching anymore."

"I know, but I just can't convince myself he's all right. What if he suddenly gets worse while no one is here? I'll feel better if I stay and make sure."

Jesse gazed at her a moment longer then shrugged and ducked out the entryway.

Kenzie sighed. There wasn't much she'd like better than to leave this stupid tipi. There was absolutely nothing to do, and she was heartily bored. For the first few days, she'd found refuge in sleep. Then she'd borrowed sewing materials from Red Blanket and sewed up the buckskin shirt she and Jesse

Three Dogs had sacrificed to take care of Adam's wound. It had taken some time to sew with the unfamiliar sinew, but now the shirt was finished, her body was rested, and the forced inactivity was driving her insane.

Yet leaving the tipi was out of the question. The few times she'd ventured out to answer the call of nature, Eagle Feather had been there, lurking right outside. The first time, she didn't think much about it. The second, she thought it was just a coincidence. But when it happened over and over, she began to realize he was purposefully waiting for her.

It didn't make much sense. Though there wasn't a mirror for miles, Kenzie had a pretty good idea what she looked like covered with scratches and bruises and wearing a pair of buckskin pants that were made for a man three times her size. She had a hard time believing Eagle Feather was overcome by her beauty. A casual comment by Jesse Three Dogs had enlightened her about the reason for the younger man's interest: male competition. Even in this century, it seemed a force to be reckoned with. Eagle Feather saw her as Whiskey Jug Johnson's property and, therefore, a prize to be won, no matter how bad she looked or how improbable the match.

Kenzie was no stranger to the peculiarities of the male ego. It was Brad's insistence that she erase every trace of other men from her life that had landed her in this mess in the first place.

What she wouldn't give for her sketch pad and a supply of pencils. Not only was she bored out of her mind with nothing to do but watch Adam sleep, she fairly itched to sketch the faces around her. Buffalo Horn and his brother Jesse Three Dogs would make wonderful character studies. So would Red Blanket and even Whiskey Jug Johnson.

Kenzie looked at him and sighed. He had reacted a little when she touched his face. Maybe she could wake him. Reaching over, she ran the back of her fingers down the side of his face. Once again, he turned toward her palm, but that was all. Her hand might have been a comfortable pillow, for all the difference it made.

As Kenzie sat there, staring down at him, she gradually became aware of the odd thoughts touching him evoked. *It's amazing how soft his beard is. I wonder what he looks like underneath it.* Her fingers traced the length of his jaw. *No weak chin there.* Still, it was impossible to imagine the shape of his face.

With gentle fingers, Kenzie brushed back a lock of hair and tried to visualize it styled. She smiled. Her imagination couldn't conjure the image any more than she could picture Brad's hair disheveled. She traced the arch of his brows and the bridge of his nose with her fingertip, reveling in her explorations. His moustache was the same texture as his beard but softer. With sudden clarity she remembered the feel of it against her mouth as he kissed her.

That kiss had taken her completely by surprise. What would have happened if Red Blanket hadn't interrupted them? Would thoughts of Brad have brought her back to her senses? Kenzie was ashamed to admit that she didn't know. In retrospect, it seemed that Adam's kiss was somehow more...*something*. Trouble was, she couldn't put her finger on what that something was. The more she thought about it, the more she wondered: Was it the way his mouth felt against hers, some magic Adam himself wrought, or just her memory playing tricks on her?

From deep inside came an irresistible urge to find out. *He'll never know,* Kenzie told herself as she leaned forward and placed her lips against his. Dozens of sensations crashed in upon her. The soft silkiness of his moustache caressing her upper lip, the hard muscles of his chest where she rested her hand, the way his mouth seemed perfectly molded to fit hers.

Intent on her experiment, Kenzie stiffened in shock when the lips beneath hers parted and began to move. Startled, she pulled back and stared down into Adam Johnson's brown velvet eyes.

"Hello, there," he said softly, bracketing her face with his hands.

Kenzie's breath caught in her throat, mesmerized by the

glow she saw in his eyes. "I didn't mean—" She raised her fingers to his mouth in an effort to make him understand.

"Doesn't matter," he whispered, kissing the tips of her fingers. "Let's see where it takes us."

"Oh, I don't think—" she began.

"That's right," he murmured against her lips. "Don't think. Just feel."

As he teased her lips apart, Kenzie's resistance melted like frost in a forest fire, and she gave herself over to the wonder of the kiss. For a moment, it was enough; they explored, open-mouthed, hungrily, the first tendrils of passion swirling between them like an errant spring breeze.

Then Adam's good arm circled her and drew her down against him. Kenzie gave a soft sigh and cuddled closer. Through the buckskin of his shirt, she could feel the heavy muscles of his arms and chest. The sensation was new and exciting. Adam's muscular body was completely unlike Brad's tall, elegant frame.

The thought of her fiancé hit Kenzie with the force of a tsunami, and she jerked away in consternation. How could she even think of kissing another man when she had Brad Marriot, the husband of her dreams?

"No!" she said, pushing herself away from him. "This is wrong."

Adam blinked at her in confusion. "But you're the one—"

Kenzie surged to her feet. "I wasn't—I never meant... Oh!" Her face flaming, she turned and fled.

Adam watched her go, with equal parts bewilderment and disappointment. He shook his head to clear his mind. It usually took him a moment or two to orient himself when he entered *Beta Quest*, but never like this. One minute he was lowering his helmet onto his head; the next, he was right in the middle of a mind-numbing kiss. Ok, so maybe it was closer to a tentative kiss at first. It had become mind-numbing when he'd put his arm around her and pulled her close. With his blood on fire and surging through his veins, he'd literally forgotten where he was—*who* he was, for that matter. If Kenzie's programming hadn't kicked in, who knew what would have happened.

Beta Quest was set up to shut down if a player tried to instigate anything of a sexual nature with any of the characters. The Sex Hex, as Annie called it, was his attempt to keep his invention out of the hands of the porn industry. Since it caused a complete shut down and resetting of the program, he'd built in a series of failsafe measures to prevent innocent activation. Kenzie's reaction must be a product of that.

Adam was conscious of a tiny ping of regret. If there was only one thing about her programming that worked, why did it have to be the Sex Hex? He pushed the thought away. The last thing he needed was to get intimately carried away with his glitch and wind up shutting the whole thing down before he had a chance to find out what was going on.

Now all he had to do was figure out why Kenzie had been kissing him when he came into the program. Not that he minded; it was a lot more fun than waking up staring Bear Bait in the face or listening to Jesse Three Dogs's snoring. Still, it seemed an odd thing for her to be doing. Apparently, the program had continued without him once again.

Adam glanced around the tipi and sighed. There was nothing here to bring him any closer to understanding. There was no help for it; he was going to have to go outside. With a grimace, he grasped one of the tipi poles with his good arm and began the painful process of getting to his feet.

Kenzie's headlong flight carried her to the center of the village. The odd looks she was getting gradually penetrated her embarrassed preoccupation and slowed her to a walk. All work around the village had ceased as everyone stopped to stare at the crazy white woman rushing through camp. Her tentative smile was met with blank expressions. Even in her day, nobody could pull off flat affect like a Native American. It was a skill she had always rather admired, but today she found it a bit unnerving.

"Oh, Red Blanket," she murmured, "where are you when I need you?" As though the words had conjured her, the old woman suddenly appeared in the entryway of a nearby tipi. "Keenzie?"

"Red Blanket, am I ever glad to see you," Kenzie said with feeling.

Red Blanket gave her a questioning look, said something in Arapaho, and gestured back toward Buffalo Horn's tipi.

Kenzie shook her head and held up her hands, indicating her lack of understanding. Red Blanket tried again, this time pantomiming a very tall person with a beard.

"Whiskey Jug?" Kenzie asked.

Red Blanket nodded and screwed her face into an expression of intense suffering.

Kenzie shook her head. "No, no, nothing like that. He's fine." *A little too fine,* she thought to herself as she felt the color creep up her face in remembered embarrassment. *Leave it to Whiskey Jug Johnson to pick the most inopportune moment to wake up.* "I need something to do." She pointed to herself then to an old woman stirring a pot. "Work."

Red Blanket looked pensive for a moment then lifted her hand to her mouth as though eating.

"No, no, I'm not hungry. I'm bored. I want to work." Kenzie pointed from herself to all the other women around the camp who had gone back to their tasks the minute Red Blanket appeared. "You know, work."

Red Blanket looked pensive for a moment, then shook her head again. Kenzie sighed. "I wish there were a few more people around here that spoke English."

"I talk English," came a husky female voice behind her.

Kenzie whirled around and felt her jaw drop in surprise. The woman's flawless nut-brown skin; long, flowing black hair; and high cheekbones marked her as a member of the tribe, but she was easily the most beautiful woman Kenzie had ever seen. Though she was dressed like the other women in the village, her eyes set her apart. Their surprising smoky gray color gave her an exotic air. Her dress was buckskin, but it fit her willowy frame as though it had been created for her by a Parisian clothing designer. The ornate beading on the dress, belt, and leggings showed hours of work at the hands of a true artist. Her clothing only added to the aura of sensuous mystery that surrounded her like a cloud.

"You are Whiskey Jug's *haw-hase*?"

"Uh, yes. My name is Kenzie."

The woman nodded. "In English, I am Beautiful Dawn."

"That figures," Kenzie muttered under her breath. "Where did you learn to speak English?"

"Whiskey Jug taught me."

"Ah, of course." A jab of something suspiciously like jealousy pierced Kenzie's consciousness, and she pushed it away in irritation. She was very nearly a married woman. It made no difference to her if Whiskey Jug and Beautiful Dawn spent all last winter rolled up together in a buffalo robe.

"You tell Red Blanket you wish to work?"

"Oh, yes. I'm so bored I could scream."

Beautiful Dawn gave her an odd look. "What is bored?"

"It means I'm tired of sitting around twiddling my thumbs and need something to do." At Beautiful Dawn's puzzled expression, Kenzie shook her head. "Look, there has to be something around here I can do to help out."

Beautiful Dawn glanced down at the basket she carried balanced against one hip. It was filled with dark purple berries, which would explain why Kenzie hadn't seen her earlier. "You pick chokecherries?"

"Chokecherries! Sure, I used to pick them for my mother all the time. She'd boil them down and add some crabapple juice and sugar to make the best jelly you ever tasted."

"Jelly?"

"It's... Never mind. Just give me something to put them in

and point me toward the chokecherry bushes."

Beautiful Dawn nodded and said a few words to Red Blanket, who frowned and shook her head. Beautiful Dawn shrugged and turned to Kenzie. "She says she doesn't think you will want to do it."

"Of course I do." Kenzie smiled at Red Blanket and pointed to the basket of chokecherries then to herself. "I would be glad to pick chokecherries for you."

Red Blanket gave Kenzie the same look she had when the younger woman had wanted to take a bath, then shrugged and went back inside the tipi.

Kenzie followed Beautiful Dawn through the village to a tipi on the far edge, where the other woman dumped the berries into a larger container. "Why doesn't she want me to pick chokecherries?"

"It is hard to know. Red Blanket sometimes has strange thoughts," Beautiful Dawn said, handing her the basket and pointing back toward the creek. "The chokecherries are there."

"Thanks," Kenzie said, smiling. Glancing up, she thought she saw of glint of sly satisfaction in the gray eyes of the other woman. It was gone in an instant, but Kenzie was left wondering if she had imagined it or if she was being set up.

As she made her way to the chokecherry bushes, Kenzie suddenly grinned to herself. Of course. It was the same old chokecherry scam she and her sister had pulled on unsuspecting friends in their childhood. The deep purple color of the berries, along with their delightful smell, made chokecherries extremely appealing. It was easy to convince the unwary to take a taste. Even those who knew chokecherries were unable to resist popping a few in their mouths. In reality, chokecherries were so bitter they immediately caused a person to pucker and left an aftertaste that was nearly impossible to get rid of. Chokecherries were probably the most aptly named fruit on the planet.

Kenzie was still smiling when she reached the chokecherry thicket. She resisted the urge to look back over her shoulder to see if Beautiful Dawn was watching as she stripped a handful of plump berries off their stem and popped a few into her mouth. The familiar bitter taste was almost pleasant as it brought back sweet memories of her childhood. Kenzie made a big show of spitting out the seeds and taking another mouthful with every sign of pleasure. So much for Beautiful Dawn's trap.

Picking chokecherries had never been Kenzie's favorite job. As a child, it seemed to take forever to fill a bucket with the tiny berries, but today it was relaxing. She didn't even have to think as her hands flew along with the familiar task. It was a joy to be outside, soaking up the sunshine, surrounded by the delightful sounds and smells of the mountain. She might as well be in her own time.

As she let her mind float, Kenzie gradually became aware of a sound that didn't go with the serene mountain setting. She paused to listen but heard only the gurgling of the creek and the sighing of the wind through the trees. After a moment, she shrugged and went back to work. Then she heard it again: a whisper followed by a childish giggle. Surreptitiously, she peeked out of the corner of her eye.

At first, she saw only an uninterrupted line of bushes stretching along the bottom of the hill. Then one of the nearby branches moved, and she spied half a dozen pairs of eyes watching her. The children of the village.

She bit the inside of her lip to keep from smiling and kept picking, gradually moving closer and closer to their hiding place. As she drew nearer, she thought she heard the word *haw-hase,* and she grinned to herself. She'd show them a *haw-hase.*

Suddenly, a boy of about nine came tearing down the hill, yelling what sounded very much like a war cry, to Kenzie's untrained ear. As he raced by her, he tapped her none too gently with a brightly painted stick and ran back up the hill, where a whole pack of boys stood watching. They welcomed him back into their fold with a great deal of delight.

Kenzie's eyes narrowed. So, they thought to prove their bravery by touching the *haw-hase,* did they? She could play that game too. Scanning the ground nearby, she spied a branch about three feet long and half an inch thick. Perfect. The next budding adolescent to run past her was going to find himself on the receiving end of that stick. All she had to do was wait and pretend like she'd forgotten all about them.

Sure enough, she had barely turned her back and started picking again when the next would-be hero headed down the hill toward her. She bent over as though checking her shoe and unobtrusively picked up the branch. When he was a foot from her, she jumped up and swung her quasi-weapon up under his stick. With a solid whack, the two pieces of wood connected. The brightly colored coup stick went sailing over the bushes and landed somewhere on the other side. The boy stood there, shock holding him immobile as he stared at her, wide-eyed.

"There," she said. "I win!" With that, she reached forward and tickled his bare stomach. The unexpected contact galvanized him into motion, and he took off like a streak. Kenzie chuckled as she watched him dash up the hill as though the hounds of hell were on his heels. She raised her hand and waved to his friends, who gave her a horrified look and joined their comrade as he disappeared over the hill.

Swallowing her laughter, she picked up her basket and turned back toward the thicket where the younger children were hiding. The whispering was even louder and more excited than before. She was close enough to see their dark eyes watching her. Kenzie was still trying to think of a way to let them know she wouldn't harm them, when she heard a rustling in the bushes, not far from where the coup stick must have landed.

The boys were back already. They must have circled around, planning to jump out and scare her. Eyes twinkling, Kenzie set down her basket of berries and picked up her stick. She looked straight at the girls and placed her finger over her lips in the universal sign for silence. Pointing toward the rustling sound, she grinned and made exaggerated motions of sneaking up on the boys. She was rewarded with a chorus of giggles.

With stick in hand, she ducked down and crept forward. The rustling sound was getting louder. They must be getting into position. The best defense was a good offense. "Gotcha!" she yelled as she jumped forward and jerked the bushes apart.

An instant later, her triumphant cry changed to a terrified scream as a huge grizzly rose on its hind feet and loomed over her with a mighty roar.

Chapter 12

"Red Blanket," Adam called as he caught sight of his aunt, "have you seen Kenzie?"

Red Blanket raised her eyes from the hide she was scraping. "*Haw-hase*?"

Adam's mouth twisted in a rueful grin. "Right."

"She goes to pick chokecherries," she said, frowning disapprovingly. "It is a job for children."

Adam's stomach clenched. *The chokecherry thicket!* The blackest part of his life had played out in that thicket, or at least its counterpart in the real world. It existed here only because he had needed to face his demons, to put his father's death and his own mauling behind him.

Adam had only tried to recreate the incident once and had caused a near disaster. It had been back before he'd put in most of his safety measures, and he'd been seriously injured. When the grizzly loomed up out of the chokecherry bushes, it had been Jesse Three Dogs, rather than his father, who had come to his rescue. Jesse had killed the bear before it had broken Adam's back, but it had been a very close call. As it was, he'd been unable to pull himself out of the program and wound up at Fort Steele being sewed up by a ham-handed post surgeon.

Adam still carried the scars. Though he could have reset the program and returned his computer-generated body to a state of perfection, he had decided to leave the scars as a reminder to himself of the potential danger in what he was doing.

Red Blanket's voice pulled him back from the bleak memories. She had continued speaking to him in the peculiar form of the Arapaho language that existed only in *Beta Quest*.

"...Beautiful Dawn," she was saying. "That one bear's watching."

Adam frowned. "Beautiful Dawn? Who—" His question

was forgotten as screams suddenly pierced the air. "Kenzie!" The next instant, he was sprinting for the brow of the hill.

The sight that met his eyes nearly brought him to his knees. The giant grizzly of his nightmares towered above Kenzie.

"Run!" she screamed as the bushes next to her parted, and half a dozen children scrambled out. The bear turned its massive head toward the sound and let out a loud roar.

"Hey! Over here!" Kenzie yelled and swatted him across the face with a willow branch she held in her hands. The bear's attention was firmly focused on Kenzie now. It took two steps toward her in its awkward upright stance. In a moment, the bear would be upon her with its fangs and claws.

The sight unfroze Adam's feet, and he started toward her, down the hill, at a dead run, pulling his knife from the sheath on his belt as he ran. His only thought was to get to Kenzie before the bear did.

The tableau seemed to unfold in slow motion. The children streaked past Adam as he tore down the hill, their frightened voices mixing with the roar of the bear in a medley of terror.

With a final threatening snarl, the bear reached for Kenzie with one massive paw. Adam was still impossibly far away.

"Kenzie!" The name was wrenched from him in an anguished cry. "Run!"

Kenzie seemed not to hear him. She was frozen in fear, just as he had been earlier. From out of nowhere, something whizzed past Adam and struck the bear in the eye with a solid *thunk*. Adam barely had time to register that it was an arrow before two more went winging past his head and buried themselves in the animal's chest.

With a pain-filled bellow, the wounded beast tossed his head and pawed at the arrows firmly embedded in his body. The shafts snapped off, but it was too late. With a final growl, it fell to the ground and lay still.

Adam reached Kenzie a moment later and pulled her into his arms, the knife in his hand falling, forgotten, to the ground.

"A-Adam?" she quavered. Then she burst into tears. "I'd

just been picking berries from that bush," she sobbed. "He wasn't there!"

"It's all right," he murmured soothingly, holding her head against his chest. "He's dead."

Adam was shaking nearly as bad as Kenzie was. It was too much like the encounter with the bear that had killed his father and landed Adam himself in a wheelchair for life. He finally understood why his father had sacrificed himself for his son. He had been willing to do the same for Kenzie Armstrong. At that moment, it didn't matter that she was only a computer glitch and no more real than a dream; her death would have been devastating. The thought made him hold her even tighter in his protective embrace. Even the pain in his healing shoulder wasn't enough to make him loosen his grip, nor was the last of the hiccupping sobs against his chest. She might be ready to pull herself together, but he wasn't.

"Three of my best arrows," said a mournful voice.

Adam opened his eyes in surprise. He had forgotten about the unknown archer that had saved Kenzie. Eagle Feather stood there, bow in hand, gazing regretfully down at the dead bear. He sighed then bent down to retrieve Adam's knife. "It is good I was near, brother." He reversed the blade and handed it back to Adam. "This knife would not have done much good against Mato."

"Mato?" Kenzie lifted her tear-streaked face from Adam's chest. "It had a name?"

"Mato is the word for bear," Adam told her.

Eagle Feather squatted next to the carcass and pulled out his knife. "His fur is thick for winter. It will make a good winter robe."

Kenzie turned her face away in revulsion as Eagle Feather began the long, difficult process of skinning the bear.

"It's customary to say thank you when someone saves your life," Adam said softly.

"Oh," Kenzie lifted her face from Adam's chest. "Th-thank you, Eagle Feather."

Eagle Feather gave her a steady look. "It is what a warrior does for the woman he wants."

Kenzie turned scarlet. "But I—"

"Kenzie already has a man," Adam said fiercely.

Eagle Feather shrugged and turned back to his task. "Buffalo Horn says she is not your wife. A woman without a husband can be won."

"Not if she doesn't want to be," Kenzie muttered into the buckskin of Adam's shirt.

Adam felt absurdly pleased with the words but was careful to wipe the grin off his face before tipping her face up. "Are you all right?"

Kenzie pulled back and wiped her eyes with the back of her hand. "Yes," she sniffed. "I'm sorry for crying all over you like that."

"You had a pretty good reason. What were you doing down here picking chokecherries, anyway?"

"I wanted to do something useful. They sent me down here. I don't get it. Red Blanket didn't seem to like the idea either. What's wrong with me picking chokecherries?"

"It's a job the women give to the children. Who told you to do it?"

"Beautiful Dawn."

"Who?"

"Oh, come on, Adam. The epitome of the Indian princess, and you don't know who she is?"

"No." He glanced toward the bear. "What about you, Eagle Feather, do you know Beautiful Dawn?"

Eagle Feather paused and looked over his shoulder at them. "I do not know anyone by this name."

"Of all the... I promise you I didn't imagine her," Kenzie said, pulling away and heading toward the village. "She's probably up there right now laughing about how the stupid *haw-hase* fell for her trick. I wonder if she knew the bear was there."

Adam frowned. "Nobody from the village would

recklessly endanger another person that way."

Kenzie turned to look at him, her eyebrows raised in surprise. "Recklessly endanger? Where would a man called Whiskey Jug get words like that?"

Adam winced. He never slipped that way. It just showed how upset he still was by the whole situation. "My father was a history professor before he came to the mountains." That much, at least, was true.

"Really?" she looked interested. "What made him become a mountain man?"

"The love of adventure, I reckon," he said, falling into step beside her.

A hint of a grin crossed her face at his deliberate use of improper English. "And here I thought they all came out to get away from jail. You sure your father wasn't running from the law?"

"My father was the most honest man I ever knew."

Kenzie sobered. "I'm sorry, Adam. I was only teasing. I didn't mean to upset you."

He shrugged. "I'm a little overly sensitive about him, I guess. He died saving my life."

Kenzie gasped. "What do you mean?"

"I got on the wrong side of a grizzly. My father came upon the scene while she was mauling me and tried to fight her off. He managed to kill the bear, but he died before help came." Once again, Adam felt the anguish of that bright summer afternoon. Unable to move, he'd lain there and watched his father bleed to death.

"Oh, Adam," Kenzie said, softly touching his arm. "I'm so sorry. Today must have been awful for you."

"You have no idea," he said with feeling. He smiled down at her. "But at least nobody got hurt this time."

"It's so weird. I had just been picking berries off that bush," she mused. "How could I have not known he was there?"

"I don't know. Maybe—" Suddenly, it all came into focus for Adam. She hadn't known the bear was there because it hadn't been. He'd been thinking about the bear. Could his own thoughts and memories have brought it back? The grizzly had been exactly where he'd put it the first time. The bear was yet another character he'd deleted from the program, but he had a sick feeling he himself was responsible for the monster's return.

"Well, well, well, look who's coming to greet us," Kenzie muttered as they reached the top of the hill.

Adam looked up, surprised by the dislike in her voice. The woman hurrying toward them was a stranger to Adam, and yet there was something vaguely familiar about her at the same time.

"Keenzie, the children have told us of the bear. You are all right?" she asked.

"I'm a little shaken up, but otherwise all right. Are the kids all ok?"

The woman gave her a puzzled look. "They are all well, if that is what you mean."

She turned her eyes toward Adam and gave him a sultry smile. "The children say Whiskey Jug save them."

Adam blinked in astonishment. "Dawn?"

"It has been long since we have seen each other, Adam." She sidled closer and walked her fingers up his chest. "I do not forget that time, though. Why did you leave while I was sleeping?"

Adam felt himself redden. "Uh… Well, I…"

He heard a snort just below his left shoulder. "Don't know who she is, huh?" Kenzie said sardonically. "Sounds to me like the two of you know each other rather well. If you'll excuse me, I think I'll go find Red Blanket."

"Kenzie, wait," he called. But she just kept on walking as though she hadn't heard him. "What are you doing here, Dawn?" Adam asked.

"I live here," she said simply.

"Since when?"

She looked up at him in hurt surprise. "Are you angry with me, Adam?"

"No, no, I'm just surprised to find you here, that's all."

"Where else would I be?"

Where else indeed? "Look, Dawn, I have some things I need to do. I'll see you later."

"And I'll be waiting," she said in a husky voice.

The look she gave him was calculated to make his blood boil, but Adam felt curiously unmoved as he walked away. This whole thing was getting weirder and weirder. First Eagle Feather, then the bear, and now Dawn. Deleted characters seemed to be coming out of the woodwork.

Dawn was the biggest shock of all. She didn't belong in this part of the program. Hell, she wasn't even Native American. Last time he'd seen her, she was a sexy redhead with a French accent. Adam rubbed his hand over his face, embarrassed by the memories she evoked.

It was Annie who had put the idea in his head. She was the one that had pointed out he had no way of knowing if all his fretting about the porn industry getting hold of his invention was realistic or just paranoia. Annie had just been making conversation, but the more he'd thought about it, the more Adam wanted to know the truth. Was it even possible to have sex within the confines of *Beta Quest*, or was he worrying needlessly?

So, he had created Dawn, a combination of the sexiest women who had ever graced the silver screen. He'd made her completely irresistible and with only one thing on her mind. She was every man's fantasy. *No*, Adam thought, determined to be truthful, *she's my fantasy, pure and simple.* The first time he saw her, he realized she represented an opportunity he hadn't even thought of.

Adam had become a paraplegic when he was barely eighteen, long before he had fully investigated the mysteries of sex. With Dawn, he'd had a chance to experience everything he'd missed in the real world, to explore to his heart's content. And explore he did. It took several weeks to create the Sex Hex. The whole time he was working on it, he was trying new and exciting things with Dawn in his spare moments.

Programmed to test the sexual limits of *Beta Quest*, Dawn was delighted with every new game and participated wholeheartedly, no matter how outrageous his requests. She was the perfect partner in every way but one: She had no emotional involvement and never would. At first it didn't matter. Gradually, though, Adam had begun to realize something was missing. He might just as well have been with a prostitute. A feeling of dissatisfaction grew within him until he'd started to think of excuses not to enter the program.

Adam had finally finished the Sex-Hex and put it in place. Then he'd gone into *Beta Quest* to see Dawn one more time. They were barely into foreplay when the program shut down. Adam had never been inclined to bring Dawn back to life. Yet here she was, anxious to take up where they'd left off.

Adam rubbed his face. Damn, what a mess. It was like having your blow-up sex doll coming to life and start talking to your friends. Talk about a man's worst nightmare! What if Dawn and Kenzie started exchanging girlish confidences?

A sudden thought stopped him mid-stride. Maybe Kenzie wasn't an aberration in the programing. Maybe she was the next generation of a Dawn-type character. Had he unwittingly created his perfect woman and been unaware he was doing it? It would explain why she was so twenty-first century. It would also explain why he was so inexorably drawn to her.

Chapter 13

"It is a celebration," Jesse Three Dogs was saying.

Kenzie plopped down on the ground next to him to watch him work the deer antler in his hand. "What are we celebrating?"

"The return of Eagle Feather."

"Kind of like the return of the prodigal son, huh?"

Jesse gave her a quizzical look then went back to his carving. "He has been gone a long time."

"What about Beautiful Dawn? Has she been gone a long time too?"

"Who?"

"Beautiful Dawn," Kenzie said sarcastically. "You know, the Indian princess that makes all the men's mouths water just to look at her?"

Jesse raised his eyebrows and looked at her for a long moment. "I do not understand what you mean by making the men's mouths water."

"It means… Oh, never mind. It's probably not even her fault. I'm just a little irritated with Whiskey Jug. He tried to tell me he didn't know her."

Jesse gazed at her in pensive silence. "I do not know a woman such as this either," he said finally.

For a single frightening moment Kenzie wondered if she was delusional, if she had imagined the other woman. Then reality intruded again. "Red Blanket does. Maybe Beautiful Dawn gave me the wrong name or something." *Actually,* Kenzie thought to herself, *that sort of makes sense. What kind of a name is Beautiful Dawn, anyway?*

"So, tell me more about this celebration," she said, deciding to change the subject.

"We will feast and dance and tell of great deeds."

"Sounds like my kind of party. I suppose the dancing is around the fire with war whoops and everything."

Jesse raised an eyebrow. "We have many different dances."

"Oh, yeah? Like what?" Kenzie asked curiously.

He shrugged. "It is decided by the drummers, but sometimes we dance the Buffalo Dance, or the Chicken Dance. The women dance too."

"Really? Do they dance like the men?"

"No, they have their own dances."

Kenzie leaned forward, openly interested. "Will you show me?"

"No." For the first time since she'd known him, Jesse Three Dog's stoic expression slipped a bit. "I do not know the women's dances."

"Oh, no, of course you wouldn't." She'd never have picked Jesse for a male chauvinist, but he was clearly offended. On the other hand, this was the nineteenth century and an entirely different culture. Her way of thinking was the one out of sync here. She didn't belong in this time any more than Whiskey Jug Johnson belonged in hers. The thought gave her an unexpected feeling of sadness.

Kenzie jumped as a large bundle landed on the ground next to her. When she turned to look at it fully, a startled scream burst from her lips. It was the bear hide, minus the bear. A nauseating odor filled the air as she stared at the hideous package.

"It is yours."

Kenzie tore her gaze away from the hide to Eagle Feather's towering form. "Mine? But why?"

He crossed his arms across his chest. "I wish it so."

"But I—"

"It is a valuable gift," Jesse Three Dogs said softly in her ear.

A *gift*? Kenzie suppressed a shudder of revulsion as she looked away from Eagle Feather's bloody hands and glanced up at his impassive face. Jesse was right; it would be downright tacky to tell Eagle Feather it grossed her out and to please take the horrible thing away. "I...I've never had anything quite like it. Thank you, Eagle Feather."

His face became slightly less austere in an expression Kenzie figured must pass for his smile. With a slight nod of his head, he turned and strode away. Kenzie couldn't help but think he'd be the perfect subject for a painting called *The Noble Savage*.

"He will challenge Whiskey Jug," Jesse observed as Eagle Feather disappeared from sight.

Kenzie's gaze flew to the old man's face. "Why?"

Jesse Three Dogs sighed and went back to his carving. "You are Whiskey Jug's woman."

"They'd fight over me?" Kenzie asked, alarmed.

"It is always the way with those two. What one has, the other wants."

"But Whiskey Jug has a wounded shoulder."

"That is why Eagle Feather waits."

"What if I tell him I'm not interested?"

"Too late," another voice intruded. "You already accepted his gift."

Kenzie whipped around to find Adam looming over her. "What do you mean?"

"You accepted the bear skin."

Kenzie's gaze flew once again to the bloody hide. "You mean he thinks I like him because I didn't throw that horrible thing back in his face?"

Adam gave her a sardonic smile. "He figured you'd be thrilled with it. Any other woman in this village would be."

"Can't I just give it back?"

Jesse shook his head. "No."

"Why not?" Kenzie argued. "I mean, it might be impolite, but maybe that will make him change his mind about me. I wouldn't care if he thought I was the rudest person alive."

"It's more than that," said Adam. "If you return it now, he'll lose face. You'll wound his pride."

Kenzie made a disgusted noise. "Male ego again. I might have known. It's the bane of my life."

Jesse looked up from his work. "What kind of eagle?"

"Never mind," Kenzie said with a sigh. She glanced up and caught Adam in mid-grin. The expression was gone in an instant, but she had the fleeting impression he understood the play on words and found it amusing. No, of course not. He was feeling smug because he thought he had the upper hand over Eagle Feather. Maybe he did. If she had to choose between the two…

Kenzie reached over and nudged the hide with her shoe. "What am I going to do with this stupid thing?"

"Tan it?" Adam suggested.

Kenzie glanced up again. This time there was no mistaking the grin on his face. He obviously knew that was the last thing she'd want to do. Wiping that self-satisfied smirk off his face suddenly became her greatest ambition. "You know," she said, getting to her feet, "that's not a half-bad idea. It will give me something to do. What do you say, Jesse? Do you think you could teach me?"

"Tanning hides is women's work," Adam said, before Jesse Three Dogs had a chance to answer. "Do you want to humiliate him in front of the whole village?"

"Oh." A glance at Jesse Three Dogs showed Kenzie Adam was right. The old man might be able to teach her how to tan the hide, but he didn't want to. "Right. It doesn't matter." She bent down to pick up the hide and very nearly collapsed in a surprised heap next to it. "Holy cow, that's heavy!"

Whiskey Jug chuckled. "What were you planning on doing with it?"

"I'll take it to Red Blanket. She'll be glad to help." She shifted the heavy burden in her arms, being careful to keep the fur on the outside. "I'm sure I can make her understand what I want. If not, I'll ask Beautiful Dawn to interpret."

She had only gone a few steps before Adam caught up with her. "About Dawn…"

"What about her?" Kenzie asked without looking up. Her full concentration was on putting one foot in front of the other while keeping her stomach from emptying its contents all over the ground. Her arms were already beginning to ache, and the smell from the hide was horrendous.

"She and I... Well, it was a long time ago."

"Mmm." Hadn't her science teacher said the sense of smell was easily fatigued? Any minute now her nose would go to sleep, and her stomach would stop rebelling. Yep, any minute now.

"I'm not really sure why she's here but—"

That got Kenzie's attention. "What do you mean you don't know why she's here? Doesn't she live here?"

He ran his hand through his hair. "Not exactly."

Kenzie looked up at him. "What the heck does that mean? Either she lives here or she doesn't."

"Look," he said with a helpless shrug, "it's kind of hard to explain."

"I'll bet."

He took the bear skin from her self-consciously. "Anyway, it's all over between us."

Kenzie gave him a sidelong glance. "Does Beautiful Dawn know that?" She watched with fascination as the skin visible above his beard darkened. Adam was blushing! "She doesn't, does she?"

"Well..."

Kenzie laughed. "Man, I'd like to be there when you tell her. I suspect she isn't usually the one to get dumped." She frowned suddenly. "Jesse Three Dogs says Eagle Feather is after me because of the competition between the two of you?"

"It's possible."

"Why me and not Beautiful Dawn?" Kenzie demanded. "Or is he cozying up to her too?"

"No."

"Why not?"

"Because they've never met."

Kenzie came to a dead stop. "They don't know each other?" she said in surprise. Slowly, she began to smile. "And tonight there's a party. This might turn out to be a very interesting evening."

Adam frowned. "Kenzie, what are you planning?"

"Nothing yet." She grinned and started walking again. "But I'm bound to think of something."

Kenzie was conscious of Adam's gaze on her as they walked along. She swallowed a giggle. His consternation was nearly tangible in the afternoon sunshine. *Good,* she thought. He deserved to be a little worried. At least that irritating smug look was a thing of the past.

Kenzie had no trouble making Red Blanket understand what she had in mind for the bear skin. It wasn't long before the older woman had the hide staked to the ground and Kenzie on her hands and knees scraping the flesh away. It was back breaking labor, but after days of inactivity and boredom, Kenzie reveled in it. Contrary to what her science teacher had said, the smell never completely went away, but Kenzie eventually became accustomed to it.

The only blot in the long afternoon was the sudden appearance of Eagle Feather. Left to her own devices, Kenzie would have sent him packing in no uncertain terms, but Red Blanket seemed to enjoy having him there.

Kenzie pretended to ignore Eagle Feather's gaze, but she could almost feel its predatory weight upon her as she carefully scraped the hide. When she didn't look up or acknowledge his presence, he finally went on his way, and Kenzie relaxed.

With Red Blanket's help, Kenzie managed to have the entire hide scraped by midafternoon. The two women washed the hide with soap weed and set it to soak.

Red Blanket gestured for Kenzie to follow her into the tipi. Once inside, the older woman rummaged around for a few minutes then offered Kenzie a bundle of buckskin.

"What's this?" Kenzie asked.

Red Blanket smiled and chattered companionably as she

shook out the beaded leather dress. Kenzie only understood one piece of what the old woman said. Beautiful Dawn. It made no sense, and even less when Red Blanket handed her the garment.

"You want me to give this to Beautiful Dawn?" she asked, pantomiming the action of giving the dress to someone.

Red Blanket shook her head vehemently. "You wear," she said in heavily accented English.

"Me?" Kenzie said in surprise.

Red Blanket nodded eagerly. "For Wheesky Jug."

Suddenly, Kenzie caught her meaning and started to grin. Red Blanket wanted her to give Beautiful Dawn a run for her money for Adam's affections. "Thank you, Red Blanket," she said, giving the other woman a hug. "I'll give it my best shot."

Red Blanket's smile widened until her whole face shone. That's when Kenzie discovered there was more to the plan than a new dress. For the next hour, she received the Native American equivalent of a makeover.

Red Blanket pointed to her hair. Kenzie made a face. "I know, it must look horrible, and it's driving me crazy." She lifted a hand apologetically. "I'm afraid there's nothing I can do about it though. My hair is naturally curly, and without any kind of a brush, it's pretty much a disaster. And why am I telling you when you can't understand a word I say?"

Red Blanket just smiled and gestured for her to sit down. Kenzie took a seat on the ground, and the other woman began to work out the snarls with a smooth, pointed stick. Though Kenzie's curls and a week without brushing made the job an especially difficult one, Red Blanket seemed endlessly patient.

Kenzie usually found someone working with her hair relaxing. In fact, she'd been known to go to sleep in the beautician's chair. There was no question of drifting off today. The constant pull and tug against her scalp was anything but soothing. Eventually, though, Red Blanket was satisfied and began to run her fingers through Kenzie's long, curly hair, combing it into some semblance of order.

Kenzie was just beginning to relax when she suddenly realized the other woman had some sort of greasy substance on her hands that smelled suspiciously like bear fat. With a start, Kenzie started to pull away then quickly relaxed. *When in Rome.* Besides, for all she knew, the bear fat would keep her unruly locks under control.

At last, every strand of hair was greased to Red Blanket satisfaction and she divided it into two long tails which she lay over Kenzie's shoulders. Instead of braiding, she produced two beaded hair thongs, which she proceeded to expertly weave around the hair.

"Oh, how pretty!" Kenzie cried as she picked up one of the tails and admired the intricate beading on the ends of the thongs.

Red Blanket beamed her approval then left the tipi, only to return a few minutes later with a bowl of warm water and a soft cloth. She pointed to the T-shirt and buckskin pants with a disapproving frown. Kenzie obediently stripped and stood shivering in the middle of the tipi in her underwear. Red Blanket indicated that she should remove those too, but Kenzie balked. There was a limit to how far she'd go to fit in with the natives. Finally, Red Blanket shrugged and handed her the water, indicating that she wash herself.

Delighted, Kenzie took a quick sponge bath and slipped into the beaded dress. The beads made it surprisingly heavy, but the soft chamois-like leather felt like heaven against her skin.

"Wow," she said enthusiastically as she smoothed the dress down over her hips. "And I thought the buffalo robe was awesome. This is better than fleece."

Red Blanket smiled indulgently as she handed her a matching belt, beaded leggings, and moccasins. With Red Blanket's help, Kenzie had soon donned all the finery and was ready to go. She whirled around in delight. "Oh, Red Blanket, you're just like my fairy godmother!" she said, giving the older woman a hug.

Red Blanket positively beamed then made a wiping motion with her hands and said something about Beautiful Dawn. Though Kenzie didn't understand the words, the meaning was obvious, and she smiled in return. "I appreciate your vote of confidence, but I doubt I'll pose any serious threat to Beautiful Dawn, even in this gorgeous outfit."

"Wheesky Jug like."

"You think so?" Kenzie chuckled. "It'll be a big surprise, at least. I haven't exactly been at my best since I've been around him."

"Go," Red Blanket said, shooing her toward the doorway. "Find Wheesky Jug."

"All right, all right." Kenzie grinned back over her shoulder as she ducked through the tipi flap. "But I'm not expecting miracles."

She straightened and collided with a solid wall of flesh.

"*Haw-hase.*" The deep voice rumbled with obvious pleasure as a strong hand reached out to steady her. "This way of dressing is good."

Startled panic knotted Kenzie's stomach. "Eagle Feather! What are you doing here?"

"I bring you the bear's brain," he said.

"The brain?"

Kenzie's horrified reaction was cut off in mid-squawk as Red Blanket emerged from the tipi behind her and accepted the brain almost as though she'd been expecting it. As she watched the older woman carefully wrap the thing and store it away, Kenzie wondered uneasily if it were destined for the evening's feast.

Kenzie was never quite sure how Red Blanket did it, but within moments, she'd sent Eagle Feather on his way and Kenzie on her hunt for Whiskey Jug.

As Kenzie wandered around the camp, she wondered what Adam would think of her in these clothes. Not that she cared what Adam "Whiskey Jug" Johnson thought of her changed appearance. His opinion shouldn't matter in the least. Except, for some reason she didn't quite understand, it did.

Nervous butterflies danced in her stomach as she spotted him with several of the other men of the village. He looked like a giant oak among the saplings. His back was toward her, but there was no mistaking that tall, broad-shouldered frame. Then he turned, and she caught her breath in stunned surprise.

The full beard he'd sported since the day she'd first seen him in the hot pool behind Rainbow Falls was gone. The face beneath it was that of a stranger—*a very good-looking stranger*, she admitted to herself as she gazed at his profile. Kenzie had always figured him to be in his mid to late thirties, but without the beard he looked years younger. You wouldn't think a strong jaw and the suggestion of a dimple in his chin would make that much difference on a man.

Just then, he smiled at something someone said, and her heart turned over in her chest. Had she thought he was good-looking? She must have been crazy. Gorgeous was closer to it.

Calm down, Kenzie told herself. *You're nearly a married woman.* If Whiskey Jug Johnson could make her hormones sit up and take notice, think of the effect he must have on the unattached women of the village.

As if on cue, the crowd shifted, and she saw who had made Adam smile. Beautiful Dawn stood gazing up at him, with her heart in her eyes.

Kenzie's stomach fell to her toes. Suddenly, the beaded dress and the hair thongs seemed like a pathetic attempt to compete. What a laugh. Kenzie turned and slipped away before Adam saw her. The missing beard made total sense now. It didn't take a rocket scientist to figure out that he'd shaved to please Beautiful Dawn.

Chapter 14

"I know why Whiskey Jug has done this," Buffalo Horn said with deep gravity. "Eagle Feather takes the hair from a bear, so Whiskey Jug takes it from his face."

Jesse Three Dogs quirked an eyebrow. "That is so, but Eagle Feather will say his bear looks better."

Adam laughed with the others and rubbed a hand ruefully over his clean-shaven cheek. "I feel like Eagle Feather's bear. I'm not so sure using my Bowie knife was a good idea." In truth he didn't know what had possessed him. Shaving inside *Beta Quest* had never even occurred to him before. If it had, he'd have bought a razor in Laramie City. For that matter, he could have come into the program clean-shaven. Yet here he was, with his treasured beard gone and his face smarting. What in the world had he been thinking?

But, deep down, he knew what had caused him to do such a thing: the Kenzie glitch. Though there seemed little chance she would choose to go with Eagle Feather, Adam had felt compelled to hedge his bets. With a full complement of coarse mountain- man hair, he was as foreign to Kenzie's twenty-first century eyes as Eagle Feather. He refused to look too closely at why it mattered.

A movement to the left caught his eye, and he turned his head in time to see a woman walk away. Though she was dressed like a woman of the tribe, she was obviously white. He didn't think he'd ever seen her before, and yet there was something very familiar about the way she moved.

"Kenzie?" Adam called, but the woman didn't even pause. A moment later, she disappeared behind a tipi, and he was left wondering if his eyes had played tricks on him or if the program had produced another odd character.

"He shaved for me," Beautiful Dawn said, smiling up at

him. "Didn't you, Adam?"

"Mmmm," he murmured noncommittally. Gazing down into her luminous eyes, he realized Kenzie was right; Dawn had no notion it was over between them.

"Dawn," he said heavily, "we need to talk."

Her smile returned instantly. "Yes," she said. "We go now."

Adam held back a sigh. This wasn't going to be easy. He took her arm and moved away from the group of men.

"This is nice," she said with a happy smile. "We have not been alone since…" Her voice trailed off and a furrow appeared in her forehead.

"Since?" he prodded gently. He was curious about what she'd say. The last time they'd been together was in Paris.

"That is strange; I am not really sure. It was a long time ago."

"What exactly do you remember?" he asked.

"Many things," she said with a smile. "Like the time you held me so we could make love standing in the fountain, and the time…"

Adam felt himself blushing as Dawn described their many adventures. Had he really done all of those things with her? But his body remembered and began to react to her words and the memories they evoked. He didn't think his state of arousal by itself would be enough to trip the Sex-Hex, but there was no sense taking chances. "Do you recall where we were?" he asked hastily.

"Of course. I…" Her voice trailed off, and she stopped walking as the furrow between her brows deepened. "I can't seem to bring it to mind."

Adam wasn't surprised. Since he'd been in the process of testing his programming in *Beta Quest*, their liaisons had taken place in some of the most exotic locations on earth, none of which bore the slightest resemblance to the Snowy Range or the Indian camp.

"Oh well," Dawn said with a shrug. "Where we were does

not matter as much as what we did." She laid her hands on his chest. "And I remember every second of it." Her smile faltered slightly as she gazed up at him. "Don't you?"

Adam started to deny it, but something in her eyes stopped him. She might be a product of his imagination, but she had feelings, just like a real person.

"Yes," he said softly, "I do." He lifted his hand and trailed his index finger down the side of her face. "You're so beautiful," he murmured, almost against his will.

Dawn gave a happy sigh as she circled his waist with her arms and laid her cheek against his chest. "You *do* still care. I knew it."

Of their own accord his arms went around her in a comforting gesture. What he had to say was going to hurt, but there was no way around it. "Dawn, I—"

"Whiskey Jug, come quick!" A small boy raced toward them.

Adam dropped his arms in alarm, imagining all kinds of disasters. "What's the matter?"

"Jesse Three Dogs told me to come find you," he said, his dark eyes sparkling with excitement. "The hand game is about to start."

Adam sighed in relief as visions of mayhem and disaster faded from his mind. The hand game was a Native American game of chance and skill that he'd learned to play in his youth, one that he was rather good at. Today it had the added bonus of delaying his difficult talk with Dawn.

"What is the hand game?" she asked curiously as they followed the boy back to camp.

"It's kind of a betting game. You and a partner each have two sticks. One of your sticks is marked and the other is plain. You put one in each hand and mix them behind your back. Then the picker comes along and points to two hands. If you and your partner both have the unmarked stick …" He grinned at Dawn's look of confusion. He remembered feeling the same way the first time he'd seen it played. "Never mind. Watch for a while, and you'll catch on."

"I have never seen this before. Is it a white man's game?"

"No, it's ..." Suddenly he wasn't so sure. His experience with the hand game had been at rendezvous and pow wows. He had no clue where it had originated. For that matter, the dances the tribe did here were ones he was familiar with. He had no idea which were modern and which had been handed down for generations. The scientist in him made a mental note to check the origins and dates of the Native American customs he'd installed in his software for *Beta Quest*. Granted, there would be few players who would know the difference, but some would. Nothing could spoil someone's enjoyment faster than an anachronism. That was the whole reason he had a team of experts researching every setting and why he'd developed the Reality Guard: to make sure the program stayed true to the time period. Neither *Beta Quest* nor *Fantasy Quest* could create anything that wouldn't exist in that time.

"Adam?"

"Hmm?"

"What is wrong?"

The note of apprehension in Dawn's voice brought him back to the present. "Oh, nothing," he said, smiling down at her to relieve her anxiety. "I was just thinking."

She returned his smile and touched his arm possessively.

As Adam put his hand over hers to gently remove it, he happened to glance up, right into the brilliant green eyes of Kenzie Armstrong. The disillusionment he saw there made him feel guilty. Not for the first time, it occurred to him he might have made his SR program a little too realistic. Though it was that same realism that the marketing team planned to capitalize on, it made for uncomfortable situations. *Sort of like real life*, he thought with a rueful smile. But, then, humans were odd creatures. They had to feel negative emotions like anger and jealousy to truly enjoy happier feelings.

What he was feeling now was an odd combination of both. Consternation for being caught in what looked like a compromising position with Dawn warred with delight as he took in Kenzie's changed appearance. He'd always known she was pretty, but he'd never seen her at her best. In fact, he suddenly realized she was the woman he had seen earlier and thought was a new character. Now, dressed like the other women of the village, with her hair under control and most of her bruises healed or hidden, she was beautiful.

Kenzie wasn't drop-dead gorgeous like Dawn; nobody was. Yet, somehow, her allure was more powerful. If Dawn was his deepest fantasy, Kenzie was the reality he secretly wished for. She was like sun-warmed earth or a crystalline brook bubbling over mossy rocks in a leafy-green glen. Looking at her made the blood run hot and heavy in his veins, but it also tapped something deeper, more primitive. Something that made him want to claim her as his own, to warn other males away.

He gave himself a mental shake. That was just plain silly. Kenzie Armstrong was a phantasm no more real than the illusion that he could walk. These odd feelings must be a reaction to the constant competitive spirit Eagle Feather always brought to the game. The solution was simple: leave the Indian village. Nobody would give it a second thought. He'd done it many times before. Perhaps that was the solution to the Kenzie glitch as well: to get on Bear Bait and ride out, leaving her here with the rest of his characters.

Maybe that's just what he'd do — but not yet. Right now, the look of determination on Kenzie's face did not bode well for someone, and his curiosity was getting the best of him. She'd promised him an interesting evening. It might be fun to see what she'd meant by that.

Chapter 15

Kenzie's eyes narrowed, and her lips thinned as she noted the possessive way Adam's hand covered Beautiful Dawn's. So much for his assurance that the affair was over. She turned away, reminding herself she didn't care. Ignoring the couple behind her, she made her way over to the center of the village, where a crowd was gathering.

Two rows of men sat on the ground, facing each other. Their hands lay on their thighs, fists closed and facing upward as Buffalo Horn walked between the rows, scrutinizing the faces watching him expectantly. The highly decorated stick in his hand and the drums pounding at either end of the row matched the cadence of his chant. He stopped before two men and pointed his stick toward their adjacent hands. Both opened their fists, revealing two small, rounded bones. Buffalo Horn nodded, pushed a marker stick toward their side and moved on.

Buffalo Horn repeated the same pattern over and over during the next half hour or so. Sometimes he awarded the men one stick, sometimes two. Other times, a groan rose from the crowd as, for no reason Kenzie could see, the marker sticks all went back to the middle, and the play turned to the other row of men.

"Got it figured out yet?" Adam said at her side.

Kenzie didn't even turn to look at him. She had no desire to see Beautiful Dawn plastered against his other side. "Not a clue. Care to enlighten me?"

"It has to do with the bones they have hidden in their hands."

"No kidding."

"Then you see the difference in them."

She could hear the amusement in his voice and resisted the

urge to grind her teeth. Adam seemed to enjoy rubbing her nose in her ignorance. Kenzie crossed her arms and gazed pensively at the two bones that were just being revealed in the game. "Sure, one is the right hind toe of a grizzly, and the other is the left front toe of a black bear, right?"

Adam chuckled. "I would have thought they were rabbit bones, myself."

Pasting a sweet smile on her face, Kenzie peeped up at him. "Very perceptive. I was just checking to see if you knew." She turned her attention back to the players, but there was no denying the odd little spurt of pleasure she'd felt when she saw he was alone.

"One is plain in each set and the other is marked," he said with a grin.

"Oh, yeah! I see now. That one has a design on it, and the other one doesn't. They just look like decorations."

"They are. Every player has his own set of bones. For every plain bone the picker chooses, the team gets a marker. If two marked bones show up, the team loses all their markers—"

"And the play goes to the other side," she finished for him. "I suppose the team that winds up with all the markers is the winner."

"Exactly."

"Cool. Can I play?"

"Well," he hedged. "it's usually the men…"

"Yeah, yeah, yeah. I know. It's another thing women don't do. I should have guessed." She glanced around and realized for the first time that the gathering was entirely male except for her. "Where are all the women, anyway? Slaving over hot campfires, no doubt."

"Somebody has to fix the food."

"Right. I suppose that's where Beautiful Dawn went, too."

"Probably." He rubbed the side of his nose self-consciously. "About Dawn—"

"Never mind." Kenzie held up her hand and turned her head away. "It's none of my business. I'm going to go join the women now. Certainly wouldn't want to be the one to upset the apple cart — er, chokecherry basket."

Kenzie swept away, with a toss of her head and a self-satisfied smile on her face. *Ha! Let him put that in his peace pipe and smoke it.*

"It may not be any of your business," Adam said, falling in beside her, "but I'm going to tell you anyway."

Kenzie frowned in irritation. Didn't he know an exit line when he heard one? "Look, Adam, I really don't want to know."

He went on, as though she hadn't spoken. "Dawn and I were involved romantically, but it was several years ago. I haven't seen her since. There's really nothing between us."

"But she doesn't know it's over, right?"

"Exactly. I tried to tell her, but I couldn't hurt her like that."

Kenzie stopped and stared at him. "I don't believe it. A man with a heart. Who would have thought?" She stared at him in wonder a moment longer, then waved a hand through the air and started walking again. "Not to worry. If my plan works, Beautiful Dawn won't even give you a second glance after tonight."

"What plan?"

"You'll just have to wait and see. You'd be surprised at the things I can accomplish when I have a mind to."

"I can see that. You've obviously made a conquest of Red Blanket."

"What makes you think that?"

"Your clothes. It's the closest thing she has to a wedding dress. You must be pretty special for her to let you wear it."

"Her wedding dress!" Kenzie gazed down at her outfit in shock. "You're kidding, right?"

"Nope, it's what she wore when she married Buffalo Horn after her first husband died. She must consider you almost a member of the family."

Kenzie swallowed a grin as she remembered Red Blanket's cryptic message about Beautiful Dawn. "Maybe she just wanted me to make an impression on someone."

"You're probably right," he said with studied nonchalance. "Eagle Feather has always been a favorite of hers."

Her eyes narrowed. He thought he was going to tease her about Eagle Feather, did he? Two could play at that game. "Speaking of Eagle Feather, he brought me another gift this afternoon."

"Oh?"

"It was so sweet of him. Oh, look, there's Red Blanket. I'll see you later," she said with a pointed look. He seemed to understand this time. She peeked back over her shoulder to see if he followed, but he was just standing there, gazing after her, with an unreadable look on his face. *Good. Let him wonder what I'm up to.* Her plan had a much better chance of succeeding if he didn't know what was going on. One of the participants in her little drama was primed and ready. Now for the other two.

At her approach, Red Blanket looked up from the campfire where she was cooking and smiled in welcome. "Wheesky Jug like?" she asked.

"He loved it," Kenzie lied. As far as she knew, he'd hardly noticed her changed appearance beyond the fact that she was wearing Red Blanket's dress. "Eagle Feather did too." That much at least was true.

Red Blanket's smile faded, and she shook her head. "*Hicka*! No Eagle Feather."

"It's all right." Kenzie grinned. "I have plans for Eagle Feather." She held up one hand. "See, this is Eagle Feather, and this"—she held up the other hand—"is Beautiful Dawn." She folded her hands together. "What do you think?"

Red Blanket looked at Kenzie's folded hands for a moment, then her face broke into a huge smile. "Yes," she said simply. "Good."

"I think so too." Of course, it was going to be a bit tricky to make everyone jealous and keep Whiskey Jug and Eagle Feather from beating each other to a bloody pulp. *Good thing I enjoy a challenge,* Kenzie thought. She made a show of looking for someone. "Where is Beautiful Dawn, anyway?"

Red Blanket pointed toward another small knot of women, who appeared to be cooking around another nearby campfire. Kenzie nodded and took a deep breath. "Ok, wish me luck."

The older woman nodded her head as though she understood what Kenzie had said. "You go now," she said with a big grin.

With a jaunty wave, Kenzie headed toward the other women. Beautiful Dawn was easy to locate among the others. She stood out like a rose in a field of daisies. Kenzie pasted a smile on her face and called out, "Hey, Dawn! I've been looking all over for you."

Beautiful Dawn looked first startled then wary. "You have?"

"Yes, I need you to act as interpreter for me. Will you ask them what they want me to do to help?"

The other woman stared at her for a long moment. "You trust me?"

"Sure. Whiskey Jug trusts you, and that's good enough for me. Besides, you're the only other woman in the village that speaks English, and the men refuse to leave their game."

Beautiful Dawn stared at her for a long moment then turned and spoke to the other women. After several minutes of conversation, to which everyone seemed to want to contribute, Beautiful Dawn pointed toward the pot on the fire. "You can help me with the chokecherry gravy."

"All right. What do you want me to do?"

"Just take the chokecherries off the stems like this." She deftly stripped a stem and dropped the berries into the pot. "And put them on to boil."

Kenzie nodded. She grabbed a handful and began to expertly strip the berries. "I used to do this as a kid when I helped my mom make jelly."

The two women worked in companionable silence while Kenzie tried to think of a good way to broach the subject of men without being too obvious. After several long minutes,

Beautiful Dawn spoke.

"I am sorry about the bear," she said hesitantly. "I did not know it was there."

"Oh, no, of course you didn't." As Kenzie said the words, she realized it was true. "You'd never have endangered the children that way," she added softly.

"No, but I did not mean for you to be hurt either."

Kenzie fought to suppress her smile. Just the opening she was looking for, "All's well that ends well. It really turned out to be a good thing for me."

Beautiful Dawn raised her delicately arched brows in surprise. "How was it good?"

"Eagle Feather," Kenzie said with a dramatic sigh. "I never realized how brave he was until he killed the bear."

Beautiful Dawn frowned. "Adam run to save you too."

"Yes, he did, but if Eagle Feather hadn't been there with his bow, we'd have both been killed. It was the most amazing thing I've ever seen. Three arrows, one through the eye and two dead center in less than two minutes."

"They say he is the best hunter in the village," Beautiful Dawn said.

"Oh, I believe it," Kenzie added enthusiastically. "Did you know he brought me the hide?"

Beautiful Dawn looked surprised. "He did?"

"Yes, and the brain too, although I'm not really sure what I'm supposed to do with it."

"The brain is to tan the hide."

It was Kenzie's turn to look surprised. "It is?"

"You use the brain of the animal to tan the hide. It makes the finest buckskin." She pointed to her own dress. "See how it is almost white? That is brain tanning."

"Really?" Kenzie was interested in spite of herself. Maybe this tanning thing would turn out to be more than just a way to prove Whiskey Jug Johnson wrong. Beautiful Dawn's dress was gorgeous. "Will it make my bear skin white like that?"

"The part you tan will be white. The fur will not change

color, but if you work the hide right the fur will be very soft. This man has given you a valuable gift."

Kenzie sighed, doing her best to imitate an infatuated teen. "I know, isn't he just the most wonderful man you ever saw?"

"I have never seen this Eagle Feather." Beautiful Dawn gave her a sidelong glance. "What of Adam?"

"What about him?"

"I thought you wanted him."

"That was before I met Eagle Feather. Don't get me wrong. Adam is a great guy and a good friend." Kenzie shrugged. "He just isn't Eagle Feather."

"I must meet this Eagle Feather for myself."

"Oh, you will. He'll be at the party tonight. It's to honor him, after all." Kenzie noted the speculative look on Beautiful Dawn's face with great satisfaction. She had her now. It was probably time to change the subject. The point had been made; any more would be overkill.

"What do we do with the juice once we've boiled it out of the chokecherries?" Kenzie asked. The conversation ebbed and flowed as they worked companionably, side by side. If Eagle Feather's name came up occasionally, Beautiful Dawn pretended not to notice, but Kenzie could see the other woman was intrigued. *Good. Two down and one to go.*

In a surprisingly short time, the food was ready for the feast. Kenzie left the women and went in search of Eagle Feather. She found him with the other men just as the hand game ended.

"Which side finally won?" she asked.

Eagle Feather glanced down at her as though surprised by her presence. "Both sides win many times."

"Really? Who won the most?"

Eagle Feather's face darkened. "Whiskey Jug, but he has much luck. It is always the way when he plays the hand game."

Kenzie fought the urge to smile. The competition between the two men was still alive and well. Of the three, Eagle Feather was going to be the easiest to set up. "I suppose that will make

Beautiful Dawn happy. She said he was the best hand game player in the village."

"This Beautiful Dawn does not know of what she speaks," Eagle Feather said sharply.

"That's what I told her, but she insists that Whiskey Jug Johnson is the best at everything."

Eagle Feather frowned. "Who is this Beautiful Dawn?"

"Oh, haven't you met her? She's new to the village, and from everything I hear, she's Whiskey Jug's woman."

"What of you?"

Kenzie sighed and shook her head. "I don't stand a chance against Beautiful Dawn. Look, there she is with him now." She gestured toward the other couple, who were strolling through camp, arm in arm.

Predictably, Dawn was at Whiskey Jug's side, though Kenzie thought perhaps she wasn't clinging to him quite as much as before. Adam was looking rather pleased with himself. Winning obviously agreed with him. At least, that's what Kenzie hoped had put that smug expression on his face. She tried to ignore the little voice inside that kept reminding her that she hadn't exactly let him in on her plan to get Beautiful Dawn together with Eagle Feather.

It was too late to worry about that now. The wheels were in motion, and she doubted if she could stop it now even if she wanted to. A glance up at Eagle Feather gave Kenzie a surge of satisfaction. His gaze was firmly fixed on the woman at Adam's side. Now, if Beautiful Dawn would just look up…

As though the other woman had heard Kenzie's thoughts, Beautiful Dawn raised her head and looked straight at Eagle Feather. As their gazes locked, Kenzie could almost see the spark. The air practically crackled with the attraction between the two of them. Kenzie heard Eagle Feather's breath catch in his chest as Dawn's lips parted.

Adam noticed Beautiful Dawn's preoccupation and followed the line of her vision. Kenzie almost laughed aloud at the expression on his face when he saw what had attracted her attention. His look of hopeful confusion reminded Kenzie of a child who wasn't sure if he was being rewarded or punished. When he finally glanced her way, Kenzie allowed herself a grin and a wink. At first, she wasn't sure Adam had gotten her message. Then he gave her a slow nod. He watched Beautiful Dawn and Eagle Feather for several minutes, apparently deciding what to do. Then he spoke to Beautiful Dawn, glanced at Eagle Feather, frowned, spoke to Dawn again, and finally led her away.

Eagle Feather stood stock still for a long moment then let his breath out in a low *whoosh*. "That is Beautiful Dawn?" he asked tightly.

"Sure is," Kenzie said in a disgruntled tone. "Did you notice Whiskey Jug didn't even look at me? She's completely turned his head."

"She is not yet his woman."

"Somebody ought to tell them that," Kenzie said in a peevish tone. "They seem to think it's a done deal."

"She is not his wife. A woman without a husband can be won." Eagle Feather headed through the crowd, after them.

It was all Kenzie could do not to giggle as she followed him. He'd said exactly the same thing about her. Now, if she could just keep the situation under control, everything would come out all right.

At first, it looked as though her biggest difficulty was going to be Adam. In fact, he seemed to be doing everything in his power to make sure her plan came to nothing. He flirted outrageously with Beautiful Dawn, even causing some of the women to wag their heads disapprovingly. Every time Eagle Feather tried to get closer, Adam maneuvered Beautiful Dawn away. All through the meal, Kenzie's frustration mounted right along with Eagle Feather's.

By the time the drums started their primal beat, and the dancing began, Kenzie was ready to wring Adam's neck. Why hadn't he just told her he wanted Beautiful Dawn and saved her all this trouble? Eagle Feather eagerly joined the dancers, anxious to show off his prowess to Beautiful Dawn. Kenzie sat on the sidelines, disgruntled and angry. Her look was far from friendly when Adam sauntered over.

"Excellent play-acting, Kenzie-girl," he said with a smile. "Anyone would think you were ready to breathe fire."

"What makes you think I'm not?"

"Because your plan is going so well."

"Is it?" she said caustically. "And here I thought you were thwarting me at every turn."

"On the contrary, I'm making sure it goes just as you planned."

Kenzie gave a disbelieving snort. "Really. How do you figure that?"

"It will only work if Eagle Feather thinks he's beating me out of something I want. If I seem too anxious to get rid of Dawn, he'll know it's a ruse and turn his attention back to you."

"I hadn't thought of that," Kenzie said, slightly mollified. "What about Beautiful Dawn? Do you think she's falling for it?"

"Oh, definitely. I don't know what you did to turn her head, but my manliness has faded significantly. To make matters worse, I didn't even want to participate in the dancing. How do you plan to get them together?"

"I haven't quite got that worked out yet," Kenzie admitted. "It's too bad the men and women don't dance together. If they had one waltz in each other's arms, we'd be home free."

"Actually, there is a dance that both the men and women do. It's called the Friendship Dance. Of course, it's closer to a get-acquainted dance than a waltz. Still, I think we can make it do the trick. They always play one."

"How will I know which one it is?"

"I'll give you a signal. All we have to do is keep them apart until the end of the dance. By the time we get done with them, Eagle Feather and Beautiful Dawn will forget either of us ever existed."

"What if it doesn't work?" Kenzie asked doubtfully.

"Then, you'll think of something else. I'd better go before

one of them notices us together."

There's little chance of that, Kenzie thought to herself as Adam walked away. Eagle Feather and Beautiful Dawn only had eyes for each other.

Several other dances came and went, some for women, some for men. Kenzie got caught up in the primitive rhythms and graceful movements. She even joined one of the women's dances, though she would have preferred the more uninhibited movement of the men's dances.

After an hour or so, it became obvious a different sort of dance was forthcoming. Two lines formed, one of men and one of women, facing each other. Kenzie sought Adam's eyes and received the expected signal. She was to get in line opposite Eagle Feather, just as Adam was opposite Beautiful Dawn.

As soon as the drummers began, the two lines converged. Eagle Feather crossed his hands at the wrist and reached for Beautiful Dawn's, but Adam was there before him, whisking her away in the dance. Kenzie could almost swear she heard Eagle Feather's teeth grind as he took her for a partner instead. In a shuffling two-step, the double line moved around the camp, weaving in and out like a giant snake. Then the leaders separated, and the two lines pulled apart, only to come together again with different partners.

Instantly, Kenzie could see how Adam's plan would work. No matter how hard he tried, Eagle Feather never wound up with Beautiful Dawn. His frustration became a palatable thing as the dance progressed, and Beautiful Dawn was partnered with every man but him. At last, Adam and Kenzie were back where they started, with Eagle Feather and Beautiful Dawn across from them. Kenzie was never quite sure how he managed it, but at the last minute, Adam seemed to stumble, and Eagle Feather leaped in to take his place.

"Just a minute," Adam protested. "That's my partner."

"No," Eagle Feather said, without even looking at him. "Mine!" A blind man could have understood his meaning. He was claiming the woman at his side for more than just a dance.

"You know, Kenzie," Adam murmured as he grinned down at her, "we might actually pull it off."

Kenzie sighed with satisfaction. "It's starting to look like it."

They finished out the dance and stood watching the other couple from a distance. Kenzie glanced up at him. "You won't mind, will you, if Beautiful Dawn winds up with Eagle Feather?"

"No, I'd say that would solve two of my three most pressing problems."

"Oh?"

"I've driven myself crazy trying to figure out what to do with those two. You solved both problems at once." He nodded toward Eagle Feather and Beautiful Dawn, who were standing toe to toe and gazing into each other's eyes like a couple of star-struck teenagers. As they watched, Eagle Feather lifted his hand to trace the curve of her face. "They'll be so focused on each other that they won't have time for anything else."

Kenzie smiled with satisfaction. "It does appear that way, doesn't it? What's your third problem?"

He hesitated. For a moment, it looked as though he wasn't quite sure what to say. "I wish my shoulder would hurry up and heal," he said, moving it experimentally. Adam frowned. "That's odd. It hardly hurts at all anymore."

Though it made perfectly good sense, Kenzie had the strangest feeling it wasn't what he meant to say at all. Still, she accepted his explanation and nodded her understanding. "Want me to take a look?"

He shrugged. "Might as well, I guess." Crossing his arms, he grabbed the bottom of his shirt and pulled it up over his head.

Kenzie had to pull her eyes away from the well-developed chest and bulky biceps. Sweet mother in heaven, but he had a nice body! Swallowing a sigh of pure appreciation, she moved forward to look at the wound. With gentle fingers, she carefully lifted Buffalo Horn's bandage and peeked beneath it. "What the heck?"

Adam glanced down at her. "What's wrong?"

"Nothing really, but this is so strange…" She pulled the bandage farther away and ran her fingers over his skin.

"What's strange? Is it infected or something?"

"No." She shook her head. "Nothing like that."

"What, then?"

"Here. Look for yourself." She reached up and pulled the bandage completely free of his shoulder.

"I'll be damned." The vicious wound that had been there this morning was nearly gone. Only a purple scar remained to show that it had ever been there.

Chapter 16

"I still don't understand why we had to leave," Kenzie said. "I wanted to stay and watch Eagle Feather's and Beautiful Dawn's romance bloom."

Adam shook his head. "We couldn't take that chance. There's no saying what Eagle Feather will do in a situation like that. I sure as hell didn't want to fight him."

"No, I guess not." Kenzie sighed and tried to settle more comfortably behind the saddle without startling Bear Bait. "I don't suppose we're headed to Rainbow Falls, are we?"

"No, we're going to my cabin."

"I was afraid of that."

"Why?"

"I just keep thinking about how nice a hot bath would feel." Kenzie brightened suddenly. "Hey, you must have some way to bathe at your cabin."

"Afraid not."

"Is that because you use the hot springs? Or because you don't bathe much?"

Adam grinned. "Don't you know it's unhealthy to bathe too much?"

"Oh, really." Kenzie's voice was flat with disbelief.

"Yep. Once a year is plenty. I've known men to sicken and die from taking more than that."

Kenzie snorted. "Right. The next thing you'll be telling me is that a string of garlic around your neck will keep vampires away."

"Don't know about vampires, whatever they are, but it will keep you from catching a cold."

"Only because no one can stand to get close enough to pass any germs to you," Kenzie told him. "Of course, if you only bathe once a year, I guess garlic wouldn't be so bad by comparison."

Adam chuckled. "Not too much garlic up here anyway. Might find some wild onions, though."

"Hmm. No, I think they'd be better in a stew than a necklace. You know, Adam, where I come from, some people bathe every day."

"Is that right?"

"Yes, and they are so healthy many even live into their hundreds."

"From bathing?"

"Not entirely, but it helps."

It suddenly occurred to Adam that the Kenzie glitch had opened the door to a whole set of questions he hadn't even thought to ask. What was her perception of what was going on? Would she be like Dawn and not be able to remember, or had she somehow developed memories? Time to find out. "Where exactly are you from?"

Kenzie was quiet for several long moments. When she finally spoke, her voice was hesitant. "I doubt you'd believe me if I told you."

"Try me."

"It's not so much a *where* as a *when*." She took a deep breath. "Adam, I'm from the future. Now, I know how strange it sounds, but somehow I've traveled back in time."

"Time travel?" Adam burst out laughing. "That's the craziest thing I ever heard."

"I knew you'd say that." Kenzie sniffed. "You probably think I'm delusional as well, but how else do you explain what's happened to me?"

"I don't really know what happened to you," Adam reminded her. "We've never really talked about it. All I know is that you showed up at the bottom of Rainbow Falls, half-dead and dressed in your underwear."

"It wasn't my underwear," she said indignantly. "It was a perfectly respectable pair of shorts and a T-shirt."

"Whatever you call them, they were indecent."

"That proves I'm from a different century. Where I come from, everybody dresses that way all the time."

"Must be interesting in the winter," he murmured, unable to resist teasing her a bit.

"Ok, so they don't wear them all the time. You still have to admit it's a style you don't see around here."

"And you still haven't told me how you got here."

Kenzie sighed. "I'm not sure. The last thing I remember was hitting a cliff."

"You hit a cliff?" Adam turned in the saddle to look at her. "Maybe you'd better go back to the beginning."

She shrugged. "Ok. I had gone to the Sinks to get rid of some stuff—"

"The Sinks?"

"It's a place. See, the Popo Agie River comes roaring down the mountain, disappears into a cave, and then comes up in a calm pool about a mile down the road. It's called the Sinks. Anyway, Brad, my fiancé…"

Adam listened to Kenzie's story with a growing sense of confusion, starting with the insecure fiancé who demanded she dispose of every token of her past loves and ending with a bizarre underground river, the details of her story were odd and completely unrealistic. Yet, it was the implausibility that somehow gave it the ring of truth.

"… and I came to in the hot pool."

"I take it that wasn't where you expected to be." He felt her shrug against his back.

"If I'd had time to think about it, I would have expected to wake up in a hospital or a morgue, not next to…well, where I was."

"Next to what?" he prompted. "A waterfall?"

"No, a naked mountain man, if you must know. You freaked me out!"

"Freaked you out?"

"Scared the pants off me."

He grinned. She made teasing her so easy. "As I recall, you

had your pants on."

"You know what I mean."

"If people walk around in...uh, *shorts* where you come from, I wouldn't think a naked man would bother you much."

"You're wrong. We may not dress the way people do here, but the important parts are always decently covered."

The vision of an actress at the last academy awards popped into Adam's head and he had to fight a smile. It was a good thing she couldn't read minds. "When did you decide you'd traveled back in time?"

"When I saw Laramie City. Up until that point, everything made sense in my time."

"How's that?"

"There are people in my century we call right-wing militants that have a not-so-secret desire to do away with the government. Some of them hide out in the mountains and live pretty much like you do, with no modern conveniences."

"Modern conveniences?"

"Right, like electricity, indoor plumbing, four-wheel drives and..." She trailed off as she apparently realized he wouldn't have a clue what she was talking about. "Anyway, they tend to be pretty dangerous characters."

"And you thought I was one of these militants?" Adam couldn't help but be amused. As though any self-respecting right-wing militant would dress in buckskin and use a muzzleloader. They were far more likely to wear camouflage and carry an assault rifle.

"Yes." She sighed. "Ok, so it seems a little weird now, but at the time, it made perfect sense."

"When we got to Laramie, though, you realized you'd made a mistake?"

"Well, yeah. I mean, I've been to Laramie, and trust me, it doesn't have dirt streets and tent saloons. At first I thought it was a movie set."

"A what?"

"A movie set. They build a make-believe town, then use it

to…" She sighed. "It's kind of hard to explain. Anyway, when I realized it was real, I knew I'd gone back in time."

"You couldn't think of any other explanation for what happened to you?"

"Like what?"

"I don't know, a dream maybe?"

She snorted. "A dream that goes on for weeks? I don't think so. Even a hallucination wouldn't last this long."

"But time travel?"

"Yeah, I know. Even in my time it isn't possible except in books. Still, I can't think of a single logical explanation for what's happened to me. Can you?"

She had him there. The way she told her story, there was no logical explanation, but then there didn't have to be. It wasn't real. Anything could happen within the confines of *Beta Quest*. The only question he wanted answered was how a computer glitch had come up with such an incredible story.

"See?" she said, apparently taking his long pause as an answer in itself. "There is no other explanation. The problem now is how do I get home?"

"You want to leave?" he asked in surprise. No other character had ever expressed such a desire. Of course, none of them knew there was a world outside of *Beta Quest*.

"What do you think?"

"I don't know, I guess I thought you were happy here."

"Oh, right. I've been battered, bruised, sunburned, scraped, scratched, bounced around like a puppet, frozen half to death, and nearly eaten by a bear. I've had nothing but fun since I got here."

"It was your own fault that you nearly frozen. Nobody made you take that bath," he reminded her.

"Which brings us back to Rainbow Falls. Couldn't we just go there on the way home? I won't complain anymore; I promise."

Adam frowned. He was going to have to go soon, and he was a little worried about leaving his body outside. It had never been a concern before the arrival of the Kenzie glitch, because the program shut down as soon as he left. If something happened to his body, he couldn't recreate it without resetting the program. He'd already proven he couldn't recreate Kenzie, and he wasn't finished studying her. No, his body had to be left somewhere safe.

Adam glanced at the sun. "I need to go hunting and find us something to eat for supper."

"How far is Rainbow Falls from here? Maybe I can hike over."

"It's an hour by horse. If you walked, you wouldn't get there until way after dark. I'm sorry, but there just isn't time today."

It would be touch and go whether he got Kenzie to the cabin before Annie showed up for his therapy session. "I can take you tomorrow."

"Why not now?"

Adam smiled at her petulant little-girl voice. It reminded him of when Zoey was small and needed a nap. "Look, we're both tired. I'll take you first thing in the morning, I promise."

Kenzie sighed. "I suppose I'll have to be satisfied with that. Will I have time to work my hide when we get to the cabin?"

Adam glanced at the sun again. "We have an hour or so until dark. I pretty much go to bed when the sun goes down," he warned.

"It shouldn't take long with my fox hide." She sighed again. "It's too bad I couldn't have brought the bear skin."

"Red Blanket was right. It was way too big a project for a beginner. You could never have worked it. This one will be much better for you."

"I know, and she'll do a better job. I just wanted to do it myself. Maybe you should have left me there so I could work on it."

"I suppose I could have." He glanced back over his shoulder again. "Of course, Eagle Feather would probably have decided he might as well have two wives as one."

"I doubt it. I have the feeling Beautiful Dawn will keep him too busy to even look at another woman."

Privately, Adam thought she was probably right, which brought him to the question he had already asked himself a dozen times today: Why hadn't he left Kenzie at the village? He'd fully intended to, right up until he started packing Bear Bait. She'd have been safe there with Jesse Three Dogs and Red Blanket to watch over her, and he'd be able to find her whenever he had time to continue studying her.

Then, for some reason, he'd decided he needed to isolate her from the other characters, and he'd brought her along. Now he was going to have to figure out some kind of elaborate plan to explain his absences when he left—and leave he would. Time was getting short. The team at Microcom planned a February launch for *Fantasy Quest* and were even now gearing up for it. They'd be less than pleased if he put them off because he didn't have the program polished to his satisfaction yet. They'd have no choice but to comply, of course; it was his company, after all, as well as his program. Still, it had taken a great deal of time and effort by many people to get this far. He owed it to his employees to hold up his end.

Kenzie shifted uncomfortably on the back of the horse. "I wish we'd get to your cabin. My backside feels like it's been pounded with a board. I think it's still bruised from my fall."

"Bruises take a long time to heal."

"I suppose so. At any rate, a good long soak in the hot pool will be just what the doctor ordered."

Adam grinned and shook his head. "You don't give up easily, do you?"

"No, I usually—hey, isn't that your cabin?"

Adam blinked in surprise. They should still be at least twenty minutes away, but Kenzie was right. A small part of the cabin's roof was visible through the trees. Adam took a quick look around. The cabin was right where it was supposed to be. It was almost as though they had been transported somehow. *How in the heck did that happen?*

A few minutes later, they dismounted. Kenzie stretched and hobbled toward the cabin as Adam tied Bear Bait to the corral fence.

"Everything looks just like we left it," Kenzie said as she opened the door of the cabin. "It's kind of a mess. Jesse and I were so worried about you we didn't take time to put things to rights." She disappeared inside the cabin. A moment later, her voice came through the open door. "It won't take me long to clean up though."

"All right. I'll go get water." Adam glanced around the cabin as he went in to retrieve the bucket. The room showed signs of a hasty departure. Blankets and furs lay in a jumble on the floor. His few dishes were stacked on the table next to the dishpan. It was impossible to tell if they were waiting to be washed or put away. For the first time he realized how concerned Kenzie and Jesse Three Dogs must have been about him, or at least the body that he'd left behind in *Beta Quest*.

He pondered the situation as he walked down the familiar path to the creek. How had they skipped the last part of the trip here? Most computer games had cheat codes that enabled that kind of thing, but he hadn't created cheat codes for *Beta Quest*.

It wasn't the first time an odd snafu had showed up in *Beta Quest*. In fact, that was the whole purpose of the program: to find errors so they could be fixed in *Fantasy Quest*. So far Adam's method had been reasonably effective. The only thing that he hadn't been able to figure out was the Kenzie glitch. Now, of course, he had deleted characters popping up all over the place and other odd quirks happening. He needed to work out what was going on.

By the time he returned to the cabin, Adam's mind was already halfway down the path to figuring out the time jump. Right now, what he needed to do was go into *Fantasy Quest* and see if his calculations were correct.

"Oh, good," Kenzie said when he appeared in the doorway, with the bucket of water. "Do you suppose you could build me a fire in the fireplace so I could heat up some of that?"

"Sure." Adam set his bucket on the table, went to the fireplace, and retrieved his tinderbox from the mantle. "You may as well learn how to do it yourself," he said as he picked up the steel and flint. "You never know when you'll need a fire, and I won't always be around to start one for you."

Without a word, Kenzie joined him at the fireplace and dutifully watched every step he took. Before long, a fire was burning cheerfully, and she turned to him with shining eyes.

"That was amazing!" she said. "I've always heard you could build a fire with steel and flint, but I'd never actually seen it done."

"Think you could do it on your own next time?"

She flashed him a crooked grin. "I seriously doubt it, but then, I suspect it takes a lot of practice."

Adam thought back to the rendezvous he attended as a small boy. Year after year, he'd try to start the fire. It had been one of his greatest frustrations. When he'd finally succeeded, at the age of twelve, it had been one of his greatest triumphs. "I'll let you try next time," he told her. "You'll get the hang of it eventually."

Unexpectedly, Adam's wrist began to tingle with the telltale vibrations of his watch. It was time to make his exit. He'd go, let Annie do her therapy session, then come back and get Kenzie set up for the night. "Look," he said, getting to his feet and replacing the tinderbox on the mantle. "I need to leave for a while."

Kenzie looked up at him in surprise. "Do you want me to come with you?"

"No, I just need to take a look around. I might even be able to scare us up a rabbit for supper."

"All right," she said doubtfully, rising to her feet. "Is there anything you want me to do while you're gone?"

"Nope. Just make yourself at home. I'll be back before you know it," he said, walking to the corral. He mounted Bear Bait then turned and waved a jaunty goodbye before riding out of the clearing. He could feel the gaze of those big green eyes on his back until he rode out of sight through the trees.

Chapter 17

With a sinking feeling in her middle, Kenzie watched Adam ride away. She'd never felt so totally alone, not even when she'd arrived here. Of course, then she'd thought she was close to the highway and home.

With a deep sigh, she turned back to the cabin. Maybe cleaning would make the time pass quickly. The kettle of water Adam had placed on the fire for her was already beginning to steam.

How do I get it out of the fireplace? She glanced around the room, searching for a pair of gloves or something that she could use to reach into the fire. Nothing.

Then her gaze lighted on a half dozen fire-blackened tools leaning up against the wall next to the hearth. Even a novice like her could tell they went with the contraption inside the fireplace that was used for cooking. Two iron bars with metal rings at the top had been driven into the floor of the fire box. A third bar was suspended between the two, with either end sticking through the rings. The open kettle hung suspended on a hook over the fire. Off to the side was a crude grill that could be moved over the coals to facilitate cooking. It wasn't pretty, but she had to admire its efficiency.

Kenzie studied the tools for several minutes, eventually deciding on a long iron bar with a hook at one end. It looked like it could be used to retrieve things from the fire.

By now, the water was boiling merrily in the kettle. It took some maneuvering, but Kenzie finally managed to get the hook underneath the bail of the kettle and lift it off the fire. It was surprisingly heavy, and she nearly dropped it twice before she got it to the table, where the dishpan was.

It took longer to get the water out of the fireplace and cool it down enough to stick her hands in it than it did to wash the dishes and tidy the cabin. Before she knew it, she was finished, and time hung heavy on her hands once again. Maybe she could get the rest of the brain solution worked into the hide before Adam returned.

Kenzie took the fox fur outside and carefully unrolled it. This one was further along than her bear hide; it was almost ready to dry. Early this morning, Red Blanket had mashed up the bear brain with water and shown Kenzie how to work it into the damp hide. They had finished the first application when Adam had fetched her. It had been Red Blanket's idea to trade hides when she discovered Kenzie was leaving with Whiskey Jug.

Kenzie made a face. She had to admit she was a little disappointed. Somewhere along the way, tanning the bear hide had become an interesting project rather than a simple "I told you so" for Adam. It appealed to her artist's soul. Still, a fox fur was better than nothing.

"I sure wish there was somebody around to tell me if I was doing this right," Kenzie muttered to herself. She carefully staked the fox hide on the ground in front of the cabin, just as Red Blanket had shown her, and began to work the brain solution into it.

"Make sure you get the edges. They'll curl if you don't."

Kenzie screamed and jerked away so hard she fell backwards. Her backside hit the ground with a hard thump, and she found herself staring up at a grizzled old trapper. The man's face was lined and leathery; his startling blue eyes studied her hide critically. His hair and beard were mostly white, with an occasional streak of dark gray here and there. He wore what she'd come to think of as the uniform of the mountain man: a fringed leather shirt, pants, and moccasins.

"That the first or the second?" he asked.

"Uh, f-first or second what?" she ventured.

He hunkered down next to the hide and tested it for pliability. "First or second coat of tanning solution."

"Oh. Um, I think it's the fourth."

"Good, I reckon it's about ready to dry, then." He glanced up at her. "You Whiskey Jug's woman?"

"I… Yes, I am," she said. No sense getting herself into another pickle, like she had with Eagle Feather. "Are you a friend of his?"

"Might say so." The man rose to his feet and leaned on his rifle. "Yep, it was me that found the little mite back when he weren't no taller than a tree stump."

A memory clicked in the back of her mind. "Then you're Cra—er…Charlie?"

His laugh grated on her ears like fingernails on a chalkboard. It was more of a cackle than anything else. "You were right the first time, missy. Crazy Charlie's what they call me, right enough." He turned his head and spit a long stream of tobacco toward the corral. "It's on account of my memory ain't so good."

"Really?" Kenzie said.

"Yep, sometimes my brain just sorta shuts down on me," he admitted. "And you be?"

"Oh. Kenzie. Kenzie Armstrong."

"Pleased to meet ya." He extended a callused right hand. Kenzie automatically put hers in it, thinking he wanted to shake hands, and found herself yanked to her feet instead.

"That's a mighty fine hide you got there," he said, dropping her hand. "You kill it?"

She looked down at the hide staked to the ground. "No, it's Red Blanket's. Do you know Red Blanket?"

"Sure do. Married to the chief, I reckon." He looked confused for a minute. "Can't rightly remember his name though…"

"Buffalo Horn."

He nodded his head and looked pleased. "Yep, that's him. How'd you get her pelt?"

"I traded my bear hide for it."

"A bear hide! Damn, girl, you done got cheated. A prime bear hide's worth ten foxes!"

"Oh, no, it wasn't that kind of trade," Kenzie hastily assured him. "Red Blanket's going to finish tanning it for me, and then we're going to trade back. See, the bear was my first hide, and she figured it would probably be too hard for me to finish by myself. She traded me this one to practice on."

He nodded his approval. "Reckon she knew the right of it. Smart woman, that Red Blanket."

"A good friend, too."

"I reckon so." He spit another stream of tobacco then looked at her questioningly. "You 'bout ready to go?"

Kenzie was startled. "Go? Go where?"

"Weren't you wantin' to go to the falls?"

"Yes, but—wait a minute. Did Whiskey Jug send you?"

He pondered this for a moment. "Don't rightly recall if he did or not." He shrugged. "Reckon he must have, else how would I know you wanted to go?"

"That's true." She glanced at the sun, as Adam had earlier. Even to her untrained eye, it was obvious the afternoon was waning and that there were only a few hours of good light left. "I wish it were closer. I suppose it's too late today."

Crazy Charlie shook his head. "Ain't all that far away. We could walk there in the time it takes to skin a rabbit."

Kenzie frowned. "Are you sure?"

"Yep." Crazy Charlie grinned. "You're thinking old Charlie's going to forget where he's goin', ain't ya?"

"Well—"

He shook his head. "I never get lost, though sometimes I forget why I was goin' there."

"It seemed a lot farther when I came with Whiskey Jug," Kenzie said.

"I know a short cut. 'Sides, I expect you didn't come here directly from the springs, did you?"

"No."

"Look, missy, if you're afraid we'll get lost, just bring your knife along and blaze a trail. That way you can find your way back."

"I haven't got a knife," Kenzie said. "Maybe I'd better just wait for Whiskey Jug. He said he'd be back soon."

"Maybe so, but I reckon he sent me so you could have your bath, and he could finish what he was doing."

"You remember talking to him, then?"

"Talk to him all the time." He hefted his rifle and turned to go. "You comin' or not?"

Kenzie chewed her lip indecisively. Adam had to have sent the old man. As Crazy Charlie had pointed out, he couldn't have known she wanted to take a bath otherwise. And hadn't Adam told her the old coot was completely harmless? He'd never have sent Crazy Charlie if there were any danger. The image of a nice, warm bath decided her. "All right," she said. "Just let me grab a few things, and we'll be on our way."

Crazy Charlie nodded. "I'll wait."

There was nothing in the cabin that resembled a towel or a bar of soap, but she still had part of her yucca root, and she could wear Adam's mother's dress while her own clothes were drying.

Crazy Charlie stuck his head in the door. "You 'bout ready?"

"Oh! Yes, I'll be right with you." There was no other choice. She grabbed the cotton dress and headed for the door. Too bad there was no way to leave Adam a note. Of course, there was no certainty he knew how to read, so it was probably a moot point. She closed the door behind her then smiled at Crazy Charlie. "I'm ready."

He nodded then reached down and pulled a wicked-looking tomahawk from his belt. Kenzie's heart leapt to her throat. Had she completely misread him after all? The thought had barely had time to form in her mind before he reversed the blade and handed the tomahawk to her, handle first.

"You can use my hawk knife to blaze a trail."

"I wouldn't have the slightest idea how to do that."

"Just put a notch in a tree now and then so you can follow them back."

"Can you show me?"

Charlie nodded. "Sure thing, missy. I'll do the first couple, then you can take over from there."

With mixed feelings of anticipation and nervousness, Kenzie followed the old man down the path and across the creek. True to his word, he showed her how and where to mark the tree with a wedge-shaped cut through the bark. After the first couple, he turned the hawk knife over to Kenzie and coached her beginning cuts. Before long, she was marking the trees he pointed out to her with the confidence of a veteran.

To Kenzie's surprise, they reached Rainbow Falls in less than 20 minutes. "Why did Whiskey Jug tell me it would take an hour?" she asked Crazy Charlie.

The old trapper grinned at her. "I told you, I know a short cut. It takes Whiskey Jug a mite longer to get here 'cause his horse has to take the long way around."

It still didn't make sense, but Kenzie decided to let it drop. Since she had left the hot pool by climbing the slopes that surrounded it, she had never seen Rainbow Falls from the front side. Now she gazed at it in awe. It fell from a high cliff, straight down into a placid pool at the bottom. Lush greenery grew in profusion on the cliff face and all around the pool, dampened by the mist that hung in the air. That same mist caught the light and split it into a beautiful spectrum that arched across the water and gave the falls its name.

"Oh!" Kenzie sighed in reverence. "It's beautiful."

"Yep, I reckon that's why Whiskey Jug's great-grandpappy built his cabin here."

Kenzie looked at Crazy Charlie in surprise. "His great-grandfather lived here?"

He frowned. "Now that you mention it, I ain't real sure. It could'a been his pappy or his grandpappy. I don't rightly recollect." He shrugged and pointed to a square hole on the east side of the pool. "It don't really matter, I guess. Anyhow, that's what's left of his cabin over there."

Intrigued, Kenzie wandered over to take a look. She was

surprised to discover that the hole went down a good four feet into the earth. "That's weird," she said. "It sort of looks like a basement, but it's not deep enough."

Crazy Charlie shook his head. "This here's the way trappers build cabins." He pointed to the hole. "See, that's the floor down there and half of the walls. You just build the rest of the walls about this high," he said indicating his shoulder, "and put the roof on it."

"Wow!" Kenzie looked at the hole with new eyes. "That makes good sense. It would only take half as long to build."

"Yep, and dirt walls are a might warmer in the winter. Snow don't blow in through the cracks, ya see."

"So why isn't Whiskey Jug's cabin built like this one?"

Crazy Charlie frowned. "Don't rightly know," he said. "Could be because he found it."

"He found it? A perfectly good cabin that just happened to be deserted? Does that kind of thing happen often?"

Crazy Charlie pursed his lips and leaned on this rifle as though considering this. "No," he said finally. "Don't reckon that makes much sense, does it? Guess you'll just have to ask him yourself when you get a chance." He spit then wiped his mouth with his arm and picked up his gun. "Reckon I'll leave you to your bath, then. I'll scout around and make sure there ain't no critters around to bother you. Holler if you need anything."

"All right, and thanks for bringing me."

"Glad to oblige," he said over his shoulder as he disappeared into the woods.

It was downright eerie. One minute he was there, and the next he was gone. Kenzie watched the spot for several minutes, trying to catch a glimpse of him through the trees, but didn't see so much as a flicker of movement. Crazy Charlie might be a senile old man, but he was as much a part of the woods as the deer and the bears.

Smiling, Kenzie turned her attention toward the falls. A bath—a *real* bath, in hot water. She couldn't wait. Eagerly, she started toward the curtain of water next to the falls, which she knew hid the hot springs.

She was about halfway there when she tripped over something in the grass. Expecting to see a rock or a tree root, she glanced down and stopped dead in her tracks. It was her journal!

Of course. She'd dropped it into the river just before she'd fallen. It had come through the same way she had. She picked it up and flipped through the pages. With a flicker of disappointment, she saw that prolonged exposure to the water had washed away most of the ink. Even the lines on the paper were nearly invisible except for a slight smudge here and there. She gave a deep sigh then suddenly brightened. The rest of her treasures could be here as well! Eagerly, she glanced around, her eyes searching the tall grass next to the bank. Nothing.

An errant sunbeam on her face brought her back to the present. The sun was already starting to sink toward the horizon in the west. She'd have to hurry if she was going to have her bath and get back to the cabin while it was still light. There would be plenty of time to explore later.

Her sense of anticipation resurfaced as she headed toward the hot pool once more. With a quick look around to make sure Crazy Charlie wasn't lurking in the bushes, Kenzie shed her clothes on the bank and stepped out onto the shelf that separated the two pools. She waded a few feet then dropped down into the pool.

The water curled around her waist in eddies of warmth. A sigh of pure pleasure escaped her lips as she closed her eyes and sank into the pool up to her shoulders. She'd never again take indoor plumbing and the ability to take a hot bath for granted.

For a quarter of an hour, Kenzie luxuriated in the warm water, swimming, soaking, and floating on her back. She could easily have spent another thirty minutes doing the same thing, but the shadows began to lengthen, and she knew it was time to get out.

When she donned the dress, the hem of the long cotton skirt stopped about two inches short of her ankle and was miles too big around. Kenzie didn't care as the yards and yards of cloth absorbed the excess water off her body. She braided her hair into two long plaits.

Kenzie paused at the water's edge, trying to make up her mind whether she should take the time to wash her clothes or not. A glance at the sun, which was already sinking below the treetops, decided her. It would be dark in less than an hour. It was definitely time to head back to the cabin. Whiskey Jug was probably there and wondering where she was. He might even be worried about her.

"Charlie?" she called. "I'm ready to go." She listened for a moment, but the only sound she heard was the tittering of birds and the stirring of some small animal in the underbrush. "Crazy Charlie?" Still no answer.

For the next few minutes, she circled the pool, calling his name. Finally, she had to admit to herself that it was useless to continue. Crazy Charlie had probably forgotten all about her and wandered too far to hear her calling. For a moment, panic swirled up through her, but Kenzie fought it down. He had told her to blaze a trail for this very reason.

At first, she couldn't find the last blaze and panic began to claw at her again. She closed her eyes and forced herself to calm down. All she had to do was remember where they had come out of the woods. Slowly, the picture began to form in her mind. It was about ten yards west of the hole. Taking a deep breath, Kenzie retraced her steps past the cabin foundation to one corner of the pool. It took another five minutes to locate the blaze, but she eventually found it. Relieved, she began her trek back through the forest.

It wasn't an easy task in the rapidly waning light. She had to retrace her steps more than once when she hurried past one of her marks. Twilight was just giving way to dusk when she finally came to the creek. With a sigh of relief, she hiked her skirt above her knees, forded the creek, and hurried up the path to the cabin.

Fully expecting Adam to be there ahead of her, pacing back and forth and worrying, she was surprised to find the cabin empty and dark. Not only was he not there now, it looked as though he never had been.

The fire had died down, but the embers were still glowing. Gradually feeding smaller then larger sticks to the fire, Kenzie managed to get it going again. Full darkness had fallen by the time she had the fire burning. It gave the cabin a cozy glow but did little to calm Kenzie's uneasiness. A complete search of the cabin turned up a few mouse nests and Adam's bullet-making supplies but nary a candle or lamp.

Even worse, there was no food. The light lunch of jerky and water had been hours ago, and hunger gnawed at her stomach the way worry gnawed at her mind. He'd only planned to be gone a short time. Where was he? Had Bear Bait bucked him off and he was lying hurt somewhere? Was he unconscious...or worse?

Worried, scared, and filled with a loneliness the like of which she had never before experienced, Kenzie curled up on the bed to wait. She finally drifted off into a state halfway between sleeping and waking.

Suddenly, she jerked to full wakefulness. A noise outside the cabin brought her senses to full alert. There it was again, a strange snuffling noise. Kenzie jumped from the bed, rushed to the door, and slipped the bar into place. Then she tiptoed to the hearth, where she picked up the hooked bar she'd used to lift the boiling water off the fire.

Eyes wide with terror, she followed the creature's progress around the cabin. It scratched at the door, but the bar held. After a growl of frustration and a mighty thump that almost had Kenzie screaming in hysterics, the animal gave up and disappeared into the night.

Kenzie slumped in relief, but it was short lived. A wolf howled in the distance and was answered close at hand. Too close. Suddenly, all the night sounds beyond the door took on new significance. Even the innocent chirp of a cricket had her tightening her death grip on the iron and staring around the confines of the cabin in wide-eyed fear.

Sometime during the interminable night, Kenzie put the last of the wood on the fire. She knew there was a huge stack of it right outside, but there was no power on Earth strong enough to make her open that door. She watched the wood burn down to nothing and the embers slowly die away.

Alone in the dark, hungry, and more terrified than she'd ever been in her life, Kenzie told herself dawn couldn't be far away. Wrapped in the buffalo hide and clutching the iron bar in her hands, she settled down to wait.

Chapter 18

"I knew it was too much to ask to keep you out of that program another day," Annie said as Adam slipped the goggles off his head.

"Yeah, well, it is my job, you know." He stripped the gloves from his hands. "I could feel you tapping on my shoulder. Been waiting long?"

"About ten minutes or so."

He backed his chair out of the station. "I'm sorry about that. I was in the middle of something."

"You're always in the middle of something. What was it this time? Hunting deer, chasing that stupid horse of yours, or visiting with one of your characters?"

"I was finding a place to build a cave."

"A cave!" She moved her stool in front of his chair and reached out to take hold of his left arm. "I didn't know it was possible to build a cave," she said as she lifted his arm to start his therapy session.

"Anything's possible in *Fantasy Quest*."

"That sounds suspiciously like an ad campaign. Lift your arm a little higher, please."

"It's a slogan I came up with."

"Ok, now move it back." Annie nodded in satisfaction. "So, I take it everything is still progressing as planned?"

"Right on schedule."

"And your glitch?"

"I've got it isolated," Adam assured her as he lifted his arm above his head. "How much longer until I can drive again?"

Annie stared at his arm in surprise. "You've actually been doing your exercises!"

Only if you count the exercising I did in Beta Quest. "Of course. I always do just what you tell me to."

"Yeah, and I'm a geisha dancer."

"Really?" Adam said with a grin. "I never knew that. You're avoiding my question. When can I drive again?"

"You don't need to drive. I'll take you anywhere you want to go. Try lifting your arm to the side."

He lifted his arm and quirked an eyebrow at her. "Anywhere? What if I want to go to a strip joint?"

"Male or female strippers?"

"I sure as hell don't want to watch some slicked-up, muscle-bound Chippendale take his clothes off."

"I was afraid of that," Annie said with a sigh. "Guess I'll have to send Todd with you, then."

"Annie, you're trying to distract me."

"Is it working?"

He gave her a look.

"Oh, all right. The doctor said as soon as you're healed and have full range of motion in that arm, you can drive again," she told him.

"Why didn't you just say so?"

"Because your idea of what healed is differs greatly from the medical community's definition of it."

"Come on, Annie. You know I won't push it too fast."

"Sure. As I remember, that's how you got into this predicament in the first place. Dr. Dowie told you to take it easy with your shoulder last spring."

"I did."

"Right, for all of about a month. Then you took a handful of painkillers, entered a race with your new racing chair, and had one of the most spectacular crashes I've ever seen. It's too bad I didn't video it. I could have posted it on YouTube and made a small fortune when it went viral."

"I didn't crash because of my shoulder."

"Oh, no? Then how come Dr. Dowie said it looked like someone had taken an atomic-powered egg beater to it?"

"Because of the way I landed. It's beside the point anyway; I'm asking about driving my pickup, not wheelchair racing."

"You and that pickup! I swear, men and their toys!" Annie hid her smile. From the day Adam had discovered the company in North Carolina that did wheelchair conversions for extended cab pickups, he hadn't rested until he had one of his own parked in the basement garage of his apartment building.

"It's not a toy any more than your car is!"

"Uh-huh. That's why you and Todd flew to Raleigh, practically camped on their doorstep while they did the conversion, and then drove it all the way back to Denver."

"How else would I get it home?"

"Oh, I don't know. Have it shipped, like anyone else would have, maybe?"

"You're trying to distract me again," Adam said, "and it's not going to work. How close am I to the full range of motion?"

"Not far," she admitted, "but it's probably going to take even longer to heal this time than it did last time."

"It actually feels pretty good," Adam said, surprised to find it was true. "It was hurting like the devil yesterday, but hardly hurts at all now."

"Yeah, yeah, and you're a super quick healer. That's what you said last spring too."

"I know, but this time is different. Look how much higher I was able to lift my arm today. You're a physical therapist, wouldn't you say that means it's healing?"

"It should," she hedged, "but there's no way I can know for sure without an MRI. Has your nurse come in and changed the dressing today?"

"No."

"Maybe I should take a peek at it."

"You just want to get my shirt off."

"Rats, I've been found out." She started to unbutton his shirt with a brisk, professional air. "I have a weakness for rippling biceps and hard pectorals." She eased the fabric off his shoulder and dislodged the bandage with careful fingers.

"For heaven's sake," she exclaimed.

"What's wrong?" he asked.

"Nothing's wrong, really. It's just… Here, check it out."

Adam experienced a weird sense of déjà vu as he looked at his incision. He half expected to see it transformed into a purple scar as it had been in *Beta Quest*. It wasn't, of course, but the incision looked as if the skin had completely grown back together already. Though he was no expert in such matters, it appeared to Adam as if the stitches were ready to come out. "See, I told you I'm a fast healer," he said

"Mmm, maybe." She looked at the incision doubtfully. "You know, I think we ought to call Dr. Dowie about this."

"What for?"

Annie already had her cell phone out and was dialing the number. "He wanted to know if anything unusual happened with your incision. I'd say this qualifies. Hello, Martha? This is Annie Bedford. I need to talk to Dr. Dowie if he has a minute. Right, tell him it's about Adam Johnson. Sure, I'll hold."

Adam pulled his shirt back over his shoulder. "What are you going to tell him? That my incision is healing too fast? He'll think you've totally lost it."

"It won't be the first time someone has thought that."

"You're a worrywart."

"Somebody has to be. You certainly don't take an interest in your health, except where it slows you down."

"Fine. I think I'll work on my programming while you wait," he said. "Let me know what he says. We'll have a good laugh." He wheeled his chair back into his station and pulled up his programming.

By the time Dr. Dowie came to the phone, Adam was so deep into his work that he was barely aware of the conversation that went on behind him until a chance-heard phrase caught his attention.

"That's kind of what I was thinking too. We can be there in" — Annie glanced at her watch — "oh, say, twenty minutes or so. Right, we'll meet you at the hospital. Thanks a bunch. Yeah, me too. Bye, now." She hung up the phone and gave Adam her don't-even-think-about-crossing-me look. "Dr. Dowie wants to take a look at it. He'll meet us at the hospital after he's done making his rounds."

"Oh, come on, Annie! I don't have time for this," Adam protested.

"Tough. I'm not giving you a choice. Dr. Dowie thinks there could be something odd going on here."

"What, because it's healing too fast? Yeah, I suppose that would get a doctor all worked up. Can't collect as much money from a patient that way."

"Ed isn't like that, and you know it. Grab your jacket, and let's go."

Adam grumbled all the way to the hospital, but it did him no good. Neither Annie nor the doctor paid him the slightest heed. A thorough examination left Dr. Dowie even more puzzled. Though he was inclined to think everything was all right, he scheduled an MRI for the morning and sent them home.

Though Adam was in a hurry to get back to his computer, Annie insisted on feeding him dinner first. She admitted she'd planned on kidnapping him all along and had put a casserole in the oven before she left home. Nearly four hours had passed by the time he'd checked out Todd's and Sam's progress on their car project, helped Zoey install some new animation software she'd bought, and eaten dinner.

When he finally got home, he had to put up with Annie's tender ministrations, making sure he was safe and secure for the night. Adam was nearly grinding his teeth in frustration by that time, but he knew better than to tell her he fully intended to work as soon as she left. She'd simply refuse to leave. *Damn stubborn woman anyway.* He wouldn't put it past her to call Todd to let him know what was going on and then to settle in for the night.

With a yawn and a stretch, he announced he was going to bed. Annie smiled sweetly, told him to have a good rest, and then proceeded to make him a little something he could pop into the microwave for lunch tomorrow.

After he was in bed, she decided to tidy up a bit. Adam fell asleep waiting for her to leave. When he woke up several hours later, he had the sneaking suspicion that it had all worked out the way she'd planned.

Getting out of bed, he grudgingly admitted to himself that he'd been more tired than he'd realized, or he wouldn't have fallen asleep. As it was, the few hours of sleep had probably helped his mental processes.

It didn't take long to reboot his computer, and within minutes he was deep into his problem. As he sifted through the programming, he discovered several small discrepancies that hadn't been there before. Cheat codes! His guess had been right after all, but how had they gotten there, and what did they mean for *Fantasy Quest*?

About two o'clock in the morning, he figured it out. The cheat codes came from inside the program. But how? He ran through everything in his mind. What had he done differently than the thousand other times he had traveled from the village to his cabin?

Then it hit him. Kenzie had wished they were back at the cabin and suddenly they were. Could it really be that simple?

Within minutes, he had connected himself to the other computer, booted up *Fantasy Quest*, and recreated the mountain-man world within the other program. Then he placed himself halfway between the Indian village and the cabin.

"I wish I were home," he said. Nothing happened. *Hmm maybe it needs to be more specific.* "I wish I were at the cabin." Nothing. He rubbed his chin thoughtfully. *What exactly did she say anyway?* "I wish the cabin was closer."

In the blink of an eye he could see it through the trees. *Damn!*

Adam could feel the adrenaline pumping through his system the way it always did when his programs did something new and exciting. He'd often thought this was how parents must feel when their children reached some new milestone in their development.

He rubbed his hands together in anticipation. *This could turn out to be great fun.*

"I wish Bear Bait was here." At first, he thought it hadn't worked, but then he caught a glimpse of black through the trees next to the cabin. The horse was in the corral, munching on a pile of hay.

Filled with anticipation, Adam strode through the trees and looked around the clearing near the cabin. What should he do? The possibilities were endless.

What can I wish for that will test the limits? "I wish I had something to eat."

Nothing happened for several seconds, then a rabbit hopped out of a nearby thicket and stared at the man for a long moment, twitching its nose, before disappearing back into the brush. *Of course! The Reality Guard.* Food will only appear on the hoof, so to speak.

So that's why the game increased. I've been subconsciously putting it there. As he glanced around the clearing, his gaze lit on Bear Bait. Maybe this was the way to fix the dunderhead's skittishness. Pursing his lips thoughtfully, he considered the proper way to word his request.

"I wish Bear Bait were calmer." Adam stood there for a long moment, waiting. Bear Bait never even lifted his head. He just continued eating as though nothing had happened.

"Well, of course not, you idiot," Adam muttered to himself. There was really no way to tell if it had worked or not. You never knew how Bear Bait would react. Sometimes he was as gentle as a kitten. Others he blew sky high with little or no provocation.

Adam crossed his arms and turned back to the cabin. He needed something more tangible, something that would test the limits. Glass windows? No, too simple. How about something way out of line, something that would push the Reality Guard?

"I wish the cabin had running water."

There was a loud thump directly behind him. Adam glanced over his shoulder and blinked in surprise. Bear Bait lay on his side, eyes closed, legs stretched out straight.

"Bear Bait?" Concerned, Adam vaulted the fence and knelt next to the prostrate horse. Bear Bait's pulse was strong and his breathing regular. Adam sat back on his heels. The dad-blamed idiot was asleep! Adam's mouth twisted wryly. He had asked that Bear Bait be calmer, and he was that. Evidently, the wishes need to be more specific.

Adam rose to his feet and stopped in stunned surprise. The creek that had formerly lay downhill from the cabin had changed course and was now running right through the front door. As he watched, the stream burbled out from under the wall at the far side of the cabin and continued on its way down the hill. The Reality Guard had done its job and kept the setting in *Fantasy Quest* honest. Though it was not at all what he'd had in mind, there was no arguing the fact that his cabin now had running water.

Chapter 19

"You sure you don't want me to come in with you?" Annie asked, leaning forward in the driver's seat and peering out through the open passenger door of her car. "I could open doors for you."

Adam slid into his chair and adjusted the footrests. "Nope. Taking me to the doctor yesterday and to the hospital this morning to get my MRI was enough. I'm just going in and going to bed anyway. Besides, the doctor gave me a clean bill of health."

"Not entirely. If you'll remember, he said you shouldn't push it yet."

"Riding up the elevator and unlocking my door isn't exactly pushing it." He shot her a mischievous look. "You know, you're going to lose all your power over me next week when Dr. Dowie clears me to drive again."

She gave a gusty sigh. "I know, and I just don't know what I'll do. You've been such a good patient and so easy to deal with. Can't imagine what I'll find to do to fill all my time."

"Todd will be finished with his big contract soon. You can spend your energy bugging him until he takes on another."

Annie returned his grin. "There is that." Her smile faded, and her demeanor became serious. "We never did thank you properly for giving Todd the Microcom contract. I'm not sure our company could have made it through our first year without it."

Adam shrugged. "We needed to beef up security, and Todd's the best in the business. Besides, it doesn't matter how good the system, the security is only as good as the person securing it. Todd's the one man I knew I could trust with *Fantasy Quest*. Now, stop trying to distract me and go bother your husband." He swung the car door shut, wheeled himself up the ramp onto the curb, and waved goodbye.

Annie rolled down the car window. "You're not getting off that easy. I'll wait until you get inside."

"Oh for… What do you think is going to happen to me between here and George?" he asked, jerking his thumb back over his shoulder toward the beefy doorman.

"Abduction by space aliens, attack by killer termites… You name it," she said. "Don't you ever watch television?"

Adam gave a laughing snort. "All right, you win. Watch my back. Shoot any aliens or insects you see. We'll worry about whether they're friendlies or not later."

"No such thing as friendly termites!" she called out the window.

It was obvious by the way George's lips twitched that he'd heard the whole thing. "Good morning, Mr. Johnson," he said, opening the door with a flourish.

"Thanks, George." Adam turned his chair, gave Annie the all-clear sign, and then watched as she drove off. "I have to humor her," he said. "Stark raving mad, you know."

George chuckled. "So you've said, sir. Would you like me to ring the elevator for you?"

"I suppose so." Adam glanced up at the other man as he punched in the code on the console Adam had installed for the apartment complex. "How long have you worked here, George?"

"About a year and a half."

"So, when do you think you'll start calling me Adam instead of Mr. Johnson?"

"When I no longer want to work here, sir."

Adam sighed. "Still living by the rules, I see."

George gave him a lopsided grin. "Yes, sir. At least until I graduate from college and can get a better job. I have a wife and baby to support. Your elevator's here."

Adam resisted the urge to sigh again as he entered the elevator and punched the button for the fourth floor. George was a nice guy, only a year or two younger than Adam. But there was to be no familiarity between the help and the inhabitants of the apartment complex.

It wasn't that he wanted the man for a friend, really. Sometimes he just wanted a friendly, "Hi, Adam. How was your day?" when he came home.

He rolled out of the elevator and down the hall to number 410. Of course, that was exactly why he'd left his mother's house. She was never happier than when she could hover over him twenty-four-seven. Even after he moved out, it had taken him almost five years to convince her he was perfectly able to take care of himself.

Which was pretty much what she told him about the deposits he put in her bank account. She even fussed a little about wasting his hard-earned money every time he sent her on a cruise or booked a tour to some foreign country. If they lived under the same roof, she'd no doubt give up her traveling and her endless round of card parties and luncheons with her friends, thinking her baby needed her.

Adam shuddered as he unlocked the door and let himself in. *No thanks.* As much as he loved his mother, there was no way he'd live with her. They both enjoyed their independence too much, and the last thing either of them wanted was to wind up resenting each other.

Adam tossed his keys on the table next to the door. Damn, he was morose today. Probably because of all the time he'd wasted at the doctor's office yesterday and the hospital this morning to find out his shoulder was healing just fine. Of course, it could have something to do with the sleepless night he'd spent. Annie hadn't been best pleased to find him at his console when she'd arrived this morning. She'd have really blown a gasket if she'd known he'd been there all night.

At least he'd fixed the cheat code problem in *Fantasy Quest.* It was still possible to use them, but only from the control menu on the outside. Voice commands could no longer alter the program by themselves. The cheat codes explained a lot that he hadn't been able to figure out. They were the reason he was able to create and change characters from inside *Beta Quest*. It was also why his virtual body had reacted to Kenzie and Jesse Three Dogs when he hadn't been on his computer. They had expected his body to react to them, and it had. It still didn't explain why the program continued to run in his absence though.

Adam yawned and stretched. He'd fix the cheat codes in *Beta Quest* later. Right now, he was badly in need of a good long nap. He eyed the recliner, contemplating whether he should make the effort to go to bed or just crash there. No, he'd wake up three hours from now gritty-eyed and stiff. On the other hand, he lacked the energy to undress and go to bed. Maybe he should have let Annie tuck him in. He finally compromised by lying down on the bed, fully dressed, and pulling a quilt up over him.

He relaxed into the comfort of his mattress. *Ah, sheer heaven!* An odd little thought niggled at the edge of his consciousness. It was as though he had forgotten something, something very important. Adam tried to capture the image, but he was too tired to grasp it. He settled deeper into his pillow. Maybe it would come to him when he was more rested.

Adam floated in a cloud of semi-consciousness, the irritating idea knocking at the edges of his comfort but not quite able to penetrate the relaxed fuzziness of his mind. He was on the verge of slipping away completely when it suddenly burst into full bloom, and he jerked awake with a curse.

Oh hell! Kenzie.

Kenzie couldn't remember a longer night. Though the mysterious midnight marauder hadn't returned, neither had Adam or her ability to sleep. It wasn't until the sun finally crept up over the horizon and a thin crack of light appeared between the shutters that she was finally able to relax into slumber.

She had no idea how long she slept before the persistent buzz of a fly brought her into full wakefulness. Kenzie threw off the buffalo robe, rose from the bed, and cautiously opened the door.

Butterflies flitted through the tall grasses near the corral, and the birds sang cheerfully in the pine trees. A black beetle of some kind scuttled across the path, but nothing else stirred. The sun was still climbing toward its zenith, indicating it was late morning. Panic skittered through her again. Where was Adam? Something must have happened to keep him away so long. A quick survey outside the cabin gave no clue as to the identity of her nighttime visitor. Everything was undisturbed.

Between her worry and the hunger that was gnawing at her, Kenzie barely registered that her fox hide hadn't become a midnight snack as she had feared. It was hard not to panic as she attempted to figure out what to do. *First things first.* Food was the most important order of business.

"Sure wish there were some wild strawberries around here," she muttered. "I'd even go for chokecherries at this point." She glanced around, wondering if she dared wander far from the cabin, foraging for food. An angry growl from her stomach convinced her.

Look back over your shoulder as you walk. That way you'll recognize it when you come back. Her grandfather's words of advice came back to Kenzie as she walked away from the cabin. It had saved her hours of searching for her car in parking lots. She glanced back, taking bearings on the clearing as she stepped into the woods.

The trees had barely closed in behind her when Kenzie spied another clearing up ahead. Were those chokecherry bushes? Moments later, she stepped out into the sunshine, a huge smile lighting her face. The clearing was lined with chokecherry bushes heavy with fruit, and underfoot was a veritable strawberry patch.

It didn't take long to realize that strawberry season was over, and the fruit long gone, no doubt gobbled up by the animals who lived there. Kenzie sighed regretfully then moved past to the chokecherries. "If this is all there is to eat, I wish they were a little sweeter," she said. "Like blueberries, or blackberries." But, beggars couldn't be choosers, and anything was better than hunger. She stripped off the first handful and popped them into her mouth.

As she peeled the flesh from the chokecherry seeds with her tongue and teeth, Kenzie's eyes widened in shocked surprise. The bitter flavor she expected didn't materialize. Instead, her mouth filled with the sweetest juice she'd ever tasted. She spit out the seeds and took another handful. The same delightful flavor caressed her taste buds, and she closed her eyes in ecstasy. She'd always heard the sharp edge of hunger would improve the taste of anything, but this was amazing. Maybe they weren't chokecherries after all.

She opened her eyes and studied the bushes, fully expecting to see that she had mistakenly identified an exotic species of berry bush. No, these were definitely chokecherries. They had the telltale dark-green leaves and a dozen blackish-purple berries growing from each long stem. Maybe it was the soil here that gave them such a wonderful flavor. Who knew? Who cared, for that matter? She was just going to enjoy.

Kenzie took the edge off her hunger then went back to the cabin to find something to put the berries into. A coffee pot, a single pan, a cast-iron Dutch oven, and a tin dishpan were all she found. At least dishes would be easy to do around here. The Dutch oven was the logical choice to use as a berry picking bucket. It was the only one that had a bail to carry it.

As Kenzie grabbed it, the pan tipped, causing the lid to fall off, and a roll of buckskin fell out onto the floor. Curiously, she picked up the roll and shook it out. Her mouth formed a perfect *O* of surprise as she gazed at the buckskin dress she held in her hands. Red Blanket's dress was beautiful, but this was gorgeous! From the soft, nearly white leather to the exquisite beading, it was a work of art. Why had it been stored inside the Dutch oven? Mice, maybe? She'd have to ask Adam when he returned. If he returned.

Now, why had she brought that up again? Swallowing the lump in her throat and fighting the worry that curled around the edges of her mind, Kenzie carefully laid the dress on the bed and picked up the Dutch oven. She was halfway back to the thicket when she heard a slight rustling in the bushes. A terrifying image of the bear rose in her mind as she frantically cast around for a better weapon than the iron pan in her hand. She grabbed a large rock then dropped the Dutch oven and whirled to face her attacker.

The noise intensified. Whatever lurked there was getting closer. Kenzie took a firmer grip on the rock. Then she could see it: a large, dark form back in the bushes. She screamed and threw the rock. It probably missed by a mile, but she wasn't going to stick around to see. She took off running as fast as she could in the opposite direction.

"Kenzie!"

The familiar voice halted her flight. "Adam?" She whipped around to find him standing on the trail. The next second, she was running across the clearing toward him as quickly as she'd run away. "Oh, Adam, you're back!" she cried as she grabbed him around the waist and hugged him with all her might. "Where were you?"

"Something came up," he said, closing his arms around her.

"I thought Bear Bait had bucked you off, or you'd been attacked by a bear or bitten by a rattlesnake."

"You're partially right. Bear Bait didn't exactly dump me, but he did take off for the tall timber. I'm sorry you were alone all night."

Kenzie shuddered. "It was awful. Some animal came sniffing around the cabin in the middle of the night. I don't know what it was or where it went, so I was afraid to open the door and get more wood."

"Then, the fire went out?"

"Yes, and I spent the rest of the night starving to death in the dark."

Adam groaned. "Oh man, I forgot to bring you any food." He dropped his arms and began to pull away. "I'll go—"

"No!" she tightened her grip on him. "No, I'm fine now. I found these berries. They're really good." She pulled him over to the nearest bush. "Here, try some."

Before he could respond, she stripped several berries from a branch and popped them into his mouth. Adam had little choice but to taste the fruit, which he did with a resigned air until the flavor hit his taste buds.

"Dang," he said as he spit the seeds out and reached for another handful. "I see what you mean. I've never tasted chokecherries like this." He rolled a few around in his mouth experimentally. "They sort of taste like a cross between a blackberry and a blueberry, only sweeter."

"I know. Great, aren't they? I was going to gather a bunch and make jelly." She cocked her head to one side. "That is, if you can get me some sugar and some jars."

"Don't know about jars, but I suppose I could get you some bottles from the saloon. Sugar is pretty expensive, and I don't have anything to trade for it."

Kenzie sighed in disappointment. "Oh, yeah, I kind of forgot we're in 1868. Rats. There ought to be something we can do with these berries."

"Pemmican."

"What?"

"Pemmican. It's a combination of dried meat, dried fruit, and bear fat."

Kenzie made a face. "Yum! Just exactly what I've always dreamed of eating."

"It's not as bad as it sounds," Adam said with a chuckle. "The children at the Indian village think of it as candy."

"They eat rattlesnake, too."

"Which you enjoyed, if you remember." Adam grinned down at her. "You know, you already have a good supply of bear fat, and we'll have jerky as soon as I get a chance to go hunting."

"Yippee," she said sarcastically.

"I'll show you how to dry the berries so we'll have them

when the time comes."

Kenzie sighed. "I suppose it's all part of getting ready for winter. It just hit me today that fall is almost upon us." She looked up at him. "That's why we had to come back to the cabin, isn't it? Because winter's coming."

He gave her a startled look. "Winter… Right, that's exactly why we came back. We have to get ready for winter."

Kenzie was puzzled by his reaction. It was almost as though he'd forgotten winter was coming. "What's wrong?"

"Oh, uh…nothing." He gave a huge yawn and stretched. "I'm just tired. Didn't get any sleep last night. I'll go get something for supper."

"No!" She saw his eyebrows go up at the nearly frantic tone in her voice, but darn it, she couldn't help it. The thought of being left alone again was more than she could face right now. "Why don't you get some sleep? Then we can go hunting together."

"You want to hunt?" he asked in surprise.

"I love to hunt," she lied. "It's one of my favorite things to do."

Adam's eyes narrowed. "Since when?"

"Since forever. Didn't I tell you?"

"No, you didn't. Come on, Kenzie, what's really going on?"

"Really?"

"Yes, really. Tell me the truth."

Kenzie sighed. "The truth is I don't want to be by myself yet. Last night was the most scared I've ever been in my life, and I don't want to go through it again."

"You know I can't stay here all the time. I'll have to leave to hunt. Bear Bait can't carry both of us and a deer or an elk."

"I know, and I won't be this way forever. I just need you here today."

Adam looked pensive. "All right," he said finally. "I guess I can sleep in the cabin."

"Of course you can. Why would you sleep anywhere else?"

"I meant I can sleep now and find us some food later."

"All right. I'm going to stay and pick berries."

Adam disappeared back through the bushes, toward the cabin. Five minutes later, Kenzie heard a rifle shot. Frightened, she dropped the Dutch oven and hurried toward the sound.

"Problem solved," Adam called as soon as she appeared. He held up the carcass of a dead rabbit for her to see. "Supper came to me."

"Oh. Well, have a good sleep, then. I'll see you when you wake up." *Talk about overreacting!* Kenzie thought as she retraced her steps and scooped the spilled berries back into the Dutch oven. Last night must have done more of a job on her than she'd realized. Brad would be laughing himself sick about now. He always did when she made a fool of herself. It wasn't the first time since she'd arrived in this nightmare that she was glad her fiancé had been left behind.

Chapter 20

"Adam, are you awake?" Kenzie whispered to the man sprawled across the bunk in the cabin. No response. She cleared her throat and tried again louder. "Adam, are you awake?" Nothing. "Adam," she said loudly. "Whiskey Jug!"

Kenzie sighed in defeat. Honestly, the man slept like a stone. He might as well be in a coma. *Maybe if I kissed him again,* she thought. *It worked once.* No, he might get the wrong idea. She could just see it. 'Oh hi, Adam. Yes, yes. I was kissing you, but I was just trying to wake you up. I didn't mean anything by it.' Kenzie sighed. It looked like she was stuck here with nothing to do until he woke up. As tired as he said he was, that might not be for hours yet.

Kenzie's problem was boredom, plain and simple. It had always been her besetting sin. She had absolutely no tolerance for it. In her own time, she always carried a book or a sketchpad with her everywhere she went. That way, she always had something to do. Doctors and dentists usually thought it amusing when they came into the examination room and found her reading or drawing, but at least she didn't get bored waiting for them.

Too bad she hadn't brought something to read with her this time. *My journal...* The image of the nearly blank pages flashed through her mind. If she could find something to draw with, it would make a decent sketchpad. She glanced around the cabin, though she knew it was highly unlikely she'd find a pen and ink. Her gaze snagged on the fireplace, and she began to smile. *Charcoal!* Not only was it one of her favorite drawing mediums, she'd learned how to make it for an art history project.

Now, what did I do with my journal yesterday? Kenzie mentally retraced her steps. The last she remembered seeing the book was when she laid it down on a rock near the hot pool.

Her thoughts turned longingly to the hot pool and Rainbow Falls. Well, why not? She could get her journal, take another bath, and wash her clothes. Thanks to Crazy Charlie and his trail blazing, she knew how to find her way. There was plenty of time before the sun went down.

"Adam!" she yelled. Still no reaction. Oh well. He'd probably sleep until she got back anyway. Within a few minutes, she had gathered her things and crept quietly from the cabin. She used a long, pointed stick to scratch a note in the dirt, on the off chance that he could read, and drew a picture of Rainbow Falls in case he couldn't. Then she picked up her supplies and set off for the falls.

Her trail blazes seemed easier to follow this time, probably because she knew where she was going. In less than half an hour she had arrived. Her journal was right where she remembered leaving it, and she spent several minutes thumbing through it. The pages were water stained, but surprisingly few were unusable.

I wish I could find the rest of my stuff so I could take it home and show Brad what I think of his demands! she thought with a surge of defiance. In retrospect, she wondered why she'd given in to his ridiculous argument. His unreasonable behavior had nearly killed her and landed her in this mess. *Ok,* she admitted to herself, *it was my reaction to his unreasonable demands. Still, it's his fault I'm here.* Her resentment toward him bubbled, and she pushed it away with irritation. Better to concentrate on her laundry.

Kenzie stripped, put on the cotton dress, and proceeded to wash her T-shirt and underwear. The buckskin pants could use a good cleaning too, but she had no idea how to accomplish that.

Before long, the pool at the base of Rainbow Falls became irresistible. It looked even more inviting than it had the day before. She glanced around as she spread her clothes on the bushes to dry. *Why not?* Adam said no one from the village ever came close to the place, and Crazy Charlie was long gone.

Kenzie eagerly shed her dress then waded out into the cold water. Thanks to the hot pool spilling over into this one, it wasn't anywhere near as cold as the creek, but still made for a nice invigorating swim. With Adam back at the cabin, sleeping like the dead, she felt like she had all the time in the world. He'd still be there when she got back.

She swam around the pool until her arms and legs were tired. Then she moved to the hot pool where she took a long, leisurely soak. This was the life. Too bad Adam's cabin wasn't here. It would be like having a spa in your backyard.

Eventually, she began to feel the effects of staying too long in the heated water and clambered back over the ledge into the cold water. Once the initial shock wore off, swimming was pure ecstasy. The water caressed her limbs like liquid velvet. After a couple of laps, she dragged herself to shore and donned the cotton dress. Then she lay back in the grass, with a happy sigh.

Kenzie's mind floated along as she watched puffy clouds drift lazily across the sky. She could almost believe she was lying out in her grandmother's pasture, daydreaming the way she had as a kid.

Adam found her, sound asleep in the grass like some sort of wood sprite. Even wearing an ugly old cotton dress three sizes too big for her, there was something irresistible about the way she slept with one arm crooked above her head and her lips slightly parted.

Adam dropped down beside her and picked a long piece of grass. Her lip twitched up as he dragged the tufted end under her nose. By the third pass, she was scrunching up her face. With a low laugh he changed tactics and flicked it across her eyelids and down the side of her face. She swiped at it with her hand. Adam's grin deepened as he dragged it across her lips.

The tip of her tongue appeared and traced the path the grass had taken. Adam watched its journey, mesmerized. The need to touch those lips with his own became an irresistible force that pulled his head down. The first contact was unbelievably sweet, like the first peach in summer or homemade strawberry ice cream.

Kenzie's mouth opened softly, and her tongue touched his. With a groan deep in his throat, Adam settled her against him and deepened the kiss. She smelled of sunshine and tasted like heaven. His hand traced the curve of her waist and the swell of her hip. Desire rose within him, hot and heavy, but there was something else too. Something he couldn't name but was so intense it seared his senses. This joyous feeling of completeness was what he'd been searching for, what had been missing with Dawn.

Dawn! The thought worked like a bucket of ice water, and Adam jerked away. For a moment he held his breath, terrified that he'd tripped the Sex Hex. If the program shut down now, he'd lose her forever.

"Mmm. Morning, Brad," Kenzie murmured, cuddling closer. "I must have fallen asleep." She opened her eyes and stared up at him in shock. "Oh! Adam, I didn't realize…uh, I didn't mean…" She trailed off in confusion.

Adam flopped over on his back, his arm thrown over his eyes. The Sex-Hex was working just fine, thank you. Nothing shut you down quite so fast as another man's name on the lips of the woman you were kissing.

Kenzie sat up and looked down at him. "What was that all about?"

He moved his arm. "What do you mean?"

"I want to know why you were kissing me, because if you're trying to start something—"

"No, no," he hastily assured her. "Nothing like that. I was just paying you back."

"Paying me back! For what?"

"I seem to remember waking up with you kissing me not too long ago."

Color crept up her neck. "That was kind of an experiment."

"So was this."

"Oh." She put her arms around her legs and stared at the waterfall. "What did you find out?"

He grinned. "That you are a very sound sleeper."

She turned her head to look at him. "What?"

"I spent a good half hour tickling you with a piece of grass, and you slept right through it."

"Liar."

"All right, so maybe it was only ten minutes. The point is I didn't get a whole lot of response."

"Look who's talking, Mr. I-could-sleep-through-an-earthquake."

"You tried to wake me?"

"Only about six times."

This could prove to be interesting. Adam was most curious to hear what his body's reaction had been. He'd left it on the bed in the cabin when he'd gone back to his apartment to sleep. "What exactly did I do?"

"Do? Nothing. I practically yelled in your ear, and you never even wiggled an eyelash. I only knew you were still alive because you were breathing."

Huh, so it looked like I was just asleep. Interesting. "That's why you left the note?"

"Sure. I didn't want you to worry when you finally woke up." She glanced at him again. "So, you can read. I wondered."

"Yes, I can read." He grinned. "But I could have figured out your cute little drawings if I hadn't."

"I'll have you know I have a college degree in cute little drawings."

"Is that so?"

"I'm a graphic artist, and I just landed a job with... Never mind about that. Where did you learn to read?"

"My father taught me."

"Oh yes, the history teacher. I forgot." Her eyes lit up. "Hey, where are his books?"

"His books?"

"Yeah. I was just wishing I had something to read. They're

210

not in the cabin or I'd have found them."

"No." There weren't any books in the cabin, because Adam hadn't thought of it. Trelane Johnson hadn't believed in taking the modern world with him when he went to rendezvous or even camping. His delight in roughing it was one of the reasons Adam's mother rarely accompanied them. Though Adam loved to read, books were the last thing he took to the wilderness.

"So, where are they?"

Adam thought quickly. "I burned 'em."

"What!" It was clear she thought burning books was sacrilege.

"Yep." He put his hands behind his head and gazed up at the sky. "Had a bad winter a couple of years ago."

"And you burned your father's books?" Kenzie was clearly aghast.

"There was a blizzard that lasted nearly two weeks," he said, getting into his story. "I had to string ropes out to the corral so I could feed my horse." He sighed. "Didn't have the shed then, and the poor blighter froze to death."

"Oh, Adam!"

"In the long run, it was probably a good thing, or I'd have starved."

"You ate him!"

"It was that or my boots. Anyway, I ran out of firewood ten days into it. I burned the corral poles and all the furniture. Finally, there wasn't anything left but my father's books." He heaved another deep sigh. "I purely hated doing it; Pa set great store by his books. I burned them one at a time to make them last as long as possible. The last one to go was the family Bible."

"Oh, Adam, that's the most terrible story I've ever heard!"

Adam bit back a grin. He thought it was pretty good. "I take it you've already had your bath."

"Yes, and I've done my laundry, too. I didn't have time for that yesterday."

"Yesterday! You were here yesterday?"

"Sure was."

"No wonder you were scared. It must have been pitch dark when you got back."

"Not quite, but if I'd waited much longer to head back, I'd have been in trouble."

Adam frowned. It was a good hour's ride to the falls from his cabin. If she had left right after he had, she'd have barely gotten there before dark. "How did you find your way?"

"Crazy Charlie showed me."

"Crazy Charlie! Where did you run into him?"

"At the cabin." Kenzie cocked her head. "I thought you sent him to get me."

"I haven't seen Crazy Charlie for a couple of months."

"Then how did he know I wanted to go to the falls?"

"I have no idea. How do you think he knew?"

Kenzie looked thoughtful for a moment. "You know, you hadn't been gone very long when he showed up. Do you suppose he heard us talking?"

"Could be." *More likely a cheat code working. She probably wished someone would show up and take her to Rainbow Falls.* With the thought, something clicked in Adam's mind. Was that why all the other deleted characters had showed up? Had Kenzie wish them into being? It made sense.

Then it hit him: Maybe that's where Kenzie herself had come from. She was a character he himself had produced from wishful thinking: his ideal woman! Not a fantasy like Dawn, but a real flesh-and-blood female who challenged his mind and kept him on his toes.

"Adam, are you listening to me?"

Adam blinked. "What?"

"I said are you planning to take a bath?"

"I guess so. Why?"

"I thought I'd look around and see if any more of my stuff came through before I head back."

Adam sat up and looked at her in surprise. "What do you mean, more of your stuff?"

"I found my journal yesterday." She held it up for him to see then walked over to Bear Bait and tucked it into the saddlebag.

"Your journal? What was your journal doing here?"

"It was one of the things I threw in the river."

Adam raised his eyebrows. "Brad made you throw away your journal?"

"It wasn't the journal," she said a bit defensively. "It was the memories that were in it."

His eyebrows went up another notch. "I think old Bradley has an ego problem."

Kenzie flushed angrily. "He does not! He's just a little—"

"Possessive?"

"So what if he is? He's handsome, smart—"

"Rich?"

"Not yet, but he will be. He's in a very competitive field, but he's one of the best. Brad will climb to the top in no time."

"On the backs of the less ruthless, no doubt," Adam muttered.

She glared at him. "The point is, he could have had any girl out there, and he chose me."

"A very great honor, obviously."

"Oh, what do you know? You aren't even from my century. Men live by a different code in my time. Things have changed."

"Not for the better, it would appear." Adam took one look at her flushed, angry face and held up his hand. "Look, let's just call a truce. You're right; I don't know Brad. You go ahead and look for your things, and I'll take a bath. We'll still have plenty of time to make it back before dark."

"I'll find my own way back."

Adam might not have a lot of experience with women, but thanks to Annie, he knew when to back off. "All right. I guess I'll see you at the cabin, then." Surely she'd have cooled off enough to accept a ride by the time he caught up with her. One thing was for sure: He hadn't created the Kenzie glitch all by himself. The Reality Guard had given her a full load of emotional baggage. On the other hand, it could have been the Sex Hex. A man would have to have a lot of courage to take that on.

Kenzie tossed her head and walked away without bothering to answer. *Jerk!* What right did he have to act like there was something wrong with Brad's love for her? She stalked through the long grass, too angry to even look for her treasures. Too bad he hadn't frozen to death with his blasted horse! Her foot hit something, and she glanced down. The cloisonné box! With a cry of delight, she scooped it up and opened the lid. Surprisingly, the contents had remained completely dry. *Must be airtight,* she thought as she pulled out a fortune stick. "True love is closer than you think." Kenzie snorted. *Sure it is!*

But the fortune made her smile, and she started paying more attention to the ground at her feet. A glint of silver down in the water caught her eye. Her thumb ring! She swooped down and fished it out of the water.

The image of a boy flashed into her mind as she slipped it on her thumb. Dave. An unrequited college love. There had been a playful tussle in the student union during which she'd taken possession of the ring. The memory lay warm and sweet in her heart. It didn't come any more innocent than that. Why *had* Brad been so insistent she get rid of the ring? She hadn't even dated Dave.

Ok, so maybe Adam did have a point—a small one. Kenzie glanced out into the pool, where he was swimming back and forth with the long, forceful strokes of a competition swimmer, and was instantly captivated. An odd little thrill ran through her as she watched. Though there was hardly any splashing, the water churned as his body moved through it. There was something erotic about the sheer, raw power of it.

As she watched, Kenzie noticed something odd—Adam wasn't using his legs. Was he doing it to build up his arms and chest? Heaven knew he was muscular enough. She watched, mesmerized, for several long moments, until he dove under the water and came up about five feet from her. Smirking, he shook his head like a wet dog. Water sluiced from his long, black hair in a spray that would have done a sprinkler proud.

"Ack!" she yelled as she jumped back. "You're getting me all wet."

"Care to join me?"

"Not on your life. You'd probably drown me. Besides, I'm still hunting."

"Find anything?" he asked curiously.

"Just my Chinese fortune sticks and my ring so far, but I haven't even gone halfway around the pool yet."

"Good luck. I'm headed for the hot pool."

He dove back under the water and swam clear to the other side before he surfaced. Kenzie looked away to give him his privacy but couldn't resist a peek as he clambered over the barrier between the two pools. Her eyes widened in wonder. The wide shoulders and well-muscled back were no surprise — she had admired them from the beginning — but it was the first time she'd seen the whole package. The long, muscular legs and taut backside made it a sight to behold. Damn, he was one fine-looking man from the back!

Kenzie tore her gaze away. Since when had she become a voyeur? Ignoring the niggling little voice inside that pointed out she'd never been inclined to sneak peeks at Brad's butt, she turned her attention back to her search. But she couldn't concentrate. Her mind kept turning to all that gorgeous maleness lolling about in the hot pool and the knowledge that he wouldn't turn her away if she chose to join him. It was definitely time to go back to the cabin. Resisting one last look toward the pool beyond the waterfall, she turned and headed into the woods.

There was no difficulty following her blazes this time; a faint trail was beginning to form in the carpet of plants where she walked. She only had to depend on her blazes where no plants grew, where trees were too thick to let sunlight filter through and footprints disappeared into a soft mat of dead pine needles on the forest floor. Kenzie was pleased. The idea that she had blazed a trail was kind of cool.

In no time at all, Kenzie was back at the cabin. She set the cloisonné box on the mantle and changed back into her clean clothing. As she went to hang up the cotton dress, she caught a less-than-pleasant odor. She held the fabric to her nose then made a face. Despite its recent use, a slightly musty scent seemed to cling to the fabric. She'd have to wash it on her next trip to Rainbow Falls. In the meantime, maybe hanging it out in the open air would help.

It only took a minute to hang the dress outside over a tree branch. Maybe she'd ask Adam if he could string some rope for a proper clothesline. On the other hand, there really wasn't much in the way of washable clothing here. Adam wore buckskin, and except for her T-shirt and her underwear, so did she.

Thinking about the buckskin made her think of the dress she'd found in the Dutch oven. There it was, lying on the end of the bed, right where she'd left it. She held it up to her. It looked like it was about her size. She glanced toward the door. Why not? Adam wouldn't be home for a while yet.

It only took a moment to slip out of her clothes and put on the dress. It was softer even than Red Blanket's. As she smoothed her hands down over the ornate designs, fringes tickled her legs, and the softness of the buckskin caressed her naked limbs in a sensual feast. Kenzie had always loved clothes, and this dress was an absolute delight. Maybe she'd just leave it on and see what Adam said. Surely he wouldn't mind, even though it was obviously a treasured memento.

All right, what now? Her gaze fell on the rabbit Adam had killed and cleaned earlier. She might not know how to cook it, but she could at least get the fire started. Eagerly, Kenzie piled kindling in the fireplace then took Adam's fire-starter kit down from the mantle. She opened the lid and stared at the contents.

There was some kind of burnt cloth in the bottom, which she ignored. She might not know much, but she did know the important pieces were the metal striker and several small chips of rock.

The striker looked like a thick metal bracelet that had been squashed into an oval shape. Kenzie picked it up and inserted her fingers through the loop. Despite the fact that it had obviously been made for bigger fingers, it was surprisingly comfortable. With her other hand, Kenzie picked up one of the rock chips she knew must be flint. She struck the rock against the metal experimentally. Nothing happened. She changed the angle of the flint and tried again. This time, a tiny spark flew.

Kenzie smiled and knelt down next to her little pile of kindling and started hitting the striker with the largest piece of flint. After many tries, she mastered the art of making sparks, but none of them seemed to do much good. Ten minutes later, the pile was as pristine as it had been when she began. Maybe the kindling wasn't small enough. She broke several sticks into smaller pieces and started again. After another fifteen minutes, she stood up and tossed the striker on the hearth.

In frustration, she leaned a hand against the wall and glared down at the undisturbed pile of tinder. "I wish the stupid thing would just cooperate and burst into flames!" she muttered darkly. With a deep sigh, she dropped her hand and headed toward the water bucket. Maybe a break was what she needed.

The dipper of water was halfway to her lips when she heard an ominous crackling behind her. Kenzie whirled around. The dipper dropped from nerveless fingers, and her mouth fell open in shock.

The whole wall where she had been leaning was on fire!

Chapter 21

Adam was still a long way from the cabin when he saw the smoke. At first, he thought maybe it was a campfire. Crazy Charlie was in the area, after all. As he watched, the gray smoke turned black and billowed out over the trees. That was no campfire! Frantically, he searched the trail in front of him. Where the hell was Kenzie? He should have caught up with her long ago.

Suddenly, he was coming out of the trees next to the cabin. The sight that met his eyes almost brought his heart to a standstill. The cabin was engulfed in flames, and Kenzie was within five feet of it, trying to quench the fire by throwing a bucket of water at it.

"Kenzie!" He swung down from the horse. The minute his boots hit the ground, Bear Bait reared back, pulling the reins from Adam's hand, and took off the way they had come. "Dammit, Bear Bait!" Adam hollered after him. "That fire isn't going to get you."

Kenzie dropped the bucket and ran toward him. "Oh, Adam," she cried as she threw herself into his arms. "I was just wishing you were here."

That explains the two-mile leap I just made. "What happened?"

Her face was streaked with soot and tears as she looked up at him. "I...I don't really know. I was trying to start the fire in the fireplace."

"Looks like you succeeded."

"No, that's just it. I didn't. I'd been trying for almost half an hour but couldn't even get it to smolder. I decided to take a break and get a drink of water." She looked back at the cabin. "That's when it started to burn."

Adam made a face. "I don't suppose you said something like, 'I wish a fire would start,' did you?"

"I don't know. I might have. Why?"

"Wishes have a way of coming true."

"Oh, come on, Adam. Houses don't catch on fire because someone makes a wish."

"No, you're right." *Which is why I need to get the cheat codes fixed on Beta Quest as soon as possible. Who knows what else might happen with a careless wish?*

"I...I'm sorry about your cabin, Adam," Kenzie said in a small voice.

"I'm just glad you got out all right." He hugged her.

"I saved a couple of things."

"Oh?"

"The bucket, the buffalo robe on the bed, and the rabbit you shot for supper."

Adam blinked. "That's an odd combination."

"It wasn't exactly on purpose. I threw the water in the bucket on the fire," she shook her head. "I swear, if I hadn't just been drinking from it, I would have thought it was filled with gasoline."

"Gasoline?"

"It's... well, it's really flammable, which means it burns like crazy. When I threw the water on the fire, it sort of exploded. The fire was almost to the door, so I put the buffalo robe over my head for protection. I grabbed the bucket to get more water."

"And the rabbit?"

"I noticed it when I reached down to get the bucket, so I grabbed it, too."

"Good thinking. I don't like my meat well done."

She gave him a watery smile. "I'm glad you can see the humor of it." She shifted in his arms and looked back at the burning cabin. "Once I got outside, I ran down to the creek for more water, but it was a waste of time."

"I think it was pretty much a lost cause when it caught fire."

"I guess. Adam, what are we going to do?"

"For tonight, we'll make a pine-bough bed and sleep under

the buffalo robe. There will be plenty of time to figure it out tomorrow."

With a crash, the roof caved in and threw sparks and flames high into the air.

Kenzie whimpered and turned her face into his chest. He tightened his arms and rubbed his hand over her back comfortingly. "It's all right, Kenzie-girl. It's just a pile of logs."

"And my clothes," came the muffled reply.

"What?"

"My clothes," she wailed. "I just realized, they're in the cabin."

He set her back a step and looked down at her. "My mother's dress!"

"I hope you don't mind, Adam, I tried it on without asking."

"So what? I was going to let you wear it the day you stole my horse."

"Oh," she said in a small voice. "Is that why you changed your mind?"

"Because you stole my horse? No, it was because we were headed to Laramie City. They'd have eaten you alive if you'd shown up in that dress."

"And they were so friendly as it was," she said with a sniffle. "Why did you want me to wear your mother's dress?"

"I don't know. I guess I just thought it would look good on you, and it does."

She sniffed again. "I'm glad you like it, because it looks like I'm stuck in it."

"If you hadn't put it on, it would have burned up with the cabin," he reminded her. "What say we cook that rabbit?"

Adam set up a pile of kindling on a piece of barren ground then lit it with a burning pine bough he stuck into the fire. Once there were enough glowing coals to suit him, he suspended the spitted rabbit over the fire and settled back to wait.

"How did you make it back here so fast?" he asked curiously.

"I used Crazy Charlie's short cut. It only takes twenty minutes or so."

"Twenty minutes! But that's impossible."

Kenzie shrugged. "Impossible or not, I've walked it six times now, and it takes twenty minutes."

"Crazy Charlie showed it to you?"

"Yes. I told him I wished it were closer so I could go that first night, and he said he knew a short cut. Then he gave me his hatchet to blaze the trail."

Adam rubbed his forehead. He needed to get back to his computer and get those cheat codes fixed before she wished for an earthquake or a blizzard or even a mall nearby. He shuddered to think what his Reality Guard would do with that. "You know, it's going to take a while for the rabbit to cook, so I think I'll take a short nap."

"You're going to sleep?" Kenzie looked at him as though he'd lost is mind.

"Only for a few minutes. I'll be right back."

"What do you mean you'll be right back?"

"I meant to say I won't be asleep long."

Her look of skepticism didn't change. "All right, but if I can't wake you up in time to eat, I might just eat the whole rabbit myself."

"Fair enough." He lay down on the buffalo robe and prepared to leave the program. "Don't forget to turn the spit." He closed his eyes and touched the stone at his throat.

The next thing Adam heard was the ringing of the telephone next to his console. "Ought to just let the damn thing ring." He glanced at the caller ID and sighed. It was his head engineer.

"Yeah, Sam, what's up?"

"Sorry to bother you this late at night, but I need some clarification on this cheat code thing."

"What kind of clarification?"

"You mean besides explaining the weird, convoluted instructions you gave me?"

Adam swallowed a sigh. He'd thought his directions were perfectly clear. "So, what else is bothering you?"

"Where do the cheat codes come from?"

"From inside the program. That's why it took me awhile to track them down. They're an offshoot of the character and setting generator."

"You mean the players can access it while they're inside?"

"Yes. In fact, that was the only way to access it before I modified it."

"How exactly does a player use it?"

"They make a wish."

"They *what*?"

"I know it sounds goofy, but all they have to do is make a wish. When I first discovered it, I decided to do a test, so I said, 'I wish I had some food.' A minute or so later, a rabbit hopped out of the brush."

Sam gave a low whistle. "Are you sure you want to get rid of it? I mean, this could be an incredible selling point."

"It could also be a complete disaster."

"How so?"

"People make wishes without thinking it through. I wished my cabin had running water. The next thing I knew there was a creek running through it."

Sam laughed. "Ok, I guess I could see where it might cause some problems, but I can't see any real danger in that."

"How about wishing you could start a fire and burning down your house?"

"Mmm. All right, that could be ugly."

"Now think about a modern setting. You could cause impossible traffic jams and horrible wrecks, start wars unintentionally, or even wipe out your whole program by dropping a nuclear bomb. In situations like that, there is a very real possibility of the player panicking and forgetting he's in a program."

"I see what you mean."

"What I came up with just moves the cheat codes from

inside the program to the control menu. That way, if there's a problem, the player won't be inside. He'll be able to shut it down and start over."

"Makes sense," he said. "Now, are you going to walk me through it?"

Adam closed his eyes in frustration. "All right, but we need to make it fast. I don't have all night."

"Oh?" Sam sounded interested. "Got a hot date?"

Adam smiled at the other man's choice of words. "Something like that. Do you have your computer on?"

"Yeah. I'm ready to go."

"All right, then." As Adam converted the cheat codes in *Beta Quest*, he walked Sam through the steps. He fought to keep his patience and acknowledged that he'd make a terrible teacher. It was difficult to explain his complex calculations to one even as intelligent as Sam. The process seemed to take forever, but finally they were finished. Adam was anxious to end the conversation and get back to Kenzie, but Sam seemed inclined to chat.

"So, who's this hot date with, Boss?"

"I never said it was a date," Adam pointed out.

"Shucks, and here I was hoping I was right."

"What do you mean?"

Adam could almost hear Sam's grin over the phone. "We've all noticed your preoccupation lately. Joe maintains the creative spirit has you in its clutches, but I said it was a female. I was so sure, too. You show all the signs of a man in love. I bet five bucks on it."

Adam was startled. His prosaic chief engineer mistook his fascination with solving the Kenzie glitch for love? How strange. "The truth is I'm spending all my time trying to fix a glitch that's developed in *Beta Quest*."

Sam was instantly concerned. "A glitch! Do you think it's serious?"

"Probably not. It hasn't carried over to *Fantasy Quest*, anyway."

"You're sure?"

"Positive. I tried to reproduce it and couldn't. Still, I'd like to figure out what's going on."

"A glitch, huh? Damn. I really hate to lose that bet. It isn't the money; it's having to admit that Fredrickson might be right."

"I see your point." Adam suddenly grinned. "Tell him I said it *is* a female that's keeping me busy."

"Your glitch is female?"

"Aren't they all?"

Sam laughed. "That's for sure! All right, I'll make sure this gets into the final programming. You need any help with that glitch?"

"No. I think I can handle it myself."

"Ok, Boss. I'll leave you to it, then. Take care of that shoulder so you can start coming back in. We miss you down here."

"Shouldn't be too long. Now, go home, Sam. Quitting time was three hours ago. Your wife is probably wondering where you are."

"As if she didn't know. I'll leave just a soon as I get this cheat code thing tied up."

"There will be plenty of time for that tomorrow morning. I'm going to check your electronic timecard. If you aren't clocked out in half an hour, I'm going to start docking your pay."

"All right, all right. You're as bad as my wife. I'm leaving right now."

"Good. The last thing I want is Mary down my back. Give her my love."

"I will."

"And thanks, Sam. I'm glad you're on my team."

"Hey, does that mean I can ask for a raise?"

"Sure, just don't expect to get it. I already pay you too much."

Sam chuckled. "Can't kill a guy for trying. Have fun with

your glitch."

"I will. Good night."

Adam glanced at his watch as he hung up the phone. Damn! He'd been gone almost an hour. Kenzie would be fit to be tied. His stomach growled, and he made a face. There was no help for it; he was going to have to eat before he went back in. No matter how nourishing the rabbit might seem to be, his body needed real food.

Annie's casserole was still in the refrigerator. Good. He could solve two problems at the same time. He wouldn't have to waste valuable time cooking something, and when Annie came next time, she wouldn't get all bent out of shape because he hadn't eaten her food.

Adam considered eating it cold to save time, but decided he was just being foolish. As he waited for it to heat in the microwave, he considered his strange conversation with Sam. It was flat weird that his co-workers thought he was involved with a woman. Where in the hell had they gotten an idea like that anyway? He hadn't had a date in years; the last one had been a complete disaster.

It had been a blind date, and the friend who had set it up hadn't thought to mention that Adam was confined to a wheelchair. The poor woman had been so ill at ease she could barely focus on her food at the expensive restaurant he'd taken her to. Adam had finally taken pity on them both and had driven her home, swearing he would never again set himself up for that kind of humiliation.

Now, instead of dwelling on his dating fiasco the way he usually did, he found himself thinking about Kenzie instead. She was a bit impetuous, and sometimes downright irritating, but at least she wasn't boring. And she'd have his liver if he didn't get back there soon.

Adam wolfed his food down in about thirty seconds flat, threw his dishes in the sink, and headed back to his computer. He smiled in anticipation as he put his helmet and gloves on, then he slipped into blackness.

A wave of water hit him full in the face just as he opened his eyes. He came up coughing, sputtering and ready to fight.

"Oh, Adam, thank God!" Kenzie grabbed his hand and tried to hoist him to his feet.

"What the hell—"

"We don't have time for questions now, Adam. Come on. You have to get up."

"I don't und—"

"Dammit, Adam," she yelled. "We're in the middle of a forest fire!"

"What?" But it only took one look to see she was right. The clearing was ringed with fire, and they were right in the center of an inferno.

Chapter 22

"Come on," Kenzie shouted. "The path to the creek is still clear!"

Adam scrambled to his feet and scooped up the buffalo robe he'd been lying on. Kenzie grabbed his other hand and started pulling him toward the trail. "Hurry, before the fire jumps into those trees!"

Adam didn't waste any more time. In two long strides he was in the lead, pulling Kenzie along behind him. They reached the creek in record time and splashed across it. Only then did Adam stop to look back. He studied the distant fire for a moment then shook his head. "I think it's headed the other way. That seems to be the way the wind is blowing."

"I know," Kenzie said. "That's why we had to come this way." She smacked him on the arm with her fist. "Why wouldn't you wake up? I thought we were both going to die."

"I'm sorry, Kenzie. Truly, I am. It never occurred to me that I was putting you in danger."

"Me? You could have been burned to a crisp just as easily as I could have."

It was true, of course, but if Adam died, it was no big deal; he could recreate his avatar from the control panel. If Kenzie died, she ceased to exist. He'd already proven he couldn't recreate her. Even though she was just a glitch, an aberration in the programming, the thought of losing her was somehow intolerable.

"What do we do now?" she asked. "Go to the falls?"

"The fire is between us and the falls."

"You're forgetting Crazy Charlie's shortcut."

"It's this way?"

Kenzie nodded and pointed to a tall spruce. "See that blaze on the trunk? That's the first one on the trail."

"Well, then," Adam said with a sweep of his hand, "lead the way." As he followed her through the trees, Adam suddenly noticed she was wearing the long cotton dress instead of the buckskin. Was this yet another manifestation of problems within the program? "Kenzie, what did you do with my mother's dress?"

"I'm wearing it."

"I mean the other dress. You know, the buckskin one."

"Oh, it's underneath." She stopped and hiked her skirt up until the fringe showed. "See?"

"Where did you get the cotton dress? I thought all your clothes were in the cabin."

"They were, but I'd hung this outside to air out. I went and got it as soon as the fire began to spread." She held up a burlap bag that he hadn't noticed. "I grabbed my fox fur too."

Adam was startled. "Where did you get the bag?"

"It was in Bear Bait's shed. I figured it was a grain sack."

Adam tried to remember if he'd ever seen the bag before. He thought he could vaguely remember something like it lying in the corner of the shed. On the other hand, she might have wished for it before he'd changed the programming. "You seemed to have had plenty of time to gather things up."

Kenzie shrugged. "It didn't take very long. Besides, the fire didn't take off all at once like it did with the cabin." She glanced back over her shoulder. "Lucky for you."

"Kenzie, stop a minute, will you?"

She turned around. "What's up?"

Adam put his hands on her shoulders. "Kenzie, I want you to promise me something."

"That depends on what it is," she said cautiously.

"If we ever get into another life-threatening situation, I want you to promise me that you'll save yourself."

"Every man for himself, huh?"

"Yes, exactly."

Her face hardened. "Does that mean you'd leave me behind?"

"No, of course not, but that's because I—"

"You know," she said, knocking his hands away, "I've about had it with this macho, male-ego thing." She turned and stalked off down the trail. "If you had saved my life, it would be fine, no problem. Hey, that's what guys do. But turn it around, make the woman the hero, and suddenly you're all bent out of shape."

"My ego has nothing to do with it."

"Ha! Like you even know what an ego is. The guy who invented egos and ids hasn't even been born yet."

"Kenzie, this isn't about you saving my life."

"Oh, no? Then why have you been such a pain in the backside since it happened?"

"Because you might have been killed. I couldn't stand that."

"Yeah, but so could you. How do you think I'd feel if you died, and I knew it was my fault?"

"You don't understand. I have ways of saving myself that—"

"Oh, so now you're Superman!" Kenzie whirled around and faced him. "You may think you're invulnerable, but you're not. Nobody is. Even Superman had kryptonite."

He lifted his palms to her imploringly. "How can I convince you—"

"You can't!" she said, advancing on him. She jabbed his breastbone with her finger. "I don't care if you get down on your knees and beg, I won't go off and leave you in danger. Do you understand me?"

"Kenzie—"

"I said, do...you...understand...me?" Every word was punctuated with a jab to his chest.

"Yes!" He grabbed her hand. "I understand. You can be my knight in shining armor if you want to."

"Knightess," she corrected him. "You know, I wish there were a dragon here right now so I could test your resolve." She missed the look on Adam's face as she turned away. "Come on, the sun will be going down soon, and I'm not positive I can find my way in the dark."

A dragon! Adam didn't even want to know what his Reality Guard would do with that.

"Do you think Bear Bait will be all right?" Kenzie asked.

"I hope so. He's such an idiot it's hard to say where he went."

"Would he go back to the Indian village?"

"He might."

Kenzie brightened. "If he does, will Jesse Three Dogs or Eagle Feather come looking for us?"

"Even if they did, they won't come near the hot springs."

"How come?"

"They think it's full of bad spirits."

She sighed. "How long would it take us to walk to the village?"

"A couple of days, if they haven't moved."

"Oh no. I forgot about the fire." Kenzie sounded stricken. "Do you think they'll be all right?"

"Positive. They will have gotten out of its way."

"Are you sure?"

"As soon as they see the smoke, Buffalo Horn will send out some scouts to see where it's going. In the meantime, the women will pack up the camp and be ready to move as soon as the scouts return."

"How will we find them again?"

Adam wondered the same thing himself. The way the program was acting, it was hard to say where the Indian village would be. "Don't worry. I'll find them. If nothing else, I'll run into Jesse Three Dogs like I did last time."

"I wish we could find them now." Kenzie sounded wistful. "Then we'd at least have a place to stay."

"Unfortunately, there's a fire between us and them." Adam looked up at the sky. No smoke was visible. "The fire still seems to be headed the other way."

"Even if the fire hits Rainbow Falls, we'll be safe in the

water."

Adam didn't point out that they weren't there yet. He wasn't entirely sure she was right, anyway.

"I sure wish you had another cabin somewhere," Kenzie said mournfully.

"It's a little late for that," he muttered under his breath.

Kenzie glanced back over her shoulder. "Did you say something?"

"No, just talking to myself. How much farther did you say it was?"

"We should be there in five or ten minutes. You've really never been this way?"

"Nope." And every minute they spent on this trail made him nervous. He had no way of knowing where they were exactly or even where the fire was. They could be walking right into the center of it, and they'd never know until they saw the first flames.

"There it is," said Kenzie, "and I can't see any sign of a forest fire."

Adam followed her out into the clearing and looked at the sky. Far off to the east, he could see the billowing smoke where his cabin used to be. He shook his head. There was no way they could have walked here so fast, and yet they had. He could hardly wait to see what the trail they'd just come down looked like in the programming.

"Where are we going to sleep tonight?" Kenzie wanted to know.

"I don't guess it matters a whole lot, as long as we're not so close to the falls that we get spray." He shrugged the buffalo robe off his shoulders and pulled out his knife. "I'll go cut some branches while you decide."

Several minutes later, he heard a small voice behind him.

"Adam, I… I have a confession to make."

"Oh?"

"You know the rabbit?"

"The one that was cooking when I, uh…went to sleep?"

She nodded. "It's gone."

"I wouldn't expect you to save everything from the fire."

"It wasn't the fire. I ate it." She sighed." I tried to save you some, but I was so darn hungry that it was all gone before I realized it. I hadn't eaten anything but those berries since last night, and I guess I was a little mad at you. At the time I thought you could just go shoot yourself another one."

With a pang, Adam thought of Annie's casserole. Here Kenzie was starving, and he hadn't even given her a second thought. "It's all right. I had some jerky, so I ate earlier. You needed it worse than I did."

"Oh, so we're back to the Superman thing again."

For some reason, her attitude irritated him. "No, we're back to the Whiskey Jug Johnson thing. I don't know who this Superman character is, and I really don't care. He sounds like a gol-darned nitwit."

Kenzie tipped her head to the side thoughtfully. "Faster than a speeding bullet, stronger than a locomotive, able to leap tall buildings in a single bound, and a gol-darned nitwit. Yes, I can see where that has potential."

Adam turned back to the tree so she couldn't see his grin. "Sounds like he's been out in the woods too long. The next thing you'll be telling me is that he runs around in his long johns and wrestles wild grizzlies."

Kenzie gurgled with laughter. "Pretty much. What do you think about putting the bed here? It's more-or-less level, and we have protection from the trees if it rains."

Adam glanced at the place she indicated and nodded his head. "Looks good. You want to help me drag these branches over there?"

"Oh? You want my help? I thought you were Mr. Macho-I-can-do-everything-myself."

"Does this fiancé of yours beat you?"

"No!"

"He must have the patience of a saint."

"For that, I should make you do it all yourself," she said

with a toss of her head.

"Which would prove my point. It's a good thing you come from the future. In this day and age, your sass would most likely get you thrown across your man's knee and paddled."

She gasped. "You wouldn't dare!"

He raised an eyebrow. "Care to try me?"

She stared at him for a long moment then began to smile. "Why, Adam Johnson, I do believe you're teasing me!"

He grinned back. "I do believe I am, at that. Now, are you going to help me make this bed or not?"

Adam enjoyed the camaraderie as they worked, but underneath the pleasure boiled something very like panic. What a mess. He'd promised never to leave her alone at night, but the comatose body he left behind when he returned to the real world posed a threat to Kenzie. She'd try to save it no matter what the danger to herself.

His only choice was to sleep inside *Beta Quest*. He'd never done so, and he wasn't positive it was safe. On the other hand, there was really no reason why it should pose any threat. His wristwatch alarm was set for 6:30 A.M. Its buzzing should wake him up. If not, Annie was due at 9:15. She'd bring him out of it if she had to shake him.

"I just thought of a problem," Kenzie said. If we put the buffalo robe under us, we'll freeze, but if we put it over us, those little short pine needles will poke into us."

"It's spruce, not pine," Adam informed her, "and it so happens I have a blanket in my cache."

"Cash? What good is money going to do us out here?"

"Not *cash*, *cache*. It's where mountain men store their valuables."

"Sort of an outdoor safety deposit box?"

"I guess so, whatever that is." He pointed toward the bank of the pond. "See that big, white rock? That's where my cache is."

Kenzie suddenly remembered him digging there the first day she had arrived. She'd thought he was digging a grave.

"And you bury stuff to protect it," she said with dawning comprehension.

"Exactly. It'll only take a minute or two to get the blanket. Why don't you get ready for bed while I do that?"

Kenzie nodded and walked back into the trees until she was out of sight. What in the world was she going to sleep in? Her underwear was out of the question. Keeping a lusty mountain man at arm's length was going to be tough enough without throwing kerosene on the fire. She considered her two options and decided on the cotton dress. The leather dress was far more comfortable, but she didn't want to damage it.

It only took a few minutes to complete the switch. She carefully rolled the leather dress into a bundle and wandered down to the pool to wash her face and hands.

Adam was already underneath the buffalo robe when she returned. Asleep, no doubt. Kenzie shook her head in amazement. She'd seen some deep sleepers in her day, but he took the cake. Maybe he had that disease where people can't stay awake — narcolepsy or something. At least he'd thoughtfully turned down her side of the bed at the far end. She couldn't decide if she was relieved or disappointed that he'd decided they should sleep at opposite ends.

Kenzie removed her shoes and slipped between the blanket and the buffalo robe. She was just settling in when he spoke.

"I never thanked you for saving my life today," he said gruffly.

"No problem. You'd have done the same for me."

"Even so, you didn't have to put yourself in danger for me. Most men would have run in the same situation."

"Good thing I'm not a man, then, isn't it?"

His answer was a deep chuckle that made Kenzie smile. "Adam?"

"Yes?"

"You wouldn't happen to have a tipi in that cache of yours, would you?"

"Afraid not. Why?"

"If we don't have a tipi, and we can't find the village, how are we going to survive the winter?"

"I'd say our best bet would be to build a cabin."

"Do you think we could?"

Adam put his hands behind his head and gazed up at the night sky. "I suppose if we had time, we could. The problem is we're into August already. The snow flies pretty early up here."

Kenzie sat up and braced herself on her hands. "What if the foundation and half of the walls were already there?"

He turned his head to look at her. "Do you know of such a place?"

"As a matter of fact, I do. Your grandfather's cabin."

"What?"

"That hole over on the corner of the pond. Crazy Charlie showed it to me. He said all you have to do is build the walls five or six logs high and put a roof on it. Would it work, do you think?"

"I don't know. We'll have to check it out in the morning."

Kenzie flopped down on her back. "We also have the problem of getting enough food. Your rifle was on Bear Bait, wasn't it?"

"That it was. I do know how to build a snare, though."

"We can't live on rabbits alone."

"No, but we could a deer."

She turned to look at him again. "You could snare a deer?"

His teeth flashed in the dark. "There is no end to my talents, woman. When will you figure that out?"

"I have a feeling the next few weeks are going to test that."

"Probably, but I always did like a challenge."

"Yeah, me too." Kenzie fell silent as she lay staring up at the Milky Way. Adam's story about burning his father's books and eating the body of his dead horse loomed in her mind. What if this winter was that harsh? Could they survive it? She shivered at the thought.

"Are you cold?"

"No, just thinking." An unexpected lump formed in her

throat. "I'm scared, Adam. What if we don't get the cabin built in time?"

"We will. Don't worry; that's my job, remember?"

"Oh, yeah, Superman. I keep forgetting." She was silent for a long moment. "Adam?"

"Yes?"

"Would you just hold me?"

Without a word, he switched to her end of the bed then turned on his side and enfolded her in his long arms. With a soft sigh, she snuggled closer into his embrace. For the first time in two days, she felt safe and secure. He might not be Superman, but nothing could hurt her as long as Whiskey Jug Johnson held her in his arms.

With the music of the waterfall in her ears and her head pillowed against Adam's strong chest, she drifted off to sleep.

Chapter 23

"That's the nicest lean-to I've ever seen," Kenzie said, looking it over with a critical eye. The structure, a cozy shelter for two, sat between two trees. The three walls—built of pine boughs layered over each other until they reached the ground—created a protected space large enough for the bed Adam had constructed inside. The fourth side was open but shielded from the elements by the lower branches of the trees he'd used as a base.

Adam gave her an amused glance. "Seen many of them, have you?"

"Ok, so, this is my first," she admitted. "However, it looks like a professional job." She twinkled up at him. "But, then, I guess it is. Being able to build a proper lean-to is part of your job as a mountain man, isn't it?"

"My father always thought so, anyway. Shall we go take a better look at that foundation?" he asked as he headed toward the corner of the pool.

Kenzie caught up with him. "I thought you said it would do."

"On first inspection it looked like it would, and I'm sure it will. We just need to take a closer look and figure out exactly what we'll have to do." He walked around the perimeter, studying the walls. "It needs a little shovel work."

"And a lot of ax work."

"Yes, and that's one thing that has me worried. I have a shovel in my cache, but my only ax was in the cabin."

"What about the one you used to build the lean-to?"

"That's a hatchet, not an ax."

"Yes, but couldn't you use it to chop down trees?"

Adam gave her a look. "I guess I could, if I wanted to take six weeks for each tree. I figure we need to have the cabin up in six weeks."

"Winter is only six weeks away?" Kenzie squeaked. Once again, panic coiled through her as the image of Adam burning his father's books flashed across her mind's eye.

"More or less. It's probably more like two months, but the first snow could come any time after the first of October."

"Can we get an ax in Laramie City?"

"Probably. The problem is we don't have any way to get there except to walk, and that would take several days—days we don't have. Besides, without a rifle, we'd be sitting ducks for any kind of predator, human or animal."

"Oh, Adam, what are we going to—"

"Shh." He held up his hand for silence and appeared to be listening intently.

Suddenly, Kenzie heard it too. Something was coming. From the sound of it, that *something* was rather large. *A bear? A moose?* She stepped behind Adam and focused on the sounds.

"Howdy, folks!" came the cheerful call a moment later as Crazy Charlie stepped out into the clearing. "Found this critter wanderin' around and figured you'd be wantin' him back."

"You found Bear Bait!" Kenzie cried and stepped forward to take the horse.

"Kenzie, be careful!" Adam said in a low, urgent voice.

"Don't worry," she said, as she took the reins from Charlie. "He likes me, don't you boy?" As if in answer the horse nuzzled her with his nose. "See?"

Crazy Charlie cackled. "Reckon she's got ya there, boy! That horse is a sucker fer a pretty face."

"Why, thank you, Charlie," Kenzie said as she rubbed Bear Bait's neck.

Adam watched for a moment then relaxed when Bear Bait showed no signs of shying.

"Figured he must have run away during the fire," Crazy Charlie said.

Adam nodded. "He did. I'm surprised he came back."

"Hard to say what a durn fool horse will do. I found him

nosin' around what's left of your cabin."

"Not much there," Adam said.

"That's a fact. Picked up what I could find and brought it along."

Adam straightened in surprise. "You found something? I thought everything would have burned up or melted down."

Crazy Charlie spit. "Nope. Found pots and pans mostly, but I found a couple of other things too." He jerked his thumb over his shoulder toward a gunny sack hanging off the saddle.

"Thanks, Charlie," Adam said, stepping forward to retrieve the sack. "You're a lifesav—"

Bear Bait chose that moment to rear back. With a high-pitched snort, he tried to jerk his head away, but Kenzie held tight to the reins.

"Hey now, big boy. It's all right," she said, pulling his head down. "Nothing's going to hurt you. Shh, settle down now." The horse calmed with the soothing sound of her voice. "Adam," she said quietly, "I think I know what's wrong with your horse."

"Terminal stupidity?"

"No. Look, I'll show you. Approach him from the left side."

It was obvious that Adam thought she'd lost her mind, but he did as she asked. He walked right up to Bear Bait and put his hand on the saddle. The horse didn't so much as flicker an eyelash.

"What does that prove? He's always been temperamental that way. One minute he's a tornado, the next he's as quiet as a mountain lake."

"Now try it from the right side," she said in the same calm voice.

"If you say so." Adam hadn't taken more than two steps when Bear Bait threw his head up in alarm.

"What the hell?"

"I'm pretty sure he's blind or nearly so in his right eye," Kenzie said. "That's why he spooks if you come at him from that side."

"Danged if that don't make sense," Crazy Charlie said. "If you let him know you're there, and walk up nice and quiet like, he'll let you close."

Adam looked at both of them as though he thought they'd lost their marbles, but after a moment he shrugged. "Whoa, there, Bear Bait," he said. "I'm going to walk up and take that sack off your saddle now."

Bear Bait turned toward the sound of his voice but stood steady as Adam walked forward.

"I'll be damned," he said. "Looks like I owe you one, Kenzie."

"Two actually, but who's counting?" Kenzie grinned at his sardonic expression. "I think I'll go give Bear Bait a drink of water and take his saddle off. He's probably ready for a good roll."

Adam nodded, his attention already focused on the sack of salvaged treasures.

In the end, it took Kenzie almost fifteen minutes to take care of Bear Bait, but she was justifiably proud of the results. Not only had she removed the saddle and blanket, she had stowed Adam's rifle safely, and even managed to picket Bear Bait in a lush patch of grass. She left him happily munching away and returned to the men.

"Don't reckon it'll hold up like an oak handle," Crazy Charlie was saying "but it'll work until better comes along."

Adam was hunkered down on the ground examining a fire-blackened ax head. "You're right about that. Now if I just had a way to sharpen it."

Crazy Charlie scratched his head. "I've got a sharpening stone somewheres...I think."

"You found the ax!" Kenzie exclaimed.

"Sure did, ma'am." Crazy Charlie spit a noxious stream of tobacco juice, and Kenzie was surprised to discover it didn't bother her anymore. "I found some of your things too," he said, pointing toward the burlap bag.

"My cloisonné box!" she exclaimed when she saw it lying

on top of the burlap. The paint was burned away and the metal blackened, but it was intact. "I guess it wasn't tin after all. Tin would have melt—Oh for heaven's sake!" Her mouth fell open in surprise as she opened the lid. The Chinese Fortune sticks had been transformed by the intense heat into perfect charcoal drawing sticks. "Unbelievable!" she said, pulling one out to examine it.

"Some pots and pans too," Charlie said, nodding toward the bag again.

Kenzie delved into the burlap bag once again. "The Dutch oven! How on Earth did you pull it out? I would have thought the embers would still be hot."

Crazy Charlie frowned. "Don't rightly recollect, now that you mention it."

Kenzie opened the lid and gasped. "Ohmigosh! My berries were still in here." She touched them with her finger. "Hey, they're not burned. In fact, they almost look..." She trailed off as she stuck her finger in her mouth. "It's good!"

Adam grinned. "It's a cobbler without the crust."

Kenzie dipped her finger in again. "And the sugar. Those chokecherries were so sweet, though, that it hardly matters. How weird."

"That's why they call it a Dutch oven, you know," Adam told her. "You bury it under the coals of your fire, and it bakes just like an oven."

"Oh!" Kenzie looked at the pot with new respect.

"Makes darn good cornbread," Charlie added. "Don't reckon you got any cornmeal left?"

Adam shook his head. "What you see right here is what we have. At least we can go to Laramie City and get supplies, now that you brought Bear Bait back."

Crazy Charlie gazed at the hole in the ground. "You say you're gonna rebuild your grandpappy's cabin?"

"Unless you have a better idea."

Crazy Charlie considered this. "No," he said finally. "Don't have time for nothin' else. You remember how to chop down a tree?"

"I think so."

"We'd best get a handle on that ax, then, and get started."

Kenzie sighed. "I guess I'll see what I can do about cleaning up what you managed to save for us."

Adam nodded and gave her a quick smile before he followed Crazy Charlie back into the forest.

The fireplace cooking apparatus, two plates, and a tin cup had survived the conflagration. They were black with soot, and the cup had a large dent in the side.

Kenzie bit her lip. The fireplace tools were fine, but how the heck was she going to get them clean enough to use? She didn't even have a bottle of dish soap or a dishrag. What she wouldn't give for a steel-wool soap pad.

Ok, time to think outside the box. She frowned as she glanced around the clearing. *No yucca. But, then, there's a good chance it wouldn't be enough anyway. Heck, even sandpaper wouldn't cut it.*

Sandpaper!

Kenzie's gaze flew to the pond. She could scrub them with sand! By the time she'd lugged everything around the pond so that she could use hot water, she was heartily glad that more hadn't survived the fire. It took at least twenty minutes of concentrated scrubbing to get the worst of the black off. Even with the soot gone, the metal was still discolored, and her hands were rubbed raw. At least the dishes were clean.

Now all she had to do was figure out how they were going to eat without silverware.

She was still trying to think of something when she heard the ring of an ax from the forest.

Adam and Crazy Charlie must have the ax fixed already. Glad of an excuse to leave her problem behind, she followed the sound back into the woods. She found them in the middle of a stand of huge pines. Crazy Charlie sat on a fallen log and looked on, giving Adam advice on how to chop the tree so it would fall where he wanted. Adam had removed his shirt to work and was swinging the ax with powerful strokes.

Kenzie's eyes widened as she took in the play of all those lovely muscles and tan skin. The word *spectacular* came to mind. So did *mouthwatering*. Brad had a membership at a gym and dutifully worked out two or three times a week. His slim, toned body was nice to look at but certainly didn't make her stomach go all quivery like this.

"Put your back into it more, son."

Adam adjusted his stance and swung again. This time the ax bit deeper into the tree, and Crazy Charlie nodded approvingly.

"Reckon you remember the way your pa taught you after all."

"Yes, but we usually did it together."

Crazy Charlie gave his cackling laugh. "Are you tryin' to tell me somethin', boy?"

Adam glanced at him and grinned. "Sure as hell am, old man." He grunted as his ax connected with the tree again. "Hurry up with that ax handle so I don't have to do this all by myself."

For the first time, Kenzie realized that Crazy Charlie wasn't just sitting idle while Adam worked. He was shaping an ax handle from a stout branch. By the time Adam had cut through both sides of the trunk, Crazy Charlie seemed satisfied with his homemade ax handle.

"Timber!" Adam yelled as the tree toppled to the ground with a crash. He wiped the sweat from his brow with his forearm. "One down, a hundred to go."

"Expect that one was the hardest," Crazy Charlie observed. "But it ain't done yet. Still got to skin off all them branches and strip the bark before you even think of notchin' it or liftin' it into place."

Kenzie thought she detected a slight slump to Adam's shoulders. "Why don't we have lunch and worry about all that later?" she said.

"Now, that's a danged good idea, missy." Crazy Charlie brightened then frowned. "What's *lunch*?"

Adam laughed. "Lunch, Charlie, means it's time to eat."

"I reckon pickin's will be mighty slim, with all your grub gettin' burned up."

"I reckon you're right," Kenzie said. "All we have is a pot of baked berries, but there's plenty of it."

"I'll be right back." Crazy Charlie walked to the edge of the trees and disappeared into the forest.

Kenzie blinked in surprise. "Where do you suppose he went?"

"Who knows? Last time he did that he came back with a brand-new ax." Adam leaned over to pick up his discarded shirt. "I don't even know what 'right back' means for sure. It might mean five minutes, or it might mean a month. You never know about Crazy Charlie."

Kenzie cocked her head to one side. "Why do they call him Crazy Charlie?"

"I think that's pretty obvious, don't you? He's as senile as they come."

"But surely he hasn't always been that way."

"As long as I've known him, he has. If you want to know the truth, I think he came into the world a few turnips shy of a load."

"But you always treat him with respect. I think you're even fond of him in a way."

"In a way, I suppose I am. He reminds me a lot of my father."

Kenzie's eyes widened in surprise. "He does?"

Adam pulled his shirt over his head. "It's only superficial."

Kenzie watched him put on his shirt with keen disappointment. With the distraction gone, she suddenly realized how much her fingers stung. She frowned down at the scratches and abrasions on the ends of her fingers.

"What's wrong with your hand?"

"Oh, nothing really." Kenzie held up her palms. "I scraped them up a little when I was scrubbing the pans."

"Let me see." Adam took her hand and winced when he

saw the abrasions on her fingertips. "Ouch. Why didn't you say something?"

"What good would that do? It's not like you can do anything about it."

"Wait here. I think I have something in my saddlebag that will help." He made his way to his saddle, reached into the bag, and dug around for a minute. A moment later, he apparently found what he was looking for and headed back. "What's all this?" he asked, holding out a bundle of letters and a book.

"Oh, my journal and my letters!" she cried with real pleasure. "I forgot all about those. I found them along the bank while you were taking your bath."

"More of your treasure?"

"Yes, and I found my thumb ring too." She held up her hand for him to see.

"I can see why old Bradley wanted you to get rid of that. It looks downright dangerous."

Kenzie's eyes narrowed. "His name is Brad, and I'll thank you to keep your opinions to yourself where he's concerned."

"You don't have to get so defensive," Adam said. "I was just teasing." He put the letters and journal on the ground, sat down on a stump next to her, and held out his palm. "Here, give me your hand."

She grudgingly put her hand in his. "I suppose you're going to use something awful."

"Afraid so. Last year's bear grease. It doesn't smell very nice, but it will make your fingers feel better and will help the abrasions heal."

"Ugh," she said, turning her nose away as he opened the bottle. "You weren't kidding. That stuff is downright nasty." But as he smoothed it on with gentle fingers, Kenzie felt the pain start to leave her sores. After a few minutes, the healing warmth of his hand seemed to flow up her arm, straight to her heart. She sat there soaking it up until it suddenly occurred to her that he'd been stroking her hand a lot longer than necessary. Kenzie glanced up and encountered a heated gaze that made sparks tingle in all sorts of interesting places.

The glow in his eyes made her think of a banked fire, one that was ready to burst into flames at any minute. Her lips parted, and she found herself suddenly short of breath. Her heartbeat escalated as he leaned toward her. *He's going to kiss me.* Just as her eyes started to drift closed, she heard a sharp intake of breath.

Kenzie's eyes popped open. Adam was staring at her with an expression that could only be described as horrified.

"Here." He jumped to his feet, thrust the jar of bear fat into her hand, and strode off into the forest.

Bewildered, Kenzie stared after him. *What was that all about?* When he emerged from the trees five minutes later, he acted as though nothing had happened—which, Kenzie reminded herself, was true; nothing had.

"Now where is this frontier cobbler you made?" he asked with a cheerful grin.

Wordlessly, she pointed toward the Dutch oven. Though the chokecherries were delicious, they were difficult to eat. They had to skin the edible part off with their teeth then spit out the large, cherry-like seeds. They were halfway through the meal when Crazy Charlie reappeared with four small bags, one filled with flour, one with jerky, another with coffee, and the fourth with battered flatware. "'Tain't much, but it'll keep you from starvin'."

Kenzie accepted the offerings with a grateful smile. "Why, thank you, Charlie, but won't this make you short?"

"Nope, got plenty more where that came from." He frowned. "Leastways, I think I do. Don't matter anyway. I can make a trip to town and get more."

The meal ended in convivial conversation, and they all trooped back to the fallen tree in high spirits. Adam gave Kenzie his hawk knife and showed her how to trim the branches. Then Crazy Charlie started chopping trees while Adam attacked the foundation with the shovel.

The afternoon's work set a pattern for days to come. They

rose at dawn and breakfasted on jerky and biscuits, then they went to work. Adam completed the dirt work in a couple of days while Crazy Charlie chopped trees and Kenzie stripped the branches. Once Adam joined Crazy Charlie, the trees seemed to fall three times as fast, and Kenzie would never have been able to keep up if Adam hadn't left every afternoon to go hunting. Whatever he brought home was supper.

Kenzie and Adam took turns using the hot pool to bathe and soak away the day's aches and pains. One would use it while the other tended the fire. After about half an hour, they'd switch. When the last one was finished, supper usually was too, which they ate before falling into bed, exhausted.

The second week, Crazy Charlie brought home a deer, and all work on the cabin stopped while they smoked the meat and stretched the hide. Two days later, Crazy Charlie went hunting and never returned. Kenzie wanted to go looking for him, certain that he was lying hurt somewhere, but Adam said he'd been expecting it. In fact, he was surprised Crazy Charlie had stayed as long as he had.

The days passed, and the cabin walls grew. Adam still hunted every day, saving the deer for winter, when game would be scarce. The rest of the time, he worked on the cabin, wearing only his buckskin pants and the odd little flat rock he wore on a thong around his neck. Day after day, Kenzie watched the sweat-slickened skin gleaming in the sunlight and the muscles moving beneath while her insides twisted in response. Even the horrific scars he bore from the bear attack that had killed his father didn't detract from his masculine beauty. As her eighteen-year-old niece would say, Adam Johnson was hot!

She was uncomfortably aware how much her attraction for him was growing and how far she was drifting from her fiancé. There were nights, when she lay in bed gazing at the stars, that she could hardly remember what Brad Marriot looked like. And there were days, as she watched Adam work, that she couldn't have cared less.

Chapter 24

"What do you mean you'll be gone all day?" Kenzie asked, looking up from the breakfast dishes she was getting ready to wash. "We haven't finished the cabin yet."

"I know, but there's no help for it. I have some things I have to do that I've been putting off."

"Like what?"

Like a corporate board meeting and a call to Scott Martin. "I want to see if I can locate the Indian village. We're getting low on supplies, and they might be able to spare some. If not, maybe I can talk Jesse Three Dogs into taking the deer hide and making a trip to town for us."

"Do you think that's safe? I mean, look what happened to him last time he was there."

"If he knows we need the supplies right away, he won't linger. He should be safe enough if he just gets what we need and leaves." Besides, Jesse Three Dogs wasn't going anywhere near Laramie City. He, Adam Johnson, the computer-game purist, was going to break his own hard-and-fast rule: He was going to use cheat codes to get what he needed.

"What about the cabin?"

"We're almost done. All we have left is the rest of the chinking."

"And I'm supposed to mix mud and fill cracks all day while you're gone?"

"No. We'll finish it together. You've earned a day off. Enjoy yourself."

Kenzie scoffed. "Yeah right. And how exactly am I supposed to do that? The nearest mall is a hundred and thirty years away."

Adam chuckled. "Whatever that is."

"Can't I just go with you? I'd love to see Red Blanket and

the rest."

"I don't know how far I'll have to ride, and Bear Bait won't be able to travel as fast carrying both of us."

"All right." She sighed. "I really wish I had thought to pick chokecherries when they were in season. I could have made pemmican, but I suppose they're all gone now."

"Maybe not. As I remember, there were some green ones in the back of that thicket by the cabin. They should be ready about now."

"Are you crazy? That thicket is probably a pile of ashes."

"Not necessarily. Remember all the aspen trees around it?"

"Yeah…"

"They don't burn, at least not like pine and spruce. As fast as that fire was moving, I'm betting a good part of those chokecherries were more or less untouched by the fire."

"You're kidding."

"It's probably worth checking out. Why don't you wait until I come back, and we'll go together?" As long as he was using cheat codes, he might as well go whole hog. That chokecherry thicket was already in the program. All he had to do was reactivate it.

"It's only a twenty-minute walk."

"Yes, but you already know how much bears like chokecherries. They'll be fattening up for winter right now, and food is scarce this year. You'd look like a nice snack to a big old grizzly."

She paled a little under her tan. "And Eagle Feather wouldn't be there to shoot it."

"No."

She gave a defeated sigh. "Ok, you win. I'll stay right here, but what am I going to do? I'll be so bored."

He waved a hand toward Rainbow Falls and the two pools. "You see before you, madam, the world's greatest natural spa. You can pamper yourself all day long."

"What?"

The moment he saw her expression, he knew he'd blown it.

There was nothing for it now but to try and fake his way through. "I said you could go swimming and soak in the hot pool all day if you wanted to."

"No, you called it a spa."

He tried to look confused. "Isn't that what you called it?"

Kenzie frowned. "I did? When?"

Adam's mind raced. *What will she accept?* "When you first got here."

"I don't remember saying anything of the kind."

"You were pretty woozy."

Kenzie gave him a suspicious look. "Are you sure?"

"What do you mean am I sure? You almost passed out on me several times, and the minute I turned my back, you took off like you thought I was the devil himself. You were worse than woozy; you were downright loony."

"No, I mean are you sure I called it a spa?"

Adam shrugged. "I thought that's what you said. Why, what's a spa?"

Kenzie crossed her arms and looked away. "It's a place you go to pamper yourself. They have hot tubs, saunas, mud baths, private swimming pools, you name it."

"Sounds like you just described this place."

"Except for a steam room and a masseuse, *spa* describes this place perfectly. It was just weird to hear you say it, that's all."

"Steam room... Is that anything like a sweat lodge?"

Kenzie looked at him. "You mean a Native American sweat lodge?" She shrugged. "I guess so. It's the same principal, I think."

"Maybe after we get the cabin finished, I can build a sweat lodge, then all we'd need is the masseuse." Adam couldn't resist teasing her a little. "What is that, anyway?"

"It's someone who gives really good back rubs." She gave him a sultry look. "Maybe I could teach you."

The thought of rubbing lotion all over Kenzie's naked body just about incinerated Adam on the spot. The temptation to take her up on the blatant invitation she was issuing was almost irresistible. Damned Sex Hex! Time to put the conversation back into safer channels. "Anything you want if I wind up sending Jesse Three Dogs to Laramie?"

She grabbed the front of his shirt in mock desperation. "A hairbrush with stiff bristles and a good comb!"

Adam chuckled. "I'll see what I can do. Anything else?"

Kenzie pulled her braid over her shoulder and wrinkled her nose. "A good pair of barber scissors if you can get them. I'm going to chop this mess off and be done with it." She reached up and brushed his cheek. "You might want to ask for a razor, too. It's got to be easier than your hunting knife."

"Or I could regrow my beard." In reality, he hadn't had to shave since the first time. He didn't expect his beard to grow, and it hadn't. It would take some concentrated effort to get it going again even if he could. He just wanted to hear what she'd say. She didn't disappoint him.

"Mmm, no." She ran the backs of her fingers down one cheek then opened her hand and softly trailed the palm down the other side of his face. "It's much nicer this way."

"What about winter? My beard keeps my face warm." His voice sounded husky even to his own ears.

"Have Jesse Three Dogs buy me some yarn. I'll knit you a scarf."

"You have an answer for everything, don't you?" He caught her hand and kissed the palm. Her eyes widened, and her lips parted with a soft gasp as though she couldn't quite get enough air. The look in her eyes kicked his hormones into overdrive. *Ah, what the hell? Just one kiss. What could it hurt?* He already knew the Sex-Hex wouldn't shut down for a kiss, and he didn't have time for anything else.

Adam brushed his lips against hers, stopping to touch the corner of her mouth with his tongue before nibbling at her bottom lip. With a moan, she melted against him like butter against a hot knife. Her mouth opened beneath his, and his tongue swept in to explore the silken depths. She tasted of the pine twig she had used to brush her teeth and something infinitely sweeter, the essence of Kenzie herself.

Lust pounded through his veins hot and heavy as he put his arms around her and pulled her close. He felt a gratifying quiver move through her body and knew she was feeling the answering tremor in his own. It was all he could do not to groan with frustration when the vibration of his timer tingled against his wrist.

Regretfully, he pulled back, feathering kisses against her lips, unwilling to break contact, knowing he must. "I've got to go," he said softly.

"Mmmm." She slowly opened her eyes and gazed up at him with a bemused look that was very nearly his undoing.

He brushed her hair back with a gentle hand and dropped a kiss on her forehead. "I'll be back before you know it."

Kenzie blinked and pulled herself together. "Take your time. I'll be lounging in the spa all day."

Adam laughed and stepped away. "If you get tired of that, you can always work on your fox fur. When you get the softening done, all you have left is smoking it. Red Blanket showed you how to soften it, didn't she?"

"Yes, but I don't have a tipi pole to rub it back and forth across." She followed him over to where Bear Bait was tied. "Any ideas?"

Adam thought for a moment. "Maybe." He untied the rope from his saddle and walked over to the edge of the forest, where he tied one end of the rope around one stout tree, then strung the rest over to another. There he took two wraps and pulled the rope taut between them. When he thought it was tight enough, he tied it off and stepped back. "There, that should work. Just remember to keep the fur side up."

"Hey, that looks like it might even be an improvement over a tipi pole. Thank you, Adam."

The look she gave him said very clearly that she wouldn't mind another goodbye kiss, and Adam was sorely tempted. But the tingling in his wrist reminded him that he had less than an hour to get to his meeting. Resisting the urge for one more kiss, he swung up into the saddle. With a wave goodbye, he rode out of camp and up over the hill.

Adam was barely out of sight when the need to leave the program suddenly intensified about a thousand percent; he could feel a hand on his shoulder. Since nothing was touching him here, it could only mean the sensation was coming from the real world.

Adam rode Bear Bait off the trail, praying Kenzie wouldn't be venturing far from camp. In spite of what he'd told her, he really wasn't too worried about the bears. If they were moving in the program, they'd be farther afield, where there was more food. He had the horse picketed in a matter of seconds then lay down under a tree. After he left, his body would appear to be asleep. Kenzie would freak out if she found him standing up. He gave one more glance around to make sure they were hidden, then reached up and grabbed the worry stone on the thong around his neck.

There was a moment of blackness followed by the blinking lights of his computer screen. With the lightning reflexes of a trained athlete, he reached up and grabbed the wrist of the person shaking his shoulder.

"You're back."

"Annie! What the hell are you doing here? You scared me half to death."

"Why?"

"Because I could feel you touching me."

"I wondered if you would. You didn't seem to be paying much attention to that timer you wear on your wrist."

"I was busy." He took the helmet and gloves off.

"How do you get yourself out of there, anyway?"

"With this." He stuck his hand in his pocket, pulled out the worry stone and tossed it on the desk.

"Didn't one of my kids give you that?"

"Seth, but it really doesn't matter what you use. It just has to be something in the real world that you're familiar with. You imagine the feel of it inside the program, and it pulls you out. I visualize this on a thong around my neck, but you could just as easily imagine it in your pocket."

"What if somebody picks the wrong thing and can't get out?"

"*Fantasy Quest* doesn't work that way, just *Beta Quest*. There are ports all over *Fantasy Quest* that you can leave through. I never got around to putting them in *Beta Quest,* since it's just a test program, and I'm the only one using it."

"Don't you have a big meeting today?"

He pushed away from the console. "As a matter of fact, I do, and I need to get ready."

"That might take a while. You look like hell. When was the last time you shaved?"

Adam reached up and rubbed his face. Unlike his beard in *Beta Quest,* this one was growing just fine. "I was thinking of cultivating a new look. How do you think I look with a beard?"

"How about... scary? It doesn't exactly fit your CEO image."

"Huh. Well, it was just a thought." He turned away and wheeled himself into the bathroom. "Why are you here, anyway? The doctor gave me the okay to drive two weeks ago."

"I came to clean your apartment," she called over the sound of running water.

"I have a cleaning lady."

"I know, but her daughter just had a baby, and she'll be gone for a couple of weeks. She said she'd tried to call and left several messages, but you never called her back. She finally gave up and called me."

"Funny, there wasn't anything on my phone. Must have left them on someone else's by mistake. Say, if you're going to hang around, would you mind finding me a shirt and tie that go with my gray suit?"

"Sure."

He glanced at his watch. "Damn, I'm going to be late. Have you seen my cell phone?"

"It's on the kitchen counter, I think," Annie said.

"Would you mind giving Carla a call and letting her know I'll be late? You know the security code."

"It's still the same as when you were in the hospital?" she asked in surprise.

"Yeah, I haven't had time to change it."

The door closed behind him. Annie frowned as she put in the complicated pattern of crisscrossed lines that he had created for her when he'd been in the hospital. Normally, he unlocked his phone with his thumbprint or eye-scan. He alternated between the two for added security. So why hadn't he changed it after he no longer needed her fielding his calls for him? As she waited for the call to connect, she idly scanned the screen. Her attention caught on a tiny icon in the corner. *Twenty-seven voice mails?*

"Adam Johnson's office. Carla Vickers speaking. I am away from my desk or on another call. Please leave your name and number, and I'll get back to you as soon as possible."

Annie left Adam's message, then set the phone back on the counter and walked into what Zoey referred to as "Adam's drive-in closet." The roomy interior could have held three times the clothes, but although Adam was the one who had designed the huge closet and had it built, he'd never gotten around to adding to his wardrobe. Annie shook her head. The man needed a wife.

The gray suit was easy to find. She picked a silk shirt and tie in a dark raspberry shade then laid them all out on the bed. That's when it hit her: Adam's bed was made up. *How odd.* He never made his bed. It only looked like this right after the cleaning lady had been here, and Annie knew for a fact she hadn't been here in almost two weeks.

Annie shrugged. Maybe he'd turned over a new leaf. She got the dust mop from the hall closet and started cleaning the floor in the bedroom. She had just finished the living room when Adam appeared.

"How do I look?"

She leaned on the dust mop and looked him over

appraisingly. The ugly eighth of an inch of beard had disappeared, and though his hair could still use a good trim, it looked stylish and businesslike. The tailored suit fit him perfectly, and the raspberry shirt was gorgeous with his dark hair and eyes. When he chose to put in the effort, Adam Johnson was one fine-looking man. "I wouldn't have thought it possible when I got here, but I think you've pulled it off. You look like the head of a very prosperous company."

"Thanks." He glanced at his watch. "Not as late as I thought I was going to be. Did you call Carla?"

"Yes. She was away from her desk, so I left a message."

"Thanks." He frowned. "Hey, how come you're here today instead of working?"

"It's my day off."

He gave her a fierce look. "Dammit, Annie, you shouldn't be here cleaning my house!" he said, wheeling himself to the door. "Your day off is supposed to be fun. Go home and pig out on the Home and Garden channel or take yourself to one of those spas for the day."

"Adam, when was the last time you listened to your messages?"

"I don't know, yesterday, maybe, or the day before. I haven't had time today." He started patting his pockets. "Where are my keys? Oh, here they are," he said, plucking them off the hook by the door. "I mean it, Annie. Go home. I'll get the lady down the hall to clean for me." He rolled out the door then stuck his head back in.

"This place better look just like it does now when I get back, or I'll take your key away!" He blew her a kiss and was gone.

"As if you'd even notice the difference," Annie muttered. She had just started on the kitchen when she spotted Adam's cell phone still on the counter. *Shoot. I wonder if I can catch him.* She glanced out the window just as the sleek black pickup disappeared around the corner. After a long moment, she picked up the phone and went to his voicemails.

Annie stood and listened to all twenty-seven. There were

at least seven from the cleaning lady, a couple from his head engineer on an important point that needed to be clarified, one from his administrative assistant to tell him this morning's eleven o'clock meeting was going to be held after lunch instead... Annie glanced at the clock. Quarter to eleven. He obviously hadn't gotten that one. Half a dozen were from his mother, who was out of town and increasingly agitated that she couldn't find her son.

Annie's frown deepened as she listened. The dates went back almost two weeks, and it didn't sound like he'd returned any of them. Adam wasn't sleeping in his bed or answering his phone. From the look of him when she arrived, he wasn't showering or shaving either. Her gaze landed on the sink full of dishes. He was eating here at least, but that in itself was strange. Adam always took the time to rinse his dishes and put them in the dishwasher. What the heck was going on?

He had been increasingly preoccupied of late. If she hadn't found him looking like some poor, homeless skid-row bum, she'd have thought it was a woman. But Adam hadn't been anywhere to meet one. After his accident, he'd pretty much shut himself away.

Suddenly, her gaze fell on the computer, and her stomach twisted. Was that where he was spending all his time? Could he even be sleeping there?

Annie walked over to the desk and picked up her son's worry stone. She pulled up an extra chair and sat down. Turning the stone over and over in her hand, she tried to remember exactly when Adam's behavior had changed. He'd always been into his computers, but he'd gotten increasingly involved since his surgery. No, it was before that, even. About the time the glitch showed up. Had it somehow affected his mind like an addictive drug or something?

There was only one way to find out what was going on. She stuck the stone in her pocket and slipped her hands into the gloves. The screen in front of her flickered to life. Her stomach fluttered nervously as she reached for the helmet. What if she got stuck? Adam had said she could come in and disconnect him. Surely, he'd be able to do the same for her.

Setting her jaw, she placed the helmet on her head, and everything went black.

Chapter 25

Suddenly, Annie was standing in a forest of tall pine trees. Birds were singing all around her, and she could hear a waterfall in the distance. Even knowing it was a computer program, she found it hard to believe that none of it was real. She felt a swell of pride for her friend. It was a good thing Adam wasn't the type to let success go to his head. When the world saw this, he was going to be more famous than the Pope.

A sound behind her made her turn. A huge black horse was watching her warily. "Bear Bait?" The horse's ears pricked forward, and she laughed. "Of course it is. Who else would it be?"

A glance to the right brought a startled cry to her lips. Adam lay sprawled beneath a tree less than ten feet from her. Her first panicked thought was that he'd come home, found her wearing his helmet, and come in after her. A heartbeat later she realized it was only his cyber body, the one he left behind when he came back to the real world.

She approached cautiously, not knowing what to expect. He looked like he was asleep. Her medical training took over. She knelt next to the body and placed two fingers on the carotid artery. His pulse was strong and his skin surprisingly warm. A scar visible through the open V of his shirt caught her eye. Adam didn't have a scar there.

Curious now, she reached down and pulled up the bottom of his shirt and gasped. Long ridges of scars ran the length of his torso—marks left by the claws of a huge animal. Though they were not unlike the scars he sported in real life, they were much more defined and more numerous. Had he been mauled here as he had in the real world? She raised his shirt higher and blinked in surprise. An exact duplicate of the incision from his latest surgery stretched from the top of his shoulder to his armpit. The only difference was that this one was no longer purple. It had taken on the white-ridged appearance of an old scar.

Suddenly feeling like a voyeur, Annie pulled his shirt back into place and stood up. She studied him objectively for several minutes and found herself somewhat surprised. Given the chance to recreate their own bodies, most people would be tempted to get rid of all their flaws and make themselves more attractive. Other than the scars, Adam looked pretty much the same as he always did, except that his hair was long, and he had a great tan. Both went with the buckskins he was wearing. Knowing Adam, he probably hadn't given his appearance any thought at all other than making himself look like a mountain man.

It occurred to her, abruptly, that there was one big difference: his wheelchair. The chair was so much a part of who he was that she'd never even thought about him being able to walk here. *Perhaps that's why...* But, no, he'd been working on these programs for a good five years. He'd been able to walk, run, jump, do cartwheels if he wanted, ever since the beginning.

All at once, Annie had a burning desire to see that: to see him whole the way she never had. She'd have to talk him into letting her come with him sometime. That is, if he ever spoke to her again after he found out she'd sneaked in without his permission.

She wasn't going to find the answers she sought here. Annie turned and headed toward the sound of the waterfall. When she'd first met him, Adam had talked about Rainbow Falls all the time. It had been a favorite place for him and his father to camp and a bright memory that he clung to during the long, pain-filled months of grief and recovery. She'd asked once whether he'd thought of putting Rainbow Falls into *Beta Quest*. He'd just grinned and said, "What do you think?" Unless she missed her guess, Rainbow Falls was right over that hill.

Annie had only walked a few yards when she came to a well-defined trail. Less than five minutes later, she topped a rise and looked down into Adam's dream world. Across the way, a beautiful waterfall tumbled down the rocks and into a tiny lake, throwing a broad band of mist into the air on its way. A rainbow arched over the water, created by the magic of sparkling sunlight and mist.

Not far from the banks of the lake stood a small cabin — a very small one; the walls were only about four feet high. As she studied the freshly peeled logs, Annie knew with soul-deep certainty that Adam had built it with his own two hands. The question was: why?

So, he wanted to build a cabin. Why not build a full-sized one rather than one so short he couldn't even stand up in it? Was he inventing a new handicap-accessible design or something? And why now? With the launch of *Fantasy Quest* only a few months away, he said he had no time to spare for anything else. He could build a cabin anytime, and it certainly wouldn't be a reason for him to sleep here. There was obviously more to this than met the eye.

It was easy to see why he wanted to spend time here, though. There was a feeling of tranquility about the place, an appeal that was hard to resist. Annie walked down hill, taking in everything as she did. The plants that grew alongside the trail were reminiscent of the lush greenery one saw in formal gardens, but with an untamed quality that added to the wild beauty of the place.

Though it was all wonderful, it was Rainbow Falls and the small pond at the bottom that kept drawing her gaze. It made her want to stand naked beneath the waterfall and let the crystal water cascade over her, to dive into the sparkling pool and swim through its shimmering depths.

With her attention on the waterfall, she nearly missed the lean-to. She'd have walked right past it if the sunlight reflecting off an ax blade hadn't caught the corner of her eye.

Annie turned her head to see what it was and found the lean-to back in the trees. She frowned as she took in the pine-bough bed. It was covered with some kind of large animal hide that had seen better days. *This is where he's sleeping!* She thought. Though it was roomy enough for the largest man, it didn't look anywhere near as comfortable as the king-sized, top-of-the-line mattress Adam had at home.

Then she saw it, he last thing she expected to see here in Adam's world but one that made sense of it all: an old-fashioned woman's dress and some modern-looking underwear hung from a makeshift clothesline, drying in the sun. So, her initial thought had been correct—he *was* involved with a woman!

Annie looked around. Where was the woman, and why was Adam taking time away from his work to play patty-cake? It didn't make sense. Adam was always so focused, especially now, when his dreams for *Fantasy Quest* were about to be realized.

Maybe the answer lay in the cabin. The heavy smell of newly cut lumber perfumed the air, and Annie sniffed appreciatively as she rounded the edge of the cabin. The door lay on the opposite side of the building, directly across from the falls. Annie smiled to herself. Adam didn't have a picture window, but he wasn't about to let that view go to waste. It would be the first thing he saw every morning when he looked out his door.

Annie looked in through the open doorway, her eyes widening. No wonder the walls were so short. Half the cabin was underground. What an incredibly clever idea! That Adam was something else.

The smile slipped from her face. Building a cabin meant he was planning to spend even more time here. If he thought he'd found true happiness here, how would she ever convince him to go back to the real world?

She glanced toward the waterfall and froze in stunned surprise. An Indian woman stood on the other side of the pond. Her hair was in two long braids, and she was dressed in a beautiful white leather dress—truly, a work of art. The intricate beading was noticeable even at this distance. It took a moment to realize that the woman was white.

Suddenly, it all came together in Annie's mind. The glitch. Adam had said it was a character that didn't fit. Ever since then, he'd been spending more and more time inside the program. Unless she missed her guess, the woman across the pool was the key to it all.

As she watched, the other woman undressed, hung her dress on a bush, and waded into the water at the edge of the pool. She stepped up onto what appeared to be an unseen ledge, walked a few steps, and then disappeared behind the waterfall.

Curious, Annie was about to follow, when she suddenly heard a menacing voice in her ear. "You have 30 seconds to get the hell out of my program!"

"Adam?" Annie jerked her head around and looked behind her, fully expecting to see him. But the clearing behind her was empty. It took her a second to realize the voice had come from inside her head. Apparently, Adam had come home and found her at his computer. She reached for the stone in her pocket then stopped as she remembered the sight of Adam's body lying so still and quiet. For some reason, the thought of leaving her body here in the open seemed like a stupid thing to do.

"Twenty seconds," came the voice again.

Annie spun on her heel and started back toward the clearing where she'd found Adam and Bear Bait. She was about halfway there when Adam himself came striding down the hill. She stopped in her tracks, stunned as she watched his long, powerful stride eating up the ground the way his wheelchair blazed around the racetrack. If he was handsome dressed as the quintessential businessman, he was downright gorgeous as a wild-haired mountain man. Wild and dangerous looking. He was close enough now to see the angry set of his jaw and the sparks shooting from his eyes. Annie swallowed nervously and reminded herself this was Adam, her friend.

"What the hell do you think you're doing?" Adam roared.

"I wanted to see this fabulous program for myself." She

gave him a nervous smile. "I've got to tell you, Adam, it's even more amazing than I thought it would be."

"Dammit, Annie, if you wanted a tour, why didn't you just ask? I'll set you up anything you want in *Fantasy Quest*."

"I know." Annie walked past him with a nonchalance she was far from feeling and headed back up the hill he'd just come down. "The thing is, it wasn't *Fantasy Quest* I was concerned about, and I knew you'd never let me into *Beta Quest*."

He fell in beside her. "Of course I wouldn't. It's a beta program; that means it hasn't been fully tested yet," he said as though he were explaining it to an idiot. "It's dangerous."

"I know. I saw the scars on your body." She looked at him. "They're worse than your real ones. Did you make those up, or did you get them while you were in *Beta Quest*?"

"My scars! What were you looking at my scars for?"

"Professional curiosity."

"Really." Adam's flat tone was one of disbelief.

Annie shrugged. "I found a body lying under a bush. I checked vital signs and did a cursory examination to make sure it was all right. What was I supposed to do?"

"Well, let's see now," Adam's voice was heavy with sarcasm. "I don't suppose you could have just left it alone since you knew it wasn't real. Besides, last I knew, you didn't need to lift a shirt to take a pulse."

They had reached the hidden glade. Annie gave him a saucy grin, doing her best to diffuse his anger. "I told you; I'm addicted to bulging biceps and rippling pectorals. I couldn't resist."

"Bull."

Annie sighed. "All right, I wanted to look at your shoulder."

"Why?"

"You're avoiding my question," she pointed out.

"And you're avoiding mine. What the hell are you doing in my program?"

She reached into her pocket and grabbed the stone. "See

you back at your apartment."

Annie opened her eyes a moment later to the blinking lights on Adam's computer console. He was sitting in his chair next to her with a second helmet on his head. He must have gotten it from his other computer. She had just removed her own and carefully set it on the stand when Adam blinked and opened his eyes.

Annie gave him a long assessing look. "I saw her, you know."

His frown sharpened. "Who?"

Annie calmly removed her gloves and stood up. It gave her a height advantage, though Adam didn't seem to notice. "The woman. She's your glitch, isn't she?"

He gave her a belligerent glare as he removed his own gloves. "Yeah, so what?"

"So, I think you've forgotten who and what she is."

"I haven't forgotten, because I never knew. "He turned and wheeled out to the kitchen, where he pulled an imported beer out of the nearly empty refrigerator. "That's the whole point. I'm trying to figure out just what she is and what she means to the program."

"What about what she means to you?"

"Kenzie means nothing to me. She's an interesting puzzle, that's all."

Annie gave him a look of pure disbelief as she crossed the kitchen and pulled open a drawer. "Sure, that's why you've started living in your program." She handed him a bottle opener then leaned back against the counter and crossed her arms.

"Living in my program?" Adam laughed as he popped the lid off the bottle and took a swig. "Whatever gave you that goofy idea?" he asked without quite meeting her eyes.

"Your bed hasn't been slept in, you haven't shaved or bathed in days, and you haven't answered your phone or checked your messages for almost two weeks. The only thing you are doing here is eating. Except, for the first time since I've known you, the dishes get tossed in the sink instead of rinsed and stuck in the dishwasher.

"So what? I'm busy getting *Fantasy Quest* ready for the launch."

"Right, that's why you haven't bothered to answer your head engineer's calls, and you've taken the time to build an entire cabin by hand inside *Beta Quest*. Tell me how that's contributing to *Fantasy Quest*."

"I want to see what's possible."

"Then, why didn't you do it before? For that matter, why can't it wait?"

Adam took another swig of beer. "Maybe I just wanted to see if I could do it."

"And maybe you're planning on living there permanently."

Now she had his full attention. "You mean inside the program?"

"That's exactly what I mean." Annie was taken aback by the dumbfounded expression on his face. If he was faking it, he was doing an incredible job of it.

"Why would I do that?"

She shrugged. "You tell me."

"Annie, what you're talking is crazy. You think I've forgotten *Beta Quest* is a fantasy." He shook his head. "I couldn't live there even if I wanted to. I have to come out to eat and go to the bathroom if nothing else. Maybe I'm spending a little more time there than usual, but I haven't lost my grip on reality."

"Then why build the cabin?"

He took another drink of his beer and frowned. "Winter's coming on," he said finally.

"What?"

"I said it's almost wintertime."

"Adam, it's the middle of November. We have six inches of snow on the ground. I'd say winter arrived last month."

"But not in *Beta Quest*." He rubbed his hand over his face.

"See, I didn't give the season any thought when I started the program. I just set it for summer. It never mattered before, because it just shut down when I left and started up again when I returned."

"And it doesn't do that now?"

Adam shook his head. "Not since the Kenzie glitch showed up. That was sometime in late summer, and the program has run continually ever since. Now fall is definitely coming. Some of the trees are already starting to turn."

"So what?" Annie said. "I mean, you can just reset the program before winter hits, can't you?"

Adam tried to look as though the idea had never occurred to him before. "Yeah, I guess so." He took another drink and avoided looking at her. "If I reset it for early summer, I wouldn't have to deal with winter, would I?"

"Only, for some reason, you don't want to do that," Annie said thoughtfully as she tipped her head to one side. "I wonder why not. Unless…"

Adam gave her an inscrutable look. "Unless what?"

"There's something in there you don't want to lose."

"I can recreate everything in *Beta Quest*."

Annie shook her head. "Except your glitch. If you shut down *Beta Quest*, it's gone forever. *She's* gone forever."

"Then my problem would be solved, wouldn't it? Remember," Adam pointed out, "I'm trying to get rid of it."

"No, that's what you originally wanted to do, but not now."

"Is that so?"

"Yes, it is. And do you know why?"

"No, but I'm sure you're going to tell me."

"Because you're in love with her."

Adam stopped with his bottle halfway to his mouth. "In love? Annie, she's a glitch, an aberration in the programming. That's all. I could no more fall in love with her than I could fall in love with my computer."

Annie snorted. "And your point is?"

"The point is she's not real."

"Then, why did you build her a cabin?" Annie asked.

"I'm not done studying her yet. I still need to know where she came from. *Fantasy Quest*—"

"Horse pucky! You already told me she poses no threat to *Fantasy Quest*. You're deluding yourself if you think that's the reason for all this."

"Since when are you such an expert on my program?" he asked. "You said you saw Kenzie. Did you actually talk to her?"

"No."

"Then, how the hell do you know what she is or how I feel about her?" Adam drained the rest of his beer and tossed the empty bottle in the trash. "For that matter, who made you my guardian, and what gives you the right to judge me or tell me what to do with my life? If I decide I want to spend every waking minute in *Beta Quest*, it's none of your damned business! You treat me like I'm one of your kids, and I'm sick of it. Why don't you just go home and leave me alone?"

Annie's gaze dropped during his tirade, and the color drained from her face. "Adam—"

Adam's anger evaporated into thin air, and remorse hit him like a tidal wave. "Oh God, Annie, I'm sorry. You know I didn't mean—"

Annie waved his apology away like an annoying mosquito. "Adam!" She raised her wide-eyed gaze to his. "You... You moved your leg!"

Chapter 26

"Hello?" Adam reached over and put the phone on speaker without taking his eyes off the monitor.

"I just had an idea."

"Annie?" Adam rolled his eyes. "I'll bet you aren't even in the parking garage yet."

"Then, you'd lose. Hear that?" The sound of a revving engine came over the phone. "I'm just getting ready to leave. Anyway, as I was saying, I'm going to call Carla and tell her to make sure you don't get sidetracked this afternoon."

"Carla has more important things to do than—"

"No, she doesn't, Adam. She's your secretary. That's what you pay her for."

"I pay her to take care of my business, not my personal appointments."

"When I tell her movement is coming back to your legs, she'll agree with me."

Adam sighed. "Look, this isn't necessary. I promise we'll go as soon as my meeting is over. Dr. Dowie said the neurologist wouldn't be able to get away for several hours, anyway."

"But you know how you get wrapped up in what you're doing and forget things."

"Annie, there's no chance in hell I'm going to forget this!"

"Still, if Carla knows what's going on, she'll make sure you get there on time."

"All right, call Carla if you want. Call the whole world for all I care. Can I please just go back to work?"

"What are you doing?"

"Deleting you from *Beta Quest*."

"I'm already gone."

"*You* are, but your body isn't."

"I guess you don't want discarded bodies lying around."

Adam grinned. "It is a little disconcerting to stumble over one. That's why I built an automatic delete feature into *Fantasy Quest's* avatar generator."

"But it's not in *Beta Quest*?"

"No, after I got the avatar generator perfected, I deleted it in order to make more room. I never bothered putting it back after I developed the Zeta server. This is how I delete characters now."

"And you've been trying to get rid of me all afternoon."

Adam's smile disappeared. "Look, Annie, you know I didn't mean—"

She laughed. "That's the third time you've tried to apologize. I should just let you wallow in your own guilt. Maybe you'll be nicer to me in the future. I wasn't paying any attention anyway."

"That doesn't excuse—"

"Oh, Adam, it just doesn't matter. You're going to walk again!"

Adam's stomach gave an odd little twist of joy, but he kept his voice level. "We don't know that yet. You know as well as I do there's a big difference between muscle twitches and walking."

"Don't be such a wet blanket!"

"Just don't get your hopes up," he warned.

"Oh, heck, I'm not even going to talk to you anymore. Go entertain yourself by dumping my body."

"It's already done," he said. "Just a little poof, and it was gone."

"Poof?"

He grinned. "Poof."

"I thought it would be more dramatic than that. Ah well," she said with a sigh, "the garage attendant is waving me on through, so I guess I'd better go. I'll see you at four."

"You can put money on it."

"Just don't stand me up."

Adam smiled as he disconnected the phone. Good old Annie. The anger he'd felt when he found her in his program was gone as though it had never been. If she hadn't sneaked into *Beta Quest*, who knows how long it would have been before he realized he could move his right leg.

He focused on it now, willing it to move. After several seconds of intense concentration, it did. Not much, mind you, but enough. Euphoria flooded him yet again. Maybe Annie was right; maybe he would walk again.

Adam glanced at his watch. His meeting wasn't for another couple of hours yet. Good, there was still time to call Scott.

Scott answered on the first ring. "Hey, Adam what's up?"

"Did you get my package?"

"You mean the new Zeta unit? Sure did, and I'm putting it through its paces." Scott made an appreciative noise. "I've gotta tell you, old buddy, that storage unit is worth more than your SR program. It's not only going to revolutionize gaming, it's going to change the whole computer industry! Hope you've got the patent tied up tight."

"I do. There are seven patents and two trademarks. It's as safe as my legal team and three patent attorneys could make it." Adam traced the edge of his desk with his finger. "That's actually not why I called."

"Oh?"

"How are your hacker skills?"

"I left hacking behind with my rebellious youth."

"As I remember, the Pentagon pretty much insisted."

Scott chuckled. "Yeah, they weren't too pleased when I broke in."

"Are you still working for the government, then?"

A cautious note entered Scott's voice. "I'm testing their computer security programs, if that's what you mean."

"Good, that's exactly what I was hoping."

"Look, Adam, you're a great friend and all, but that information is classified."

"No, no, I don't want anything like that."

"Then, what do you want?"

"I want you to try to break into my SR program."

"What for?"

"For the same reason the government hires you: to see if you can."

"You think you have a hacker?"

"No. It's been acting oddly, and I just want to make sure everything is still secure. With the launch so close, I don't want to take any chances."

"All right," Scott said, "but there *is* the matter of my fee."

Adam didn't even hesitate. "Name it."

"I want my own autographed copy of *Fantasy Quest* the day it hits the market."

Adam smiled. "Done! Anything else?"

"Nope. I figure that will someday be worth enough for me to retire comfortably."

"As if you haven't made enough money on your own."

"My dad always says you can't have too much." He paused. "But, then, he's a rancher, so his vision is a little warped. I asked him once what he'd do if he won the lottery, and he said he'd just keep on ranching until it was all gone."

Adam laughed. "Now I know where you get your sense of humor. So, do you need any information to get started?"

"Adam, Adam, what challenge would there be in that? Figuring it all out is half the fun."

"I suppose. I never got into hacking, myself."

"That's because you were too busy building your own programs to worry about breaking into someone else's."

"Then, what's your excuse? You've created quite a few programs yourself."

Now it was Scott's turn to laugh. "True, but I got into hacking while I was teaching my friend Lucas computers. No better way to train. Lots of great programmers tried their hand at hacking."

"Sounds like I missed out."

"Not really. It shook me up pretty bad when the Army

brass showed up at my house, demanding my head on a platter for breaking into NORAD. I think my father seriously considered handing me over to them right then and there. He might have if I hadn't been sixteen."

"Instead, they hired you to test their security."

"I always did live under a lucky star. By the way, did you ever figure out your glitch?"

"Not exactly. She's still just as out of sync as ever, but she's been very useful."

"How so?"

As he told Scott about the wishing fiasco, it struck Adam how much the Kenzie glitch had taught him about his own program. Without her, he wouldn't have known that characters could be recycled or about the cheat codes until *Fantasy Quest* hit the market. She'd probably saved him a fortune in future lawsuits.

By the time Adam had finished telling about calming Bear Bait and the running water in his cabin, Scott was laughing so hard he could hardly catch his breath.

"Oh man, I wished I'd been there to see your face."

"I felt pretty stupid," Adam admitted. "That's when I began to wonder if it was a good thing or a bad thing. At first, I thought having the cheat codes inside the program might be a great innovation. You know, kind of an every-wish-comes-true sort of thing. Then I realized we don't always make intelligent wishes. Some are downright dangerous."

"Dangerous! How do you figure that?"

"My glitch wished she could light a fire and wound up burning down the whole cabin. In fact, by the time it was all over, she'd started a forest fire that we almost didn't survive."

"Ok, I see your point. The cheat codes had to go."

"Not entirely. I left them in the menu part of the program so that players could still access the fun part of it without putting themselves in danger."

"You know, the more I hear about this program, the more I want to play it," Scott said admiringly. "You've decided to keep your glitch, then?"

The question took Adam by surprise. Had he decided to keep Kenzie? Maybe he had, at that. The whole point of the cabin was so she'd be safe during the winter, after all. "I don't know. I think she might turn out to be more trouble than she's worth," Adam said ruefully.

"I'll get started on your hacking this afternoon and let you know the results in a day or two."

"Thanks, Scott. I appreciate it. Let me know when I can return the favor."

"Don't worry; I will."

His conversation with Scott brought Adam's feelings about the Kenzie glitch into sharp perspective. Even though he treated her like a real person, Adam was very aware that Kenzie was just a complex piece of computer animation. Yet her reactions were as unpredictable and confusing as those of a real, flesh-and-blood woman. He couldn't shake the notion that she might not be a glitch at all. What if she'd been created by the cheat codes instead of a malfunction? Had he wished her into existence?

Scott's question nudged his mind again. So what if he had decided to keep Kenzie? It wasn't like she was any threat to the program. Once the cabin was finished, he'd have plenty of time to concentrate on *Fantasy Quest*. Kenzie wouldn't even question it if he went "hunting" every day, as long as he brought game with him when he returned. He thought about what it would be like to have her there, welcoming him home every night, her smile banishing his loneliness and warming his heart.

Suddenly, he had to see her, to share his joy with her, even if he couldn't tell her the reason. He glanced at his watch. If he set his timer for forty-five minutes, he'd still make his meeting, even if he ran into heavy traffic. In a heartbeat, the timer was set and his gloves in place. Adam smiled in anticipation as he settled the helmet on his head. Then everything went black.

Bear Bait nickered a greeting as Adam blinked his eyes and sat up. Five minutes later, he rode up to the cabin and dismounted. Kenzie was nowhere in sight, though the fox fur was tossed on the top of a stump as if she had just set it down for a moment. The skin felt supple to his touch. She'd obviously spent some time working it this morning. He laid the fur back down and looked around, wondering where she'd gone. It couldn't be far, since her cotton dress and underwear were drying on the rope he'd strung before he left.

Adam grinned. If he'd thought about it, he'd have expected sensible underwear, not these tiny wisps of satin and lace. Though they were nearly worn out from constant wear, they still were the very essence of femininity. His grin became rueful. On the other hand, seeing her underwear was definitely not a good thing. They evoked erotic images he was better off not having. Knowing what was underneath would make even the ugly cotton dress sexy as hell. Now he was going to have to do his best to forget what he'd seen. *Good luck with that!*

Still grinning, Adam turned away. Wherever she was, she wasn't wearing much. His mother's buckskin dress was the only thing missing from her wardrobe. Imagining what was under that was going to be even worse than the underwear. There was only so much temptation a man could take. If he had any intelligence at all, he'd turn around and leave right now before he saw Kenzie and tripped the Sex Hex just by looking at her.

From what Annie had said, Kenzie had just entered the hot pool when he'd come home. With everything that had happened, an hour or more had passed, so she had surely finished bathing by now. He smiled to himself. Knowing his Kenzie glitch, she'd probably gone to check out the chokecherry patch without him. At least he'd remembered to reset it in the cheat codes when he erased Annie from the program.

Adam was conscious of a sting of disappointment. There wouldn't be time to go find her. The berry patch was too far away to get there and back in time for his meeting. He considered leaving the program and going to the menu so he could enter at the site of the old cabin, but he'd never be able to explain how he got there or why he had to leave without her a few minutes later.

Life is full of little disappointments, he told himself. When he came back from seeing the neurologist, he might have even more to celebrate with her. His feeling of well-being and euphoria returned full force. Maybe he'd bring a bottle of wine and tell her Crazy Charlie had given it to him or something.

As long as he was here, he might as well have a good, long soak in the hot pool. It was sure to relax him, and that would make his meeting go better.

Adam skirted the pool and stopped next to the waterfall to strip off his shirt. He dropped it to the ground and kicked off his moccasins. A small sound behind him stopped him in the process of reaching for the button on his pants. He was just starting to turn when two hands gave him a hard shove from behind.

Unable to catch himself, Adam fell forward into the cold water of the pool. He came up sputtering and ready to fight. Flipping the wet hair out of his face, he jerked his head around, looking for his enemy, but there was no one there. Then he caught a flash of movement out of the corner of his eye. He turned just in time to see Kenzie disappear behind the waterfall, wearing nothing but their one and only blanket.

Little bushwhacker! Adam scrambled out of the water, intent on revenge. Icy spray cascaded over him as he stepped through the curtain of water at the edge. Astonished, Adam stopped in his tracks. He'd never been behind the waterfall before. Instead of the rugged rock wall he expected, a cave yawned before him.

A muffled giggle from inside galvanized Adam into action again. She probably didn't know he'd seen her run behind the waterfall. Quietly, he edged his way along the cliff until he reached the entrance. He listened intently for several seconds, but the roar of the falls drowned out any sound from inside the cave.

Figuring a surprise attack was the only way he was going to catch her, he gathered himself and sprang around the corner, effectively blocking the entrance. To his surprise, Kenzie was nowhere to be seen. The cave consisted of a small room with two tunnels branching off of it. Adam scrutinized the floor of the cave, looking for some clue as to which tunnel his quarry was hiding in, but it was impossible to tell. The mist in the air condensed on the floor of the cave, obliterating all signs of footprints. He looked at the tunnel entrances. Which would she take? It was doubtful that she had gone very far into either of them. The only light came through the waterfall from outside and was too dim to penetrate far down either passage.

As he stood there, studying the situation, a sound came to his ears. The echo of rock clattering against rock was barely discernible over the roar of the water behind him, but it was enough to tell him where she was. With a smug grin on his face, he started forward. The tunnel was darker than he'd expected, and he stopped at the entrance to allow his eyes to adjust to the darkness.

"Honestly, Adam, you are too easy!"

Realizing he'd been duped, he whirled around just in time to see Kenzie give a saucy wave and duck outside again. The little wretch had been right inside the entrance all the time.

This time, though, Kenzie had made a fatal mistake. She hadn't reckoned with his long legs and determination. He caught up with her on the ledge of rock between the two pools.

Kenzie glanced back over her shoulder, her eyes widening when she saw how close he was. She feinted to the right when he reached for her then twisted to the left at the last minute and jumped into the hot pool.

Adam was left standing there, holding the damp blanket in his hand, as Kenzie swam to the other side of the pool.

"Ha," he said, tossing the blanket aside. "I've got you now. You're trapped like a rat."

She gave him a smug look. "You aren't coming in after me."

"You think not?"

"Getting even with me isn't worth destroying your buckskins," she pointed out. "You told me yourself that the mineral water would ruin them, and you don't have a spare."

Adam gazed at her for a moment then reached for the button on his pants.

Kenzie sucked in her breath. "You wouldn't dare!"

"I've never had much use for modesty," Adam admitted as he stripped off his pants and tossed them onto the bank before stepping down into the hot pool. "Being naked doesn't bother me at all."

"If you're trying to scare me, it won't work." She stood up and started toward him. "I'm not afraid of you."

Adam struggled to keep his eyes focused on her face as he gave her his best sinister look. "Maybe you should be."

"I don't think so." Kenzie stopped a few feet from him as though daring him to do something about it. "Why would you be dangerous all of a sudden?"

"There's the little matter of a sneak attack."

"That wasn't a sneak attack!" she said indignantly.

"Could have fooled me." He took a step forward and put his hands on her shoulders. "Come here."

Kenzie came willingly, her eyes shining expectantly as he drew her near. "What is it you want?" she asked in a husky voice that sent rivers of lust coursing through his veins like molten steel. She ran her hand up his chest and gazed up at him with a Mona Lisa smile.

Adam felt like a starving man at a smorgasbord. He didn't know what to focus on, the intricate patterns she was tracing on his skin or her naked breasts just inches from his chest.

Distracted, he missed the mischievous twinkle in her eye. He was completely unprepared as she hooked her foot behind his knee and jerked. Adam went down like a felled tree, and she jumped away with a giggle.

"Now *that*," she said when he came up for air, "was a sneak attack."

"You're going to regret that." He started toward her menacingly.

Kenzie dove under the water and came up on the far side

of the pool, laughing. "Not if you can't catch me."

"We'll see about that," he said and disappeared under the water.

They chased each other around the pool, laughing and splashing, cavorting like two adolescent otters. Kenzie neatly evaded every trap Adam set for her, spinning away just as he got there or throwing water in his face so she could make an escape.

After one particularly close encounter, she surfaced near the middle of the pool. Adam was nowhere to be seen. She quickly scanned the water around her, but not so much as a ripple betrayed his presence.

She squealed as the water directly behind her erupted, and Adam wrapped his long arms around her.

"I've got you now." His voice caressed her ear. "Revenge is mine."

"What are you going to do?"

"Torture, I think."

She gave a delighted shiver as the strong arms pulled her closer until her back was pressed against the rock-hard body behind her. "What kind of torture?"

"The best kind." He touched his lips to the tender spot where her neck and shoulder met. "Long and slow," Adam murmured as he lifted her wet hair out of the way and trailed kisses down the back of her neck. "I plan to show no mercy." His teeth grazed her ear lobe, then he turned her to face him. "No matter how much you beg."

She put her arms around his neck. "Is that a promise?" she asked in a low, sultry voice.

"You can bank on it."

Kenzie stood on her tiptoes and pulled his head down for a kiss. "So, get started," she whispered against his lips.

Her kiss was sweetly erotic as she pressed her lush body against him. Adam obligingly lifted her to his level, and she wrapped her legs around his waist.

The hot water swirled around them, caressing their skin as

their tongues danced together. Adam couldn't get enough. He wanted to touch her everywhere at once, and he wanted her to touch him.

Adam hardly remembered crossing the pool to where the cliff formed a natural couch. The water had flowed over the surface until it looked as though it had been shaped and smoothed by a giant hand to fit the contours of the human body. It became their lovers' bower as he gently laid Kenzie against the smooth surface and gazed down at her with smoldering eyes. "This will teach you to dump me in the water."

She gave him a slow sexy smile. "Do your worst."

"My worst is very, very good," Adam murmured against her lips.

Kenzie sucked in her breath as his lips began a sensuous journey downward. Telling himself to go slow, to savor every second, he traced the sensitive cord of her throat with tender kisses, sipped water from the small hollow at the base of her throat and kissed his way across her chest.

Adam's goal was the tips of her breasts that lay submerged just below the surface of the water. He wanted to bring her desire to a fever pitch that matched his own, to make her want him as badly as he wanted her. The nearer he came, the more she squirmed beneath his questing lips. Kenzie's hands tightened in his hair, and her breathing accelerated as he made first contact with his tongue.

"Oh," she gasped as he paid homage to first one breast and then the other. With a warm, wet finger, she traced his ear as she slid her foot up the inside of his thigh. She smiled as a tremor ran through him. Kenzie continued her sensual onslaught, touching here, kissing there, tracing every part of him she could reach with her hands and feet. His final undoing was when she ran her tongue around the shell of his ear.

A groan came from deep inside, and he raised his head to look at her. With one hand, he captured both of her wrists and held them above her head. "Do you have any idea what that does to me?" he asked in a voice thick with passion.

Kenzie smiled and moved sensuously beneath him. "Why don't you show me?" she whispered.

With another deep groan he buried himself in her willing body and closed his eyes against the exquisite pleasure. Willing himself to stay still, he tried to get his rampaging desire under control, to prolong the moment for them both. But Kenzie would have none of it. With a few calculated movements of her body she drove all thought of restraint out of his mind.

At first, the buoyant water made them awkward and unsynchronized, but they soon found the rhythm and moved together in the ancient dance of love. Higher and higher they spiraled, reaching the top only to discover another higher plateau. On and on they went, far beyond the limits either had ever thought possible. At last they reached the ultimate pinnacle and burst into a thousand brightly colored fragments that drifted back to earth, mixing and blending together until it was impossible to tell where one began and the other ended.

Adam wrapped his arms around Kenzie and rolled onto his back in the rock depression then settled lower into the warm waters of the spring as their breathing slowed.

Kenzie was practically purring. "That was incredible," she said. "If I'd known it was going to be like that, I'd have seduced you sooner."

"Is that what this was, a seduction?"

"More like spur-of-the-moment inspiration. If I'd left it up to you, we'd have never gotten around to it. Am I forgiven?"

Adam kissed the top of her head. "What do you think?"

Kenzie sighed as she snuggled her head into the hollow of his shoulder. "I think we should try it again soon, just to make sure it wasn't some kind of fluke."

Adam chuckled and closed his eyes. He absently stroked her back as he considered what had just happened. The Sex Hex was obviously a bust. When he'd tested it with Dawn, he'd fully expected it to shut the program down, and it had, probably because of the cheat codes. This time, his animal instincts had taken over, and he hadn't given the Sex Hex a thought. Today was the first time it had actually been put to the test, and it had failed miserably.

Not that he minded, really. In fact, the primitive male deep inside was very, very glad it hadn't worked. Still, there was no way he could let *Fantasy Quest* go out on the market like this. The porn industry would turn it into a triple-X-rated product in a matter of days, and *Fantasy Quest*'s image would be irrevocably tarnished. It could take months of intensive work to find out what was wrong and to fix it.

Two facts were blindingly clear. First of all, *Fantasy Quest* probably wasn't going to be ready in time for the February launch; the delay would probably cost him millions. Secondly, he could make love to Kenzie any time he wanted. Adam smiled. Life was good.

Chapter 27

Kenzie drifted along in a warm cocoon of bliss. She hadn't planned on pushing Adam into the water, and the last thing she had expected was to wind up where they were now. She'd only meant to tease him a bit, not turn him into a sexual dynamo. She smiled and snuggled closer. Not that she was complaining, mind you. Not when she'd just experienced the best sex of her life.

This world might not be of her own choosing, but there were some very nice compensations. She was cuddled up to the best of them right now.Kenzie tipped her head back and looked up at him. "Happy?"

"Mm-huh. How about you?"

"Totally." She kissed his chest then reached up and traced his collarbone with her finger. "Why did we wait so long, anyway?"

Adam was silent as though considering his answer. "Well," he said finally, "I seem to remember a fiancé somewhere in the picture."

Kenzie shrugged. "Not in this picture. Brad is 150 years in the future, Adam. He doesn't even exist here."

"So, it's okay if you sleep with both of us?"

"I've been *sleeping* with you for the last month. What you mean is having sex, and I'm not having sex with Brad."

"Are you saying you never had sex with him?"

"No, I'm not saying that, not that it's any of your business. What I meant is that I'll never have to choose between you, because you'll never be in the same time."

"That's convenient."

Kenzie sat up. "No, Adam, that's reality. I'm being honest with you. I know you want me to say I'd choose you over Brad, but the truth is you're not in competition with each other. He's part of my past, one I'll probably never be able to return to."

"Would you?"

"Would I what?"

"Choose me over Brad?"

Kenzie made a disgusted sound. "Haven't you been listening? It doesn't matter, because I'm never going to have to make that choice. You're both incredible men in your own setting, but Brad would be as out of place here as you would be in my world."

Adam stared at her, his expression unreadable as though he couldn't quite figure her out. Suddenly, he looked down at his wrist. "Damn. I've got to go."

Kenzie blinked in surprise. It had looked for all the world as if he was glancing at a watch. "Go? Go where?"

But he had already climbed out of the hot pool. "I'll see you tonight," he called over his shoulder as he scooped up his pants and disappeared through the mist of the waterfall.

"Adam, wait." Kenzie scrambled out of the pool to follow, but by the time she'd wrapped the now-soggy blanket around her, Adam had his pants on and was skirting the freshwater pond. As she watched, he pulled his shirt over his head and broke into a jog.

Kenzie fought down a feeling of panic. He was angry. She couldn't let him leave with this unresolved between them. Adam didn't understand that he was asking her the impossible. In her mind, it wasn't a matter of choosing between the two men as much as it was choosing between her own time and this one. People still died of pneumonia and simple infections here. What if she got a cavity? The tooth would rot out, and she'd wind up having to have it pulled without anesthetic. As much as she cared about Adam, she wasn't sure she was ready to commit to staying here the rest of her life.

It took Kenzie several minutes to retrieve her leather dress from the bush where she'd hung it and put it on. By then, Adam was nearly to the cabin. "Wait!" she yelled. Then she broke into a run. Either he couldn't hear her over the roar of the waterfall, or he was ignoring her. He mounted Bear Bait and turned toward the trail.

Kenzie briefly considered crossing the pond to get there faster, but she quickly discarded the idea. It would take her longer to strip down and swim across than it would to go around. Besides, in spite of their recent intimacy, she didn't feel comfortable running after Adam stark naked.

By the time she'd rounded the pool, the distance between them was actually less than before. Maybe if she followed him until he was out of earshot of the waterfall, he'd hear her and stop. Refusing to let herself think about the fact that he could be ignoring her, Kenzie sprinted to the trail. A painful stitch in her side slowed her down, but she finally managed to reach the top of the hill only a few minutes behind him.

There was no sign of Bear Bait or Adam. How could he have disappeared so fast? Kenzie bent over and rested her hands on her thighs as she tried to catch her breath. Her legs were shaking like so much gelatin, and her heart felt as if it might burst out of her chest at any moment. Gradually, though, the rasp of her breathing slowed, and her heart settled down to a more normal pace.

At last she straightened and stared down the trail, feeling frustrated and helpless. "Damn you, Adam Johnson!" she shouted, knowing full well he couldn't hear her. "Why do you have to be so blasted…male?" It didn't make a lot of sense, but at least it vented some of her aggravation.

Kenzie was just turning to go when a sound from nearby brought her head around in astonishment. She listened intently for several minutes. There it was again, the unmistakable clank of a chain. Creeping forward, she followed the sound to a nearby thicket, where trampled grass formed a faint trail leading through the brush.

Carefully pulling branches aside, Kenzie made her way through the bushes until she found herself in a small clearing. She frowned in confusion. The sound she had heard came from the picket chain attached to Bear Bait's leg. What in the world was Bear Bait doing here, and where was Adam?

Then she saw him, and everything else went out of her head. He lay on the ground, so still she thought at first he must have been thrown. Then she shook her head. *No, of course not. He dismounted and picketed Bear Bait first.* With her heart pounding, Kenzie knelt on the ground next to him. Though she examined him closely, she could find no sign of injury, not even a bump on the head. With worry clogging her throat, Kenzie tried everything she knew to wake him up, but to no avail. The mysterious sleeping sickness had returned. He must have felt it coming on and had the wherewithal to picket Bear Bait before he passed out.

As she worked to revive him, she suddenly realized she was crying. "Come on, Adam, you can't leave me here like this, not after what just happened between us." At last she sat back on her heels. Letting him lie here until he decided to wake up was not an option. This illness, whatever it was, needed to be treated.

Buffalo Horn! He'd know what to do. The problem was she had no idea where the Indian camp was or how to get Adam there. She'd never be able to get him onto Bear Bait by herself, and she didn't really know how to build a travois or how to hook it to the horse. "Where is 911 when you need it?" she muttered.

"Funny place to take a nap," said a familiar voice behind her.

Startled, Kenzie looked over her shoulder then sagged in relief. "Crazy Charlie! Boy, am I glad to see you."

"I'm a mite tickled to see you too. Been sorta lonely lately. Thought I'd come by for a visit." He glanced down at Adam. "You and Whiskey Jug have a fight?"

Kenzie frowned. "No. At least, not really."

"Then how come Whiskey Jug's sleepin' up here instead of down by the cabin?"

"There's something wrong with him. We have to get him to Buffalo Horn. Do you know where the Indian camp is?"

"Yep." Crazy Charlie narrowed his eyes thoughtfully.

"Leastways, I think I do. I can find 'em, anyway." He turned and headed out of the clearing.

"Wait!" Kenzie cried. "Where are you going?"

"To cut two poles for the travois. You best go find a blanket or hide to stretch across them."

A moment later, Kenzie heard the sound of him chopping nearby and gave a sigh of relief. *Who needs 911 when you have Crazy Charlie?*

Adam drummed his fingers on the arms of his chair then glanced at his watch for the umpteenth time. Twenty minutes he'd been sitting here waiting for the doctors to return. About ten minutes ago, Annie had disappeared too, murmuring something about calling home to let them know where she was. She'd been gone too long for a simple phone call. Maybe she'd decided to take a bathroom break while she was at it. Without her constant chatter, boredom had set in rapidly.

He'd been fifteen minutes late for his meeting, but it had all gone well otherwise. Everything was online for the launch. The board was happy; stockholders were happy; even his employees were happy. He'd decided not to drop the bomb about the Sex Hex. After all, he hadn't even attempted to fix it. For all he knew, the solution might be as simple as the one for the cheat codes. The thought of fixing it had him grinning from ear to ear. The obvious place to start was by reenacting this afternoon's tryst. He was still smiling to himself when the door opened, and Annie came in with the two doctors.

Dr. Dowie and Dr. Frank were complete physical opposites. Dr. Dowie was tall and lean, while Dr. Frank bore a strong resemblance to the cookie elves on TV commercials. Frank was a friend of Dowie's, who just happened to be one of the top neurologists in the West. Adam had never met the man before today, but he'd liked him on sight. Right now, the two doctors were practically vibrating with excitement.

"So," Adam said, trying to be nonchalant. "What's going

on with my leg?"

Dr. Dowie sat down on the corner of the desk. "To be honest, Adam, we don't really know, but whatever it is seems to be repairing your damaged nerves."

"Repairing? You mean like rebuilding?"

"We can't be sure, but that's exactly what it looks like!" Dr. Frank was practically beaming. "It reminds me a bit of the results we've had stimulating muscles using electrodes, but that's been on patients whose muscles haven't had time to atrophy. I've never seen anything like this. Without looking at your records, I would never have guessed you'd been paralyzed for ten years."

"Wait a minute," Adam said. "Are you telling me the muscles in my legs have changed?"

Dr. Dowie nodded. "If I didn't know better, I'd think you'd been doing a strenuous workout every day."

Adam thought about all the work he'd been doing on the cabin in *Beta Quest*. His brain had almost certainly been sending messages to his legs, but the damage to his spinal cord should have stopped the nerve impulses dead before they ever got there. "What about my spine?"

"We don't know yet," Dr. Frank told him. "There wasn't time for many tests this afternoon, and it will take a while to get everything I need set up here. I'd like to run a full battery the day after tomorrow, if that's all right with you."

"Sure. Whatever you want. I just... This is all pretty hard to grasp."

"The important question is, will he be able to walk again?" Annie asked in her usual direct manner.

The two doctors exchanged a glance, then Dowie shrugged. "It's too early to know at this point, but I wouldn't say it was impossible."

Annie let out a loud whoop and gave Adam a hug. "I knew it!"

"Calm down, Annie," Adam said as she continued to dance around. "It wasn't even a definite *maybe*." But he couldn't quite keep the grin off his face or the exultation out of his voice.

They spent several more minutes making arrangements for the tests and discussing the astonishing turn of events. Annie was still bubbling as Adam drove her home. He gave up trying to persuade her that she was jumping the gun a bit and just enjoyed her optimistic view of the future. "There you are," he said, pulling his pickup to the curb in front of Annie's house. "Home sweet home."

"Service with a smile, as always," Annie said as she climbed out and shut the door. She glanced at the truck in the driveway then put her folded arms on the window of the pickup. "Todd's home. Are you sure you don't want to come in and tell him your news?"

"I'll let you do it. I have a ton of work to do if I'm going to spend an entire day being poked and prodded."

"All work and no play will make Adam a dull boy."

"Better dull than broke."

"Okay, then, go play with your computer. I'm still expecting you for dinner Friday night."

"I'll remember."

"I know you will, because I'm sending Todd to pick you up!" Annie pushed away from the pickup. "Remember to call me the day after tomorrow and let me know how the tests went."

"Will do, and Annie? Thanks for going with me."

She lifted a hand and waved goodbye as he pulled away.

Adam cranked up his music. Damn, but he felt good. He was almost afraid to let himself hope, but it was impossible not to. He wanted to shout it to the heavens or plaster it on billboards across town. The image of such a billboard brought a smile to his face. The truth was what he really wanted to do was share it with someone special: with Kenzie.

Adam parked his pickup, took the elevator to his floor, and was fitting the key in the lock when his phone began to vibrate. He unlocked the door and fumbled to get his phone out before it went to voicemail. Scott Martin's face flashed on the screen as he rolled across the threshold and shut the door behind him.

"Hi, Scott, what's up?"

"Bad news, I'm afraid. Someone's breached your firewall."

"Damn! I thought *Fantasy Quest's* protection was foolproof—"

"No, not *Fantasy Quest*. It resisted everything I threw at it. The problem is with your beta program."

"*Beta Quest?*"

"Yeah, it wasn't easy, but I finally managed to get in. That's not the worst of it, though."

"No?"

"Someone had been there before me."

Adam frowned. "Could you tell how they got in?"

"No, and I don't know who it was, either, but I'm working on that."

"How are you going to figure that out?"

Scott chuckled. "Hey, you're not the only Boy Wonder when it comes to computers, you know. I've just turned my attention in different directions. I'll get to the bottom of it eventually. So how are things going with your glitch?"

Adam couldn't help the sappy grin that covered his face. "Pretty well, although she crashed another one of my programs."

"Oh? How did she do that?"

"I'm not really sure. To be honest, I'm not even sure it was working properly in the first place. When I tested it out, the result I got could have just as easily been caused by the cheat codes."

"You mean you expected certain results, so you got them?"

"Exactly. I even thought for a while that the cheat codes might have created my glitch."

"But now you don't."

"No, she's too irrational to have come from my imagination."

"Oh?" Scott sounded surprised. "I thought we agreed last time that women's thought patterns were incomprehensible."

"True, but her basic intellect would be based on mine, right?"

"I guess so."

"Well, I finally asked her where she came from. Know what she said?"

"Outer space?"

"That's at least in the realm of possibility. She thinks she's traveled back in time! There's no way my subconscious would come up with something as crazy as time travel."

There was a long silence on the other end of the line. "Time travel isn't necessarily crazy. Didn't you ever study Einstein?"

"Theoretically, sure, but no one with any sense really believes it."

"I'll have to introduce you to my friends Brianna and Lucas Daniels sometime," Scott said with a soft chuckle.

"Lucas… The one who got you into hacking?"

"In a manner of speaking," Scott said. "I see your point, though. Your glitch shouldn't believe in something you thought impossible."

"Wait a minute," Adam said. "What if the glitch was put there by the hacker?"

"Wouldn't he have to have the basics of your programming to add something that complex to it?"

"I suppose so, and if he had that, he wouldn't need to hack into it in the first place."

"Unless… Of course. Why didn't I think of that before?" Scott said, excitement coloring his voice. "What if he created the glitch unintentionally? What if it had been created by the link itself? Is that possible?"

Adam pondered this for a moment. "You know, I'm not sure. The cheat codes are certainly capable of creating a character. They've done it before. To tell you the truth, after everything that's happened with this program, I wouldn't discount any possibility."

"It would explain why you've never been able to delete her from the programming."

"And why I could never change her."

"Anyway, it sounds like she's been more of a help than a threat."

"True, but she still represents an enigma, and I don't like enigmas, especially when they're in my program." Adam toyed with a paperclip on his desk. "Does your aunt still work for the IRS?"

"For now, she does, though she's planning on retiring this spring."

"Could you have her look up someone for me?"

"Adam, old buddy, she can't give out confidential information any more than I can."

"I just want to check out a name to see if he really exists."

Scott was quiet for a moment, considering. "I guess it wouldn't hurt to ask. Who did you have in mind?"

"Brad Marriot. I did a search and found seventeen of them."

"And you want me to narrow it down for you?"

"Right."

"Ok, what do you know about him?"

"He just graduated from college last spring with a degree of some kind, so I'm guessing there are student loans as well as college records."

"What is his degree in?" Scott asked.

"Computers, though I don't know what field specifically."

"Anything else?"

Adam thought for a moment. "Only that he sounds like a control freak, but that's not going to help much."

"All right, I'll give her a call and get back to you."

"I appreciate it. I owe you, man."

Scott chuckled again. "And I don't ever intend to let you forget it. Talk to you soon."

As he hung up, Adam suddenly realized he hadn't told Scott his news. It would have been interesting to see what the other man thought about the possible connection between *Beta Quest* and nerve damage reversal.

Adam sighed. Somehow, the edge had worn off his excitement. The need to see Kenzie was greater than ever, but the uncertainty of who the hacker was and where he'd come from had ruined the mood.

With a deep sense of foreboding, Adam put the helmet on his head, and everything went black.

Chapter 28

"What the hell?"

The loud exclamation brought Kenzie's head around with a jerk. "Charlie, stop," she said as she saw Adam sitting up on the travois. "He's awake!"

She slid off Bear Bait's back, where she'd been perched behind Crazy Charlie, then rushed back to the travois just as Adam started to stand up. "Oh no, you don't," she said, pushing him back down. "You're not getting up until Buffalo Horn says you can."

Adam glanced around the empty mountain meadow. "Buffalo Horn?"

"We're headed to the Indian village. You're sick, Adam, and he needs to look at you." She chewed her lip. "Though I don't know if he'll know anything about this."

"There's nothing wrong with me." He struggled to get up again.

Kenzie put her hands on his chest and pushed him back down. "Adam, please. This sleeping you do isn't normal. I'm afraid you have a disease called narcolepsy."

"Oh, for pity's sake. I'm just a deep sleeper, that's all."

"No, Adam, it's more than that. Nobody sleeps that deeply. I did everything I could to wake you up. You never even stirred."

"I'm not riding to the Indian village on a travois. I can walk."

Kenzie shook her head. "I'd feel better if you stayed where you are. There's no sense in taking chances."

"And I'd feel better if I didn't have to lie back here like an invalid."

"Somebody has to. All three of us can't very well ride Bear Bait at the same time. We have to stop so he can rest every fifteen or twenty minutes anyway."

"All right, then, how about if you ride back here with me?" He wiggled his eyebrows suggestively.

"Oh, I don't think—"

"Might as well, missy," Crazy Charlie put in. "I reckon it's the only way yer gonna keep him on that travois."

"That's right," Adam said, rolling on his side and patting the blanket next to him. "Come on now. You wouldn't refuse a sick man his medicine, would you?"

"Since when am I your medicine?"

"Since this morning in the hot pool," he murmured. "You cured everything that ailed me." The look he gave her just about melted her bones.

Heat spread from her toes to her hairline, three parts embarrassment and seven parts arousal. "All right," she said as she sat on the edge of the travois, "but not because I think it will make you feel any better."

"On the contrary," he said with a slow, sexy smile, "I feel better already."

"You two all settled back there?" Crazy Charlie called out.

"Not quite." Adam raised an eyebrow. "It sticks in my mind we did this once before."

Kenzie nodded. "This is how Jesse Three Dogs got us to the village the first time."

"How exactly did we both fit?"

Kenzie felt herself coloring again. "You don't remember?"

He shrugged apologetically. "I was asleep."

"Well, you were lying down flat."

Adam obligingly flopped over on his back. "Like this?"

"Right. And I just kind of fit myself in alongside you," Kenzie said, snuggling down next to him.

"I see." Adam put his arm around her. "Are you comfortable?"

"Mm-hm. How about you?"

"Definitely. All right, Charlie, we're ready."

The travois started with a slight jerk, and Kenzie settled

back against Adam's shoulder.

"This is nice," he said.

"Yes, it is," she agreed. "It sort of reminds me of relaxing in my grandmother's hammock when I was a kid."

"Speaking of relaxing, how was your day at the spa?"

"Great. I didn't quite have the courage to try a mud bath, but everything else was top notch." She tipped her head and gave him a saucy look. "I especially enjoyed the massage."

A smile flickered across his face. "Your massager was all right, then?"

"He's called a masseuse, and he was fabulous."

"Is that so?" His voice was low and husky and sent lightning bolts of sensation through her. Time to get some emotional distance. There was a difference between what you could do in the privacy of your own hot pool and what was seemly here with Crazy Charlie less than ten feet from them. Playing huggy-bear-kissy-face was definitely out of the question.

"You know, Adam, I didn't mean to make you mad back there at the hot pool."

"What makes you think I was mad?"

She craned her head around to look at him. "What makes me... Adam, we were right in the middle of an argument when you made some goofy excuse and left."

"It wasn't a goofy excuse, and we weren't arguing."

"Could have fooled me. Where were you headed in such an all-fired hurry, anyway?"

"I wasn't in a hurry."

"Oh, right, that's why I couldn't catch up with you. It looked like you were late for... Wait a minute. You felt a sleep attack coming on, didn't you?"

Adam raised an eyebrow. "A sleep attack?"

"You didn't want me to see you go into your sleep coma, so you left in a hurry before it hit."

"You have a vivid imagination."

"Do I?" Kenzie said, refusing to let it go. "Then, why did

you hide yourself and Bear Bait in that thicket?"

Adam frowned. "How did you find me, anyway?"

"I tried to stop you, but you didn't hear me, so I followed you. When I got to the top of the hill, I heard Bear Bait's picket chain rattling, so I went to investigate."

"Why were you trying to stop me?"

"To apologize."

"For what? I keep telling you we weren't arguing."

"Oh, come on, Adam. That was hardly a friendly little discussion."

"You mean about choosing between Bradley and me?"

"It's Brad, and yes, that's exactly what I mean."

"I thought you didn't want to talk about it."

Kenzie gave an exasperated sigh. "I don't, but it's obvious you don't understand where I'm coming from. It really doesn't have anything to do with you and Brad, you know."

"It doesn't?"

Kenzie didn't even need to see Adam's incredulous expression to know he found her statement a tad ridiculous. "Okay, yes, it does, but not as much as you think. See, I wouldn't be choosing between you and Brad as much as I'd be choosing between the nineteenth century and the twenty-first." She shivered. "I don't think I want to spend the rest of my life here, no matter how great some of the compensations are."

Adam was silent for a moment. "What compensations?"

"The people here are great." She tipped her face up and gave him a steady look. "And some are nearly perfect," she said softly.

"This is as far as I go," Crazy Charlie announced as the travois stopped with a jolt.

Startled, Adam unwound himself from Kenzie and rolled out of the travois. "Why? What's going on?"

Charlie dismounted and reached up to unfasten his rifle and scabbard from the saddle. "Nothin's goin' on. Blue Sky Woman and me had words last time I was here. I don't much want to tangle with her again."

"Blue Sky Woman!" Adam looked surprised. "I've never heard her say a sharp word to anyone."

Crazy Charlie took off his hat and scratched his head self-consciously. "Never said they was harsh words. Fact is, she's got her heart set on a weddin'."

"Why, Charlie, you old dog. Have you been playing fast and loose with her affections?"

Crazy Charlie's face turned red. "Ain't never touched her that way. I was friends with her husband, see. When he died, she took it into her head that he'd want me to take care of her. Can't quite figure out why."

"Probably because she knows what a wonderful person you are," Kenzie said, rising from the travois. "Maybe you should give it a chance. You might change your mind."

Crazy Charlie shook his head. "That sort of thing is for you young'uns, not an old coot like me. Besides," he said over his shoulder as he walked away, "I ain't ready to settle down."

"I'll be damned," Adam said as they watched Crazy Charlie disappear into the woods, back the way they came.

"What's wrong with Blue Sky Woman?" Kenzie wanted to know. "Is she old and ugly or just bossy?"

"Blue Sky Woman is about thirty-five or forty, I'd guess. She's sweet tempered, quiet, and rather pretty."

"Another of the tribal beauties?"

"She doesn't look like Beautiful Dawn, if that's what you mean."

Kenzie snorted. "Who does?" She looked up at him quizzically. "Why do you suppose she wants Crazy Charlie? I mean, he is half crazy."

Adam shrugged. "Your guess is as good as mine. The tribe believes there is strong magic in such people; maybe she figures he'll last longer than her first husband." He glanced toward the trail again. "I expect we'll find the village just beyond those trees."

"Let's go, then."

Adam grabbed Bear Bait's reins, then stuck his foot in the

stirrup, and vaulted into the saddle. Once he was settled, he took his foot out of the stirrup and reached his hand down to help Kenzie.

"Just about perfect, huh?" he said as she swung up behind him.

She grinned against his back. "Of course. Don't you think Buffalo Horn and Red Blanket are amazing?"

"Jesse Three Dogs too," Adam added after a slight pause.

"And Eagle Feather."

"Not to mention Beautiful Dawn."

Kenzie's grin deepened. "You're right. I wasn't going to mention her."

Adam chuckled. "Now, why? I thought you were grateful to her for getting Eagle Feather out of the way."

"I got rid of him myself," she said primly. "Beautiful Dawn's part in it was carefully plotted by me, I'll have you know."

"Is that so?"

"Yes, it is."

"You won't mind if he's riding out to greet us, then."

"No, of course not. I wouldn't mind at all." She peeked around Adam's broad back uncertainly. "Is he really?"

Adam laughed outright at that. "He and half a dozen other men are riding this way, but I suspect they're going out hunting rather than coming to meet us." He called out something in Arapaho.

When Eagle Feather replied, Adam chuckled and shot back an answer that had all of the other men laughing. They were all still laughing as they rode away.

"What was that all about?" Kenzie asked.

"They just wanted to know whether we'd seen any game or not."

"Sure, and that's why they all laughed, right?"

Adam shrugged. "I guess so."

"Oh, I get it now. It's a man thing. I'm supposed to pretend like I believe you were talking about elk and moose and forget about it, right?"

"Smart girl!"

"Men: They're all the same, no matter what century they come from," she grumbled.

"Looks like you'll get your chance for revenge. Unless I'm much mistaken, the women are coming out to meet us."

"Really?" Kenzie peered around him again as they rode into the village. Sure enough, the women were calling greetings and waving.

"They're all glad to see us."

"I'm glad to see them, too, but it's not like I'm going to get even for whatever you said to the men."

"Why not?"

"The only one I can talk to is Beautiful Dawn. Of course, I guess we could sit and trade stories about you and Eagle Feather."

"Uh, I'm not sure that's a good idea."

Kenzie grinned to herself as she heard the consternation in his voice. "Really?" She couldn't resist the temptation to tease him a little. "Why not?"

"It... I just don't think it's a good idea."

With a start, Kenzie realized Adam was afraid of what Beautiful Dawn would tell her. A vivid image of what had transpired at the hot pool flashed through her mind. For all she knew, Adam and Dawn had been together there too. Even if they hadn't, they'd almost certainly been intimate at one time or another. With sudden clarity Kenzie knew she'd far rather remain ignorant of what had gone on between them.

"No, probably not," she said. "Beautiful Dawn strikes me as the jealous type. Even though she's obviously smitten with Eagle Feather, she still might be holding a grudge for me leaving with you. The last time I got on her bad side, I almost got eaten by a bear."

"That's not what I—" Adam was cut off as the women surrounded them with obvious excitement. "Whoa, Bear Bait," he said trying to calm the nervous animal.

The crowd of women parted as Red Blanket came out of Buffalo Horn's tipi and hurried toward them. "Keenzie, Wheesky Jug!" She seemed to be in the grip of some strong emotion as she gazed up at them, tears sparkling in her eyes.

"Red Blanket, what is it?" Kenzie asked, instantly concerned.

"You live," she said simply.

"She is happy to see you," Beautiful Dawn said. "We thought you had died in the fire. Jesse Three Dogs went to your cabin."

"And found it burned to the ground," Adam murmured. "So that's what Eagle Feather meant."

"What?" Kenzie asked.

"He said it was good to see us among the living."

She looked at him in surprise. "That doesn't seem very funny to me."

"That's not what they were laughing at."

"Somehow I don't think it was about elk and moose, either."

"No. It was sort of in the way of warning Eagle Feather off. I was afraid he'd try to go after you again."

"All right, buster, fess up. What exactly did you say to them?"

He scratched the side of his nose self-consciously. "I told them it would take more than living with a female grizzly to kill Whiskey Jug Johnson."

There was a long moment of silence. "A female grizzly, huh?"

"It was supposed to make Eagle Feather think twice about picking up his suit. I didn't really mean it."

"I see."

Beautiful Dawn drew herself to her full height and glared up at him. "Eagle Feather has no use for another wife. One is plenty for him."

"You got married?" Kenzie squeaked.

Beautiful Dawn's face relaxed into a happy smile. "Yes,

Eagle Feather is my husband."

"Oh, Beautiful Dawn, I'm so happy for you!" Kenzie said as she slid off the horse. "I wish I could have been here for the wedding."

Red Blanket asked for an explanation of their conversation and Beautiful Dawn interpreted for her. The old woman turned a brilliant smile on Kenzie. "Keenzie and Wheesky Jug next wedding."

"Well..."

Red Blanket waved aside her protest. "I say. It happen."

"Don't I get a say in this?" Adam protested.

All three women looked up at him as though he'd grown another head. Then Beautiful Dawn shook her head and turned to Kenzie. "Are you sure you want him?"

"I don't know," Kenzie said. "Can you believe he called me a female grizzly?"

Beautiful Dawn shook her head. "Adam does not deserve you."

"You're probably right," Kenzie agreed. "But never mind that. I want to hear all about your wedding. I'm sure it was wonderful."

Beautiful Dawn smiled. "Yes, I tell." The two women linked arms and strolled away, with the others clustered around and everyone chattering like a pack of chipmunks.

Adam watched in confusion as the women walked away. How had he become the bad guy? One minute, Kenzie hadn't even wanted to talk to Beautiful Dawn, and now they were best friends. And she said men were impossible to understand. Shaking his head, he went to find Buffalo Horn and Jesse Three Dogs. At least Kenzie had forgotten about his supposed narcolepsy. He was going to have to do a better job of hiding his body in the future.

Chapter 29

"You're so beautiful," Adam murmured as he trailed kisses down the side of Kenzie's neck and tasted the hollow at the base of her throat. He heard her swift intake of breath as his teeth grazed her collar bone.

"Oh, Adam, what you do to me." Kenzie's breathless whisper went straight through him.

He straightened and smiled as he gently traced the curve of her face with his hand. "Tell me," he said.

"You turn my knees to rubber," she said.

"Rubber knees." He kissed her forehead. "And…?"

Her eyes drifted closed. "And you make my blood boil."

"Boiling blood." He kissed her eyelids. "Anything else?"

Her arms encircled his neck, and she melted against him. "I want you so bad I can taste it."

"Mmm, taste." He kissed the corner of her mouth. "That one is the best of all," he whispered against her lips. They came together in a magical kiss that rocked them both with its intensity. With his left hand resting on the swell of her hip, Adam began a slow ascent up her rib cage with his right. His thumb grazed the tip of her breast through the thin fabric of her shirt, and he felt it harden. Kenzie's moan vibrated against his mouth as she pushed her breast more fully into his hand. Desire rose within him, hot and insistent. He reached for the buttons on her shirt.

Then everything went black.

"Damn!" Adam pulled his helmet off and glared at his computer monitor. No matter how he played it out, or with whom, the program shut down the minute anything got the least bit interesting. The Sex Hex was working just fine now.

He glanced at his watch. Three hours he'd spent on this, and he was no closer to figuring out why the Sex Hex had failed in *Beta Quest* than he had been when he'd started. The only thing he'd accomplished so far was to make himself crazy. He'd never been so sexually frustrated in his entire life.

The sound of the doorbell brought his head around in surprise. "Oh, great, company! Just what I need." He set the helmet aside and peeled off his gloves.

"Hold your horses," he called as the doorbell sounded again. Adam wheeled himself over to the door and unlocked it. "Come on in, Annie."

"Either you're not using the security camera," came a deep male voice, "or you need glasses. There's no way you could think I was my wife."

"Todd!" Adam said in surprise as the door opened, and Todd Bedford walked in. "What brings you over?"

"A friend of yours has been trying to get hold of you all day. You weren't answering your phone, so he called Annie. You'd given him her number for emergencies, and I gather this is something of an emergency."

Adam frowned. "Someone from work?"

Todd shook his head. "No, Scott Martin. He said it was important that he talk to you right away. Said he'd hit pay dirt and that you'd know what he meant."

"He found my hacker!"

Todd raised his eyebrows. "Somebody hacked into your program?"

"Not *Fantasy Quest*," Adam explained as he picked up the phone, "but still a problem. Excuse me, will you? I need to make that call."

"Sure."

"This won't take long. You got time for a beer?"

Todd glanced at his watch. "Yeah, I guess so. Annie won't be home for dinner, so the kids and I will probably order a pizza. They won't be home for another hour yet."

"Great. You know where the beer is," Adam said as he dialed Scott's number. "Help yourself."

Todd opened the refrigerator, then glanced back over his

shoulder. "You want one too?"

"Yes, thanks."

Todd took out two beers, opened one and set the other on the counter. Then he wandered over to Adam's computer console and stared down at the screen. "Looking for your hacker?"

"No, I've got a problem with the Sex Hex. I've been—Hello, Scott?"

"Hi, Adam. Boy, you're one tough man to reach."

"I was working. So, what have you got for me?"

"I tracked down that name you gave me yesterday."

"Already? Your aunt works fast."

"Didn't have to go to my aunt," Scott said. "I did another search on the internet and figured out which one was the Brad Marriot you were looking for."

"How did you figure that out so quickly?"

"He has a website."

"I should have known. What did you find out?"

"He fancies himself one of us."

Adam frowned. "What do you mean?"

"According to his website, he's invented more software than Bill Gates." The sarcasm was heavy in Scott's voice.

"But you don't buy it?"

"I might have, but I dug a little deeper."

"Oh?"

"According to his bio, he went to my alma mater and even pledged my fraternity. So, I put in a call to an old friend who's still at the university, working on his doctorate."

"And he never heard of Brad Marriot, right?"

"No, he'd heard of him, all right. His advisor was on the board of inquiry that investigated Brad Marriot halfway through his junior year. You'll never guess what the charges were."

Adam frowned. "I'm not going to like this, am I?"

"Probably not. It seems there was some question about who had created the programs Marriot claimed were his."

"He stole them?"

"That's what my friend figures. Says Marriot's one hell of a hacker but hasn't got an ounce of creativity in him. Anyway, this guy from the Midwest shows up one day, claiming Marriot had hacked into his computer and stolen his program. He had no proof, and everyone pretty much blew him off."

"What prompted the inquiry?" Adam asked.

"Over the next two years, a teenage computer geek from California and a Canadian software engineer made similar accusations against our friend. The department head decided where there's smoke there's at least a smudge pot, so he called for an investigation."

"And?"

"And nothing. If Marriot was guilty, he was good at hiding his tracks. Nobody could prove a thing. The Board of Inquiry closed without even a reprimand."

"So, if he is a thief, he's a clever one and good at covering his tracks."

"Looks that way," Scott agreed. "But that isn't the worst of it."

"No?"

"In spite of the cloud of suspicion around him, my friend said Marriot got a plum job as soon as he graduated."

"I'm almost afraid to ask."

"Vid-Tech."

Adam swore. "It would have to be my top competitor, wouldn't it?"

"I wouldn't put it past Pete Saunders to have hired him specifically to try and steal *Fantasy Quest*, either," Scott added. "It's just the sort of thing Saunders would do."

"You think Marriot is my hacker?"

"It wouldn't surprise me. Where did you get his name, anyway?"

"From my glitch."

There was a long moment of silence. "You're kidding."

"No, she's been talking about him since she first showed

up. Says he's her fiancé. I don't suppose his website said anything about a wedding?"

"Nope, but I got the feeling he wouldn't think a fiancée important enough to mention."

Adam's mouth twisted. "A little self-centered, is he?"

"That's the way it seemed to me."

"What's the address for Marriot's website?"

"I'll message it to you." There was a pause as Scott tapped on his computer keyboard.

Adam experienced a feeling of unreality. How could Kenzie's fiancé be real?

"Oh, by the way, I almost forgot to tell you," Scott said. "I think I may have found the hacker's physical location."

Adam blinked. "Really? Where?"

"That's the weird part. It seems to be coming from a hospital there in Denver."

"What?"

"I know. It makes even less sense than your glitch knowing the name of a hacker."

Adam sighed. "The deeper we get in to this, the less I understand."

"You know," Scott said. "Maybe you need to apply Occam's Razor here."

"You mean the simplest explanation tends to be the correct one?"

"Right."

Adam pondered this for a moment. "And the simplest explanation in this case would be…"

"Maybe she's not a glitch at all. Maybe she's another player in your game."

Adam felt as though a fist had slammed into his gut. "You can't live inside the program," he protested. "She's been there day and night for two months. If she were real, she'd have starved to death by now."

"Unless she leaves when you do."

"What would be the point of an elaborate masquerade like

that?"

"My guess would be industrial espionage. Of course, it might not be that at all. Maybe she just has the hots for you."

Adam closed his eyes and pinched the bridge of his nose. Was Kenzie a spy bent on stealing his program? It seemed unlikely, but if she were a real person rather than a computer-generated graphic, much that was unexplainable suddenly made sense. "Let me know if you find out anything else. Maybe more of the facts will help make sense of all this."

"Mind if I go hunting for your glitch in the real world?"

Adam sighed. "Sure. Knock yourself out. I already tried and didn't find a thing."

"I'll see if my aunt can find anything. Call you tomorrow."

"Right. Thanks."

"He found your hacker?" Todd asked as Adam hung up the phone.

Adam ran his fingers through his hair roughly. "I don't know. It's turned into one big, confusing mess."

Todd opened the other beer and handed it to Adam. "What's going on?"

"I wish I knew." Adam filled Todd in on everything Scott had told him.

Todd gave a low whistle. "No wonder you look hassled."

"I guess it's time to ask my glitch some pointed questions."

"Why don't you just shut the program down?" Todd asked. "That would take care of the whole problem, wouldn't it?"

"Probably, but I still haven't figured out what's going on with the Sex Hex."

"You mean your anti-porn program?"

"Right. It isn't working, and my glitch seems to be involved somehow. It's one feature that absolutely has to be perfected before *Fantasy Quest* hits the market."

Todd looked surprised. "How do you know it isn't working?"

"It didn't shut down when it was supposed to."

"You had sex with your glitch?"

Adam felt himself redden under his friend's questioning look. "The point is that the program didn't shut down."

Todd looked pensive. "Are you sure it shuts down when both characters are real people? I mean, if it was created to work with computer animated characters, it might not recognize another human."

Adam stared at him. "You know, that never occurred to me. It ought to be easy to check out. Just find two people who are willing to go into the program and try to have sex."

"Hey, maybe I can talk Annie into it," Todd said with a chuckle. "She's been nagging me to take her on an exotic weekend getaway. Of course, I'd be willing to bet it's already been tried. It's like space sex."

"Space sex?"

"Sex in space. You've never actually heard of any of the astronauts trying it, but you know they have. It's just the way we humans operate. Give us a new environment, and sex is the first thing we try out, just to see what it's like."

Adam grinned. "And you think my employees couldn't resist trying it out in *Fantasy Quest*."

"I'd put money on it."

"The problem will be getting them to talk about it."

Todd shook his head. "Nah, bragging is another pretty popular human foible. Once you let them know there won't be any reprisals, they'll be tripping all over themselves to tell their tales."

"You could be right. I'll check it out in the morning."

"Once the word gets out about what you want to know, you'll probably have half of your employees volunteering to have cybersex with the other half in the name of research."

"And I'll have my answers." Adam raised his beer. "To human foibles."

Todd clinked his bottle against Adam's. "Long may they reign."

Chapter 30

This time Adam woke up right where he expected to be, deep inside a cave he'd created with his cheat codes. Though it wasn't terribly handy, and his skin was downright chilly to the touch, it was safe from the eagle eyes of his Kenzie glitch.

Kenzie occupied his mind as he made his way out into the mellow light of an autumn sunset. What was he going to do about her? Until he'd looked at the situation through his friends' eyes, he'd been able to delude himself that he had to keep the game inside *Beta Quest* going. The truth was, he really didn't need *Beta Quest* anymore. Everything here could be recreated in *Fantasy Quest*: the forest, Rainbow Falls, the Indian village, even the characters. Everything except his glitch. And that was the crux of it: He didn't want to lose Kenzie.

That's why he was here instead of inside *Fantasy Quest* solving the problem with the Sex Hex. He had to figure out who or what Kenzie was, once and for all. After his conversation with Scott, he'd searched all the popular social media sites looking for her. He'd found several Kenzie Armstrongs, but none of them were *his* Kenzie. Was she a real person bent on stealing his secrets, a clever computer virus planted there by the hacker, or a complex glitch in his own programming? He had to know.

Adam looked around at the familiar mountain and sighed. Lord, but he was going to miss this. Todd was dead right about shutting the whole program down though. *Beta Quest* had become a liability he couldn't afford. The hacker hadn't stolen anything yet, but he could find his way to the heart of the program at any time.

Though *Beta Quest* lacked the refinements of *Fantasy Quest*, enough of the basics were there. Someone like Pete Saunders, with a team of crack software engineers and unlimited resources, could develop their own version; they might even be able to beat Microcom to the marketplace. Once that happened, it would be Adam's word against the older, richer, and more prestigious Pete Saunders. He was still mulling the whole problem over in his mind without any real progress when he reached the village.

"Adam! There you are." Kenzie spied him the moment he appeared and hurried toward him with a huge smile on her face. "I've been looking all over for you."

"I've been out hunting," Adam said, trying to ignore the way his heart skipped a beat when he looked up and saw her. Kenzie's honest delight in his return felt warm and welcome. How could he ever consider her a threat?

"I know. Buffalo Horn told me. He also said there's nothing wrong with you. You've always been a sound sleeper."

Adam shrugged. "I told you."

"I still think it's abnormal, but if you've been doing it since you were a kid, I guess it isn't life-threatening. Anyway, that's not why I came to find you."

"Oh?"

"Look!" Kenzie opened her arms wide and whirled around, displaying the fur she had wrapped around her. "Red Blanket finished my bear skin. Isn't it gorgeous?"

"Incredible." But he wasn't looking at the hide. With her hair down and her face alight with pleasure, Kenzie rivaled Beautiful Dawn for beauty.

"I thought it would be kind of coarse, but it's incredibly soft."

"And you decided to wear it as a coat?"

"Not really. It's just too heavy to carry any other way. I didn't realize that darn bear was so big."

Adam blinked. For the first time, he focused on the bear hide. It was half again as large as it should have been. "I didn't either. That hide could almost wrap around you twice."

"Not quite." She gave him a sultry smile. "But it might go around both of us."

Adam quirked an eyebrow. "Is that an offer?"

"It could be." Kenzie batted her eyes playfully. "We might have to check it out later."

"You know you're wearing it inside out, don't you?"

She looked down at it in surprise. "I am?"

"The fur should be on the inside, next to your skin."

"Mmm, now that's a pleasant image."

"What is?"

"The fur against my naked skin."

Adam felt his blood pressure soar. The image of her naked body nestled against the bear fur wasn't exactly what he'd describe as pleasant. Erotic and mouth-watering maybe, mind-boggling even, but certainly not something as tame as pleasant.

"Come on," she said, taking him by the hand. "Red Blanket has been waiting for you to come in so she can feed you. She made your favorite."

"Rattlesnake stew?"

Kenzie looked back at him and stuck out her tongue. "You got me with that once, but you won't again. It's rabbit stew this time, just like it was then."

Adam grinned. "Are you sure?"

"It's what I choose to believe." She tossed her head. "Now, come on, before she gives your supper to the dogs."

Adam meekly allowed her to lead him over to the fire, where Buffalo Horn and Jesse Three Dogs were already eating. They greeted him with every evidence of pleasure, and the feeling of welcome washed over him again. As he settled into a cross-legged position and accepted a bowl of stew from Red Blanket, it occurred to him that *Beta Quest* was more of a home to him than his posh apartment in the expensive Denver high-rise.

The talk tonight centered around the success of the hunting party he and Kenzie had met. They had come home with a moose and two elk, a welcome miracle with winter so close. The meat would go a long way toward seeing them through the cold months ahead. Eagle Feather's prowess as a hunter was discussed at length, then they moved on to plans for another hunting party to set out the next day.

Through it all, Adam's mind kept straying from the topic. All he could think of was Kenzie laid out on the bear skin, naked and wanting. The invitation in her eyes every time he looked her way did nothing to cool the fire in his blood. He shook his head, trying to clear it. The last thing he needed was a distraction right now. There were questions he needed answers to, and he wasn't going to get them if he couldn't keep his mind focused.

At last the meal and conversation were over, and Buffalo Horn retired for the night. Adam was ready to call it a night too, but not in a tipi filled with other people. What he needed was privacy. The next time he caught Kenzie's eye, he smiled. "Care to go for a walk?" he asked.

"I'd love to. Just let me finish helping Red Blanket clean up."

Red Blanket shook her head. "No, you go Wheesky Jug."

"If you're sure," Kenzie said doubtfully.

The old woman pointed up at the full moon then smiled and flapped her hands at the two of them, indicating they should go enjoy the moonlight.

"All right, then. I will." Kenzie smiled and put her bear hide around her shoulders.

"Thanks, Red Blanket." Adam dropped a kiss on Red Blanket's cheek. "I owe you one," he said in Arapaho.

"You brought me Kenzie," she replied in her own tongue. "That's thanks enough."

Kenzie looked back over her shoulder as they walked through camp. "You know, I can't figure out if she's always known more English than I realized or if she's learning it from being around me."

"You've got me there. It does seem like she understands more than she lets on, doesn't it?"

Kenzie gazed up at the heavens and sighed. "You know what I love most about these mountains of yours?"

"What?"

"The stars. There must be a bazillion of them up there. You don't see them in town, you know."

Adam looked up. "My father used to tell me stories about the constellations. I didn't realize he was teaching me Greek mythology until years later."

"Oh, look, a falling star!" Kenzie closed her eyes tightly and scrunched up her face.

Adam was amused. "What are you doing?"

"Making a wish."

"Ah."

"Don't you want to know what it was?"

"Won't that keep it from coming true?"

"Not this time. In fact, I think I'll have a better chance of it coming true if I tell you." Kenzie looked up at him with a half-smile on her face. "I wished you would kiss me," she said softly as she ran her hand up his arm. "And I wished you'd make love to me right here under this beautiful sky."

The moment she touched him, all thought of the unanswered questions between them disappeared in a swirl of emotion that threatened to overwhelm everything, including his better sense.

"Your wish is my command." He bracketed her face with his hands and stared down into her eyes. "You're so beautiful," Adam murmured as he trailed kisses down the side of Kenzie's neck and tasted the hollow at the base of her throat. He heard her swift intake of breath as his teeth grazed her collarbone.

"So are you." Kenzie melted against him, her arms going around his waist in sweet surrender.

Adam raised his head and looked down at her in surprise. Every time he'd used that line in *Fantasy Quest*, her response had been, "Oh, what you do to me."

"What's the matter?"

He shook his head as though to clear it. "Oh, nothing. I just… I guess I was expecting you to say something else."

"What?"

"Never mind." He kissed the tip of her nose.

Kenzie frowned. "Adam, what's wrong?"

"Nothing's wrong."

"Then, why are you acting so weird?"

Adam sighed and rested his forehead against hers. "You know, you're making this very difficult."

"What?"

"This seduction."

Kenzie giggled. "This is a seduction?"

"Isn't that what you wanted?"

"Maybe in the beginning, but now I've changed my mind."

"But you said—"

"I know what I said." She gave him a slow, sexy smile. "But now I've decided I'd rather be the seducer."

"Oh, really?"

"Yes, really. You got to do it last time. I think it's my turn."

A feeling of unreality washed over Adam. This had to be the strangest intimate conversation there ever was. "You're certainly playful tonight."

Kenzie put her arms around his neck and brought his head down to kiss him. "So, let's play," she said in a husky voice.

The moment her tongue touched his, Adam was lost. When her hands slipped under his shirt to caress the muscles of his back and chest, he thought he might go up in flames. His arms went around her and crushed her to him. After several long, delicious moments, she started to struggle, and he instantly released her.

"You're wearing too many clothes," she said, trying to tug his shirt up over his chest.

Adam grabbed the bottom, pulled it over his head, and tossed it to the side. "Better?"

"Oh, yeah." She traced his shoulders and arms with her hands. "Do you know how long I've wanted to touch you like this?" she murmured, running her fingers reverently over the heavy muscles of his chest. "You have the most beautiful body I've ever seen." A shiver of pure lust rocked him as she leaned forward and circled a masculine nipple with her tongue.

"Enough," he growled, sweeping the bear skin from her shoulders. He spread it on the ground, fur side up, then turned back to her. "Now it's my turn," he said when she protested.

"I'll freeze to death without my hide."

"Don't worry." He pulled her into his arms again. "I'll keep you warm." His mouth came down on hers as he untied the single leather thong at the neck of her dress.

Kenzie stepped back several paces, her mouth curved into a sexy half-smile. Without a word she crossed her arms, grasped the sides of her dress and slowly pulled it up over her head.

"Dear God in heaven." Adam breathed as her body came into view an inch at a time. Standing there, bathed in the moonlight and wearing nothing but two tiny wisps of satin and lace, Kenzie was the embodiment of every fantasy he'd ever had.

Unable to move, he watched, mesmerized, as she undid the hook between her breasts and slowly revealed the skin beneath. Her eyes blazing with desire, she dropped the lacy confection to the ground and reached for the matching satin at her hips.

"No, let me." Adam's voice, raw and raspy, sounded harsh in the velvet night, but Kenzie only smiled a mysterious, feminine smile and held out her hand.

With a groan deep in his throat, he swept her up into his arms and took three steps to the bear skin. Sinking to his knees, he claimed her mouth and toppled over backwards onto the soft fur. Lying there, with Kenzie stretched out on top of him, her breasts nestled against his naked chest, Adam was sure he had reached heaven. His hands trembled with suppressed desire as he touched the soft skin between her shoulder blades and followed the sensuous indentation of her spine down to the flare of her hips.

Adam slipped his fingers under the elastic of the sexy little panties and dispatched them with a few quick movements.

Kenzie reached for the button on his pants. "Time to get rid of these," she said, nipping at his ear.

With a groan, Adam rolled to his side and stood up. He stripped off the offending garment then stood there for a moment, his eyes feasting on her. She lay upon the fur, looking like a pagan goddess, with her hair spread around her in a cloud. His imagination had fallen far short of reality.

"You take my breath away," he murmured, knowing that the picture before him would be forever seared into his memory.

Kenzie's eyes smoldered with passion. "Come here," she said, crooking her finger at him. "You promised to keep me warm."

She sighed in satisfaction as he settled next to her on the fur and kissed her again. As their mouths danced — one minute harsh and demanding, the next barely touching — their hands eagerly explored, intent on a journey of passionate discovery. At last, when they had driven each other to the limit of their endurance, he rolled her beneath him.

"Oh, my." Kenzie gave a soft gasp of pleasure as he claimed her. She held him close and buried her head against his shoulder. "I love you, Adam," she said, her voice breaking and cracking as the waves of ecstasy rolled over them both.

The words struck Adam's heart like a bolt of lightning then were forgotten in a maelstrom of desire that drove them both to the brink of insanity before bursting into a shower of multicolored sparks that blended with the stars before drifting slowly back to earth.

They held each other while their breathing returned to normal, and the heat from their bodies dissipated into the cold night air.

Kenzie gave a delicate little shiver and snuggled closer to him.

"Cold?" he asked.

"A little," she admitted, "but I don't want to move."

"Let's see how big this hide really is, then." It took a little adjusting, but Adam managed to get the fur wrapped around them and covering everything but their heads and the lower part of his legs. They had to squish together to accomplish it, but neither saw that as a negative point.

Adam dropped a kiss on her head as Kenzie settled against him with a deep sigh of contentment. "You know," he said conversationally, "it just occurred to me that we've never discussed this future world you supposedly come from."

"No."

"I think it's time we did."

Kenzie tipped her head up to look at him. "Why?"

"I don't know," he said with a shrug. "Just curious, I guess."

"I can't tell you much."

Now it was his turn to be surprised. "Oh? Why is that?"

"What if I told you about a terrible flood? Only, because you knew it was going to happen, you got people out of the way."

"Saving lives would be a good thing, wouldn't it?"

Kenzie shrugged. "Maybe, but what if it changed the future? What if someone who was supposed to die lived and wound up marrying the president's mother, so the president was never born or something?"

Adam chuckled. "Sounds like a pretty convoluted plot, but I see your point."

"Then you understand why I can't tell you about the future."

"Why don't you just tell me about your life, then?"

"What do you want to know?" she asked cautiously.

"For starters, where were you born?"

"In a tiny little Wyoming town that probably doesn't even exist yet."

"Brothers and sisters?"

"Three brothers and one sister."

"I always wanted to be part of a large family," Adam said wistfully.

"Yeah, I guess we did have a lot of fun together."

"What was it like growing up?"

Kenzie looked up at him and grinned. "Chaos!"

He smiled back. "Tell me."

Almost before she knew it, Kenzie was telling him her life story, and Adam listened intently. The more she talked, the sicker he became. This was a real life she was describing, filled with all the details that came only from truly living.

Along the way, Kenzie started dropping little tidbits to see if she could pique his interest. "When I left for college, I thought about flying but finally decided to drive so I'd have my car."

Adam almost smiled at her transparent attempt to interest him in the marvels she'd seen growing up in the twentieth century. "I suppose that's where you met Brad Marriot?" he said, refusing to take the bait about flying.

"Right, in my junior year."

"Love at first sight?"

Kenzie laughed. "Hardly. It was a blind date set up by his roommate and mine. I wouldn't have gone out with him in the first place if Nancy hadn't tricked me into it."

"Oh?"

"She didn't tell me he was a geek. I don't date computer types."

Her remark took Adam by surprise. It felt like a slap in the face and proved beyond a shadow of a doubt that she wasn't from his imagination. "But Marriot changed your mind?" he managed.

"Oh, Brad isn't like other geeks. He's handsome and suave, a good dresser, the life of the party. You'd never know what he is by looking at him."

"And you love him." Adam's voice sounded bleak even to his own ears.

Kenzie raised her head and looked at him. "I thought I did, but it was nothing like what you and I have. I love you, body and soul. What Brad and I had has nothing to do with us. If I had a choice to go back to my own time or to stay here with you, I'd stay."

Adam stared up at her for a long, pain-filled moment then, with a strangled groan, pulled her back into his embrace and rolled her underneath him. This time there was desperation to his lovemaking, as though he could somehow pull her inside himself and keep her there. She met him halfway, stroke for stroke, surrounding him with her love and absorbing his essence into her soul.

When they were finished, he lay there clutching her, holding her next to his heart, storing up memories for a life that stretched out before him, unbearable in its loneliness.

Sensing something of his mood, Kenzie reached up and touched his cheek with her fingers. "What is it, Adam?"

He looked down at the woman cuddled against his chest and felt his heart break. "Nothing. I just don't want this night to end, that's all."

"Neither do I." She snuggled even closer. "Do you think they'll come looking for us if we stay out all night?"

"No."

"Good." She yawned. "It's so warm and cozy. I'm getting a little snoozy."

Adam put his hand on her head and pushed it back against his shoulder. "Shh, sweetheart. Go to sleep."

"Promise you'll wake me?"

"Mmm," he said noncommittally. Though he balked at it with every fiber of his being, Adam knew what he had to do. He held her long after she drifted off to sleep, her breath whispering across his chest in soft puffs that stirred him to the depths of his soul. He judged it to be about midnight when he finally felt her stir in his arms and knew it was time. Closing his eyes against the pain, he gave her one last, lingering kiss then reached for the stone around his neck.

Adam removed his helmet and stared at his computer screen for a long, bitter moment before taking off his gloves. Then he began typing feverishly before he lost his nerve. After about ten minutes of concentrated effort, a message appeared on the screen.

Are you sure you wish to delete this program and all related peripherals from the Zeta-unit?

Adam gritted his teeth and hit the *Yes* button with a savage stab of his finger. His Zeta-unit whirred for a moment, then another message appeared.

Beta Quest has been successfully deleted. Do you wish to delete another program?

Ignoring the question, Adam disconnected the Zeta-unit that held the master program and shut down his computer for the first time since Kenzie Armstrong popped into his life. He watched the tiny rainbows of light dance across the polished surface inside. This was the prototype—the only one not housed in a shiny metal case with Microcom's familiar electric blue and white logo emblazoned across the top—the home of Beta Quest. For a moment, he saw Kenzie's face reflected there instead of his own.

Where is she now? he wondered.

With an angry twist of his lips, he dropped the zeta unit on the hardwood floor then rolled the wheel of his chair over it. There was a sickening crunch as it broke apart. Adam rolled his wheel back and forth over the plastic until it lay shattered in a dozen jagged pieces...just like his heart.

Chapter 31

Adam's kiss blended perfectly into Kenzie's dream. It was long and lingering. She smiled softly when he ended it. Then, suddenly, he was gone, probably off to answer the call of nature. In her half-wakeful state, she wondered how he'd managed to wiggle out of their cozy cocoon without her knowledge. Doggone it. He'd promised to wake her. Oh well, no matter. He'd be back in a minute or two. She let herself drift back into oblivion.

"Dammit!"

The exclamation brought her awake instantly. But when she opened her eyes Kenzie stared around in blank amazement. Instead of the starry sky and trees, she saw a dimly lit room and a startling variety of bottles, tubes, and machines that seemed to be connected to her.

"Come on, baby," the voice came again. "You can't shut down on me now when I'm finally this close."

Kenzie looked toward the sound. A man sat at a small table several feet from her. Though his handsome blond head was bent over a laptop computer and his face turned partially away, Kenzie knew him instantly. "Brad?"

His head jerked up, and he stared at her as though he was seeing a ghost. "Kenzie! You—you're awake?"

"Either that or I'm having a very vivid dream." She looked around the room again. "I think I'll opt for the dream."

"That's right, it's a dream. You're not really here. Close your eyes and go back to sleep."

"Of course it's not real," she muttered as her eyes drifted shut again. "I'm waiting for Adam, not Brad. Silly brain is playing tricks on me."

Kenzie dreamed of Brad several more times during the night. Each time, she would wake in the dimly lit room to find him bent over his computer. The second time she spoke to him, he gave her a bitter pill, saying it would help her sleep. After that, she didn't even bother talking to him. Brad seemed increasingly agitated over whatever was on his screen, but Kenzie found she really wasn't interested. All she wanted was to stop having this weird dream and wake up in Adam's arms, where she belonged.

Finally, she opened her eyes to bright sunlight streaming in through the window. The worst of the grogginess seemed to have passed, and the room had lost its dreamlike fuzziness. The tubes and machines were still there. So was Brad's computer, though he was nowhere to be seen.

Kenzie was still studying her unfamiliar surroundings, trying to make sense of it all, when a nurse came into the room.

"Good morning," Kenzie managed, though her tongue and throat felt strangely dry and unwieldy as she spoke.

"Oh my stars!" the nurse exclaimed, very nearly dropping the chart she held in her hand. "You're awake!"

Kenzie frowned. "Yeah, I guess I am." She rubbed her forehead. "I thought this was a dream, but you seem pretty real."

"Oh, no, sweetie, this is no dream. You're in University Hospital in Denver."

That explains all the tubes and machines. "Have I been sick?" Kenzie asked uncertainly. "I don't seem to remember."

"Tell you what, I'll get your vitals then go call Dr. Edgerton," the nurse said as she took Kenzie's temperature. "He'll answer all your questions."

"Who's Dr. Edgerton?" Kenzie asked.

"He's been on your case since the beginning," the nurse said, fiddling with one of the many pieces of equipment attached to Kenzie's arm.

"The beginning of what?"

"Since you came in."

Kenzie's mind whirled in confusion. This was no dream. When and how had she returned to her own time? The next second, the reality of the situation crashed in on her. *Adam! I left him in 1868!*

"Oh no," she whispered as the machine beeped.

The nurse looked at her in surprise. "It's just telling me it's done," she said. "Nothing to worry about."

Kenzie didn't even bother to explain as tears of grief filled her eyes. *How could this have happened? How could I have lost him now, just as I realized I'm willing to give up everything to be with him?* She closed her eyes against the pain. The tears spilled over as she mourned a man a hundred years dead.

"Hey, it's okay."

Kenzie jumped and opened her eyes as the nurse touched her arm in what was meant to be a soothing gesture. "No, you don't understand."

"It's bound to be a little overwhelming at first." The nurse gave her a sympathetic smile and handed her a tissue from the box on Kenzie's hospital tray. "Everything will turn out all right."

A noise at the door distracted the nurse, and she glanced over her shoulder. "Oh, hi!"

"Hello, there. Aren't you a little early this morning?"

"Actually, I'm at the end of my shift. Susie's going to be late this morning, so I said I'd do her vitals for her. But, Brad, look!" She stepped out of the way so he could see Kenzie.

"Kenzie!" he exclaimed. "Oh, thank you, God!" In four long strides he was across the room and pulling her into his arms. With all the tubes and cords hampering the process, it was more of a one-armed hug than a passionate embrace, but Kenzie hardly noticed. Why was he pretending he didn't know she was awake?

"Weren't you here last night?" she asked.

The nurse smiled. "Oh, yes, he's here every night, all night. I've never seen such an attentive friend."

Kenzie's gaze met Brad's. "Friend?"

"Definitely." The nurse gave him a blinding smile. "Such dedication."

Kenzie frowned. "How long have we been friends?"

Just then, a buzzer sounded down the hall.

"Gotta run," said the nurse. "I'll call Dr. Edgerton and get him here ASAP."

"You act surprised that I'm here," Brad said, dropping a small sack he carried onto the bedside table as the nurse hurried out.

"Actually, I'm more surprised to find out we've been downgraded to friends," Kenzie said. "Last I knew, we were getting married."

"You're overreacting to an unfortunate choice of words. She was so excited to see you finally awake that she misspoke."

Kenzie rubbed her head. "I'm confused."

"I know, darling." He turned his back to pour a glass of water from her pitcher then sat down on the edge of the bed and smoothed back her hair. "Here, this will help you relax." He smiled encouragingly at her as he held the glass to her lips.

Kenzie took a swallow, then recoiled. "Yuck, that's nasty!"

"There's nothing wrong with this water," he said.

"Then what's that bitter taste?"

Brad looked surprised. "What bitter taste?"

"Try it."

He shrugged, then put the glass to his mouth and obediently took a sip. "Tastes fine to me. You're just not used to Denver water, that's all."

She pushed the glass away with her hand. "No, thanks. I'm not thirsty."

"I'm afraid I'm going to have to insist, darling," Brad said with a gentle smile. "Your body's been through a rough time, and I want you to get better."

"Nasty-tasting water is going to make me feel better?"

"The water's fine. You need hydration to get back to normal. I want the woman I love back in my arms, where she belongs." He lifted her hand to his lips and kissed it. "Please, darling. For me."

A soulful look from his brown puppy-dog eyes melted her

resolve the way it always did. "Oh, all right," she grumbled. "But then I want some answers."

"Of course, darling. I'll tell you anything you want."

He continued to watch as she lifted the glass to her lips. She made a face, then took a deep breath and downed the entire glass.

Brad gave her a big smile and took the glass from her hand. "There, now, that wasn't so bad was it?"

"It was horrible! I want bottled water from now on."

He leaned forward and kissed her on the forehead. "Your petulance is a product of your illness. Now, what was it you wanted to know?"

"For one thing, how did I get here?"

"The Flight for Life helicopter."

"Wh...what?"

Just as he opened his mouth to answer, the phone rang, and Kenzie automatically reached for it.

"It's probably for me," Brad said, taking it out of her hand. "I had all my calls from work forwarded here."

"You did? Why?"

But he just smiled and picked up the phone. "Hello? Ah, good morning, Pete. No, not quite. I nearly had it last night, but an unexpected snafu developed... Right, but I think I've figured out a way around it..."

Then, I wasn't dreaming last night, Kenzie thought. *Brad's frustration was real, so why is he pretending not to know I was awake?* There didn't seem to be an answer to that one, so Kenzie turned her mind to the question of how she'd traveled back to her own time.

When she awoke in the past, she'd had a memory of the accident that took her there. This time, there was nothing but a bout of mind-blowing sex with Adam and a last lingering kiss. Nothing there to fling her back into the future.

The thought of Adam brought a lump to her throat, and she struggled to keep the black grief at bay. *I don't have time for that right now. If I can figure out what happened, maybe I can find a way to get back to him.*

While trying to pull together everything she knew and make sense of it, Kenzie gradually became aware that the fuzzy, dreamlike quality of the night before was starting to come back. Before long, she could hardly hold her eyes open. Just as she was drifting off, Brad ended his conversation and hung up the phone. She could have sworn she saw a glimmer of satisfaction on his face as her eyes closed.

The next time she woke up, Brad was gone, and a dark-haired woman was sitting by her bed, crocheting. "Mom?"

"Oh, Kenzie, you're awake," she cried, dropping the yarn.

Enveloped in her mother's hug, Kenzie closed her eyes and let the spicy smell of apples, cinnamon, and love wash over her. "Oh, Mom."

"I'm sorry I wasn't here when you woke up. The doctor called me yesterday morning, and I caught the first flight out, but you were asleep by the time I got here. I've been waiting ever since." She settled on the edge of the bed and held her daughter's hand as if she were afraid to let it go

Kenzie pulled back and looked at her mother. "Yesterday? I've been asleep since yesterday?"

"Honey, you can't expect to bounce back immediately. You were in a coma a long time."

Kenzie's eyes widened in astonishment. "I was in a coma?"

Danelda Armstrong nodded and smoothed back her daughter's hair. "We weren't sure for a long time if you were going to make it."

For the first time, Kenzie noticed her mother's dark brown hair had added several streaks of gray, and there were wrinkles around her mouth and eyes that hadn't been there before. "How long?"

"Eighty-five days."

"*Eighty-five days*! That's almost three months!"

Her mother nodded. "That's why I wasn't here, baby. I used up all my sick leave and had to go back to work. Thank goodness for Brad. He's the one that convinced us to bring you here instead of Salt Lake so he could be near you."

"He's been with me the whole time?"

"Oh, yes. He spends a big part of every day here. His boss was nice enough to let him work outside the office." She patted Kenzie's hand. "Maybe you can get a job there when you're on your feet again."

"Vid-tech? No, I don't think so. I decided a long time ago that Brad and I shouldn't work together. It would put too much strain on our marriage." Kenzie frowned. "I don't suppose I still have my job, though, do I?"

"I don't know. They were very understanding about the whole situation. Maybe you could reapply. I wouldn't worry too much about it just yet. I don't think you'll be ready to go back to work for a while."

"Probably not. I just can't believe I've been here so long." Distractedly, she ran a hand through her hair and stopped in shocked surprise when her fingers came to the end of it a mere three inches from her scalp. "My hair!" she cried. "What happened to it?"

"Oh, honey, they had to shave it all off on the right side to deal with your injuries. I thought it would be best if we just cut it all so it could grow out the same. I know it's awfully short still, but it's actually kind of cute on you. "

"Mom, what happened to me?"

"What's the last thing you remember?"

Kenzie had a sudden image of her and Adam lying together wrapped in a bearskin, their clothing scattered all around. Somehow, she didn't think her mother would be impressed. It had nothing to do with whatever had happened to her anyway. "I don't know. Everything is kind of fuzzy still."

"We don't really know why, but you had taken Brad's car up to the Sinks."

"The Sinks? You mean up above Lander?"

Her mother nodded. "Right. Anyway, you somehow managed to fall into the river and were swept into the cave."

"I remember that." Kenzie frowned. For the first time, it

occurred to her how strange it was that neither Brad nor her mother had mentioned her three-month absence. If her mind hadn't been so fuzzy, she'd have thought of it before. "You must have freaked out when I disappeared for so long."

"Oh, I freaked out all right. So did your father. If there hadn't been a couple of college boys there getting ready to go spelunking, you'd have drowned for sure. As it was, you sustained a very nasty head injury when you hit the rock wall."

A horrible suspicion began to niggle at Kenzie's mind. "Mom, what's the date?"

"The date? November sixteenth or seventeenth, why?"

Kenzie felt a knot of lead form in her stomach. "I was never missing, was I?"

"Missing? You mean physically? Heavens, no. Why would you think such a thing?"

Kenzie closed her eyes. Had it all been a dream, then? Surely not. It had been too vivid, too real. There had to be some way to prove it had all really happened. "My tennis bracelet," she said suddenly. The last time she'd seen it, Adam had stuck it into his pocket at the saloon in Laramie City.

"What about it, dear?" her mother asked.

"It's gone," she said, triumphantly holding up her wrist. Proof positive that she'd traveled back in time to 1868 and a certain long-haired, obstinate mountain man.

"Oh, right. It's here somewhere." Her mother dug around in her purse for a minute then pulled out a small plastic bag, which she handed to Kenzie.

Kenzie's heart sank as she saw the familiar sparkle through the plastic. "You had it?"

"I decided it would be safer if I kept it."

"For how long?"

"Since the accident. I took it off your wrist before they put you on the helicopter."

Her mother's words were like a knife in her soul. Was the whole thing a figment of her imagination? It was hard to believe, and yet what other explanation could there be? *I can't go back!* The thought brought a twist of pain. There was nothing to go back to. Adam Johnson wasn't dead. He never existed. She was in love with a dream, a phantasm no more real than an imaginary dragon.

This time when the grief came, she let it engulf her and allowed the tears to flow down her cheeks unchecked.

Chapter 32

"Hi, Adam," Seth said as he opened the door. "You were right, Dad. You don't have to go get Adam. He came on his own," he called over his shoulder.

Seth moved out of the way and let him in. The first thing Adam saw when he entered the living room was Todd grinning from ear to ear as he lounged on the couch, the magazine he'd been reading forgotten on his lap. "You owe me five bucks, honey."

Annie stuck her head out of the kitchen door. "Adam! You're here."

"You told me Friday night at six."

"Oh, like that's ever made any difference."

Adam exchanged a look with Todd. "I think she's mad because I found the house by myself."

Todd nodded. "And on time, too, just like I told her you would. She hates it when I'm right." He raised his voice slightly and looked toward the kitchen door. "Which I usually am if she'd just admit it."

A wadded-up dishtowel sailed out of the kitchen, narrowly missing his head.

"I see what you mean," Adam said, shaking his head. "She does seem to have trouble accepting the obvious."

"You two might find yourselves ordering out for pizza!"

Todd winked at Adam. "What, and pass up Annie Bedford's famous stroganoff?"

"I brought a bottle of your favorite wine." Adam called out with a hopeful note in his voice. "I don't think it will go with pizza."

The doorbell rang before Annie could respond, and Seth came thundering through the living room. "I've got it," he yelled back over his shoulder. "Hey, Kirk. Good to see you, man. Come on in."

"Zoey's latest boyfriend," Todd explained in a low voice as a tall, dark-haired teenager was duly escorted in.

"…so if it's okay with you," Seth said, throwing a furtive look toward the stairs, "I'll catch a ride to the movie with you guys and then go home with Tom."

"Sure. Fine with me."

"Yes!" Seth said, punching the air. "I'll go get my stuff." He started for the door then stopped. "Oh, yeah. This is Adam Johnson. Adam, Kirk Roberts."

The boy's eyes widened. "Hey, you're the computer guy."

Adam grinned. "Yeah, I guess I am, at that."

"Zoey says you practically invented VR," Kirk said as he flopped down in an easy chair.

Adam's mouth twisted into a wry smile. "No, I'm just trying to take it another step."

"She says you've got a program coming out soon."

"In February."

Todd closed his magazine and dropped it on the coffee table. "Say, Adam, didn't you tell me your marketing department was going to hire some people to try *Fantasy Quest* out before it hits the market?"

Adam nodded. "They wanted to use the reactions of the average man off the street in the ad campaign."

"I was just thinking Kirk here might be interested."

The teen's eyes lit up. "Boy, would I! That would be so cool."

"It will entail three or four nights after school for several weeks and maybe a Saturday or two," Adam said.

"No problem. I messed up my knee, and the doctor says I'm out of basketball till the end of the season. Testing the program would give me something to do."

"Great." Adam pulled out his case of business cards and handed one to Kirk. "Have Zoey take you to my office sometime this week and give this to my receptionist. She'll get you signed up."

"Wow!" Kirk stared at the card for a long moment then reverently stuck it in his pocket. "Thanks."

"Kirk?" Zoey appeared at the top of the stairs. "Why didn't anyone tell me you were here?"

"Uh…" Kirk's eyes widened, and he cast a helpless look at Adam and Todd.

"All right, everyone, dinner's on," Annie called from the dining room.

Adam was hard put not to laugh at the intense look of relief that crossed Kirk's face. It was the first time since he'd shut down *Beta Quest* two days ago that he'd felt the least bit like laughing. No matter how hard he tried, a black cloud of gloom seemed to have settled around him. He knew it was because he missed *Beta Quest* and even admitted he'd developed a dangerous addiction to the program. He steadfastly refused to consider any other cause for his depression.

Annie's dinner invitation was the perfect cure for what ailed him. It was impossible to remain morose amid the lighthearted chatter and warm family love that surrounded him. Even the inevitable spat that arose when Zoey discovered Seth was going to the movie with Kirk and her was more amusing than uncomfortable. It was settled in minutes, and the three teens left in good humor.

"You know, they're still awfully young, but this one might be a keeper," Todd observed as the door shut behind them.

Annie snorted as she rose to her feet and began to clear the table. "You just think that because Kirk's such an incredible athlete and likes to tinker the way you do."

Todd shrugged. "There are worse things. By the way, thanks for giving him the job, Adam. He can use the money. There are four younger ones at home, and Dad's on disability for a back injury that happened last summer. Kirk hasn't said anything, but I imagine things are pretty tight money-wise."

"I always need good testers, and I really value the teen perspective, since that's who a good chunk of my customers are. If he does a good job for me, I might be able to put him on part time during school and full time in the summer."

"Speaking of your employees, how did your research on the Sex Hex go?" Todd wanted to know.

Adam smiled. "You were right. I had half a dozen people come forward the first day to confess they'd tried it and another ten who were willing to be guinea pigs."

"And what did you find out?"

Adam sighed. "That's the weird part. We didn't find out anything conclusive. For the most part, the Sex Hex seems to be working just fine, but there were two times when it didn't. We did an intensive questionnaire with each subject then disaggregated the data, but we couldn't find any connections."

Annie looked up from loading the dishwasher. "What kind of things did you look at?"

"Everything we could think of. We started with avatars and settings within the program, the time of day, weather, that kind of thing. Then we checked out personal information like age, sex, education, religion, race, socio-economic, even what kind of life they had as a child."

"What about relationships?"

"Huh?"

Annie put in the last plate. "Did you look at the relationships of the couples it shut down on as opposed to those it didn't?"

"Like?"

"Were any of them married?"

"Yeah, most of them were."

"I meant to each other," Annie said with disgust.

"Oh." Adam frowned. "A few were, but I don't think there's any connection there."

"Why not?" Annie paused in the act of adding the soap. "Were the ones it didn't shut down on single?"

"No, my head engineer and his wife made it malfunction, but the other couple were only coworkers."

"Oh? Coworkers in what sense?"

"He's my chief accountant, and she's his administrative

assistant."

Annie smiled mysteriously. "Perfect."

"What?"

"I think I know what's going on with your Sex Hex."

"Don't keep us in suspense," Todd said. "Tell the man."

"Nope, you'll both just laugh at me." She shut the dishwasher and pressed the wash button. "Todd, do you still want to try out Adam's program?"

Todd raised his eyebrows in surprise. "Sure, but what does that have to do with this?"

"If I'm right, the Sex Hex won't work for us, either. What do you say, shall we give it a whirl?"

Todd grinned at Adam. "I think I've just been propositioned."

"Looks that way," Adam said. "You know, if you can shed any light on this, I'd consider it a big favor."

"Can you do the space station?"

Now it was Adam's turn to grin. "Sure can. Astronaut training is one of the industrial applications of *Fantasy Quest*."

"Then, what are we waiting for?"

Within the hour, Todd and Annie were sitting in Adam's extra bedroom watching him set up *Fantasy Quest* for their SR adventure. "Do you want the run of the whole Space Station?" he asked.

Todd exchanged a look with his wife. "Sure, why not?" he said. "We can get naked and chase each other around."

"Todd!" Annie smacked him on the shoulder and turned bright red.

"Geez, honey, what was that for?" he asked.

Annie tossed her head "You know perfectly well, Todd Bedford!"

Adam just chuckled and made the necessary selections on the setting menu. "Do you want to go in as yourselves?"

"You mean we can be someone else?" Annie asked. "I didn't get to choose an avatar when I went into your program before."

"That was *Beta Quest*. *Fantasy Quest* has 500 different characters programmed in. You can even build your own if you want. There is a bank of 2000 features to choose from."

"Wow!" Todd looked intrigued until he glanced at his wife's frowning countenance. "Uh, I think we'll just be ourselves this time," he said.

"All right, then." Adam made a few more clicks with his mouse. "I think we're ready. Just move your chairs over here, and I'll get you hooked up."

It only took a few seconds to move the chairs and don the gloves. Then Adam handed them each a helmet.

Todd reached inside and touched one of the many pads. "How exactly do these work?"

"Those are strategically placed sensors that connect with your hearing, vision, kinesthetic, and speech centers, as well as other parts of the brain. Once you have the helmet in place, you won't be able to tell *Fantasy Quest* from reality. Want a quick rundown?"

When they both nodded, Adam gave them a fast lesson on the program and how to stop it when they wanted to leave. "Ok, then, whenever you're ready," he said.

Annie glanced nervously at the computer monitor. "Will you be able to see what's going on?"

Adam shook his head. "Nope, my graphic artists are currently working on a dynamic graphics loop that will play on the final version, but for now, there's nothing to see but a blank screen."

Annie looked at her husband. "Are you ready, honey?"

"Ready, willing, and able."

"Ok, then. I'll see you on the other side."

Adam watched as they slipped on their helmets. Simultaneously, the expressions slipped from Todd's and Annie's faces and their hands dropped to the arms of their chairs. He sighed and rolled out to the living room, his depression settling over him like a dark curtain once more.

For a moment, he toyed with the idea of loading *Fantasy*

Quest onto the computer in his living room, but then he thought better of it. The only scenario Adam wanted to play out was the last one his saner self needed. With another deep sigh, he picked up the TV remote and started flipping through channels. A program finally caught his eye, and he watched it until he realized he had no idea what it was about. He was focused entirely on the heroine's long hair and remembering the way Kenzie's had curled around him in glorious abandon as he'd made love to her.

With a curse, he switched off the TV and tossed the remote onto the seat of his recliner. He prowled his apartment, looking for something, anything, to distract him from his thoughts and what he knew was going on in *Fantasy Quest* right in the next room. When the phone rang, he answered it with a feeling of relief. Right now, he wouldn't even mind talking to a telemarketer.

"Hey, Adam," Scott Martin said without preamble. "I think I found your glitch."

Adam's heart jerked in his chest. "What do you mean you found her?"

"I'm not exactly sure it is her," he admitted, "but everything fits."

"Your aunt found a Kenzie Armstrong in the IRS records?"

"No, but she did find a McKenzie Armstrong."

"McKenzie?"

"It was my aunt's idea. She pointed out that Kenzie could be short for McKenzie."

"Does she work for Vid-Tech like Marriot?"

"I don't know if she does now, but last year her occupation was listed as *student*. That's all the information my aunt would give me, so I did a search on the internet."

"I suppose she has a web site, too."

"No. In fact, she doesn't seem to have any social media presence at all."

"None?"

"Not on the big three. I even checked some of the sites the kids use and couldn't find anything except a cell phone number. Want me to text it to you?"

I suppose."

"So, are you going to confront her in the program?" Scott asked.

"Can't."

"Why not?"

"I shut the program down and destroyed the zeta server for my beta program."

"Good," Scott said approvingly. "There's no way Marriot can touch you now."

"Unless he already got part of the program."

"That's true. Of course, we don't even know for sure that it's him.'

"No, but we have enough circumstantial evidence and weird coincidences to make it nearly impossible for it to be anyone else." And Kenzie was a spy, though his silly heart refused to accept the truth of it. While he was making love to her, she was selling him out to the enemy.

"Do you want me to keep looking for information on McKenzie Armstrong?"

"No, there really isn't any reason for it now." He told himself it was the only way to fight temptation. If he didn't know anything about her, he wouldn't be able to go looking for her.

"All right, if you're sure. I don't really mind, you know. Kind of enjoy the challenge."

"You've already gone above and beyond. By the way, I haven't shared the latest development with you." Adam told Scott about the reversal of his nerve damage and how the doctors were at a loss to explain it. Scott eagerly agreed that *Beta Quest* was undoubtedly involved somehow, and the two of them began speculating on exactly what was going on.

By the time Scott finally hung up, half an hour had passed. Adam suddenly realized he hadn't heard anything from Todd and Annie. A peek into the other room showed them sitting side by side, still and expressionless. Adam glanced at his watch and wondered what was taking them so long. He returned to the living room and tapped the arm of his chair restlessly. Surely they'd be out soon, and he'd have the answer he was waiting for.

Time hung heavy on his hands. Unbidden, his eyes kept straying to his phone. Finally, when he could stand it no longer, he opened the message from Scott and stared at Kenzie's number for a long moment. Then, calling himself a hundred times a fool, he hit dial. His mouth was suddenly dry, and his stomach twisted into knots by the time he heard the telltale click on the other end of the line.

"We're sorry, you have reached a number that has been disconnected or is no longer in service. If you feel you have reached this recording in error, please check the number and try your call again."

As he hung up the phone, Adam was surprised how bitterly disappointed he was that his one lead was a dead end.

"I've got to tell you, Adam, that is one hell of a program," Todd said enthusiastically as he and Annie emerged from the back room. "I want a copy the day it comes out."

"Glad you liked it. How was the space station?"

"Great! I could have spent another hour just exploring it, but Annie reminded me you were waiting."

Adam glanced at his watch. "I gather the Sex Hex didn't work?"

"Nope." Todd looked at his wife and grinned. "And once we figured out the zero-gravity thing, that was the best part, wasn't it, honey?"

Annie blushed. "It was what we went in to check out. I wasn't surprised, though. My theory is obviously right."

"It sure looks that way," Adam admitted. "So what exactly do you think is going on?"

"It's quite simple really. The Sex Hex was designed to shut down when two people have sex, right?"

"That's the general idea."

"It didn't work on Todd and me because we made love."

Adam frowned. "I don't follow."

Annie sighed. "Don't you see? For us, it's more than an act of lust. The Sex Hex didn't work, because it's designed to recognize lust. That's why it didn't shut down with your head engineer or for us."

"What about my accountant and his administrative assistant?"

Annie smiled. "I think they care far more about each other than either of them lets on. My guess is *Fantasy Quest* opened their eyes. If I were a gambler, I'd be willing to bet they'll be married within the year."

"So, what exactly are you saying?" Adam asked.

"That the Sex Hex is working fine and that you can go ahead with your February launch just as you planned. The porn industry won't be able to touch it."

Adam looked at Todd. "Do you understand what she's talking about?"

"Sorry, she lost me when she said having sex and making love weren't the same thing."

Annie rolled her eyes. "Men! Shall I put it in language you will understand?"

"That would be nice," Adam said.

"If you try to have sex with someone the program shuts down, right?"

"Yes."

"So, if it doesn't shut down, then it can only mean one thing."

"And that is...?

Annie smile was triumphant. "That you're deeply, passionately in love with that person."

Chapter 33

Kenzie had fallen from paradise straight into hell. Her first week back from the brink of death, she'd discovered she was in love with a dream. The irony of it still made her want to cry. Hard on the heels of that came the realization that she no longer trusted her fiancé. Unless she was very much mistaken, Brad Marriot, the man she'd planned to spend the next seventy years with, had been systematically drugging her.

Kenzie felt foolish and paranoid for suspecting him, but no matter how she figured it, she kept coming back to the same conclusion. At first, she'd dismissed the bitter taste of her water as a side effect of her brain injury. It was the bottled water Brad brought her that had finally convinced her of that. When it tasted slightly better than the hospital water, she'd fallen right into Brad's hands by drinking only the bottled water he so thoughtfully provided every day.

The charade had lasted right up until this morning, when she drank a glass of fresh ice water with her breakfast. It had a slight chlorine taste, but none of the bitterness. Even then, she might have dismissed it as part of her recovery if Brad hadn't hurried in on his way to work with a dozen roses and her water for the day. After he'd left, she'd opened a bottle of the water and tasted the familiar bitterness. She'd been drinking the hospital water ever since.

More damning yet, this was the first day since she'd come out of her coma that she'd been alert and hadn't slept away most of the day. The nurses had all commented on it, and her mother was thrilled. Kenzie kept her suspicions to herself, thinking perhaps paranoia was a side effect of spending the better part of three months in a coma. There was, after all, no reason she could think of that Brad would want to drug her. Besides, by all accounts he'd spent most of the last three months hovering protectively over her. It was only since her mother could be here with her that he'd gone back to work.

The more she dwelled on it, the less sense it made. What she needed was something to distract her. Her mother had gone on some mysterious errand several hours ago and told her not to expect her back until late afternoon. As usual, when Kenzie's mind wasn't occupied, her thoughts turned to her dream and the man her imagination had created.

One thing that continued to puzzle her was how she had come up with someone like Adam. She had never particularly liked primitive types, and the way he'd first appeared to her had been downright frightening. Whiskey Jug Johnson was about as different from Brad Marriot as you could get. Brad was suave, with a practiced charm that had turned her head. He had wined and dined her at expensive gourmet restaurants, taken her to the ballet and classical concerts. He'd made her feel sophisticated, classy, but there was always a niggling doubt in the back of her mind that maybe she wasn't quite good enough for him.

Kenzie hadn't exactly been happy with Brad when she'd gone to the Sinks that day. Taking over her social media accounts and then manipulating her into promising to get rid of her treasures had made her seriously rethink their relationship. Could her mind have created Adam as the antithesis of Brad? From the long hair and beard to his rough, overly-protective attitude, the rugged mountain man was Brad's opposite in every way.

As she thought back over it, Adam had changed dramatically over the course of the dream. Whiskey Jug Johnson was the epitome of the mountain man, as wild and untamed as the grizzlies and cougars. But as time went on, he'd gradually mellowed into something quite different. Where Whiskey Jug was gruff and intimidating, Adam was thoughtful and caring. He'd even developed a sense of humor. It had taken awhile, but her imagination had eventually molded and honed Adam's persona into her perfect mate.

"Good morning."

Startled, Kenzie looked up. A strange woman stood at the door of her room. The chart in her hand and the name tag pinned to her shirt indicated she was a hospital employee. "McKenzie Armstrong, right?"

The woman's infectious smile was impossible to resist. Kenzie smiled back. "Kenzie."

"Kenzie it is, then." The woman made a note on the chart in her hand. "I'm Annie, your new physical therapist."

Kenzie frowned. The young man who usually did her physical therapy had gone out of his way to make her comfortable. "What happened to Mikale?"

Annie shook her head. "He was hot dogging out on the ski slope yesterday and managed to break his leg in two places. The doctor says he's not to even think about coming back to work for a couple of weeks. I told him I'd help out with his patients if I got to do his physical therapy when he's ready for it." She grinned at Kenzie. "He said it was a high price to pay, but since he didn't have any other options, he took it."

"He mentioned he was going snowboarding and seemed really excited about it," Kenzie said. "It's too bad about the accident."

"The sad part is I doubt that he learned a darn thing from it. If I know Mikale, he'll be back on the slopes before the end of the season." The therapist glanced at the chart then set it aside. "So, let's take a look at you. Mikale said you were his star patient."

"Really?"

"Sure enough. Says he's never seen anyone bounce back so fast."

"He told me he thought I could start walking very soon," Kenzie said hopefully.

Annie smiled. "Then, we'd best get started."

It didn't take Kenzie long to decide she liked her new therapist very much. Mikale had been conscientious and thorough, but Annie had a relaxed, professional air that only years of experience could create. She kept up just the right mixture of encouragement and conversation as she put Kenzie through her range-of-motion exercises.

"You know, Mikale was right," Annie said in the middle of a particularly grueling leg stretch. "You're amazingly flexible for someone who has been in a coma for three months."

"Really?" It suddenly occurred to Kenzie that here was someone who could probably answer her questions without wondering what prompted them. "Have you had a lot of experience with comas?"

"I'm certainly no expert, but I've dealt with a fair number over the years."

"Have any of your patients had strange…sensory things afterwards?"

Annie raised her brows questioningly. "What do you mean?"

Kenzie shrugged as though trying to think up an example. "Oh, I don't know. Maybe things smelled weird to them or tasted funny. You know, like flowers smelled like garlic and water tasted bitter or something."

"Hmm." Annie considered as she worked Kenzie's ankle. "I don't know that I've ever heard those symptoms exactly, but I suppose it's possible. Why?"

"I was just curious," Kenzie said, unwilling to admit her suspicions of Brad out loud.

She gave Kenzie a shrewd look. "I'd say anything like that ought to be reported to the doctor. It's probably a transitory thing, but sometimes unusual smells or tastes are related to malfunctions in the brain."

"I was wondering, that's all. I had a friend who was in an accident and lost her sense of smell."

Annie appeared to accept this explanation and moved on to the other ankle.

Kenzie obligingly wiggled her toes and stretched the muscles in her calf. "So how soon do you think I'll be able to walk?"

"I'd say we could try it with a walker as soon as tomorrow." Annie shook her head. "Frankly, I thought Mikale was exaggerating when he told me how far advanced you were, but if anything, he understated the case. Heck, you'll be out of here and back to work before you know it. You are one lucky lady!" She glanced at her watch. "That's enough for today. If you feel up to it later, you might try a few repetitions of the exercises we did."

"Will that help me walk sooner?"

"Couldn't hurt." Annie picked up her chart. "I'll see you tomorrow."

"Ok, I'll be here."

Annie left with a wave and a smile, taking Kenzie's cloud of depression with her. *Lucky.* For the first time since she woke up in a hospital bed, Kenzie realized she was indeed lucky. The accident could have killed her or turned her into a human rutabaga. At the very least, it should have left her impaired in some way, but so far everything was normal—no, better than normal. Every medical professional she'd come in contact with was amazed by her swift recovery.

Suddenly, the future seemed full of possibilities rather than bleak emptiness. Instead of grieving for a man who never existed, she should be thanking God for such an awesome gift. Instead of losing three months of her life, or drifting in and out of a confusing nightmare, she'd been given a beautiful fantasy, one she would remember her entire life. Maybe she should try writing a book or a screenplay. Her dream would make a great time-travel romance. She'd bounce the idea off her mother.

When her mother arrived later that day, though, the idea of writing a book was the last thing on Kenzie's mind. She was trying to get into a TV program with little success when her mother arrived, but Danelda Armstrong was not alone.

"Surprise!"

Suddenly, Kenzie's bed was surrounded by a noisy crowd as her father and all four of her siblings followed her mother into the room.

"What are you all doing here?"

James, her eldest brother, gave her a bone-crunching hug. "We came to celebrate your birthday."

"My birthday's in September!"

Her sister Frances plopped down on the end of the bed. "Yeah, well, you weren't in any condition to celebrate it then."

Sean nodded. "Andy came up with the idea of waiting until you woke up."

Her father kissed her cheek. "And here we are."

"Where's Wonder Boy?" Andy asked, glancing around.

"Andy!" Danelda glared at her youngest son. "I thought we agreed this family is deeply indebted to Brad for the way he's looked after your sister."

Andy shrugged. "I just asked where he was."

"Oh," Kenzie said suddenly. "That's why he brought me flowers today! I wondered."

"Ooh." Frances reached out and touched the peach-colored petals. "Those are gorgeous. Brad has incredible taste."

"Of course he does," said Kenzie's father. "Look who he picked to marry."

Andy snorted, but the rest of the family ignored him and began to pull gifts out of coat pockets and hand bags.

The lively group completely banished what remained of Kenzie's depression. Her heart was light, and her sides ached from laughter by the time the nurse's aide arrived with her dinner at five.

"That's our cue to leave," Danelda said.

Andy stood up and stretched. "What are we doing for dinner?"

"How about Chinese?"

"No, Mexican."

"Italian."

"Seafood!"

Herb Armstrong laughed and shook his head. "We'll let your mother decide." He winked at Kenzie. "Be glad you have your dinner delivered. It will probably be midnight before we get this crew fed and settled for the night."

Kenzie wrinkled her nose. "No matter where you eat, it's bound to be better than hospital food."

"Don't worry," Sean announced in a stage whisper, "We'll smuggle you in some decent food tomorrow."

"So, what will it be?" Andy wanted to know. "Pizza, donuts, popcorn?"

Kenzie closed her eyes. "A hot fudge sundae, with the fudge sauce all warm and oozy and the ice cream just starting to melt."

"And just how are we supposed to get that up here without it turning into chocolate soup?" Frances asked.

Kenzie batted her eyes. "Beats me. I'm the birthday girl. I don't have to do anything but sit here and look pretty."

Her siblings groaned.

"Hello, everyone. I see you all made it." Brad strolled in. He rather pointedly set his briefcase on a chair and crossed the room to kiss Kenzie. "What did you think of your little surprise?" he asked with a smile.

"It's wonderful!" Kenzie found herself wondering why it irritated her that Brad spoke as if it had all been his idea when she knew darned well it wasn't.

"We were just getting ready to go get something to eat, Brad," Danelda said. "Would you like to join us?"

Brad managed to look regretful as he shook his head. "No, I grabbed something on my way over, but thanks for asking."

"Maybe next time," Herb said.

"Right."

Sean leaned down and gave Kenzie a kiss on the cheek. "See ya later, pipsqueak."

One by one, the rest of the family took their leave, until Andy was the only one left. "Nice suit, Marriot," he commented as he sauntered over to his sister's bed. "They must pay you well at Vain-Tech."

"It's Vid-Tech, and yes, they do." Brad gave Andy's T-shirt and jeans a disdainful glance. "Maybe I can get you a summer job after you graduate from high school next spring, Andrew."

"No, thanks. I don't much like their product line." He tapped Kenzie's nose with his knuckle. "See you tomorrow, sis." He gave Brad a veiled glance, then turned his gaze back to his sister. "Don't take any wooden nickels."

Brad's lips thinned as he watched Andy slouch out of the room. "It has always amazed me how your parents put up with his insolence."

"You bring out the worst in him, Brad. He hates it when you call him Andrew."

"It's his name."

Kenzie rolled her eyes but dropped the subject. The hostility between Brad and her baby brother was long standing. It stemmed from the passion they shared: namely, computers. Brad considered Andy a smart-aleck kid, and Andy thought Brad was a puffed-up snob who didn't know his head from a hole in the ground. Kenzie was tired of being caught in the middle. She changed the subject, and the evening passed in relative peace.

The only moments of discord came when Kenzie told him what the physical therapist had said.

His eyebrows crashed together, and a frown marred his handsome countenance. "They're pushing you too fast," he said severely. "You almost died. I think you should just focus on resting for now."

Kenzie blinked in surprise. "According to all the doctors, I'm healing really fast. They say it's practically miraculous."

"Doctors don't know everything."

Kenzie glared at him. "If I didn't know better, I'd think you didn't want me to get well," she snapped.

"It's just that I worry about you, darling." He glanced over at her bedside table. "You haven't touched your water today. If you aren't careful, you'll get dehydrated."

"Frances brought me a bottle of the brand she drinks. It tastes so much better I think I'll switch."

Kenzie could have sworn she saw a flicker of something in

his eyes, but it was gone so fast she wondered if she'd imagined it.

"Of course, darling. Whatever you want."

The next four days passed with a whirlwind of visits from her family. Over the weekend, Frances's husband and James's wife arrived with all the nieces and nephews in tow. Kenzie thoroughly enjoyed them all.

Meanwhile, her physical therapy program was progressing at an astonishing rate. She spent less than two days using a walker before graduating to using a brotherly or sisterly arm as support. By the time her family went home, she was walking short distances by herself.

She barely saw Brad at all. From what everyone said, he'd hardly left her side when she was unconscious, even bringing his computer to the hospital so he could work. Yet, now that she was awake, he was never here.

Kenzie had long suspected Brad wasn't fond of her large, boisterous family, and his conspicuous absence seemed to confirm it. As much as she loved them, Kenzie knew being around her family was difficult for someone who had grown up in a quiet, staid household like Brad's. She had almost as much trouble dealing with his parents' aloofness as he did with her family's open, friendly ways. Before her accident, it had seemed like a problem that would work itself out once they were married. Now she wasn't so sure.

The day her family left, Brad came in after work, wreathed in smiles. "I have a surprise for you, darling."

"Oh?" she said, masking her irritation at his obvious delight that her family was gone.

"The doctor said you'd be able to leave next week, right?"

Kenzie nodded, surprised at his pleased smile. It was completely at odds with his former attitude.

"I think I got you a job!"

"What?"

"I put in some calls today. It looks like you'll have a job waiting for you as soon as you get out of the hospital." He beamed at her, immensely proud of himself.

"You took it upon yourself to get me a job without even asking me if it was something I wanted?" Kenzie fought to hold on to her temper. It was just this sort of high-handed management of her life that had gotten her into this fix in the first place. "How do you know what I want to do once I leave here?"

"Because it's doing what you were trained to do. Two weeks from today, you can expect to start work in the Art Department of an up-and-coming computer firm."

"I already told you, I won't work for the same company you do," she told him in a flat voice.

"No, no, no, it's not with Vid-Tech." He gave her the wide, toothy grin that used to give her butterflies. Today, she found herself curiously unmoved.

"If it's not with Vid-tech, then how did you manage to get me a job without so much as an interview?"

"Because, my dear, you already had the interview four months ago."

"What are you talking about?"

"I got you a second chance at the job you landed just before your accident."

Kenzie's eyes widened. "You mean —?"

Brad nodded. "If everything goes the way I planned, you'll start December fifteenth at Microcom!"

Chapter 34

"You're alone?" Annie's glance took in the whole room and swung back to Kenzie.

"My family all had to go home yesterday. Everybody had to go back to work except my little brother, and he had school."

"And your fiancé?"

"He was glad to see them go."

"No, I meant where is he?"

"Oh. He's at work." Kenzie sighed. "He's not crazy about my family. I guess they're a little hard to take."

"On the contrary, they're delightful!"

Kenzie smiled as she swung her legs over the edge of the bed and stood up. "Maybe to you, but Brad's an only child, and I think that makes a huge difference."

Annie looked doubtful as she handed Kenzie her bathrobe. "Not necessarily. I have a friend who is an only child and something of a recluse, besides. He adores my family, and my kids think he's the greatest thing since the invention of the internet." Annie seemed to realize her comment was less than comforting. "Brad will probably come around once he gets to know them better."

"Maybe." Kenzie shrugged into her bathrobe. "What are we going to do today?"

"I thought we'd go for a hike."

"A hike?"

Annie grinned. "Yes, clear to the end of the hall."

"Wow!"

"Today the hall, tomorrow the world!"

Kenzie chuckled. "Next thing I know, I'll be walking a marathon."

"I've known stranger things to happen." Annie helped Kenzie into her bathrobe and slippers.

Annie's words suddenly reminded Kenzie of the idea she'd forgotten to bounce off her mother. Annie might even be more honest about it. Mothers tended to try to shield their children from disappointments.

"Speaking of strange things," she said, as Annie helped her stand. "I've been thinking of writing a book about my experience while I was in my coma."

"What a great idea. Others will be inspired by your quick recovery."

"That wasn't exactly what I had in mind."

"Oh?"

"Actually, it would be a novel. A fantasy, really." She glanced sideways at the therapist. "I had an amazing dream while I was asleep."

"Right or left," Annie asked as they reached the door.

"Right, I think."

"You had a dream?" Annie prompted as they stepped in to the hallway and turned right.

Kenzie nodded. "A pretty involved one. At the time, I didn't realize it was a dream. I thought I'd traveled back in time to 1868."

"I want to read it already," Annie said, intrigued. "I love time travel!"

"That isn't the strangest part. I woke up in a hot pool with a mountain man."

"A mountain man?"

"Yes, and he was stark naked, to boot."

"Whoa! I take it this was an X-rated dream?"

Kenzie giggled. "No, though there were a couple of love scenes at the end." She smiled a little sadly, then gave herself a shake. "Anyway, I thought he was a right-wing militant at first and was scared to death of him."

"I imagine. Watch your step here," Annie cautioned as they skirted an area marked by two wet floor signs. "Ok, so why was he naked?"

"We were in the hot pool, and he couldn't wear his

buckskins in the water. Of course, I didn't realize that at the time and thought he was some kind of nutcase."

"Yes, I can see why."

"I escaped the first chance I got, but he followed me. He eventually circled around and got far enough ahead to set up camp. When I saw the fire I thought I'd found help at last and walked right in. I almost freaked out when I saw who it was."

"You know, Kenzie, this sounds like a great story," Annie said. "I think you should go ahead and write it."

"You do?"

"Yes, I do. This is as good as any plotline I've ever read."

"Then, you don't think it's weird I had a dream so vivid that I thought it was real?"

"Unusual, yes. Weird?" Annie shrugged. "Scientists still don't know what makes the brain tick. They have some theories, but that's it. The brain does some amazing things. Who's to say what's normal and what isn't, especially in the case of a severe injury like this?"

"I guess you're right."

"Time to turn around," Annie said when they reached the end of the hall. "Was this mountain man of yours the only other person in the dream, or will your book have a cast of thousands?"

Kenzie smiled. "Not a cast of thousands, though there was a tribe of Indians and an old trapper with Alzheimer's. Mostly, though, it was just Whiskey Jug Johnson and me."

"Whiskey Jug Johnson?" Annie frowned. "That name sounds familiar for some reason."

"In my dream, his parents named him that because his father bought him at a rendezvous for a jug of whiskey."

"You know, that rings a bell too."

Kenzie tipped her head. "Really? I wonder where I got it. Maybe it was something I studied in Wyoming History class in high school or something. Now that I think of it, I'll bet it has something to do with Laramie. That's where Adam got hurt."

"A-Adam?"

Kenzie nodded. "My mountain man. Anyway, when we went to Laramie, somebody knifed him in a fight. He was cut from here to here," she said, drawing a line down her shoulder.

"Oh, my Lord!"

"That's an understatement. He probably would have bled to death if I hadn't sewed up the wound with a piece of hair from a mule tail, only it got infected, and that's how we wound up at the Indian village." Kenzie suddenly realized that Annie had stopped walking and was staring at her in astonishment. "What's the matter?"

"The wound," Annie said faintly. "What happened with that?"

"Oh, you mean Adam's?"

Annie nodded, and Kenzie rolled her eyes. "That was one of the scariest parts. I thought he was going to die and leave me there all alone. Luckily, it healed in a matter of days. One day it was barely closed, and the next it was completely healed."

Annie took in a deep breath. "The glitch," she murmured.

"Pardon me?"

Annie shook her head. "Oh, nothing. I was just thinking out loud. What else happened?"

"Are you sure you want to hear it? I mean, it's pretty long."

"You have me hanging on every word."

"You're not just humoring me?"

Annie shook her head. "Definitely not. I can't wait to hear it all."

"All right, if you're sure," Kenzie said doubtfully.

"I'm sure. What happened after this wound healed?"

"There was this handsome Indian man, named Eagle Feather, who decided he was in love with me, mostly to irritate Adam, I think. He considered Whiskey Jug Johnson his arch rival, you see. Anyway..." Kenzie launched into the tale. She found herself going into much more detail than she had intended, but Annie appeared fascinated by it all. They had walked the full length of the hall twice before either of them realized it.

"Goodness!" Annie said as they were about to pass Kenzie's room for the third time. "I got into your story so much I forgot what we were doing. You must be exhausted."

Kenzie stopped in surprise and took stock of herself. "No, not really. It actually feels good to get up and stretch."

"That's definitely enough for one day." Annie took her arm and led her back in to her room. "Let's get you back into bed."

"You think I actually ought to try writing my story, then?" Kenzie asked as she shed her bathrobe and slippers.

"I think it's one of the most amazing stories I've ever heard," Annie told her truthfully.

"The problem is, I've never really written anything but a paper here and there in college. I don't know if I can actually do something like this."

"I guess the only way to find out is to sit down and start writing." Annie looked at her thoughtfully for a moment. "You said there were two love scenes?"

Kenzie got a far off look in her eyes. "Three actually, but I'm not sure I can share those with the world. They were...incredible," she said softly.

"You're in love with him, aren't you?"

"Oh, yes, so much that it hurts." Kenzie gave her a slightly bitter smile. "Ironic, isn't it? I have a wonderful fiancé that most women would kill for, and all I can think about is a man I created out of thin air."

Annie smiled mysteriously as she fluffed Kenzie's pillow. "Oh, I don't know. These things have a way of working themselves out."

Adam had to force himself to stay focused as the meeting droned on and on. Normally, he enjoyed a gathering of his company's department heads. His staff was an interesting collection of people, chosen more for their free thinking than the vast array of fancy college degrees that many of them possessed. Today, though, he was restless and cranky and wanted to be just about anywhere but here.

"...so everything is right on schedule for the launch in February." Jamie Jorgensen finished his presentation then sat down.

"Thank you, Jamie. Anyone have anything else to discuss?" Adam asked, surveying the faces around the table.

Lucinda, an older woman with short, dark hair and a loud voice raised her hand. "We've come up with another market for *Fantasy Quest*. Sex therapists and marriage counselors are going to *love* the Sex Hex angle."

"*Everybody* loves the Sex Hex angle," piped up Joe Scranton, the head of accounting. A wave of laughter swept the meeting. Everyone knew the Sex Hex test was responsible for getting Joe and his fiancée together.

Adam smiled. "What do we need in place to exploit Lucinda's idea to the fullest?"

"A manual," Lucinda said promptly, and the others started throwing out ideas.

"Too accessible. Then anybody could set themselves up as an expert."

"It needs to be exclusive somehow, so people will see it as special."

"How about a training program?"

"Ooh, yeah, and the trainees earn a special license at the end of it?"

" — and the right to use the logo. We could make a special logo couldn't we, Larry?"

"They'd have the right to use a special version of the program, too."

"And the only way to get that special version would be to take the training."

Everybody looked expectantly at Adam, who sat at the head of the table, his fingers steepled against his mouth. Usually, he was an active part of these brainstorming sessions, but today his creativity was in hibernation. "The training program sounds good to me. Legal ramifications, Laura?"

"I'd say we'd need to have an expert in the field— preferably one with a recognizable name—in on the creation of such a training program. That would cover our backsides for practicing psychology without a degree, and we'd need a limited liability clause, of course."

Adam nodded. "This is something that we can focus on after the launch. Carla, put it on the agenda for April. In the meantime, everybody jot down any ideas you have, and keep your eyes open for an expert that might be interested in the project. Anything else?"

A young man with black hair and a moustache raised his hand. "We've run into a problem in the Art Department."

"What's that, Larry?"

"With Denise out on maternity leave and Henry leaving at the end of the week, we're way behind on the graphics loop."

Adam frowned. "What would you need to put you back on schedule?"

"A couple of top-notch graphic artists would do it."

"I think I may have a partial solution," the personnel manager said doubtfully, "but it could be a little risky."

"By all means, Tom, share it with us."

"We hired a young woman fresh out of college early last summer. I interviewed her myself and was very impressed. Unfortunately, she had an accident before she ever started. It was a crying shame."

"What relevance does that have for our situation now?"

"I got a call yesterday from her fiancé saying she'll be ready to work in a couple of weeks."

Adam raised an eyebrow. "But…"

"But it was a traumatic brain injury. There's no certainty that she can still do the job."

"The worst-case scenario would be that she couldn't, right?"

"Uh…right."

"Then I say we give her a chance. If she can't do the job, we won't be any worse off than we are right now. On the other hand, if she's as good as she was before her accident, she may be our solution."

Tom nodded. "All right. I'll give her a call and see how soon she can come to work."

"So, we still need at least one more graphic artist, maybe two if this one doesn't pan out," Adam said. "How soon can we get one on board?"

"That's just the problem. None of the freelance graphic artists we usually use are available. Word is Vid-Tech is gearing up for some big project and hired all of them and a dozen more last week."

Adam frowned. "Any word what the project is?"

Everyone looked at each other and then shook their heads. A mousy-haired woman at the end of the table hesitantly raised her hand.

"Did you have something, Leandra?" Adam asked.

"I'm not really sure," she admitted, "but I overheard something at Randolph's a couple of nights ago."

"Adam asked for facts." A large, red-faced man cast a scornful sneer in Leandra's direction. "Don't waste our time with barroom gossip."

Adam pinned the man with a look. "I've never known Leandra to waste our time before, George. I doubt she will this time, either." Then he gave Leandra a gentle smile. "What were you saying before Mr. Fredrickson interrupted?"

She glared at George Fredrickson then turned her attention to Adam. "I was sitting next to a couple of women from Vid-Tech, that I know from when we all worked there. They were talking about their new programmer, a hot-shot named Brett Marionet or Brand Martinet or something."

Adam's gaze sharpened. "Brad Marriot?"

"Yes, I think that's it. Anyway, most of the conversation had to do with what a charmer he is, so I didn't pay much attention. Then one of them said if he didn't deliver the SR program like he promised, Saunders would have his head on a platter. Then the other one said Marriot had just had a little set back but was trying something new and would come through just fine."

Adam felt the hair on the back of his neck rise. Tossing his spy out and destroying *Beta Quest* should have sent the SOB running for cover. There was no way he could touch *Fantasy Quest*. Had he managed to download a piece of *Beta Quest* before it was destroyed? "Did they say what he was trying?"

Leandra shook her head. "No, and I had the feeling they didn't know."

"Thank you, Leandra. I think you may have stumbled on to something."

"Excuse me, Adam." His secretary, Carla, put her hand over the receiver of the phone she had just answered. "Mrs. Bedford is here to see you. She says it's urgent."

"I think we're just about done." He glanced around the group. "Anything else?" When no one spoke, he turned back to Carla. "Tell her I'll be right there."

Carla nodded then spoke quietly into the phone as Adam turned back to the group. "We don't know for sure that Marriot is after *Fantasy Quest*, but forewarned is forearmed. Keep your ears and eyes open and report anything odd to me right away." He smiled. "Have a restful weekend, and I'll expect you all back bright and early Monday morning."

His employees were still filing out when Adam slipped through the door between the meeting room and his office. Annie was pacing the floor, more agitated than he'd ever seen her. "What's happened?" he asked in alarm.

"Oh, Adam," she cried, her eyes shining. "I've found her."

"Who?"

"Your glitch! Her name is Kenzie Armstrong, and she's as real as you and I."

"Oh, hell," he said flatly, as he rolled around the side of his desk to the computer and set the brakes on his chair. Annie watched in dumbfounded silence as he switched on the monitor.

"Didn't you hear me? Kenzie wasn't a glitch at all."

"I heard you," he said, without looking up. "She's the reason I shut *Beta Quest* down."

"What?"

"She's an industrial spy, Annie."

"A spy... Oh, come on, Adam. You're being paranoid."

"Am I? Did you know she has a fiancé named Brad Marriot?"

"Yes, but—"

"And do you know who Marriot works for?"

"Some computer company."

"That's right." He stared at his computer screen. "Vid-Tech."

Annie sat down in the chair on the other side of his desk. "As in your biggest competitor?"

"As in the company that has sworn to drive Microcom into the ground."

"But you can't be sure Kenzie's involved with Vid-Tech."

"Can't I?" He sat back and started ticking things off on his fingers. "Someone hacks into *Beta Quest*. A glitch appears in the program, a glitch that freely admits to being in love with Brad Marriot, a man who has been accused of stealing programs not once or twice but three times. Marriot lacks the skills to create his own SR program, but Pete Saunders hires him to do just that. I shut down *Beta Quest*, and Marriot runs into major problems with the SR program he's promised to Saunders."

"That's Brad, not Kenzie."

"Right. How do you suppose she got into my program in the first place? You have to be hooked up to a computer, you know. It's not like he could put her in without her knowledge. Oh, she's involved all right, clear up to her pretty little neck."

"I'm not so sure, Adam. I've spent the last week with her and—"

"Dammit, Annie," he said, slamming his hand down on the desk. "Don't you get it? Kenzie Armstrong is a lying, scheming bitch. Think about it: our relationship isn't exactly a secret. The minute she can no longer get to me, she suddenly shows up in your life. Pretty odd coincidence if you ask me. She knew who you were and how you're connected to me. You played right into her hands. She probably even instigated a conversation about me, didn't she?"

"But the Sex Hex didn't work," she said.

"Yeah, and that's because I'm the biggest dammed fool in the universe! For God sake, Annie, just drop it, will you?"

Annie dropped it, not because she was convinced of Kenzie's guilt, but because Adam had finally raised his eyes to hers. She hadn't seen so much naked pain there since he'd awakened to find his father dead and his own legs useless lumps of flesh.

Chapter 35

"It's McKenzie, right?"

Kenzie looked up from the form she was signing and smiled. "Kenzie."

"Tom Branchard." The man stuck out his hand. "Head of personnel. I interviewed you last summer."

"Yes, I remember," Kenzie said, shaking his hand.

"We really appreciate you coming in a week early," he said. "We've found ourselves in something of a bind, or we certainly wouldn't have asked it of you. I understand you just got out of the hospital."

"Last week, actually.". Kenzie felt herself relax. This was the same welcoming atmosphere she'd loved last summer when she'd interviewed. It was a modern building, but there was a feel of warmth here that had as much to do with the personnel as the interesting combination of chrome and glass interspersed with warm woods.

"If you find you aren't quite up to a full day of work yet, don't hesitate to let us know. We can make arrangements."

"Thank you, but I'm fine, really."

"Great." He glanced at the employment forms. "I'll take you over to the Art Department as soon as you get those filled out."

"I just finished signing the last one," she said, scooping up the stack. "Who should I give them to?"

"We'll drop them off with my administrative assistant, and she'll send them over to HR." He took the papers and indicated with a sweep of his hand that she should precede him across the room.

"I want to thank you for giving me a second chance," Kenzie told him. "I don't know of any other company who would have done it."

"You'll find we have a somewhat different attitude about that sort of thing here at Microcom. Besides, we really need you, especially if you can still…" The man's ears reddened slightly. "Uh, I mean…"

Kenzie gave him an understanding smile. "You mean if I can still do the job? To be honest, I was a little concerned about that myself, so I spent some time last week practicing. I was a tad bit rusty at first, but it came back pretty fast."

They had reached the office door, where Tom Branchard's administrative assistant was talking into a telephone headset. "Yes, I'll see that he gets the message," she said, jotting a note on an electronic notepad. "Thanks. You have one too." She pressed a button then looked up expectantly at Kenzie and Tom.

"This is our newest graphic artist, Kenzie Armstrong," he said. "Kenzie, this is my administrative assistant, Pia Clark."

"Welcome to Microcom, Kenzie," Pia said with a smile.

Kenzie smiled back. "Thank you. I'm looking forward to working here."

"It's a great place to work," Pia assured her as the light began flashing on the phone. "Oops, duty calls," she said, adjusting her mouthpiece. "Microcom. How may I help you this morning?"

"Good morning." A tall, dark-haired woman walked into the office and set a pile of forms similar to Kenzie's on Pia's desk.

"And this," Tom said, "is Carla Vickers."

The woman was middle-aged and looked frightfully competent, but she smiled at Kenzie as she offered her hand. "You must be the new graphic artist."

Kenzie shook the other woman's hand and smiled back. "Yes, I'm Kenzie."

"Carla is the unofficial vice president in charge of everything and everybody's Girl Friday," Tom said with a grin.

Carla gave an unladylike snort. "Forget it, Tom. I'm not taking you off the hook. The boss put you in charge of the

Christmas party, and in charge of it you'll stay." She winked at Kenzie. "I'm Adam Johnson's administrative assistant."

"A-Adam Johnson?" The floor rocked under Kenzie's feet as she stared at Carla Vickers in astonishment.

Carla nodded. "The boss, our one and only CEO."

"How long" — she swallowed — "has he worked here?"

Carla blinked. "Oh, honey, he's been here since the beginning. He owns Microcom."

"He started it while he was still in high school," Tom added. "Guess you could say Adam Johnson *is* Microcom."

It suddenly clicked into place for Kenzie. *Of course!* She heard the name when she was here for her interview last summer. That's where her subconscious had come up with it. For all she knew, she might even have met Adam Johnson himself. There had been so many people at all the different interviews she'd done last summer that their names and faces had blurred together into a confusing mishmash.

"Tom," Pia said, "it's that call you've been waiting for from Seattle."

"Oh good. I'll take it in my office. I'm sorry Kenzie. I have to take this call. I shouldn't be more than ten minutes or so. Then I'll finish showing you around."

"I can do it," Carla said.

"If you wouldn't mind."

Carla waved her hand. "No problem. I was just dropping these off on the way to the break room." She pointed to the pile she'd set on Pia's desk. "It's the paperwork for that teenager Adam hired to test *Fantasy Quest*."

"Thanks," Pia said. "Did Adam ever decide when he was going to start the test?"

"As soon as the schools get out for Christmas vacation if he has enough teens, but that shouldn't be a problem. Once the word gets out, they'll be falling all over themselves to volunteer. Well, Kenzie, are you ready for the grand tour?"

"Sure."

"We're not a huge company," Carla said as they left the

Personnel Office, "but it's a really cohesive staff. You'll find most everyone is friendly and good to work with."

"That's what I remember from when I was here last summer. It's one of the reasons I decided I wanted to work here." Kenzie glanced up at her companion. "Did I understand you to say Microcom is looking for teenagers to test a new program?"

Carla nodded. "Adam decided he wanted a cross-section of teens to do a market analysis with. Why, do you know someone?"

"My brother Andy would do just about anything for a chance to test a new Microcom program," Kenzie said. "His favorite games are Microcom games. In fact, he's the one who convinced me to apply here. I think he was as excited about me getting this job as I was."

"Does he live here?"

"No, but he's coming to spend Christmas break with me. I'm positive he'd jump at the chance. I can call tonight to make sure."

"Great. Let me know, and we'll get him signed up." She pointed toward an office that appeared identical to the one they had just left. "That's Accounting over there, and Marketing is right next door. That way we have all the bean counters together. And over there," she said, pointing to a pair of double doors across the lobby, "is where the engineers hang out. I'll show you around there as soon as your security clearance comes through."

Kenzie chuckled. "That's ok, I've seen software engineers before."

"And if you've seen one you've seen them all?"

"Something like that. What's this?" Kenzie said as they passed a large glass case. "I remember wondering about it when I was here last summer."

"Oh, that's the trophy case. Microcom supports all kinds of kids' sports. See, there's our little league team," she said, pointing to a wall of pictures, "and junior hockey, softball, boys' and girls' basketball, and even an Odyssey of the Mind team."

"Wow, that's a lot." Kenzie was impressed.

"Adam says kids are our future and organized sports teach them the skills they'll need later. Even when they don't win, which they often don't, Adam throws a party at the end of the season. Everybody has a great time, and it doesn't hurt Microcom's image, either."

"I'll bet the kids love it."

"So does Adam, though he won't admit it. If he didn't, he'd just let me set up the parties and be done with it, instead of showing up for every one he possibly can." She pointed to a collection of trophies near the back of the case. "Those are the ones Adam has won himself. His mother brought them in and insisted they be displayed along with the rest. The staff agreed with her because we're all pretty proud of him. He doesn't like it, but he's outvoted, so there they stay."

Kenzie focused on a picture next to one of the larger trophies. The man was seated in a sleek machine that looked like a cross between a wheelchair and a racing bicycle. There was a triumphant smile on his face as he held the trophy aloft. Kenzie's heart gave a jerk then started pounding so hard she thought Carla must be able to hear it. It was Adam, or at least a modern version of him. His hair above the sweatband was short, and a T-shirt stretched across the impressive expanse of his chest instead of buckskin, but the muscular arms extended above his head were the same; so was his smile. "Oh!" she murmured.

"I know," Carla said proudly. "He's something isn't he?"

"How long has he been in the wheelchair?" Kenzie heard herself ask.

Carla shrugged. "As long as I've known him. I've heard there was some kind of an accident when he was in high school, but I've never asked. Why?" Her voice had a hint of warning in it. She was obviously very protective of her boss.

"It's just that he looks really familiar," Kenzie admitted. "I didn't realize he was in a wheelchair, though, so I guess I've never met him." Now it all made sense. The trophy case had drawn her last summer the way it had today, and she'd seen the picture of Adam Johnson. Somehow, she had created an entire fantasy around him. She'd seen the face and heard the name; her brain had done the rest.

As they entered the break room, Kenzie realized she felt better than she had since leaving the hospital. Somehow, the fact that her fantasy man really existed eased some of the loneliness in her heart. Even though he wasn't really *her* Adam, she'd be able to see him again.

Carla finished the tour in the Art Department, where everyone was friendly and welcoming. The supervisor, Larry Boyd, was just the sort of creative personality Kenzie enjoyed working with. By the time she was settled in her spacious workstation with everything she needed—including state-of-the-art equipment—at her fingertips, she knew she was going to love working at Microcom and could hardly wait to get started.

Larry appeared to be quite satisfied with the preliminary work she did for him and put her on the same project everyone else was involved with. Though she wasn't quite sure what kind of program it was for, they were designing a graphics loop to run during downtime. Larry said the more creative and dynamic it was, the better. Just the sort of thing Kenzie loved to get her teeth into. It felt so good to be working again that Kenzie was surprised when five o'clock arrived.

Her jubilant mood gradually faded as she neared home. The condo she and Brad had found in June had lost its appeal. Brad had hired an interior decorator who was both tasteful and expensive. The result was gorgeous, and yet somehow it seemed cold and sterile to her. Brad, of course, loved it, and dismissed her reservations with something very like contempt.

Kenzie told herself she was just missing the well-worn furniture of her youth and the friendly clutter of her family. But in her heart, she knew it was more than that. It was Brad himself. Though he was as attentive as ever, she had begun to suspect there was little warmth or true feeling behind it. She even found herself thinking he was much like their apartment, nice to look at but hollow on the inside. Not for the first time, Kenzie found herself toying with the idea of getting her own apartment, at least for a while.

As usual when her thoughts took that sort of turn, Kenzie took herself to task. It wasn't Brad's fault he didn't quite measure up to Kenzie's dream man. Who could? Unlike a real flesh-and-blood man, an imaginary lover could be perfect. Kenzie smiled at the image. Adam, perfect? Not hardly, and yet it was his imperfections that made him so loveable. Kenzie pushed the thought away with irritation. It was bad enough that she couldn't bring herself to sleep with Brad.

Kenzie could hear the phone ringing as she let herself in through the front door. She dropped her coat over the back of the white leather couch and grabbed the designer phone. As usual, she felt a flash of irritation as she held the awkward receiver to her ear. Kenzie had argued that they didn't really need a land line, but the phone fit in perfectly with the theme and ambiance of the room, so it stayed. It was also a nightmare to use.

"Hello?"

"Hello, could I speak to McKenzie Armstrong, please?"

"This is she."

"Ah, good, I'm glad I finally caught you. This is Sonya Carothers from Prudent Life. We've been trying to get in touch with you about your life insurance policy. There are a couple of places you forgot to sign."

"Boy, that was fast. I just filled out those forms this morning."

There was a slight pause on the other end of the line. "Pardon me?"

"I said that was really quick. I expected it to take more than a day to process my employment form."

"I'm sorry, I don't understand." the woman said

uncertainly.

Kenzie frowned. "Isn't this about the life insurance policy that comes with my new job at Microcom?"

"No, ma'am, this policy was purchased" — Kenzie could hear the rustle of a page turning — "on July eighth."

"July eighth! But that's impossible. I was—" A horrible suspicion suddenly struck Kenzie. "Who is the beneficiary?"

"Let me check." More paper rustling. "That would be Bradford Marriot."

"Just how much is this policy for?"

"Five hundred thousand dollars."

"I see." And Kenzie thought she did, perhaps for the first time. Later, she couldn't remember exactly what she said, but when she finally hung up the phone, the policy had been cancelled and her resolve set. She was in the process of packing her things when Brad got home.

"Kenzie, you have got to get into the habit of picking up your things," he said with irritation when he saw her coat and purse still flung across the couch. "This isn't your mother's house, you know."

"No, it isn't, is it? As a matter of fact, it isn't mine, either. Brad, I think it's best if I find my own apartment."

"What?"

"You heard me. I said I'm moving."

"Why?"

The expression on his face was so close to panic, it gave Kenzie pause. Maybe he did care. "I just need some time to rethink my life, and I can't do it here."

"What about our wedding?"

"I need to rethink that, too."

He sank into the overstuffed chair that was tastefully upholstered in contrasting accents to the couch and the wall paper. The fact that he didn't put his briefcase away first made Kenzie realize just how upset he was.

"Kenzie, I love you. Doesn't that matter anymore?"

"I'm not so sure," she said. "I know about the insurance

policy."

"What insurance policy?" He looked so honestly perplexed that Kenzie had another moment of doubt.

"The five hundred thousand dollar one you took out on me while I was in a coma. I keep wondering how you managed that, by the way. Don't they usually require a physical or something?"

"Oh, that," he waved his hand deprecatingly. "I bought that in May; it just took a long time to process."

"Two months? Besides, don't you think half a million dollars is a little excessive?"

"No, I took the same out on myself. I was just planning for the future and our children."

"We don't have any children."

"Of course not, but we will. You know, darling, the doctor did say you might still have some residual problems. I suspect that's why you're out of sorts. You'll feel better in the morning. Please give our love another chance. You know I couldn't live without you." He gave her a pleading look.

Kenzie seriously doubted she'd feel any different in the morning, but his explanation for the insurance policy had been plausible. Besides, he seemed genuinely distressed by the thought of her leaving. Maybe she did owe him a second chance. In the end, he convinced her to stay, but only because she decided going to a hotel was stupid. She went to bed that night in the guest room, vowing to go apartment hunting the next day after work.

"I can't believe I lost her," Annie said, looking into the bathroom mirror as she removed her makeup.

"You didn't lose her. She was discharged from the hospital on your day off," Todd pointed out. "Not that it was your job to keep track of her, anyway."

Annie looked at him over her shoulder. "You know what I mean."

"I know you're messing where you don't belong and that Adam won't thank you for it."

"Don't you understand?" Annie wiped her face with a washcloth. "Adam is in love with Kenzie Armstrong, and she loves him back. If you could have seen the look in her eyes when she talked about him."

"She's an industrial spy," Todd reminded her.

Annie stopped drying her face and glared at him in the mirror. "Baloney! There's no way she was trying to steal his program. She thought it was a dream. Besides, Kenzie Armstrong was in a full coma for the whole time. I checked."

"Then, how do you explain her being in Adam's program?"

"I can't," she said, smoothing on her night cream. "But I know she would never harm him in any way. It was that fiancé of hers, somehow. I'd put money on it."

"And just how do you know that?"

"Call it female intuition."

"No, call it female interference. Stay out of it, Annie. Adam is hurting bad enough without you making it worse."

She whirled to face him. "Oh, Todd, you know I'd never hurt him."

"Not intentionally. Look, I know you mean well, honey, but this is one time you can't fix it."

"I worry about him," she said, turning off the bathroom light.

"Adam's a grown man. He doesn't need you to find the answer to his problems for him."

Annie sighed. "I just can't help thinking she *is* the answer to his problems."

Chapter 36

"Adam!" Zoey waved at him from across the room.

Adam raised his eyebrows and made his way through the testers' computer stations to where she was sitting. "Since when are you one of my employees?" he asked. "I thought we agreed you and Seth wouldn't be able to give me an unbiased viewpoint."

"No, you and Dad decided that. Seth and I said we could be as unbiased as anyone else. We'd tell you exactly how wonderful we thought it was, just like they do. Anyway, I'm not testing. I'm here with Kirk." She pointed at the pair of boys at the next computer. "He and Andy are doing the fighter pilot scenario, only they changed it a little."

"Oh?"

"They're in outer space fighting cyborgs."

Just then both boys whipped off their helmets. "Whoa, did you see that?" Kirk said excitedly. "I think we just blew up their base camp."

"Damn straight we did!"

They did an intricate dance of half a dozen different handshakes, then turned shining eyes to Adam and Zoey. "This is the coolest program ever, Mr. Johnson," Kirk said enthusiastically.

The other boy's eyes widened. "Johnson? You're Adam Johnson?"

Adam nodded. "That I am."

The next second, his hand was being wrung enthusiastically. "Oh, man, you're awesome! I've been playing your games since I was a kid. They're the best."

"Thanks," Adam said with a grin when he was finally able to withdraw his hand from the teenager's grip. "I don't think we've met."

"Oh, this is Andy," Zoey said. "He's spending Christmas vacation with his sister and testing your program while he's here."

"I see. I certainly appreciate you taking the time to give me feedback."

"Are you kidding? I'd do this for free. Heck, I'd even pay you to let me do it!"

"I hear you've been altering things inside my program."

The boys exchanged a wary glance. "We only changed the year," Kirk said.

"And the setting." Andy held his thumb and forefinger about a quarter inch apart. "But just a little."

"Darn!" Adam feigned disappointment. "I was hoping you'd test *Fantasy Quest*'s limits for me."

The boys looked at each other again. "We did try a few other things," Andy admitted.

"Oh? Like what?" For the next ten minutes, Adam sat and listened as the two teens went into details about exactly what they'd been doing in *Fantasy Quest*. Every once in a while, he'd stop them to ask a question or make a comment, but mostly he just let them talk. It was the first time he'd had reviews from someone other than his staff, and he derived a great deal of pleasure from listening to the boys' animated description of *Fantasy Quest*. They had indeed pushed its limits and were wildly enthusiastic about the results.

As they talked, Adam found himself oddly intrigued by Andy, and soon began to gain a great deal of respect for the boy. It was obvious that playing games wasn't his only computer skill. "Are you planning to make computers a career?" he finally asked.

"Definitely. I'm going to school as soon as I can make enough money to afford it. I'm hoping to find something in the computer field this summer, but I can flip burgers if I have to."

"When do you graduate from high school?"

"In May."

"Come see me when you do," Adam said. "We always have

some summer openings. There's also a scholarship program that may interest you."

"Wow, really?"

"You bet." Adam's cell phone buzzed, and he gave the three teens an apologetic smile as he reached for it.

"Of course he's serious," he heard Zoey say. "He's already hired Kirk as one of his steady part-time employees. I told you he was the greatest."

Adam hid a smile. Zoey was one of his biggest fans.

"You asked me to call and remind you of your meeting with Larry," Carla said over the phone. "He's just walking in the door now."

"Great, tell him to go in and make himself comfortable. I'll be right there."

"Looks like I have to get back to work," he said as he hung up. "You guys keep pushing *Fantasy Quest,* and let me know what you discover."

"Can't I at least look at it, Adam?"

Zoey looked so woebegone that Adam laughed. "Oh, I suppose, though you know what your mother will say."

"That I have you wrapped around my little finger."

"Exactly, and she's probably right. Might as well tell your brother he can come in, too."

She squealed and jumped up to give him a hug. "Thanks, Adam, you're the best! You won't regret this."

"Good," he said dryly. "Then, you can help get me out of hot water with your mother."

She just smiled, but as he left, he overheard her say, "I told you I could get him to let me try it."

Adam swallowed a grin. *Little wretch.* She'd probably been badgering the boys to let her try *Fantasy Quest* since they'd gotten there. That they hadn't given in to her put both young men higher in his estimation. She was pretty hard to resist.

Larry Boyd was sitting in a comfortable chair, staring out the huge picture window, when Adam arrived. "Sorry to keep you waiting," he said.

"No problem." Larry held up a steaming mug. "Carla has been plying me with hot spiced cider. I could sit here all day."

Adam chuckled. "I swear she serves a gallon of that stuff a day, and that doesn't count what she puts in the break room. The Christmas spirit gets her every year, but this year it's especially bad. Did you get some of her home-baked sugar cookies?"

Larry held up a half-eaten Santa.

"Good. The more you eat, the less I will." Adam patted his flat stomach. "If she keeps this up I'll weigh three hundred pounds before the new year! So, what have you got for me?"

Larry gestured toward the desk with a cookie. "Take a gander. These are the ones the Art Department picked out of a hundred or so."

Adam rolled over to the desk and looked at the pictures spread across it. "That's a pretty impressive collection."

"I have a few more here if we need them." Larry set his snack aside and walked over to the desk. "I've got to tell you, that new graphic artist Tom found for us is a wonder. Some of the best ones are hers."

"That's good news! Are we back on schedule yet?"

"Not quite, but we're getting close."

"These are exactly what I had in mind," Adam said, as he studied the pictures on the desk. "How many did we choose out of the people series?"

"Eight."

"So if we put in ten of these scenics, we'll still have room for the action shots?"

"Right."

"Okay, let's get started." Adam picked up a scene of palm trees, sand, and a turquoise lagoon. "Is this one of yours, Larry?"

"How did you know that?"

"I recognize your style." He looked up, his eyes twinkling. "Not to mention the dream vacation in the South Seas you keep talking about. Anyway, this one we definitely keep. It's restful." He put it to the side and reached for another.

They sorted through the pictures, putting some in the "save" pile and discarding others. "What's this?" Adam pulled out a picture that had slipped under the edge of his desk calendar. A beautiful waterfall plunged down a rugged cliff into a placid pool at the bottom. The spray broke the rays of the sun into a spectrum of color that arched over the falls. A small, rustic cabin sat next to the bank, and there was the hint of another pool beyond the mist. "Rainbow Falls," he murmured in astonishment.

"Wow, talk about the perfect title," Larry said, peering over his shoulder. "That's one of Kenzie's."

It was as though a giant fist closed around Adam's chest, forcing the air from his lungs. He momentarily lost the ability to speak or even to breathe.

"I told you she was good." Larry missed the expression on Adam's face as he shuffled through the pile of extra pictures he had in his hand. "I think there's another one in here with the same feel to it. Yeah, here it is." He handed Adam a picture of an Indian village. The first light of dawn gilded an early-morning mist that curled around the tipis in a glowing haze. The picture evoked a sense of peaceful wellbeing.

"Who did you say did these?" Adam asked in a strangled voice when he was finally able to force air into his lungs again.

"Kenzie Armstrong. The new artist Tom found for us. She's working on an awesome one of a giant grizzly for the action series, though I don't know if we'll want to use it." He shook his head. "It makes my blood run cold just to look at it."

Larry continued to expound on various pictures his staff had created for the graphics loop program, but Adam had stopped listening. A few of the pictures he already knew. He'd seen them as sketches in a water washed journal. Righteous rage blasted through him. Kenzie, here in his inner sanctum, and he hadn't even known it! He almost admired the sheer gall of the woman. It took guts to waltz in here as though nothing had happened and pick up right where she left off. "Has she been anywhere near the programmers yet?" he said suddenly.

Larry broke off in the middle of what he was saying. "Who?"

"Kenzie."

He gave Adam a puzzled look. "No, she hasn't gotten her security clearance yet."

"I'll bet that's driving her crazy."

"Not that I've seen. She's perfectly content to sit at her desk and work all day. If Carla didn't come in and drag her down to the break room once a day, she'd never leave the Art Department."

Adam's gaze sharpened. "She cozied up to my secretary?"

"Not really," Larry said hesitantly. "As far as I know, it was Carla who made the first overtures. She had a fit when she found out the new girl was eating at her desk and promptly marched into the Art Department to get her. They've become friends since then, but I think it has more to do with the fact that they read the same kind of books than anything else."

"What about the rest of the staff? Has she wheedled her way in with any of them?"

"Not that I know of. Everybody likes her, but I don't think she hangs out with any of them. Why, is something wrong?" Larry was beginning to look at Adam as though he'd lost his mind.

His expression made Adam realize how crazy he sounded. He rubbed his hand over his face. "No, the launch has me on edge, that's all. I guess I'm paranoid."

Larry looked slightly relieved. "That's understandable. With Vid-Tech breathing down our necks, we're all a little on edge." He shook his head. "But honestly, Adam, I don't think you have a thing to worry about with Kenzie Armstrong. She's really busted her backside since she's been here. When you meet her, you'll realize what a great person she is."

"Sounds like you're ready to nominate her for employee of the month," Adam said dryly.

Larry grinned. "Not a bad idea," he said. "Her picture

would look a lot better on the wall than Martha Stone's. Kenzie is pretty easy on the eye."

The memory of Kenzie lying on a bearskin wearing nothing but her come-hither smile flashed through Adam's mind. *Easy on the eye but hard on the heart.* He knew better than to follow his immediate inclination, which was to go to the Art Department, confront Kenzie, and then throw her out into the street. There was surely some way to use her presence to his advantage. He just needed time to think it through and act rationally.

It took supreme effort, but he managed to pull his mind away from Kenzie and focus on the pictures for the graphics loop. There were only one or two more from *Beta Quest*, but Adam soon discovered that he could tell which ones were Kenzie's. There was a certain style that marked her work, some trick of light that made the scene glow with hidden warmth. In spite of his anger and disillusionment, he had to admit Kenzie Armstrong was a talented artist. To all appearances, she'd been a positive addition to his staff.

"That's the last of them," Larry said finally, as he jotted down the numbers of the ones they had chosen. "What did we wind up with?"

Adam spread the chosen prints across the desk. "I make it an even dozen."

"That's what I have too. It's more than we wanted."

"True, but I like what we have. Why don't we wait until we have the action pictures before we make the final choices?"

Larry nodded. "Makes sense to me." He gathered up the extra prints then reached for the ones in Adam's hand.

"I think I'll keep these here," Adam said. "I might be able to cull one or two more."

"Good idea." He put the other pictures back in his portfolio then picked up his cup and cookies. "I'll see you tonight."

"Tonight?"

"At the Christmas party."

Adam was mildly surprised. The Christmas party was tonight? Had he known that? Probably. Carla kept him up on such things. "Right. Thanks for bringing these in."

Adam was barely aware of Larry leaving his office. His mind had already turned to Kenzie and what he was going to do about her. He laid the pictures out on his desk. The Indian village drew his gaze. It was so incredibly lifelike that Adam almost expected to see Red Blanket bent over the cook fire in front of Buffalo Horn's tipi. Besides Rainbow Falls and the village, there was a picture of a moonlit meadow beneath a thousand stars. It was the image that drew his attention repeatedly. All it lacked was a giant bear skin and two naked bodies wrapped in each other's arms. The question was: Why had she drawn it?

At first it had seemed obvious what Kenzie's objective was. By ingratiating herself with his employees, she was setting the stage to finish what her boyfriend had started: stealing *Fantasy Quest*. Yet, somehow, that didn't fit with the quality of the pictures she'd done for the graphics loop. Why would she put so much effort into creating something for Microcom if she were on Saunders's payroll? It could be some complex scheme to gain everyone's confidence and lull them into relaxing their diligence, but it didn't seem likely.

Then there were the pictures themselves. Why had she chosen those scenes? She had to have known Adam would see them at some point, which would completely blow her cover. Adam frowned. Except she didn't have a cover. She hadn't even changed her name. Maybe she didn't know he was onto her, that he'd shut the program down on purpose. Still, why all the pictures from Beta Quest? It didn't make sense.

No matter how he looked at it, things didn't add up. He needed to see her face to face, to let her know he knew what she was up to and to see her reaction. Only then could he judge for himself what was going on.

He picked up his phone and pressed the button for intercom. "Carla, could you have Kenzie Armstrong come to my office, please?"

"How come?"

Adam's brows snapped together. "What do you mean, how come?"

"I mean, why do you want to see her?"

"Since when do I have to ask your permission to talk to one of my employees?"

"Since you started growling at everyone around here and acting like a cat with his tail caught in a wringer. Larry just asked me if you were feeling all right. He said you were worried about Kenzie Armstrong not having her security clearance."

"What does that have to do with anything?"

"We can't afford to lose any more artists, with the launch only two months away. Besides, Kenzie's a nice girl and about the best thing that ever happened to that Art Department."

"How do you figure that?"

"Have you looked at her pictures? They're brilliant; you can feel the emotion in them. I'm not going to let you run her off."

"Maybe I want to tell her how much I like what she's done and ask to see the rest," Adam said in exasperation.

There was a moment of silence on the other end. "Is that really why you want to see her?" Carla said suspiciously.

"Oh for—" Adam sighed. "Look, I don't have the time or energy to argue with you right now. Just get her in here."

"All right, but you'd better toe the line, or you'll have me to deal with."

Adam glared at the intercom as it went dead. He was surrounded by women who thought they had the right to tell him what to do. If it wasn't Annie, it was Carla. They were worse than his mother.

Right now, though, he didn't have time to worry about it. In a few minutes, Kenzie Armstrong would walk through that door—not a computer-created version of her but the real, live, flesh-and-blood woman. His heart began to pound, and a surge of emotion threatened to overwhelm him. The trouble was he couldn't tell if it was anger or anticipation.

Chapter 37

"Hey, Kenzie," called Marty as she hung up the phone. "The boss wants to see you and your portfolio in his office."

Kenzie looked up from her drawing. "Larry? He isn't even back yet."

"Not Larry. Adam."

Kenzie's heart started pounding. "A-Adam Johnson wants to see me? Why?"

Marty shrugged. "Larry just took the scenic collection in. Adam probably wants to see more of your work. He knows the rest of us and our style. You're the new kid on the block." She winked. "Not to mention the fact that you're damn good."

Kenzie felt as if her throat was swelling shut as she gathered her artwork and shoved it into a folder. She'd known the time would come when she'd have to face Adam Johnson, but she hadn't expected it to be quite so soon—or so private. She'd seen him from a distance several times, but never up close. The trick was going to be keeping her heart out of her eyes. If she just kept reminding herself that this was not her Adam, but rather a stranger who had the power to fire her, she might be able to pull it off.

"Hey, Kenzie, don't worry," Marty said as Kenzie hurried past. "Adam's cool."

Kenzie gave her a distracted smile but didn't stop to chat. All across the lobby, she steeled herself for the coming meeting. Almost before she knew it, she was there.

"Boy, that was fast," Carla said approvingly. "Adam will be impressed. I'll let him know you're here."

Kenzie glanced nervously around the office as she waited. The spicy smell of cider gave it an unexpected homey feel, as did the garlands draped over the windows and the small artificial tree in the corner. It was obviously all Carla's doing, but not every boss was so lenient.

Carla hung up the phone. "You can go in. Oh, don't look like that," she said when she saw Kenzie's face. "He won't bite."

Kenzie mustered a small smile and opened the door to the inner office. Her smile faltered a bit when she thought she heard Carla mutter, "At least he won't if he knows what's good for him."

Adam Johnson's office wasn't like other corporate offices she'd been in. It was filled with complicated-looking equipment, not the least of which were three different computers and a laptop. That was one difference between this Adam and hers. This one was the quintessential computer geek. The observation made her feel a little more comfortable.

Adam sat with his back to her, staring out the huge picture windows at the city below. Kenzie took the opportunity to study him from behind. It was amazing how closely her imagination had captured him. The set of the wide shoulders and bulk of his upper arms were quite apparent in the cotton dress shirt he wore. An expert barber was responsible for the short, stylish cut, but his hair was the same odd hue, somewhere between brown and black. The wheelchair and a set of exercise bars at the side of his desk gave her a little jolt. Consciously, she knew he was a paraplegic, but somehow the reality of it always came with a tiny shock of surprise. Still, he was more like her Adam than he was different. Kenzie was still tracing every familiar line, when he suddenly turned to face her.

Though she had prepared herself, the sight of the dearly familiar face stunned her. She could tell herself this wasn't her Adam until the cows came home; her heart thought otherwise. It was all she could do not to run across the room and throw herself into his arms.

For an impossibly long moment they stared at each other, neither of them saying a word. With a start, Kenzie realized he was waiting for her to speak. He was no doubt wondering why she was just standing there gawking at him. "It's good to finally meet you, Mr. Johnson" she said, crossing the room with her hand out. "I'm Kenzie Armstrong."

He seemed startled by her direct approach and shook her hand almost as an involuntary reaction to her extended palm.

Kenzie sucked in her breath as his touch sent an electrical charge through her. It appeared her heart wasn't the only part of her under the illusion that she knew this man intimately.

"So, that's the way we're going to play it, huh?" she heard him mutter.

"Pardon me?"

"Have a seat." He indicated a chair on the other side of the desk.

"Thank you." Uneasy, she settled on the edge of the comfortable office chair. She had the distinct impression he was angry with her.

"Are you enjoying your work at Microcom?"

"Yes, very much. Everybody has been exceptionally kind." *Up until now,* she thought to herself.

"Can't wait for your security clearance to come through, though, I'll bet."

Kenzie blinked in surprise. "I hadn't really thought about it. Why, is there a problem?"

"You might say that. Doesn't your fiancé work for Vid-Tech?"

"Yes, but I don't see—"

"Are you aware that Microcom is about to launch a ground-breaking simulated reality program?"

"I knew we were working on something big, but I didn't know what it was."

"Vid-Tech wants it badly and has gone to great lengths to steal it. We stopped the latest attempt and suddenly here you are."

All at once, she understood. "You think I'm passing information to Brad!"

He shrugged. "Not yet, but then, you don't have access to

anything he can use."

She jumped to her feet. "How dare you accuse me of such a thing? You don't even know me."

"No, I really don't," he said regretfully. "I thought I did, but it was just a clever ruse all along."

Kenzie was confused. How could he think he knew her when they'd never even met? "What do you mean?"

"Oh, come on, Kenzie, drop the act.

We both know it's pure bull, and frankly I'd like to have honesty between us, just this once."

"If I had a clue what you were talking about—"

"Maybe these will clear it up a bit." He tossed three pictures on the desk. "Did you think I wouldn't recognize them?"

Kenzie stomach twisted uncomfortably as she stared at the three scenes she'd done from her dream. He said he recognized them, but how could that be, unless—

"Did you think cutting your hair short would be enough of a disguise, or did you just figure I'd never notice one more person wandering around the office?"

"I don't understand," she whispered. "It was a dream."

Adam snorted. "A three-month-long dream? Right! That makes almost as much sense as the time travel angle that you came up with before."

"Time travel?" Kenzie sat back down with a thump. "Oh my God, you were there! It was real?"

"No, it was simulated reality, as you well know."

Kenzie rubbed her suddenly aching forehead. "What are you talking about? None of this makes any sense."

"You want me to lay it all out for you?"

"That would be nice!" she said with a touch of asperity.

"Fine. Three months ago, a character showed up in my test program, a character that didn't fit the mountain-man setting I was in. When I went to delete her from the program, she didn't appear to exist."

Kenzie's eyes widened in surprise. "Me?"

"You. I thought my program had developed a glitch, one I

needed to figure out, so I played along to see what would happen. The next thing I knew, deleted characters were popping up everywhere, and all kinds of crazy things were happening. I thought you were destroying the whole program. It wasn't until we…" He paused, apparently rethinking what he had been about to say. "I finally began to suspect that you weren't a glitch at all, but another player in my game."

"But how—"

"How did I figure it out? Simple, really. You told me the name of your accomplice, and I did a little research. It's not the first time he's hacked into someone's computer and stolen a program. Only, *Beta Quest* was a little too sophisticated for him."

"Brad!" she said in a horrified voice.

"Precisely."

"That son of a bitch," she muttered through gritted teeth. "All that time everyone thought he was being the model fiancé, and he was using me to steal your program."

"Oh, and I suppose you had no knowledge of it?"

"Of course I had no knowledge of it. I was in a coma!"

Adam gave a humorless laugh. "Right. And I suppose you didn't know Annie Bedford is a close friend of mine."

Kenzie frowned. "What's Annie got to do with this?"

"After I shut the program down, you tried to get to me through her. When that didn't work either, you and Marriot went back to your original plan."

It was all beginning to make a horrible kind of sense to Kenzie. Though she hadn't a clue how Brad had gotten her into the program in the first place, he'd been less than pleased when she'd come out of it. He'd even tried to drug her back into the coma. "And what exactly was our original plan?" she asked.

"Infiltration. It was a simple matter of Vid-Tech hiring up all the graphic artists so that you were the only one available."

"You think I had something to do with that?"

"I know you did. You've spent the last two weeks pulling the wool over everyone's eyes, making them all think you were part of the team and loyal to Microcom."

"I've spent the last two weeks busting my butt for you and your stupid program," she said angrily. She tossed the folder of her artwork onto his desk. "How do you explain those?"

"All part of the plan to get everyone here to trust you. It was working, too. They all love you. I hope what Pete Saunders is paying you is worth selling out your friends."

"Who's Pete Saunders?" she asked in confusion.

"As if you don't know."

"Look," she said in exasperation, "just humor me and tell me who the hell he is."

"The head of Vid-Tech."

"And Brad's boss."

"So it would seem."

"Adam, I had nothing to do with any of this."

"I spent the better part of three months with you," he pointed out. "How can you deny you were in my program?"

"I didn't say I wasn't in your program, but I don't know how I got there. I didn't know it wasn't real, either."

"You said you thought it was a dream."

"I did after I woke up and my mother said I'd been in a coma for eighty-five days. When I was there, I thought I'd traveled back in time."

He gave her a disbelieving look.

"Oh, all right, so that was probably a stupid conclusion, but what else was I supposed to think? You did your best to persuade me I was living in 1868."

"Which, if I recall, you denied vehemently."

"Until I saw Laramie City. That was pretty darn convincing."

"Your story doesn't hold water," he said after a moment. "I only shut the program down four weeks ago and you've been here for two of those. If you were hurt so badly that you were in a coma for three months, how is it that you recovered so fast?"

"Beats me. All the doctors were amazed."

"I'm sure they were."

Kenzie dropped her head against the back of the chair in frustration. "Nothing I say is going to convince you, is it?"

"I doubt it."

She sighed in defeat and stood up. "I guess there isn't any reason for me to stay, then, is there?"

"No, probably not. There's not a chance in hell of you ever getting a security clearance. Without that, you're useless to Pete Saunders."

"I'm useless to him anyway, since I don't even know the man and wouldn't tell him anything if I did."

"So you say."

"Do you know the worst thing about waking up?" she asked softly.

"No."

"Losing you. When I realized you'd been dead a hundred years, I wanted to die too. All I could think of was finding a way to get back to you. I never imagined our reunion to be like this." She turned and walked to the door.

"You forgot your pictures," he said, pushing the folder across the desk toward her.

"No, they're yours; you paid for them." She gazed at him for a long moment, memorizing his face. "I know you'll think I'm lying, but I love you with my whole heart and soul." With that, she turned and walked through the door. The click of the catch sounded like a rifle shot in her ears, or maybe it was the cracking of her heart. It was hard to tell.

Carla took one look at her face. "Kenzie, what's happened?"

"I think I just lost my job."

Carla's eyes widened in astonishment. "He fired you?"

"I didn't give him the chance." She shuddered. "It doesn't matter. He doesn't want me here."

"What do you mean he doesn't want you here?"

Kenzie continued toward the door. "I'll leave as soon as I clean out my desk."

"No, wait, you can't go! We need you." Carla jumped to her feet and hurried to catch up with her. She grabbed Kenzie's arm to keep her from walking through the door. "Adam has been in a bad mood all month and sometimes gets completely unreasonable. He didn't mean to make you feel like you need to leave. I know he didn't."

"Yes, he did." Kenzie finally looked at Carla. "He has his reasons, too, or he thinks he does." She turned and gave the other woman a hug. "You've been a good friend, Carla. I've enjoyed knowing you." Then she turned and walked out the door.

"Kenzie, wait—"

Kenzie just kept on walking, dazed by all that had happened, oblivious to everything around her. She was halfway across the lobby when she nearly collided with another woman.

"Oh, excuse me," the woman said. "I wasn't watching where—Kenzie?"

For the first time, Kenzie looked at her. "Annie! It's true, then. You are friends." She shook her head. "I should have known. God has a twisted sense of humor." She shook her head and walked away.

Stunned, Annie turned and watched her disappear into the Art Department. "What on Earth?" she murmured under her breath. When Kenzie didn't reappear, Annie set her jaw and headed toward Adam's office. He'd obviously fumbled badly.

Annie was surprised to find the outer office empty. Carla was always at her desk this time of day. Feeling the first fingers of alarm, Annie hurried into the inner office. Adam was staring out the window, his face set as though carved from granite. Carla was sorting through a pile of papers.

"What's happened?" Annie asked in alarm.

Carla raised her head and started to speak, but Adam cut her off. "I don't want to talk to either of you right now."

"Adam—"

"I said out! For once in your lives, just do as I ask."

The two women exchanged a look. Then Carla inclined her head toward the outer office. With one final worried look at Adam, they left.

"I've never seen him like that," Annie said as the door closed behind them. "What's wrong?"

"I don't know for sure." Carla motioned for Annie to follow, and they moved to the other side of the room. "He had words with one of the artists," she said in a hushed voice. "But I'm not sure what's going on."

Annie's eyes widened. "One of the artists... You mean Kenzie?"

Carla nodded. "Kenzie Armstrong."

"She works here?"

"Yes. Or, rather, she did. She seemed to think he'd fired her for some reason, but he denies it."

"Oh my Lord. She's his glitch."

"His—" suddenly Carla's eyes widened too. "You mean the one he thought was an industrial spy?"

"Yes, only I don't believe it for a minute."

Carla shook her head. "No, neither do I." She glanced down at the pictures. "She left these in his office. I found them scattered all over the floor. I think he had a temper tantrum. Take a look."

Annie took the stack of pictures and began leafing through them. "She's very good."

"I know. That's why it doesn't make sense that he fired her," Carla said, looking over Annie's shoulder.

There were about a dozen pictures in all, about half of them depicting life in an earlier time. The two women flipped past the portrait of an incredibly beautiful Native American woman gazing soulfully up into the face of a clearly smitten man, a character study of two elderly Native American men who looked like brothers, and one of an old trapper, hunkered down by a frozen creek.

"She must have done those for the people sequence," Carla said. "It's the action pictures that are the most interesting.

Look."

Annie gazed down at a picture of a man who bore a striking resemblance to Adam. He was naked to the waist, with heavy muscles bunched across his back as he swung an ax against the trunk of a large tree. Every detail was lovingly rendered, right down to the sweat beaded on his skin. "Oh my," she said.

"That's what I thought too," Carla agreed. "And how about this one?"

A forest fire raged out of control in the background. The smoldering remains of a cabin gave mute testimony to the probable cause of the blaze. Nearby, a woman knelt by the still figure of a man who lay on the ground unconscious. Her soot-streaked face was filled with terror as she tried to wake him. The observer could almost feel her panic as the fire closed in around them.

"She won't leave him," Annie murmured.

"I know. Kind of tears at your heartstrings. It's Adam again, isn't it?"

Annie nodded. "I have a funny feeling Kenzie wasn't making this up, either." She looked at Carla. "Do you know how he figured out the Sex Hex wasn't working?"

"No, but I have wondered."

"It was her. They made love, and it didn't shut down like it was supposed to."

"But I thought that only happened when there was a deep love commitment on both sides."

"Exactly."

They stared at each other for a long moment. "He isn't going to like it," Carla said finally.

"I know, and my husband threatened to disown me if I mess in Adam's life any more. He wasn't joking, either."

"I'll probably get fired."

They looked at each other again. Finally, Carla shrugged. "Oh well, I was looking for a job when I found this one."

Annie nodded. "And Todd's never managed to stay mad at me for more than a few weeks. Besides, nothing ventured, nothing gained."

Kenzie was still numb when she reached Brad's apartment and let herself in. It was time for a confrontation. He wasn't home yet, but then, she hadn't really expected him to be. She glanced around the spacious living room and shook her head. The small apartment she had found with Carla's help was so much more welcoming. Brad hated it, of course, which only made Kenzie like it more. She'd moved everything to the new apartment last evening with Andy's help. Her brother hadn't even tried to hide his satisfaction.

She flopped on the couch and closed her eyes. There was so much to think about. Adam was as real as Brad! It still boggled her mind. As she thought about it, a sad little smile crossed her face. Faced with a choice between the two of them, Brad wasn't even in the running. She'd rather have Adam, even as mad as he was now.

A natural optimist, Kenzie couldn't help thinking there would be some way to make Adam understand she would never betray him. She was still mulling over various ideas when the doorbell rang. She answered the door to find a uniformed delivery man.

"Sign here," he said, handing her a clipboard.

"Hey, it's for me," she said, eyeballing the address on the large box at her feet as she signed.

After he left, Kenzie carried it back to the living room and went to the kitchen to get a knife to open it. She had ordered several things for this place. Maybe whatever it was would work in her apartment. But when she wrested open the box and looked inside, she gasped in surprise. Then, for the first time all day, she burst into tears.

Chapter 38

It was after ten o'clock when Kenzie finally heard Brad's key in the lock. She had dozed off on the couch waiting for him, but it hadn't blunted her anger one bit.

"Kenzie!" he said, with every evidence of pleasure as he crossed the room. "Decide to come home?" He bent to kiss her, but she ducked away.

Kenzie wrinkled her nose. He smelled of expensive bourbon and another woman's perfume. She was vaguely surprised to find she didn't care. "You're late tonight," she observed.

"Yes." He shrugged off his sport jacket and hung it up before dropping into the easy chair. "Had to put in some extra hours at the office." He loosened his tie. "So, having second thoughts about moving to that hole in the wall?"

"I've had second thoughts, all right, but not about my apartment."

He gave her a wary look. "What now?"

"First, I think I should return these." She put her engagement ring and her tennis bracelet on the coffee table between them. "It's time we called off this farce."

Brad glanced from the jewelry back to her face. "You know the doctor said you shouldn't make any big changes in your life for a while. Traumatic brain injuries like yours—"

"Can it, Brad! There is no so-called brain injury. The doctors are all still congratulating themselves on my miraculous recovery."

"Doctors don't know everything," he said sullenly.

"You're beginning to sound like a broken record. By the way," she said conversationally, "I got fired today."

Brad stiffened. "What?"

"Yes, I thought that would make you sit up and take

notice."

"What did you do? Is there any way you can get your job back?"

"No, because you see, I didn't do anything. You did."

Brad looked taken aback. "Me! I've never even been inside the Microcom building."

"Maybe not, but it appears you've been inside Adam's program."

"What are you talking about?"

"I'm talking about how you somehow put me inside Adam's simulated reality program while I was comatose. Don't even try to deny it. I'll know you're lying."

"You're having delusions."

"Am I? I met my boss, Adam Johnson, for the first time today. Only it turned out it wasn't the first time. It seems I spent the last three months with him inside his test program." She glared at Brad. "What I thought was a dream turned out to be a marathon simulated reality experience."

"Now I know you're having delusions. Why would Johnson let you run loose in his top-secret SR program that he's spent millions protecting? Doesn't make sense."

"He thought I was a glitch in the programming. When he found out I wasn't, he decided I was an industrial spy and disconnected his program. That's when I woke up."

"So that's why. I wondered." Brad relaxed against the back of the chair.

Kenzie blinked in surprise. "You aren't even going to deny it?"

"Why should I? It was an accident."

"Oh, right," she said sarcastically. "You weren't intending to break into Adam's program. You just sort of stumbled in by mistake."

"I didn't say that. I spent all last summer trying to get into his system. I could never get past his firewall, until you helped me."

"What are you talking about? I never helped you!"

"Ah, but you did. I'm still not quite sure what happened, but you were the catalyst that finally got me inside. I had used the wireless network in the hospital several times before but couldn't get anywhere. Then, one afternoon, there was a power surge, and your brain monitor started going haywire. The nurse got everything back to normal, but when I went back to my laptop, I was in." He frowned. "You can't imagine how frustrating it was to sit there for three months watching the data flow back and forth and not be able to touch it. I tried everything I knew and invented a hundred new techniques, but I couldn't break the code."

"You knew I was somehow connected to a computer program, and you did nothing?"

"I wasn't exactly sure you were connected. For all I knew, his computer was just talking to your brain monitor."

"And you didn't much care as long as you had access to Adam's program."

He shrugged. "They were keeping close watch on your vitals. There were times when your heart accelerated, but it was never any worse than heavy exercise or a good scare would produce. Besides, I had a deadline to meet."

"A deadline?" Her eyes widened. "Those accusations in college. They were true! You did steal those programs."

"The charges didn't stick, remember? I took those feeble little attempts at programming and improved on them. Those programs were mine."

"Oh my God. Adam was right. It *is* industrial espionage."

"Is that why you got fired?"

"Let's just say he wasn't pleased to find me working for him. He thinks I'm in cahoots with you and your slimy boss."

Brad rose from the chair and walked into the kitchen. "Good. I think this will work out after all." He took a glass from the dishwasher and put it under the ice dispenser on the refrigerator door. "Pete Saunders knows nothing about this, by the way. It's our little secret."

"It won't be for long. I'm going to blow this thing wide

open and throw you to the wolves."

He gave her a sardonic smile as he pulled a bottle of bourbon out of the cupboard. "No, you're not."

"And just how are you going to stop me?"

"I won't have to." He filled his glass and sauntered back to the living room. "You see, I finally managed to download a little of Johnson's programming the night you woke up. Unfortunately, it isn't enough to give Saunders. It is, however, enough to implicate your brother."

"My brother?"

"Johnson suspects it was me, but he has no proof. He also knows you couldn't have done it alone. Enter Andrew Armstrong. You two played right into my hands on that one. I didn't even have to suggest you get him a job there. You did that all by yourself."

"What are you talking about?"

He sat down in the chair and crossed his legs. "In a few days, I'm going to discover a thumb drive. When I realize it's part of a program stolen from Microcom, I'm going to return it immediately and suggest they check out my future wife's younger brother. He's been making thinly veiled threats against Microcom for a long time."

"You'll never get away with it."

"Oh, I think I will. I have no doubt that Andy has spent the last few days impressing everyone with his computer knowledge. It might be a stretch to picture him at my level, but I think I can convince Johnson. During the investigation, they'll uncover evidence that will implicate Andrew as the thief and you as his accomplice. You may get off, but your brother is definitely going to jail." He held his glass up in a toast. "Cheers."

He'd do it, too. Just like he did in college. "You bastard!"

"Now, now, my pet, is that anyway to talk to your fiancé?"

"Really, Brad, who says that? You sound like a cartoon villain. And by the way, it's ex-fiancé." Her eyes narrowed. "There's more to this, though, isn't there? Saunders is still expecting you to come up with a SR program. If you don't, you'll lose your job, and he'll make sure no one else will hire you."

He gave her is best smarmy smile. "You know, I have always admired your intelligence. It's one of the things that attracted me to you in the first place. It's too bad you won't let yourself be guided by those older and wiser than yourself."

"It's called thinking for myself, and right now I'm guessing you're about to make me a proposition I can't refuse."

"See, now, that's just what I am talking about," he said admiringly. "Look how much time you saved me not having to explain it all to you."

"All right, Brad, cut the crap. What is it you want me to do?"

"You're going to steal me a copy of Johnson's SR program."

Kenzie laughed. "Right, and how am I supposed to do that? I don't work there anymore, remember?"

"No, but Andy does. He's not as brilliant as he thinks he is, but he has enough knowledge to get the program for me. As soon as you deliver it to me, I give you the evidence against your brother."

Which you'll no doubt keep a copy of, Kenzie thought. Still, the only way out of this mess was to play along with him. "It won't work. Lots of people have seen Adam's program, and you'll never be able to convince the world he stole it from you."

"Oh, my dear, the world will never know. My greatest talent is improving on what others have created. By the time I'm done with *Fantasy Quest*, not even Adam Johnson will be able to prove it was originally his. It won't matter anyway. Pete Saunders is geared up to start production. He'll easily beat Microcom to the marketplace. In this business, timing is everything. Vid-Tech is big enough to dominate the market. With this program, Saunders will be able to squeeze all the little guys out. In six months, Adam Johnson will be bankrupt. He'll be nothing more than another out-of-work cripple."

Kenzie felt the bile rise in her throat as she watched him

gloat over Adam's downfall. Why had she never realized what a truly despicable person Brad was? Right now, she needed to keep her wits about her if she was going to come out of this all right. The only thing she had on her side was that he never failed to underestimate her. "I won't do this," she said defiantly.

"Of course you will," he said with confidence. "That's what I love about that sickeningly close family bond of yours. You'll do anything to save your brother." He sipped his drink. "I'll give you thirty-six hours to think it over. If you haven't delivered a copy of *Fantasy Quest* to me by Thursday morning at nine, I'm taking my evidence to Adam Johnson."

Kenzie stood up and grabbed her coat off the back of the couch. "Then, you better plan on going to Microcom Thursday, because I'm not falling in with your scheme." She dropped her purse into her box and scooped the whole thing up into her arms.

"What's that?" he asked.

"Oh, just something I bought for the apartment." She thrust it under his nose. "Isn't it great?"

He recoiled instantly. "What is that revolting thing?"

Kenzie balanced it against her stomach and walked to the door. "That," she said with a satisfied smile, "is proof that you truly can get anything online."

"Why? What is it?"

"A brain-tanned bear hide." Brad's horrified expression was the last thing she saw as she closed the door behind her. The image of it got her all the way to her car with the heavy load. While the car was warming up, she called Andy on her cell. He answered before it even rang on her end.

"Hey, sis. You ok? I was starting to worry about you."

"I'm fine. Brad was just late getting home. It didn't take long once he got there."

"So, Wonder Boy is history?"

"Yes," Kenzie said, "but you don't need to sound so happy about it. I just broke off a year-long engagement, you know."

"Yeah." She could almost hear his grin over the phone. "How did he take it?"

"Surprisingly well, but my broken engagement is the least of our worries." She sighed. Brad was right. There was no way she was going to let him frame her baby brother. "Andy, I'm going to need your help."

Adam was in a foul mood, and he didn't care who knew it. Carla and Annie had been at him like two annoying mosquitoes all day. His irritation, though, wasn't focused entirely on them. Most of it was aimed at himself. All they had done was point out what he already knew. He'd been brutally unfair to Kenzie. In all the time he'd known her, she'd never once given him any reason to think he couldn't trust her. She'd even risked her life to save him.

As unlikely as Kenzie's story was, he should have at least listened to her. According to Annie, her coma had been real. There was an entire medical staff that would attest to that and to how banged up she'd been when they life-flighted her in. They also said Brad Marriot and his laptop had rarely left her side during the whole three months she was unconscious. His bad mood was caused by a guilty conscience, pure and simple.

Adam glanced at the picture on his desk. It could have graced the cover of a romance novel or been a Christmas greeting card. A man in buckskins stood before a small, rustic cabin. His rifle leaned forgotten against the log wall, and warm light spilled out onto the snow from the open doorway, highlighting the woman he held in his arms. Neither seemed aware of the snowstorm swirling around them or the darkness beginning to fall. They were too lost in the kiss they shared. The word *Homecoming* penciled in on the back of the picture said it all. The picture somehow managed to capture the essence of his deepest longing.

It was the one picture from Kenzie's portfolio that he hadn't swept off his desk in a fit of rage. For the hundredth time, he wished he hadn't let his temper get the best of him. Now that he was cooled off, he would have very much liked to look at them again. He knew Carla had cleaned up the mess and doubtlessly had the whole collection safe somewhere, but he was too embarrassed to ask for them.

The phone rang, and Adam welcomed the interruption. He really didn't want to be alone with his thoughts right now. "Yes, what is it?"

"Scott Martin is on the phone," Carla said. "He says it's very important."

"Put him through."

"Hello, Adam?"

"Yeah. You got something for me?"

"As a matter of fact, I do. I found McKenzie Armstrong, and you'll never guess where."

"In my employment records."

"You already knew?" Scott sounded disappointed.

"I figured it out yesterday. It was something of a surprise."

"I suppose so. You know about her brother, then, too, right?"

Adam sat up. "Brother?"

"Actually she has three of them, but there's only one working for you."

Adam's stomach twisted uncomfortably. "What's his name?"

"Andrew Armstrong, but he goes by the name of Andy. He's apparently quite the computer prodigy, and—"

"Oh, hell! Scott, I've got to go. I'll call you back later." He cut the connection and punched in another number.

"Program Testing," came the voice over the line.

"Jackie, did Andy Armstrong come in this morning?"

"Sure did. Showed up at eight o'clock. He was waiting for someone to let him in when I got here."

"I'll be right there! Don't let him leave." Adam slammed down the phone and tore out of his office.

Carla looked up as he burst through the door. "Adam,

what's wrong?"

"Something I need to check out," he called over his shoulder. Andy was sure to know where Kenzie was. The fact that he was here was positive proof of her innocence. In two minutes flat, Adam was in front of Andy Armstrong's station in the lab. But the chair was empty.

"Where is he?" Adam asked the girl in the next station, fighting to keep his voice calm.

"Andy?" she asked. "He left about an hour ago."

"Did he take anything with him?"

"Just his jump drive."

Adam felt a giant fist close around his throat. "What jump drive?"

"You know, the one you gave him. He said you wanted him to access the higher levels of the game. He had just finished downloading what he needed when I got here." She frowned. "He said to tell you he was sorry, but he didn't tell me for what."

But Adam knew. Andy had downloaded the deepest secrets of the program—everything Brad Marriot and Pete Saunders needed to recreate *Fantasy Quest.*

Chapter 39

"Just a minute," Adam mumbled as he rolled over and grabbed his phone from his bedside table. "Hello?"

"I'm afraid I've got bad news for you, Adam."

"Scott?" Adam blinked the sleep out of his eyes. "What time is it?"

"Almost five. Sorry to wake you, but I knew you'd want to hear this."

"If it's worse than your last news, I'm not so sure I do."

"It appears your hunch was right. My friend at Vid-Tech says they're gearing up for something big. Word is Marriot came through, and they've got their SR program."

Adam closed his eyes and pinched the bridge of his nose. "That's it, then."

"Aren't you going to fight?"

"Sure, for all the good it will do me." Adam sighed. "He's going to beat us to the marketplace. Knowing Pete Saunders, he'll sue when we launch *Fantasy Quest*, saying I copied his program."

"What if *Fantasy Quest* comes out first?" Scott asked. "How close are you?"

"I don't know. We could probably pull it off by the middle of January if we cut back on the promotion."

"I'm betting that would be soon enough. Even if Saunders does have three times your staff, he's not going to be able to get his program out any sooner. If you hit the market within a week or two of each other, you'll at least start out on even footing."

"You're right." Adam grabbed the bar overhead and pulled himself upright. "I'm going to need help, though. Would you be willing to come down to Denver for a month or so?"

"I thought you'd never ask. Can't wait to see this program for myself! Want me to bring a couple of friends to help out?"

"No, thanks. We'd never be able to get a security clearance on them in time. That's what got me into this mess in the first place."

"I see your point. All right, I'll come alone. Expect me tomorrow morning at the latest."

"I look forward to it."

"We'll give Saunders and Marriot a run for their money."

Adam smiled to himself as he hung up. With Scott Martin added to the mix, Pete Saunders and Brad Marriot didn't stand a chance. His improved mood only lasted until his morning shower. The warm water cascading down around him always made him think of the hot pool, and today was no exception. With it came the thought of Kenzie and her betrayal. It lay dark and heavy against his soul.

Three days ago, he'd been convinced he'd falsely accused her, that the story of the coma had been true, and that Brad Marriot was the villain in the piece. Then his world caved in. *Fantasy Quest*, his baby, the program he had spent the last five years creating, had been delivered into the hands of his worst enemy, an enemy sworn to destroy him at any cost. Worst of all, Kenzie had disappeared. Even her family had no clue where she and her brother had gone.

Only when it became clear he might never see Kenzie again did he realize how much he loved her. She had single-handedly destroyed him and everything he had worked so hard to build, sold him out, and betrayed him, yet all he could think about was how bleak his life would be without her. Which made him about the stupidest chump on the planet. He shut the water off with an angry twist and grabbed a towel. For the first time in his life, he could identify with a biblical character. He'd played Sampson to her Delilah as surely as the sun was going to rise in the east this morning.

Adam was eating his breakfast when the doorbell rang. He glanced at his watch and raised his eyebrows. Six-fifteen? Who on earth would be coming to visit this early?

For once, he was glad of Todd Bedford's security system,

but when he switched it on, all he saw was George, the doorman, standing patiently outside his door with a large box.

"Good morning, George," he said when he opened the door. "To what do I owe this honor? I thought you never left your post."

George grinned. "I'm not officially on duty until six-thirty, so I offered to run this up to you. Do you want me to bring it in?"

"Sure." Adam backed out of the way and pointed toward the table. "Just set it over there. Where did you get it? It's too early for the mail or any of the delivery companies."

"A teenage boy brought it by," George said, setting it on the table. "I ran it through our metal detector just to make sure it's safe."

"Thanks for bringing it on up. Got time for a cup of coffee?"

George shook his head. "No, but thanks." He glanced at his watch. "Bruce will be wondering where I am."

"Right. Well, have a Merry Christmas."

"You too, Mr. Johnson." George touched the brim of his hat and was gone.

Adam retrieved a knife from the kitchen and cut through the tape holding the top shut. The flaps sprang open, and he peered inside the box curiously.

"What the hell?" He removed the gift from the box and spread it out over the table. As he did, a card fell out onto the floor. It said only, "Merry Christmas." It wasn't signed, but Adam could only think of one person who would send him a brain-tanned bear hide.

Adam felt good for the first time in three days. For once, Kenzie wasn't the foremost thing on his mind. He'd just had a meeting with his department heads, and their enthusiasm warmed his heart. His employees weren't satisfied with just fighting Vid-Tech; they were planning an all-out war! Let Pete Saunders have the game market. They'd exploit the two facets of *Fantasy Quest* that he didn't even know existed: psychological and medical.

The planning stage for the marriage counseling and sex therapy had gone into full swing. Personnel was stepping up the search for a psychologist, and marketing was working on a new ad campaign. Half of the art staff was going to focus on designing new packaging, while the other half put the finishing touches on an abbreviated graphics loop for the game version.

Adam himself was going to be their poster boy for the medical slant. Even though he had yet to walk, his progress was bound to bring customers by the thousands. Going public with his infirmity was a bit daunting to Adam, but there was no denying the impact it would make. During the brainstorming session, it occurred to Adam that *Beta Quest* could also be responsible for Kenzie's seemingly miraculous recovery from a coma, but he'd pushed the idea away with irritation. Why couldn't he just accept her duplicity and be done with it?

Determined to live up to his staff's expectations, he'd come straight back to his office and started on the exercise routine he and Annie had worked out. He wanted to be warmed up and ready to go when she arrived for his daily therapy session, but by the time he finished his exercises she still wasn't there. He looked at the walking bars consideringly. Annie might not be best pleased if he tried it by himself, but if he fell, he fell. It wouldn't be the first time nor the last.

Adam locked the wheels then pulled himself out of his chair and stood upright between the walking bars. He was still using his arms to support himself, but gradually his legs seemed to be holding up more and more of his weight. Every day he could feel himself getting closer to taking that first step. As he concentrated on staying upright, he heard his office door open behind him. Annie had arrived.

"You're late," he said, jokingly. "I decided to start without you."

"On the contrary, I think I'm early."

Adam nearly fell as he jerked his head around. "Kenzie!

What the hell are you doing here?"

"Annie said you were making amazing progress," Kenzie said, walking toward him. "But I had no idea. She's not coming today, by the way, so what do you want me to do to help?"

"Nothing!" He maneuvered himself back into his chair then glared up at her. "Haven't you done enough?"

She gave him a crooked little smile. "I hope so, but I'm not precisely sure."

"What's that supposed to mean?"

"As someone told me just the other day, timing is everything in this business." She perched on the corner of his desk and glanced at the clock on the wall. "You should be getting a phone call in the next few minutes that will explain everything."

"And if I don't?"

"Then, I'll save you the trouble of turning me over to the police by calling them myself."

"What's to stop me from calling them right now?"

"Nothing, except maybe Carla, who has control over your phone. I imagine you could get around her if you had a mind to." She shrugged. "Anyway, what difference will ten minutes make?"

"You tell me."

"I'm hoping it will get a few questions answered. I know I have all kinds of them. Surely you do, too."

"A few. Like where have you been the last three days?"

"Annie was the one that suggested I should probably make myself scarce. Todd didn't approve of what we were planning, so I couldn't very well go there. Carla volunteered to let me stay at her place, since her husband is out of town all week."

"Planning what?"

Kenzie held up her hand. "One question at a time, please. Now it's my turn. Annie and I managed to figure out a lot of this by comparing notes, but one thing we couldn't get was the knife fight in Laramie. The cut on your shoulder was exactly the same as your incision."

"Cheat codes."

"What?"

"Codes you put into computer games that make it possible to cheat—"

"I know what cheat codes are. What do they have to do with anything?"

"Quite a lot, as it turns out." As Adam explained the cheat codes and the way they'd worked in the program, he watched her face change expressions. His heart turned over in his chest. Suddenly he knew that no matter what she'd done, he'd lay his life on the line for her. He loved her so much it hurt.

"So that's where Eagle Feather and Beautiful Dawn came from?" she asked.

"They were both characters I had retired. You somehow wished them back into existence."

Kenzie looked thoughtful for a moment. "That still doesn't explain the cut on your shoulder."

"Oh, that. I'm not positive, but I remember thinking about my surgery as I walked out of the saloon. That's when I left the program. I suspect the cheat codes created the incision I imagined."

"You never spoke again once you got on the horse that day," she murmured. "That does make sense, but how come you talked in your sleep and reacted to things Jesse Three Dogs and I did if you weren't connected to the program?"

"Cheat codes again. You expected me to react, so I did. Or, rather, my virtual body did. You probably also expected the cut to get infected. Otherwise it would have healed fine. Now, it seems to me I've answered more than one question."

"Oh, all right, your turn, then. What do you want to know?"

"Why did you send me that bear hide this morning?"

"Because a black bear was the closest I could get. Grizzlies are endangered, and it's illegal to buy or sell their skins. I was sort of impressed I found a brain-tanned bear hide at all."

"That's not what I meant. Why did you send it to me?"

406

"For the same reason I ordered it in the first place." Kenzie smiled softly. "And if you can't figure that out, you're not the genius Annie thinks you are."

"Kenzie," Carla's excited voice came over the intercom, "he's on the phone."

Kenzie closed her eyes and sighed in relief. "Okay, put the call on speaker phone." She opened her eyes and smiled at Adam. "It's Pete Saunders."

"Pete Saunders. What the hell—"

"Trust me just this once, Adam."

Staring into her eyes he found that, in spite of everything, he did trust her. He reached over and switched on the phone. "Morning, Pete."

"You win, Johnson."

"Pardon me?"

There was a deep sigh. "Ok, we'll play it your way. Look, I had no way of knowing Marriot wasn't legit. He graduated at the top of his class. I hired him because he said he was an expert on SR. I had no way of knowing he was after your program."

"Didn't you check his background?"

"Sure. So what?"

"Weren't you a little suspicious that he'd been accused of stealing programs before?"

"Accused, not convicted. I was willing to give the guy a second chance."

"Then again, maybe that's *why* you hired him. After all, you knew what I was working on."

There was an explosive curse on the other end. "You think I hired the little slime-ball to steal your program?"

"It did occur to me, especially when I found his fiancée working for me. I figured you hired her too."

"Marriot's fiancée? Somebody's feeding you a line of bull. Last I knew, his fiancée was a vegetable over at University Hospital."

Adam looked at Kenzie, but all she did was raise an eyebrow. "So, she never worked for you?"

"Hell no. Look, Johnson, I'd love to chat all day, but in about twenty minutes your little virus is going to destroy my whole damn network. You've proved your point, now send your hot-shot over and get this cleaned up."

Adam gave Kenzie a questioning look.

She grinned and mouthed the words *He's on his way.*

"He's on his way."

"Good. Tell him to hurry up."

Kenzie scribbled something on his note pad and held it up. "Aren't you forgetting something?" Adam read.

There was a long silence on the other end of the line. "All right, all right. I'll have the papers ready when he gets here, but I'm only drawing it up for five years. Ten is asking too damn much!" There was a distinct click, and the line went dead.

Kenzie already had her cell phone out. "It's a go," she said into the phone. "But be careful." There was a pause while she listened. "Okay, call me as soon as you're finished."

"What was that all about?" Adam asked.

Kenzie hung up her phone and slipped it back into her pocket. "That was your hot-shot programmer. He's headed over to Vid-Tech with Seth Bedford, Kirk Roberts, and half of a high-school football team as protection. Seems you have a lot of fans among the male teenage population."

"Do I know this hot-shot programmer of mine?"

"My brother Andy. I don't know if you remember, but you met him once. You made quite an impression on him."

"Yes," Adam said dryly. "I remember him."

"Anyway, the boys are going over to Vid-Tech to fix a little problem they have."

"The one Saunders just mentioned, perhaps?"

"It's the oddest thing. They seemed to have caught a virus. One of their programmers had perfected his SR program, you see, and they were so anxious to get it into production that they didn't check it out very closely."

"Let me guess, Brad Marriot?"

"Aren't you the clever one? Anyway, the first thing the

virus did was erase everything that had been on the original disk, and then it went after the network. About forty-five minutes ago the same message popped up on every computer at Vid-Tech."

"I'm almost afraid to ask."

"It told about Brad's chicanery and made certain demands."

"Including an apology?"

Kenzie grinned. "That and the promise that Vid-Tech wouldn't market a simulated reality program for a certain amount of time."

"Ten years?"

"It was worth a try." She leaned back on the desk. "Five years is about four and a half more than I figured he'd go for. I'd hoped for six months."

"Exactly how did *Fantasy Quest* wind up crashing Pete Saunder's network?"

"It's a long story."

"I've got time."

Kenzie began with her accident and how she had wound up inside his program. As she talked, Adam's jaw tightened, and his hands formed into fists more than once. If he ever met Brad Marriot in person, he was going to be hard put not to use the self-centered, egotistical jerk for a punching bag.

"And the rest is history," she said finally, "or will be as soon as Andy calls back."

"Are you telling me your brother reprogrammed what he downloaded from my computer before he gave it to Marriot?" Adam asked.

"Not really. It was more like he wound the virus through the programming that was already there. That way, no matter what Brad did to change it, the virus would still exist. He tried to explain it to me, but I didn't exactly understand it."

"Your brother must be one heck of a programmer."

Kenzie nodded. "He is. I think that's one reason why he and Brad never hit it off. Andy's better than Brad, though of course Brad would never admit it. Andy did tell me that he'd never get this virus past you, but Brad would be too stupid to see what was right in front of his nose. It appears he was right."

"Why didn't you just come to me with all this?" Adam asked.

"For one thing, we thought you might be a little squeamish about setting out to destroy Vid-Tech. Andy had no such problem. Taking Brad down was the highlight of his young life, I'm sorry to say. For another, you weren't exactly listening to me last time we talked. If you remember, you had just fired me because I might be passing information to Brad. I didn't figure you'd be inclined to fall in with a plan that did exactly that."

"I didn't fire you," he pointed out. "You got up and left."

"Good, because I really like my job here."

"I'm not so sure I won't change my mind," he said. "I think you might be more dangerous than I first realized. How exactly did you pull my administrative assistant and my physical therapist into this?"

"I didn't. They came looking for me."

"What?"

Kenzie rose from the edge of the desk and walked over to him. "For some reason, they think I'm important to your happiness." She smoothed the hair back off his forehead. "I hope so, because you *are* my happiness." With her hands bracketing his face, she bent down and brushed her lips across his. "I love you, Adam Johnson," she whispered.

With a soul-deep groan, he scooped her into his arms and settled her across his lap, with her legs draped over the arm of his wheelchair. Her kiss wasn't practiced or seductive, but it nearly fused the wheels on his chair with its intensity.

"Mmm, I think that's what I missed the most," she said when they finally came up for air.

"My kisses?"

"That and what came afterwards. I'm so glad all those lovely muscles are real," she said, settling against him.

"And here I thought you loved me for my brain."

"That too." She ran a playful finger down his chest. "The rest of you isn't bad either. Did you do any, uh…enhancing when you built your body in *Beta Quest*?"

"No, it never even occurred to me."

She leaned over to nibble his earlobe. "I can't wait to get you naked and see if you're telling the truth," she whispered.

"Kenzie! Behave yourself."

"Oh, all right, if you're going to be a party pooper."

"Wait until we don't need to worry about Carla walking in on us, and I'll show you party pooper," he said with a wicked gleam in his eye.

She grinned at him. "Promises, promises. I want you to know, I plan for us to be very naughty once we're married."

"Oh, we're getting married now?"

"After I spent the better part of three days hiding out from the police and the last hour convincing you I wasn't a conniving bitch, I figure you owe me."

"You do, do you? It just so happens I don't think that's reason enough to get married."

"You don't?" Kenzie's look of sudden doubt went straight to Adam's heart.

"No, I don't want to marry you because you think I owe you. I want to marry you because I love you madly and passionately and want to spend the rest of my life with you."

"Really?" She gave a happy sigh.

"It won't always be easy, you know."

"Nothing ever is."

"The doctors still don't know if I'll ever regain full use of my legs. I may be in this wheelchair for the rest of my life."

"Oh, Adam, do you think that matters? I've known you were in a wheelchair for the last month, and it hasn't changed the way I feel about you one jot. You're the man I want to spend the rest of my life with, to fight with, to make passionate love to, not to run races with. Besides, you need me. Hasn't it occurred to you that your recovery has slowed down since you shut down the program?"

"The doctors figure that's because I'm reaching a plateau."
Kenzie shook her head. "Nope."

Adam raised an eyebrow. "No?"

"It's because there are therapies in *Fantasy Quest* Annie can't do with you."

"Like what?"

"Running from forest fires, building cabins, chasing each other around, unbridled passion…that kind of thing." Slowly her smile faded. "Adam, did you really get rid of *Beta Quest*?"

"Yes, I did. I couldn't take the chance of another break-in."

Kenzie bit her lip. "So, Jesse Three Dogs, Buffalo Horn, and Red Blanket are all—"

"Right here," he said with a grin as he leaned over and plucked a small external hard drive off the shelf. "I destroyed the program, but I saved the setting and all the characters."

"Then you can load it into *Fantasy Quest*?"

"As easy as falling off Bear Bait. Watch, I'll show you." Working with Kenzie sitting on his lap was a bit difficult, but she seemed disinclined to move, and Adam wasn't about to let her go. Even so, it only took a few minutes to download the contents of the drive. With a click of his mouse button, a picture of the staging area appeared on the screen.

"The program starts right by our cabin!" Kenzie exclaimed.

"It always did. Rainbow Falls and the hot pool were the first things I created. Luckily, I used a real place that I was completely familiar with, or else who knows how it might have wound up."

"Is that Bear Bait?" Kenzie asked, pointing to the side of the screen.

"Sure is. Look." He clicked on the picture and a menu of faces suddenly appeared.

"Oh, Adam, there they are. Red Blanket, Jesse Three Dogs, Buffalo Horn, Crazy Charlie, even Eagle Feather and Beautiful Dawn. I'm so glad you saved them."

"I couldn't destroy all my friends because of one stubborn glitch."

She leaned back and kissed him. "I think we should have them at our wedding."

"Somehow, I don't think our parents will agree to a wedding inside a computer game."

"Oh, we'll have one for them too. We'll even have my mother's big fancy reception where we smash cake in each other's faces and get tipsy on champagne. Only you and I will know it isn't the real wedding."

"The real one will be in *Fantasy Quest*?"

Kenzie nodded. "With Jesse Three Dogs, Red Blanket, and Buffalo Horn."

"What about Eagle Feather and Beautiful Dawn?"

"Especially them. If it hadn't been for those two, we'd have never left the village."

"No, I suppose not."

"And we'll spend our honeymoon at the cabin."

"Don't you want to go someplace exotic?"

"Mmm, maybe later. I can't think of a better place to consummate our vows than in the hot pool."

He traced the curve of her face with his hand. "You know, neither can I."

"Do you have another one of these?" she asked, tapping his helmet.

"Sure, right next to the monitor."

"Is it hooked up?"

"Yes. Why?"

"We're going to the hot pool to practice."

"You want to practice our wedding night?"

"Why not? Haven't you ever heard of a wedding rehearsal?"

He laughed. "I don't think that includes the wedding night."

"But there's never been a simulated reality wedding before. We can make up our own rules."

"What if the Sex Hex kicks in?"

"It won't. Annie told me. It only works on gratuitous sex,

not on love. The brain waves are different."

"Annie's a blabber mouth."

"I knew there was a reason I liked her. Now quit arguing with me and put on your helmet."

"There you go, bossing me arou—" But she cut him off with a kiss. Adam felt the helmet slip over his head. Then everything went black.

If you enjoyed this book, please leave a review at Amazon. com

Books and Series
by
Carolyn Lampman

Meadowlark Trilogy
Meadowlark
Silver Springs
Wild Honey

The Cheyenne Trilogy
Murphy's Rainbow
Shadows in the Wind
Willow Creek

Cheyenne Trilogy Companion books *
Murphy's Rainbow Companion*
Shadows in the Wind Companion*
Willow Creek Companion*

The Time Tech Series
A Window in Time
Love Bytes

The Pinkerton Trilogy
The Jinx and the Pinkerton
Winter Hawk
Jessup*

*Coming soon

Samples of these books are available at

www. carolynlampman.org